STORM RISING

BOOKS BY RONIE KENDIG

THE BOOK OF THE WARS

Storm Rising

THE TOX FILES

The Warrior's Seal: A TOX FILES *Novella*
Conspiracy of Silence
Crown of Souls
Thirst of Steel

THE BOOK OF THE WARS • 1

STORM RISING

RONIE KENDIG

BETHANYHOUSE
a division of Baker Publishing Group
Minneapolis, Minnesota

Published by Bethany House Publishers
11400 Hampshire Avenue South
Bloomington, Minnesota 55438
www.bethanyhouse.com

Bethany House Publishers is a division of
Baker Publishing Group, Grand Rapids, Michigan

Printed in the United States of America

Library of Congress Cataloging-in-Publication Data
Names: Kendig, Ronie, author.
Title: Storm rising / Ronie Kendig.
Description: Bloomington, Minnesota : Bethany House Publishers, [2019] | Series: The book of the wars ; 1
Identifiers: LCCN 2018053260| ISBN 9780764231872 (trade paper) | ISBN 9780764234071 (cloth) | ISBN 9781493418626 (ebook)
Subjects: | GSAFD: Spy stories. | Suspense fiction.
Classification: LCC PS3611.E5344 S76 2019 | DDC 813/.6—dc23
LC record available at https://lccn.loc.gov/2018053260

Cover design by Kirk DouPonce, DogEared Design

Author is represented by The Steve Laube Agency.

19 20 21 22 23 24 25 7 6 5 4 3 2 1

Acknowledgments

Special thanks to Dr. Joseph Cathey for his continued creativity and expertise on all things related to ancient writings and texts. So grateful for you, friend!

Many thanks to Elizabeth Maddrey, Ph.D., for your help with Mercy's geek-speak and expertise. You are awesome!

Many thanks also to Amory Cannon for your crazy-cool scientific mind, helping me seem smart. Ha! Appreciate you, friend—now get back to writing!

And I'm incredibly grateful for the Rapid-Fire Fiction QRF (Quick-Reaction Force) and your loyal, rabid excitement about my books, as well as your many and varied efforts to help these stories reach more readers. Hooah!

Prologue

UNDISCLOSED LOCATION NEAR CUBA

He'd never killed a woman in cold blood before, but now was as good a time as any.

Boots pounding the concrete as he sprinted through the bunker, former Special Warfare Operator Leif Metcalfe knew he could not let her escape. Not again. He'd never live it down. The guys wouldn't forgive him. Everyone was sick of her ability to slip through their fingers like a well-oiled serpent.

"Runt," came the tight, controlled voice of Director Iliescu through the comms, "I don't have to tell you—"

"Nope"—*huff-pant*—"you don't." Nobody had to tell him what would happen. What letting her get away meant.

"Get her and get out. Radar's lit up with a storm. AWACS is heading back. Personnel are evac'ing. GTHOOD ASAP."

Curious. Storms had happened the first time he'd chased this chick in Greece. But it had to be big for the Airborne Warning and Control System plane to turn away. "Copy," Leif grunted between breaths, focused on one spot—the end of the bunker tunnel where he'd seen the operative vanish. Shuffling to a slow jog, breath heavy in his lungs, he snapped up his M4A1 as he closed in. He needed

Iliescu's warning like he needed to eat another bullet. He'd get out of Dodge as soon as this operative was down.

His huffs rang loud through his comms as he slid up to the juncture. He plastered his spine to the wall. Glanced back in the direction he'd come, seeing the bobbing approach of a half dozen more men. He couldn't wait for them. It was only thirty, maybe forty-five seconds, but that was plenty of time for her to give him the slip.

Not this time.

Peering down the length of his weapon, he eased into the turn.

Crack! Pop!

Feeling the sting of concrete shards on his face, Leif jerked aside. Out of her line of sight. He cursed. Grunted a few more breaths and mentally jotted down what he'd seen: Her frame. The light behind her. Water rippling.

She'd been to his eleven. Moving away?

He heard frantic steps. Running.

"Entering tunnel," he radioed as he stepped in. Shoulder to the wall, he kept his head swiveling. Adrenaline jacked.

"Careful," came the warning growl of former Army Ranger Adam Lawe. "This one's not afraid to force-feed you lead."

"No kidding," Leif hissed, sure he had tiny pieces of wall embedded in his cheek from her attempt to shove it down his throat.

Releasing a shaky breath, he advanced. He did not want to die here. Each plant of his boot, each exhale, felt like a homing beacon for her. "Come to the island, they said," he murmured. "It'll be safe, they said. . . ."

He snorted. This was a remote military location full of elite operators carrying out training exercises and maneuvers, and somehow the Wild Rose of Peychinovich slithered through it. This chick had to be out of her skull to tempt the trigger fingers of SEALs, Green Berets, and Pararescuemen.

And yet she'd handed them their butts. Taken off with ease and the prized Book of the Wars.

Following the trajectory he recalled from that split-second recon of the tunnel opening, Leif slowed. Drew on the memory of the maps on the wall. To his ten, a small terrace overlooked a drop-off into the sea. To his three, a curtain of water. The placid pool that engulfed the rest of the area was easily fifteen, maybe twenty feet deep.

So, left. Unless she'd drowned herself in the pool or waterfall.

If she didn't, I'll help her.

Something moved in his periphery.

With the M4A1 pressed to his cheek, he snapped to his nine. Firmed his grip. Relaxed his stance. Scanned the sparkling water that tossed light and spray in his face. He blinked but advanced, tense.

She blurred around a passage of jutting rock winding up a cleft in the wall.

Leif eased back the trigger. Fired a short burst. Which she'd anticipated.

He felt more than saw the ambush as she came at him.

Her booted foot flew at his face. He released his weapon. It bounced against his chest, thanks to the strap. Deflecting the strike, he shoved her leg back. Drove a fist into her side.

With the roar of the waterfall and his adrenaline, he didn't hear the air leave her lungs. But the way her shoulders hunched in . . .

She landed smoothly. Effortlessly. Dropped into a fighting stance. Something in her gaze tempted him to stand down. Think back to what she'd said. What she'd done.

Made a fool of me—twice. Because he'd bought her story.

Not this time. Leif snatched his thigh-holstered handgun. He had to end this—end *her.*

Viorica was already there with a cadence of strikes and kicks. Knocking away his weapon. Advancing. Pushing. Forcing him to surrender ground. Rock dug into his spine.

He ducked her next blow. Slipped under her swing and pivoted, flipping their positions. With a roar, he threw himself at her.

Jammed his forearm up against her throat. Used his weight to pin her. "Where is it?"

She remained focused and calm, not an ounce of worry in her expression as she cuffed his wrist with one hand and his elbow with the other. She'd twist it if he gave her the chance.

Not happening. He leaned in, arm pressed harder into her throat. Cut off her air. Trained his Glock on her cheek.

Her eyes widened marginally. Aware—finally—of what he was willing to do.

"Where's the book?" he demanded.

She coughed, her face reddening.

"Runt, what's going on?" Iliescu commed. "We've lost visual and audio. Do you read? Over."

The waterfall must have been interfering, blocking his transmission. Hopefully they'd figure it out. "The book!" Leif shouted, applying more pressure. His shoulder right on her breastbone squeezed off what little air remained in her lungs, refusing her another breath.

"Yo, Golden Boy," came the teasing voice of combat medic Dai Saito through the comms. "She finally pop you for us? Report your position so we can retrieve your corpse."

Viorica shoved him. Leif stumbled, gravity trying to yank him into the pool. He skidded around it, then came up straight. All that remained of the operator was a shadow.

The cleft!

He bolted after her. Slowed when she appeared at the edge of the cave structure, her silhouette framed in the setting sun.

Cradling his Glock, he closed in. "Nothing there but ocean, Viorica. Give up. Or let me shoot you in the back, and the sharks dine on prime assassin." He shortened the gap. "The book. Give it up—tell us where it is."

Even as he erased the distance, the blood of the sun drained into the water and turned gray. The sky darkened. What? His gaze skipped over the horizon.

"—ack here!" a voice crackled in his ear. "There's—all—storm. Now!"

Facing the churning waters, Viorica glanced over her shoulder and smirked. "Letters of Marque," she said, twisting her wrists.

"*Don't!*"

She bent her legs and shoved off the cliff.

PART ONE

ONE

ONE MONTH EARLIER
VOLGA DISTRICT, RUSSIA

"Weak!"

With a grunt, Iskra Todorova threw another hard right, followed by an uppercut.

"You are weak!" Ruslan growled as he held the bag. "This—*this* is why you fail him. This is why he thinks to send you back."

The pointed truth stung, because she heard the gloat in Ruslan's words. He'd warned Hristoff she couldn't be trusted, that she would let him down.

After a left hook, Iskra followed up with a round kick—nearly nailing the bodyguard in the temple.

He flinched back, eyes wide with shock, then glowered at her. "Do that again, I'll teach you a lesson you won't forget."

Iskra hid her smile but savored the small victory. Ruslan had always been hard on her—hated her, hated that Hristoff Peychinovich, their employer, kept her in luxury and showed her favoritism. She didn't want for anything—as long as she kept Hristoff happy. As long as she did what he said.

The door to the training room flung open. Face pale, chest rising and falling, Iskra's assistant, Lesya, stopped short, clinging to the knob as if it could somehow protect her. She gathered herself and straightened. "He wants you."

Hristoff hadn't spoken to or acknowledged Iskra since she'd failed her last mission to retrieve a priceless Cellini sculpture.

"And," Lesya gulped, "they're here."

Ruslan stalked toward her, shoulders drawn. "Who?"

"ArC—Mr. Veratti."

"You mean his people," Iskra said, steadying the bag.

"No." Lesya moved farther into the room. "It's *him*. Mr. Veratti himself."

"Veratti never *visits*," Ruslan gruffed. He pointed a meaty finger at Iskra. "This is your fault."

Though she didn't want to admit it, didn't want to give Ruslan that pleasure, he was right. Her failure, the same one that had angered Hristoff so much that he gave her the cold shoulder for two weeks, had brought Ciro Veratti to Russia.

"This is bad," Ruslan warned.

Iskra unraveled her wrist bindings as he started for the door. "No," she said, tossing aside her gloves, "it's *very* bad."

Veratti held more sway over Hristoff than anyone else and evoked more fear in him than all his enemies combined. On several occasions the Italian billionaire had brought Hristoff to his virtual knees. Though her boss gave lip service to the Armageddon Coalition, his loyalty stopped there. Hristoff had one master: greed.

Ruslan's phone buzzed, and he looked at it. Then at Iskra. "He wants you."

With a nod, she said, "I'll shower—"

"No." He held up his phone. "Now."

She thought of the Lycra pants and tank top she wore. Sweat plastered her dark hair to her face and head. Would Hristoff beat her again for appearing before power players in "inappropriate attire"? Or would he want them to see her toned body, a sign of her physical prowess?

They hurried through the palatial mansion that had been her residence—never would she call it home—for the last twelve years. Iskra glanced out the windows that lined the hall. On the helipad, a sleek black helicopter lurked with two guards.

As they approached the main gallery where Hristoff entertained guests, voices filtered across the marble floors. She slowed at hearing a pleading, placating tone. She almost didn't recognize it, but that was Hristoff's voice.

Dread churned in her stomach as Ruslan gave a light rap on the wooden door and stepped in. He said nothing but inclined his head to Hristoff, who was perched on a settee.

Hristoff's hair was cut short around his temples and crown but curled along his collar. The goatee, which he'd added in recent years, somehow gave him a dignified air. Enough women fawned over him to keep his ego large and healthy. But she had never been able to think of the man who held her leash that way. He was an animal.

Swirling a snifter of amber liquid, Hristoff did not seem happy. Then again, when had he? He speared her with a look that warned her to behave. She crossed the room, sensing more than seeing the other man, who instilled fear as easily as plants gave off oxygen.

"Ah." Veratti's tone was neither amused nor pleased. "There she is." He did not seem dwarfed by the large fire roaring in the floor-to-ceiling hearth. In fact, the flames seemed to amplify his dark persona.

Iskra walked behind the settee and stood at Hristoff's right. Out of trained habit, she let her hand rest on his shoulder. When only his jaw muscle moved at her touch, she lifted her head.

"I've seen photos of your Wild Rose, Hristoff, but you oaf! She's half your age."

Hristoff slowly came to his feet, and Iskra feared what he would do. He had never been known for restraint. "She's here."

The way he said it startled her. Pushed her gaze in the direction she'd avoided—toward Veratti. He was terribly handsome with black wavy hair, a chiseled jaw—no surprise in Italian nobility—and broad shoulders that taunted the stitching of the suit he'd probably spent more on than most did on a car.

Why had Hristoff said "she's here" that way? It held meaning. As if Veratti had asked for her. Or . . .

Veratti's gaze raked her body. "Well, at least there is one area she's not lacking."

Disgust thickened her thoughts, but she'd learned long ago to bury those feelings. She considered giving Veratti a lesson in exactly where she wasn't lacking, but one thing held her back. His handsome appearance was coupled with dark eyes that held a dangerous glint, and they were still locked on her. She'd seen the same look in Hristoff's eyes the first time he saw her, when Papa offered her in repayment of a debt. Barely a teen, she had become his property. Later, she had become more.

Chin tucked, Veratti seemed especially amused. He strode to the nearby high-backed chair. "You're putting a lot of trust in a woman, Peychinovich."

Fury reddened Hristoff's face as he too recognized the predatory look. But perhaps he saw his own vulnerability in this situation, as he merely tossed back a gulp of liquor. "Because she can do it." Though he stood and swaggered to the bar, there was a hesitancy in his actions.

Sliding his hands into his pockets, Veratti gave a cockeyed shrug. "She didn't last time."

Again, he studied her. Assessed her. Left her with the distinct feeling of being flayed over an open flame. If it did not come with such a high price, she would leave. Be free. Not the prized working cow these two were verbally sparring over.

"She *will* do it," Hristoff growled, slamming the snifter down on the marble counter. He hated being questioned or contradicted. Years tethered to him warned Iskra that he would not hold his temper much longer. Surely he wouldn't lose it with the Italian billionaire, the founder of the notorious organization ArC, which had been described as worse than ISIS.

Iskra went to the bar and opened the fridge. She retrieved a water bottle, then stood beside Hristoff. He'd told her before she was a calming presence, and he definitely needed that right now. But was that still true after her massive failure with the Cellini?

Hristoff flicked the glass across the counter. Iskra caught it, preventing it from crashing into the sink. He gave the billionaire a smug smile. "What is the artifact? Tell her, and she will get it done."

Veratti again considered her.

Annoyance flared, and she itched to make him look away. But that penetrating gaze left a deadly impression on her psyche, a warning. Her life depended on this mission, that was clear. So she stowed her irritation and remained implacable.

"There is a book," Veratti finally intoned as he returned to the fireplace and stared into its dancing flames. "It is called the Book of the Wars, and it is imperative that I recover it."

"*Recover*." Bringing his attention back to herself wasn't what Iskra had intended, but his word choice was significant. "Then you had it at one time?"

He hunched over the fire as if protecting it. "No." He downed some liquor before facing them. "Not in its entirety. We had only a page. Discovered a few decades earlier, it is but a clue that the book exists. It had been thought lost to history."

"And it's not now?" she persisted.

"Iskra," Hristoff hissed. "Quiet."

"No," Veratti said, wheeling around. "It is good that she asks. Unlike you, Hristoff, she seems interested in cooperating with ArC, which makes her a very clever, beautiful woman."

Iskra skidded a glance at Hristoff, sure he would be livid by now. Fists balled, he was reaching below the counter. The Ruger.

She drew in a breath at the thought of him challenging Veratti. Nobody challenged the Italian prime minister.

"If she intends to succeed and remain alive, then she will want every vestige of knowledge about the Book of the Wars."

Her mind snagged on his last sentence. Remain alive? Her understanding of the relationship Hristoff had with this man radically shifted with those words. Hristoff owed Veratti a sizable amount of money, and her failure with the Cellini had greatly impeded his ability to repay it. But since when was he subordinate to Veratti?

"It is not a question of *if* it will be found," Veratti said. "The first leaf has been decrypted and revealed where the book's journey began."

"And you're a cryptologist or linguist that you know this?" Iskra's stomach tightened. She'd gone too far with that, teasing in sarcasm, and she saw the same thought darken his expression.

"I am not," he said, his words controlled, "but someone who owed ArC a great debt was part of decrypting the leaf." His black gaze ensnared hers again. "You want to live, yes, Iskra?"

"I prefer it." Going after this was her last hope. Her last chance.

"And you would do everything in your power to stay that way, yes?" He wanted to taunt her. Make her squirm. Which was why he was inching closer, peering at her from beneath those thick brows.

"Yes."

But not for the reason he believed. That was her secret alone, and one that fueled a treacherous thought. It hung in her mind, taunting, tempting—Hristoff's fear and submission, Veratti's anger. A plan hatched in the fertile soil of desperation. She might—just maybe—have the answer she'd been looking for. But it would be the most dangerous mission she'd ever taken. Her heart thundered.

"And you would do anything to get the Book of the Wars back, yes?" He crossed the room. Towered over her.

"Yes." She felt his hot breath fan her cheek. And she saw his meaning and intent. Did he see hers staring back?

"Good. It's in the salt mines of Israel."

She gave a sharp nod.

He grabbed her ponytail and jerked her head back, forcing her to look up at him.

Her fists and anger coiled.

"Fail *this* time, and *I* will own you."

TWO

ROCKVILLE, MARYLAND

"Two protons walk into a black hole."

The attractive bartender grinned at him. "Yeah, and?"

"That—" Leif deflated. That *was* the joke. He shook his head, knowing he probably shouldn't have tried that one on her. He felt bad she didn't get it. He'd just humiliated her without trying. "Never mind."

She set aside a buffed-clean glass. "You know most of your jokes go over my head, Handsome."

"Yeah. Sorry." He'd thought about asking her out. Considered it every time he sat here. But she didn't need that kind of trouble in her life.

When he stood, she smirked at his glass. "Will you ever actually *drink* what you buy?"

He snorted. Pivoting away, he lifted a hand. "'Night, Mallory." He shoved out of the bar and past a crowd of rowdy patrons heading in, the nightlife just getting started.

As he drove his Jeep back to the house, Leif wrestled the thoughts he'd intended to drown in liquor. The same intention he had every Thursday night. He wasn't trying to drown the memories. It was the emptiness. The void of . . . anything. Nothing. No memory. He just wanted to know what was missing. But the last several years had taught him to leave it alone.

He turned onto his street, and his headlamps struck a sleek black sedan in front of his house. Government plates. "What the . . . ?" The dash clock showed 2228 hours.

Was something wrong with his mom? He eased alongside the vehicle and saw the face of the driver. "Not Mom," he muttered as he pulled into the driveway and parked. Bouncing his keys in his palm, he stalked up the sidewalk, where the man met him. "Director. Kind of late for a briefing, isn't it?"

Dru Iliescu nodded to the door of the house. "Need to talk. May I come in?"

What choice did he have when the deputy director of the CIA showed up at his house? "Come on."

Inside, Leif flipped on the light and stalked to the kitchen. He tossed the keys on the counter and grabbed some water from the fridge, watching the director take his time joining him.

Leif tried to stuff down his anxiety, but it was dancing like a bird on a live wire. "Guess you have a good reason for being here. Because it feels like an invasion of privacy." Not that he had any. Not after what happened.

Was *that* what this was about? His gut roiled—with excitement, then dread. No, it couldn't be. They'd agreed.

"Take this position, work with the team, and I can get your record buried. No more questions. Nobody will be nosing in the shadows of your past."

"Kind of hard to know if someone is nosing around when you can't remember."

"I know. We'll make it work for us. It's a chance, Leif. A chance to start over."

"Is it about—"

"It's not," Iliescu said with a breath that hinted at both regret and relief.

Leif wasn't sure whether to be aggravated at still not having answers or relieved they weren't going to touch that void. It always felt like playing fetch with a land mine.

Iliescu motioned to two recliners facing the TV. "Please. Let's talk."

Roughing a hand over his mouth, Leif noticed the stubble on his face for the first time as he bent forward in one of the chairs, elbows on his knees. He'd given himself permission to slack off while Wraith wasn't on mission.

"You drunk?" Iliescu asked.

"Not in years."

"You were at The Lone Star."

Leif wasn't surprised they were keeping tabs on him, but it still ticked him off. And that leaked into his response. "So?"

"You've been there every Thursday night for the last two months."

"Three," Leif corrected without regret.

Iliescu considered him for a long minute, his features tight and disapproving. "You go in and order a vodka tonic. But you never drink it. Not once."

Masterful at not reacting, Leif stowed a twitch. Stowed the anger. They were prying into his life. Again. Heat thrummed through his veins. "Do you know how much toilet paper I used when I hit the head, too?"

The director's blue-gray eyes burrowed past the smart-aleck remark and seemed to test the darkness of that black hole in Leif's heart and life. "I think you're searching for answers that don't exist."

"They exist," Leif countered. In fragmented, out-of-order pieces.

A shower of rock and debris. Dust clouds plumed.

To his nine, Krieger grinned. "I'm too pretty—"

Crack! Crack! Crack!

Krieger froze.

The ground was rending. Leif lunged toward his teammate.

A chasm opened below Krieger. He dropped.

"Oh, they exist." The ferocity bleeding into his own words surprised Leif. He thought he'd buried it. Accepted after all these years that it was better left alone.

"It will drive you into the ground, son."

"I'm not your son," he growled, wishing he'd downed that vodka tonic. "My dad died eleven years ago, but thanks for the sentiment." He wiped his face again, then straightened. "Is there a reason this psych eval couldn't wait till morning?"

His gray hair in a high-and-tight, Iliescu nodded and glanced at the wood floors. "I'm taking you off Wraith—"

Leif punched to his feet. "Nothin' doin'."

Iliescu slowly lifted his head and squinted at him from the chair.

"I have not had an ounce of liquor since you pulled me from the drunk tank five years ago. I don't smoke. I am there, one hundred percent, to the mission, for the team." He was growling, so he dialed it back, knowing that didn't go over well with Dru. "Never have I wavered in that commitment. There is no reason to pull me." He huffed, the thin cords that held his mind together straining. "I should've known you wouldn't keep your word. I know you two have a mission to save the little brother, but Canyon—"

"Doesn't know about this."

Leif stilled. His older brother had fought hard and long to attach him to a team, to get his head out of the fog of hopelessness and dead-end intel hunts, and back in the game.

"And he won't."

"So you just screw everyone who's loyal to you?"

Iliescu shook his head, a near-smile pinching his gaze. "It's a good thing I like you. Now sit down and shut up." Squeezing his hands together, he sighed. "I'm pulling you from Wraith to give you your own team."

Leif jolted. *Didn't see that coming.* Especially after mouthing off. "Seriously?"

"I need your expertise with linguistics and . . . other skills."

Other skills. Leif lowered himself back into the chair. "Bull." He felt the world cratering around him. "This has nothing to do with my *linguistic* skills. That specialty is a dime a dozen in this field. This . . . this is about . . ."

"Let go! Let go!"

"No," Leif growled, eyeing the boulder. If it came down, it'd crush his guy like a cockroach.

"Chief." Krieger locked onto him. "Let. Go."

Heat skidded across Leif's shoulders, knowing how that had ended. And he didn't want a repeat. "No."

Dru frowned.

"No team. I'm not . . ." He hung his head. Balled his fists. He was not hauling out his private arsenal of *skills*. He couldn't explain them except to say he'd come out of Egypt . . . different. He'd always been a quick healer, but what his body could do now—docs couldn't break it down into comprehensible science, but they wanted more tests. He'd refused.

Those skills were unexplainable, and using them only stirred questions and concerns. Made him a freak. Surreal endurance, the ability to shut out pain, to heal crazy-fast, and to remember. *Everything.* Save six months of his life plus one day.

He gritted his teeth. Swallowed the bile. "I thought we weren't going to do that," he said quietly, despite the buzzing at the base of his brain.

"I know."

"I thought we agreed"—it took every semblance of restraint not to go ballistic—"that the less of *that* we introduced into the equation, the safer it was—*is*—for everyone."

The mere mention of opening that vault, that side of himself . . . Leif coiled his fingers into a fist. No. He wasn't going there again. Wouldn't sit on a plane again with nine flag-draped coffins. Wouldn't watch wives and families sobbing into one another's arms. Wouldn't listen to one hundred twenty-six rifle cracks at Arlington. Not again.

He'd played on the game board Dru had created. "I joined Wraith. It worked, kept questions minimal. They were impressed but not concerned. I did it—buried myself and that mission." Breathing hurt. "Now?" He choked out a laugh. "Now you're saying bring them out. Show them around." He squinted. "Seriously? Do you realize how messed up—"

"Indirectly," Iliescu asserted with a nod, "I'm adhering to our agreement. Nobody will know what you're doing or can do. But

I think your abilities will prove not just useful but vital for what I'm sending you after." He had the gall to meet Leif's gaze without regret or hesitation.

Didn't he get that the very abilities he wanted to use—against Leif's will—could also put him in a coma? Or a grave?

"This isn't adding up," Leif said. "I hid these things because *you* said it was best. *You* told me to play it close to my vest while you dug. It's been five years. I've done that. But we have no answers. No progress. Are we even getting closer?"

"I know, Leif. I know I did. And . . . some things are beginning to emerge from the shadows—"

What? The words punched the air from his lungs. *What things?*

"—but they are still in the shadows. I can't call it. I don't have definitive proof. You know me. I've put my own assets on the line for you." Dru scowled. "What I'm asking of you isn't easy."

"Convince me, because this smells like a big dung pit right now."

"An artifact—"

"That's Wraith's game."

"—before an enemy coalition gets it first."

"Again, Tox and Wraith."

Annoyance scratched at the deputy director's face. "We aren't the only ones chasing this thing. Of particular concern is a notorious operative named Viorica and a German power player—a businessman—named Rutger Hermanns. Viorica is the bigger concern. She's effective, lethal."

She. Okay, that intrigued him. "What artifact?" Why was he even asking?

"An ancient text called the Book of the Wars. Honestly, brass has been tight-lipped about this one. I just know we need to get it first. But trust me, I'm digging hard to find out why they want us to retrieve this at all costs."

All costs. Leif had heard that before. Experienced that. "So." If the director claimed ignorance on the artifact, then . . . "You're not holding the leash." Which was a game changer.

"Yes and no. Ultimately, DoD and DIA want this thing."

Leif drew back. "DoD." Military. He'd been attached to the CIA after the DoD threw him out. It'd been better to get away from the military, because someone was keeping secrets about the hole in Leif's life. DoD had their way with him and didn't want to touch him after the Sahara. "How come?"

"This book," Iliescu said after a lengthy pause, "has information. I don't know much more than that."

"But you do know *more*."

Conflict teased the edges of the director's mouth. "I do," he admitted.

"And you're not going to tell me."

"I can't. Not yet."

"Just like the things in the shadows."

Dru dropped his gaze.

Leif let the pause linger, irrationally wishing it would coerce Iliescu into saying more. "This doesn't make sense." He leaned back in the chair. "None of it. We don't know what happened to me. Six months of my life are missing—me, who never forgets anything—and you want to dig that up. Send me out half-cocked."

"You aren't half-cocked, Leif. You have the best instincts I've seen on a SEAL. Do some research. Learn about Viorica. She works for a steel magnate cum crime lord out of the Volga District, Hristoff Peychinovich. They're some serious trouble—if he gets his hands on this, there are world powers he could sway, powers he could manipulate and control."

Leif noted the way the director's face twitched. "Like America."

"Among many."

"But we don't care about 'many,' because we're Americans. We're just here to protect American interests and lives, right?" Leif said, feeling confrontational. Sensing the thrum of anger. It vibrated his veins full of adrenaline.

"No," Iliescu countered, sincerity creasing the corners of his eyes. "That's not true in this scenario." He cocked his head. "We do care about the many, because this book—if it's true what they say, it . . ."

"You know," Leif said slowly, "I've never seen you hesitate so much."

"Maybe that'll help you understand my position. There's a lot at stake." Iliescu rapped his knuckles on the table. "We do care about the many because those are the lives at stake. We need that book, Leif. Need eyes on it and control."

"The last time you were this worked up . . ." Leif swallowed, remembering that night. Cuffs biting into his wrists. Rough hands wrangling him into compliance. Things would've been so different had Iliescu not intervened.

"Yes." A placid guy who cut it straight, the director grew more animated. "Yes, it's on that level." He scooted to the edge of his chair. Stabbed a finger across the gap between them. "I *need* you on this, Leif. And believe me, I know what I'm asking." Ferocity bled into his expression. "I know it's not kosher, and both of us would rather wash our hands and go our merry ways. It could blow up in our faces, and there could be a boatload of trouble from Langley and Belvoir."

"We've stayed low, stayed quiet." To stay off their radar. To placate the brass who wanted Leif deemed a threat to society and sent to Leavenworth. Now it felt like all that was unraveling. "I don't want a team. Not again."

"Let go! Chief. Let. Go."

Iliescu expelled a ragged breath. "I know. But if you do this, if you succeed, I vow to help you get those answers."

Setting off a nuke wouldn't have had the impact of those words. "Don't do that."

Iliescu frowned.

"Don't dangle fruit you can't deliver to buy my cooperation."

"I—"

"Because if I find out you had a way to get this thing sorted, that you knew more than 'things in the shadows' and you sat on it?" Leif lifted his eyebrows. "That you didn't bring to bear every resource at your disposal to find out what happened to nine special operators?" He fought the tempest within. Shook his head, bringing it back under control. He splayed his fingers. Pulled his spine straight. Met the director's gaze. "Don't do that."

Palms out, Dru eased back. "Leif, I'm not hiding anything about that black hole. About what happened to the Sahara Nine. Do I have threads I'm chasing? Yes. Absolutely. I promised you that, and when I have something I can bring into the open, I will." He lowered his head and peered through a tense brow. "Hear me?"

Leif ground his molars.

"You've trusted me for the last five years. Please—do it one more time."

Though Leif searched for signs of deception, he found none. He waited it out, knowing if there was more, the uncomfortable silence might pluck it from Dru. Then again, he was the deputy director of the CIA.

This was a no-win scenario.

Leif had nothing to lose. It would keep him busy and his nose out of trouble. "You gave me a life, put me to use, stopped them from locking me away." He nodded, conviction and dedication to the man sitting in his living room rising to the cause. "What do I need to know?"

THREE

DEAD SEA, ISRAEL

"What was the prime minister of Italy doing at the house?"

Iskra huddled in the dark, phone to her ear. "Punishing us. I failed the last mission."

"You must be better than that, Viorica. Your life is not the only one on the line!"

"Don't you think I know that?"

"Yes, yes. Of course you do." Bogdashka huffed. "You are alive. That is good—it means he has a mission for you. What is it?"

"I'm in Israel. Hunting an ancient text called the Book of the Wars."

The rasp of Bogdashka sucking in a sharp breath rattled the connection. "You know this for sure? He said it?"

Iskra's left eye twitched as she sighted the tunnel entrance to the salt mine a hundred yards north of where she stood. "I would not be here if I wasn't."

"This is good. Very good. You have no idea." Bogdashka muttered a dozen praises to the Virgin Mother. "He has it, Viorica. He has the page that tells of the book. He must. How else would he know where the Book of the Wars is located?"

Irritation and the damp, salty air beat against Iskra's patience. "Is there a point, Bog—"

"This is how you will find him. The book is the answer. You must find it and get it to Vasily."

Scowling, Iskra shook her head. "No, I must bring it back, or we are both dead."

"Yes, bring it to them eventually, but to Vasily first. You must. Swear it to me, child."

Iskra looked at her watch. "I must go."

"Swear on her life."

Iskra ended the call and prepared for the task ahead.

"It's set." The husky voice of Imran spiraled through the tiny black piece in her ear.

"In position," she replied.

"Okay, Viorica. The Meteoroi has been activated. You have fifteen minutes from the first strike until things break loose."

She hated this. Hated that Hristoff had the power of Zeus at his fingertips. But for now, it worked in her favor. A quick glance up at the sky, a blanket of black glittered with diamonds, warned Iskra to work fast. A prickle of electricity made her hair stand up. She pushed away from the dank alcove and moved silently through the alley, eyes locked on her target: the mine entrance.

Two men shifted on either side of the opening. They did not have the rigid postures of guards posted for security, but it was still obvious in their crisp haircuts and hands loose at their sides, almost anxious to grip their holstered guns. Their bearings spoke of experience. Of willingness. Of threat. Their gazes struck hers in tandem, then bounced away, clearly not wanting to reveal the purpose or objective of their presence at the entrance to the white passages of the mine.

"Go another way," one of the guards barked, waving her aside.

Taking full advantage of her dark hair and Middle Eastern features, Iskra feigned confusion. Hesitated, hugging the bundle of blankets she held. "I was told come here," she said in deliberately broken English. "I pay!" A little righteous outrage by a woman went a long way.

"*Nein*," the other said. "*Es ist* . . . closed."

German. So. Rutger Hermanns was after the book, too. She resisted the groan working its way up her throat. He was a brilliant businessman and sometime archaeologist, and a full-time pain in the backside. He wasn't going to win this time. Wouldn't take her prize or sought-after freedom.

She looked around, still acting the part. "But I must." She whimpered. "I need the mines!" The medicinal benefits of the salt pools were proven, irrefutable.

Tears or anger? Sometimes it was a toss-up, but these two seemed as prone to brutality as Hristoff. Hysterics would only feed the monster within. So, anger.

"No!" She raised a fist. "I pay. Lot of money. They tell me come here. Sleep. A bed"—she shuffled forward—"there is bed for me!" She thumped her breast. Coughed. "I must. I need it!"

The first thug reached for a weapon. The second was more reticent, but both were unwilling to allow more trouble to pass their checkpoint.

Where was that lightning strike? She could use—

An explosion of light splintered the sky. It snaked and crackled, trailing in its wake a wicked concussion.

Crack! Boom!

The thugs jerked toward the sky.

Iskra seized upon their confusion. She slammed a knife-hand against the first thug's throat to silence him, make him grope for breath. This allowed her to disable his buddy before he got his wits and that weapon. She swept the second thug's leg out from behind him. Used her other hand to shove him backward. He landed hard, his head bouncing against the ground. She dropped a knee to his chest and coldcocked him. She might be a foot shorter, but speed and surprise made up for that.

Lightning snaked and crackled, seizing and retracting.

Having confiscated the second thug's weapon, she tucked it into her waistband at the small of her back, then sprinted into the white halls of the salt mine. With the clock ticking down to the rigged storm, she had no time to lose. The nearly mile-long passage that took her out well beneath the Dead Sea could become her worst enemy if she didn't beat the deluge created by the Meteoroi.

Chest tight and calves aching, she rounded a bend. Ahead, a cluster of cots and failed bodies littered the passages. She slowed, skittering forward. Most of the inhabitants and those making pilgrimages for health and medicinal purposes were asleep at this late hour.

Hand trailing the wall of chalky salt, she froze when a dark form slipped through the passage, moving from one room to another. Rutger. Thick-chested and thick-skulled, he was formidable. Always armed. Always prepared.

That makes two of us.

Irritation pulsed through her at the realization that she must resort to violence. Again. She was done with this. She would readily leave Rutger with shame and empty hands. It was a better punishment for him. But it would not be enough—he'd come after her with an unrelenting lust for her blood. Leaving a man like him alive meant *her* death.

She had to.

She stopped to consult her map, making sure she didn't get lost in this maze. Vibrations generated by the storm wormed through the bedrock. Rocks dribbled down, pulling her confidence with them. Then a scary thought struck. Had the cave walls been shored up enough to withstand the storm surge?

She prayed they had. Or would the God so many prayed to decide she had done enough wicked things? She had not killed the thugs at the entrance. That was to her favor. Maybe she would not need as many prayers to whatever god was listening or paying attention tonight. There was always one who deigned to punish her. Always.

But not tonight.

Tonight she *would* win. She must buy freedom. Rip it right from Hristoff's hands by delivering this book to Veratti.

The idea—the look on his face—bolstered her. She eyed the tunnel and froze. While she'd been distracted, tension had filled the passage. Twenty yards from where she'd stopped, three men emerged from a room that backlit them. One turned to her. Face framed by brown hair threaded with silver. Neck dense with muscles. A stupid rectangle of a mustache beneath his hooked beak.

Rutger Hermanns.

She cursed herself for letting down her guard.

Now he had the advantage. His smirk confirmed that he knew it. And mocked her. Threatened.

Iskra eased into a fighting stance, right foot back. Noted what he held. What he waved in the air with a smile and acknowledging nod.

He'd come for the same artifact. And beaten her to it.

"That is a dangerous book," she warned, feeling a tickle in her shoes. The storm. Thunder throwing its fit, stomping its feet and tossing around bolts of anger. Had the rain started yet?

Rutger's lips quirked. "*Ja*. True. Dangerous to those who do not have it." He dipped his head. "Like you." His large, thick hand motioned to the cots that littered the passage between them. To the people sleeping, innocently unaware of the stirring threat. "It is a terrible thing."

She glanced at them. Heavy blankets covered a woman and her young son—four, maybe five years old. The boy shifted on the thin material, scowling at her, then Rutger. An elderly gentleman with scraggly hair and beard lay in the next bed. His frail shoulders seemed barely enough to support the wool blanket. Several beds held millennials who'd come for the same reason hippies in the '70s had gotten high—to feel connected to the earth.

"I have heard," Rutger said, one of his men assisting him into a jacket so that he never released the tube containing the Book of the Wars scroll, "that the infamous Viorica is vicious and lethal when dealing with her enemies."

She arched an eyebrow, grateful he'd made her point. Understood what she'd do.

"But I have also heard that she will not abide innocents dying." He snorted, his attention drifting to the boy and his mother, then lifted a weapon. "Especially children."

"You're right," she said, heart in her throat as she inched forward.

"I can't abide the death of children. But if you've heard that, then you also know I won't beg for their lives." Begging never worked on his ilk, and the thought of what would happen, what she'd do, stirred a frenetic cadence in her bloodstream. "But I will return the favor."

Another lazy smirk as he inclined his head. "An eye for an eye, that's what Viorica says."

She hated that he knew so much about her, but she was growing bored with the dialogue.

"But then you're still left with a child's death on your conscience."

"A death atoned by the bloodletting of the one responsible." She lifted a shoulder. Reached for the weapon at the small of her back. "There's only one exit, Rutger, and it's behind me. And you have to navigate fifteen sleeping people without getting killed by me."

Confusion—or was it fear—flickered across his face. He shifted, stepped back. Where did he think he was going? "But can you save them all?"

Now she was confused.

Until he lifted his weapon. Aimed it at the hewn ceiling and fired.

She ducked and scowled. "That was—"

Crack. Boom!

"—stupid."

A jagged line raced across the ceiling.

Oh no. "Wake up! Get up!" she shouted, her gaze skidding toward Rutger, who was grinning.

"Can you save enough to appease your soul, Viorica?" He retrieved a hefty pack from the ground. Shouldered into it. "Or will you forever hear their screams?" As he lifted a rebreather, he grinned again. "Assuming you live."

This didn't make any sense. Rebreather? But the storm deluge wouldn't—

They were under the sea. If the tunnels were damaged, the passages would fill with water. He'd intended to flood it all along. Make everyone believe the Book of the Wars was lost in the disaster.

But he had it.

She lunged at him.

Pop-pop-pop! Crack. Boom!

Whoosh!

She glanced back.

The cave ceiling collapsed, heavy rock thudding to the ground. Narrowly missing the old man. Water roared into the passage. Screaming, the boy jolted upright. His mom gathered him into her arms.

Seeking an exit, Viorica pivoted to the pitch-black end of the tunnel. It was *much* closer than before. How—

She sucked in a hard breath. That wasn't the passage. It was a wall of water barreling at her.

Turning, she spotted one of Rutger's men. She corkscrewed at him. Caught his shoulder. He twisted to dislodge her. She slipped away, the water an insipid foe, shoving her. Tearing at her clothes. With a growl, she again lunged. Scraped his face. Dug her fingers into his neck, her other hand into the pack. He howled, but she reached for the rebreather. Caught the mouthpiece. Snagged it. Tore the pack free.

But water seized her. Yanked her backward. Flipped her. Tossed her. Spat awful, salty water into her mouth. She gagged but fought the rebreather into her mouth. Struggled into the pack. Opened the oxygen as water pushed her back, back.

The torrent slammed her into something. She heard an *oof*—the young mother. She stumbled, her son in her arms. They plopped face first into the water. The mother surfaced, her arms empty.

The boy! Iskra's gaze connected with the mother's. Grieved fingers strained toward the water. Viorica spun around. Saw arms and legs and face tumbling amid the foamy wake down the passage. His body thudded into the wall. There was no more thrashing. No more movement, save the powerful hands of the waters.

Diving in, Iskra swam, frustrated at the buoyancy that fought her efforts. Finally, she touched the boy's shoe but lost him. Salty water stung her eyes. Made them feel like they were bleeding. She threw herself forward again, her movement slurred. She struggled toward the boy.

The roaring water thrashed him. Tossed him up out of reach. Then slammed him back down. Iskra dove at him. Hooked his neck. Pulled him against her chest. Held tight. Tried to guide their trajectory. But the sea was just as furious as she was—it smacked her into the walls. Pain exploded through her shoulder and neck. It yanked her back only to shove her again. Violent. Furious. Beat her against the salt mine passage.

Then vomited her out.

She landed with a thud that knocked the breath and rebreather from her. Bloody warmth filled her mouth. A tooth had probably broken. Her lip had split, and the saltwater was a cruel addition. She spat. Rose onto all fours, amazed the water was only shin deep here but had engulfed them in the passage. She gripped her knees, gasping. Swiped her face, tears streaking down her cheeks from the sting of the salt.

The boy. Where was the boy?

She straightened and looked around. Ten meters away, the boy's mother clutched him to her chest, slumped in the waters. Crying. Sobbing. Rocking.

Viorica trudged out of the water, the salt grains gritty beneath her clothes and rubbing her raw. Much like Rutger's cruelty.

Rain poured from the sky, cleansing her face. Lightning shot through the clouds, prickling the air. But the howl that drew her attention was that of grief. She peered over her shoulder. Watched the woman railing at the sky, shaking her son. Screaming.

The terror of losing your child in such a wretched, awful way . . .

Hands pawed at Viorica. She pivoted and thrust a hand at her attacker.

"Easy!" Imran said, palms flashed up in reassurance. "We lost comms and got worried."

Trembling beneath the rain and her defeat, Viorica turned away. She'd lost. Lost the boy. Lost the Book of the Wars. Lost freedom.

FOUR

BETHESDA, MARYLAND

"You know it'd never work between us, right?" At the security checkpoint, Leif stalked up behind Mercy Maddox, the crazy-smart computer analyst he'd met while working with Wraith who had a penchant for superheroes.

Mercy dug through her brown messenger bag with one hand and managed a Styrofoam cup in the other. She drew back, objection perched on her lips. Or maybe some snarky remark. She was full of them. And a lot of attitude. Like the look she threw him, considering him as she searched for her ID. "Why's that, Runt?"

He palmed the control pad, and authorization came in the form of a mechanical *thunk* that disengaged locks and engaged her surprise, clearly noticeable in her raised eyebrows. He winked. "You picked the wrong universe."

She frowned, either because he had access and she still had to provide ID, or because she didn't get his joke.

Back to the door, he pushed through the security hub. "I'm a DC guy."

Now she scoffed, eyes alight. "How many ways can you spell *loser*?" she tossed after him with a laugh, gaze never missing a thing—like the fact that he was gliding through security.

He shrugged, lifting his hands. "Hulk, Thor, Iron Man, Wolverine . . ."

Her lips parted, stunned. Then she sprang forward. "No, you did not!"

Two armed security officers swept in front of her, blocking her path. "Sorry, ma'am, but—"

"You'll pay for that, *Runt*!"

He grinned as he hustled down the steps into the command bunker of the new section of the CIA's Special Activities Division. He'd worked with Tox Russell and his team under the umbrella of the Artifact Retrieval and Containment subbranch. Now, specifically for this endeavor, they had a new team, a new no-name unit. Their official designation was a series of numbers that meant nothing to anyone other than the doc retrieval specialists.

He accessed the final corridor, pleased to find a couple of new team members already waiting. "Saito!"

"*You?*" Dai Saito huffed. "That's it. I quit."

"Can't," Leif said, catching Saito's hand and slapping his back in greeting. "We're not official yet." Turning, he nodded to the wall of muscle that came out of a chair. "Lawe."

"Runt." Adam Lawe had a little too much pride and ego keeping him from a warm welcome. "Not sure this is shaping up to be much of a team."

"Thanks for the confidence," Leif said. "But I think you'll change your mind when you see the rest of the team."

Lawe considered him. "Yeah?"

"Well, bust my britches!" A twangy voice boomed through the bunker. "Isn't that the biggest Runt of the litter crowding my hallway?"

This was great. Like old times. "Culver." Laughing, Leif eyed the guy ambling out of the elevator in well-worn boots, jeans, and an OD-green T-shirt. "Glad you signed on."

Culver Brown doffed his ball cap. A Navy SEAL like Leif, he specialized in tactics—and guitar. "Well, gigs are slow right now." He had a good voice, so he'd tried to get into country music, to the mocking chagrin of his band of brothers.

"That's right. Forgot about that."

Culver thumped Leif's chest with the back of his hand. "Naw, ya didn't. Just trying to make this Southern boy feel better." He turned to the guy who'd come in with him and slapped his shoulder. "'Sides, Jake here needed someone to keep him out of trouble."

"Not sure there's enough power in the world for that," Leif said, hooking hands with the shorter Jake Klein, a Special Forces operator he'd run a few missions with.

"Good to stay busy," Jake said with a laugh.

"It smells like a guys' locker room in here." A feminine voice cut through the din of chatter.

A low whistle pierced the air as one of the most beautiful women to set foot in a combat theater sauntered into the coffin wearing jeans, a black T-shirt, and the killer smile that flatlined every soldier she encountered. But the real reason Peyton Devine was beautiful wasn't that she'd once been an NFL cheerleader, but because she'd traded her sparkling, skin-tight uniform for ACUs, a tactical vest, and a sniper rifle.

"Peyton," Lawe breathed, drawing her gaze.

"You have got to be kidding me," Saito hissed at the same time.

Klein elbowed him. "Introduce us?"

"Not if you want to live." A scowl snapped onto Lawe's face. "Show some respect."

While Leif wouldn't ever call Lawe a dog, he went rabid when it came to Devine. Behind his brawn and tactical precision lay a molten-eyed puppy where she was concerned. They'd had a rocky start to a relationship six years ago on an op gone wrong. Leif wondered if the same had happened to their relationship.

"Hey, Lawe," Peyton said, her cheeks pink—but was that makeup or a blush? She smiled at Leif. "I appreciate the request, Runt. Corporate life was boring me to tears."

"Not many opportunities to unload stress with a carbine or M4?" Leif grinned. He checked Lawe with a smirk. "Still got doubts?"

Lawe shook his head, but maybe he wasn't answering Leif's question as much as trying to wrap his mind around working with Devine again. The big guy squared his shoulders and looked anywhere, it seemed, but at Peyton. "This it?"

"Not yet."

As if on cue, a door opened. Iliescu emerged from an endless glaring white corridor. It wouldn't surprise Leif if it led directly to CIA headquarters or some off-site location, allowing the director to come and go unnoticed. Behind him appeared another man dressed in a zip-up hoodie, ball cap, and—

"Well, look at that big cheesy grin," Culver Brown said with a laugh as he crossed the room, extending a hand to the newcomer.

At six three, the Afghanistan native had a casual comfortableness about him and a ready-but-crooked smile that made him seem like he was always up to mischief. The crew gathered around him.

Lawe clapped Leif's shoulder as he strode past. "Nice."

"Who's that?"

Leif flinched, not realizing Mercy had finally cleared security and joined them. Seeing the Afghan still left a wad of guilt and regret in his mouth. And yet—a relief unlike anything Leif had experienced before. "Baddar Amir Nawabi. An Afghan commando we worked with for a couple of years over there. The best."

Mercy quirked an eyebrow at Leif. She wasn't your typical operator. In fact, she wasn't one at all, but she had razor-sharp skills when it came to hacking and communications—and reading people. Her history was as much a protected mystery and secret as Leif's, though he wasn't sure whose record was more redacted.

And Mercy came with baggage. Their last mission together left him feeling like he owed her something. Or maybe he knew what it was like to need to stay busy after a traumatic incident. She'd lost the love of her life in that mission. Though he'd teased her about them not belonging together, they both knew he hadn't meant anything by it except a bit of humor. Granted, with her long auburn hair, amber eyes, and wit, Mercy had a lot to offer.

To someone else. She had a little too much scathe for his tastes.

Arms folded, Leif took in the team reconnecting with Baddar. He liked the camaraderie. Hoped the Afghan could eke out a life now that they'd gotten him to the States. But it would never be enough to replace what he'd lost.

He felt Mercy's gaze on him still. "What?"

"What you said about the commando sounded a lot like sentimentalism, Mr. Metcalfe. If I didn't know better, I'd say you grew a heart since we last met." She smiled at the Afghan, who stalked toward them.

"Baddar." Leif extended his hand, hoping the commando would accept the peace offering. If not—

Baddar hauled Leif into a hug. Slapped his back. "Heard it is you I should thank." He caught the back of Leif's neck and pressed their foreheads together. "*Shukraan lak 'akhi.*"

The sentiment, thanking him and calling him "my brother," dislodged something in Leif. Heads still together, he patted Baddar's forearm. Then stepped back. "Negative," he said. "Fates aligned, that's all. Glad you could make it." He looked around the room, noting the others eyeballing them.

"Okay," Iliescu said, waving them to a table. "Let's get down to business."

Saito thumped Leif's shoulder, nodded to Baddar. "Classy."

Though he'd called them over, Iliescu stepped to the side, where a khaki uniform met him. The way the two stood blocked Leif's view of the officer.

"That Braun?" Culver asked quietly. "She's a tough one."

Braun? Seriously?

"You seem to have won a lot of approval bringing this commando into the mix," Mercy said quietly on Leif's other side. "I look forward to finding out why."

Iliescu returned to the table, motioning the officer with him. Average height and build, but there was nothing *average* about the intelligence behind Rear Admiral Alene Braun's brown eyes. Or the way she ran her ship—figuratively and literally. She'd fought hard to earn her position, and as a result, she expected everyone to pull their own weight and then some. She never gave anyone slack, including herself.

There had been a few rocky encounters between the rear admiral and Leif in the past, so when Iliescu tasked him to Wraith, she'd disagreed. Said Leif was unpredictable, irresponsible. Leif had to agree—what kind of team leader lost all nine men under his command?

Iliescu planted a hand on his belt. "As you—" He waved someone into the room. "You have it?"

An affirmative answer came a split second before the person entered.

Leif snorted at the familiar face. "You gotta be kidding me."

Barclay "Cell" Purcell had been Wraith's comms guy. Smart mind and smart mouth. They hadn't exactly gotten along, especially on their last mission when Leif had assumed lead.

"Oh, Barc. Just can't stay away from me, can you?" Mercy teased.

"Thought the same of you, Merc." Cell smirked at Saito, Lawe, and Leif. "What is this, the Three 'Bully' Goats Gruff?"

"Some of you know Mr. Purcell," Iliescu introduced. "He's been promoted and has accepted an assignment as senior technical analyst. He will be in direct communication with you and will liaise with me. He'll take any data retrieved, analyze it, fill in the gaps, then funnel it to the appropriate person or persons."

Interesting. Cell out of the field.

"Miss Maddox," the director continued, "will be your communications officer *in* the field. She is not tactical." He nodded to the others. "We'll leave that to the rest of you. You've worked together before, so I trust your ability to pull together for this unit."

"What exactly is our purpose?" Culver asked, his reddish blond hair and beard catching the ceiling light.

"Must be some kind of special," Klein noted as he scanned the room, "with the variety of skills you have gathered. Especially right here in this chair." He pointed to himself.

"What's so special about you?" Lawe barked.

"Besides seven years as a Special Forces operator and that I have the same birthday as Ronald Reagan—minus a few decades?" He nodded to Iliescu. "But what I'm guessing the deputy director is interested in would be my degree in the Hebrew Bible and that I've been working on my masters in Semitic epigraphy."

"Your expertise—"

"That's a generous word," Klein said. "I'm just a beginner."

"Well, what you know was deemed beneficial, but it was Chief Metcalfe's confidence that landed you this assignment." Iliescu considered Klein. "What do you know about the Book of the Wars?"

A half-amused, half-confused smile flashed over his face. "You serious?"

"Dead."

Klein swiveled in his chair, roughing a hand over his jaw. "It's a lost book. Mentioned in the Bible. Numbers, I think." He shrugged. "There are guesses about what it contained, but the title sort of gives it away. Nobody really knows because"—he nodded as if he'd made his point already—"it's *lost*."

"And it's your first mission," Iliescu said.

Saito and Lawe shared a scowl.

Klein dropped forward. His smile vanished. "Seriously? It's found?"

"Hold up." Saito lifted a hand. "I'm a medic. Why am I chasing a *book*?"

"You're a soldier, too. And this book is said to reveal some very lethal secrets," Iliescu said. "Metcalfe, Purcell, and Maddox were previously attached to SAARC, a sister branch that hunted down artifacts."

"And while Wraith was fully trained and operational, we didn't have a combat medic on board." Cell nodded at Saito. "Hope you're okay with insides boiling out and skin sliding off people."

"Cell," Leif muttered in warning.

"Just sayin', Mr. Usurper."

Leif snorted. "Still hung up on pecking order."

"That's where you're wrong. With recent personnel changes," Cell said, squaring his shoulders, "I am technically your superior."

"Superior what? Jerk?" Lawe asked, a smile never cracking his thick dark beard as laughter skittered around the room.

"Reel it in, ladies." Iliescu stiffened. "Apologies to the *real* ladies, who are acting more mature."

"The Book of the Wars needs to be retrieved," Braun said, her voice surprisingly loud despite her petite frame. "And it needs to be done ASAP, because we are not the only ones after it. We just received intel that the Germans, at the behest of Rutger Hermanns, raided a secret laboratory in the salt mines of Israel and stole the book. The race just hit warp speed."

"What's so great about this book that it's a high-value objective?" Culver asked.

"It is said to record the outcome of several wars," Braun said.

With a laugh, Lawe lifted his hand. "I have a $150 history textbook from college you can buy off me that tells the outcome of those wars. I'll cut you a killer deal, too."

"Wait," Saito said, "you went to college?"

"I'm more impressed the guy can read," Cell muttered.

Lawe lurched forward in mock attack. Cell flinched, then laughed because he was too far away to reach.

"It's prophetic," Iliescu asserted.

"Boom!" Cell said. "The truth-bomb drops."

"Wait. How do we know it's prophetic if we don't have it?" Klein asked.

"Before Hermanns absconded with it," Iliescu explained, "the experts who unearthed it said the book recorded the outcome of wars that have not yet happened."

"And we . . . what?" Saito said. "We believe that? Believe in the book's . . . *prophecies*? What is this? A sci-fi drama or something?"

Glowering, Iliescu stabbed the table. "Start training, get familiar with each other, and be prepared to deploy at a moment's notice."

"Hang on a sec," Lawe said, stroking his beard. "So it was found . . . then lost?"

"Not lost, *stolen*," Cell said, surprising everyone by speaking for the brass. "The book is under lock and seal . . . somewhere. We don't know yet where Hermanns took it. But he knows agencies and black ops teams around the globe are ready to pound the ground to recover it. So it's heavily protected."

"But you have something that's going to help us beat the rest," Leif suggested, reading Dru's confidence.

"You're dead straight," Cell said. "I managed to figure out trigger words connected to this book to scan for and—y'all can thank me later—I've convinced the brass to get you in decent proximity to that area."

"What area?"

"Where the most consistent use of the trigger words occurs," Cell said. "So when we get a lock, you can jump on it." He lifted his arms in victory. "That decent proximity?" His grin was nuclear. "The Bahamas."

"Booyah!" Culver proclaimed.

"Arrogance is a poor substitute for intelligence, Mr. Purcell," Braun said, smiling.

"I've been trying to teach him that for the last year," Leif put in. "So, this book—you said it has trigger words. What are they?"

Braun shifted. "That will not be disclosed at this time. Suffice it to say, we cannot let that book get into any other hands."

"Unfortunately, gentlemen," Iliescu said, "according to our sources, it seems the operative known as Viorica is as intent on this book as we are. She nearly intercepted Hermanns in Israel."

"But we're better. So we'll get it from the Germans." Saito glanced around when nobody responded. "We *are* better, aren't we?"

"Dude," Lawe said with a jittery laugh, "that's one psycho bi—"

"She's good," Braun affirmed. "Impressively and violently so. Beat her or defeat her."

"How 'bout both?" Lawe suggested.

"Always were afraid of women, huh, Lawe?" A lot of innuendo lurked beneath Devine's words and expression. Whatever had happened between Lawe and Devine after that mission in Afghanistan hadn't made it in the after-action reports.

"Ohh, ouch," Saito said around a laugh.

"Uncalled for," Lawe objected, raising his hands. "It was a unique situation—"

"One you were ill-equipped for?" Mercy joined the bashing.

"I'll have you know I'm very equipped—"

Chortles burst through the room.

"Not like that!" Lawe scowled. "You dirty-minded people should be ashamed."

A cacophony of laughter choked any legitimate conversation about the briefing. Leif laughed so hard his side hurt.

"Enough!" Braun barked, then shook her head with a disgusted sigh. "What is this? High school all over again?"

"Maybe junior high," Cell offered.

Braun glowered. "Mr. Klein, ask around, see if you can gather more intel about this book for us."

"Yes, ma'am."

"The dossiers on Hermanns and Viorica are already downloaded to your tablets. Get familiar with them," Iliescu said. "In fact, I recommend all of you get caught up on those files while you're funnin' and sunnin'."

Lawe thrust both fists in the air. "Bahamas, baby!"

FIVE

VOLGA DISTRICT, RUSSIA

Never again. She vowed it to herself. For herself. For her own dignity and sanity.

Once Hristoff had retreated from her suite, Iskra rose from the bed and hurried to the bathroom. She pitched herself at the toilet and vomited. Tears and sobs came quietly as she curled in on herself. The price was too high. Because she'd lost the scroll, she'd had nothing to offer him upon her return from the salt mines. And he took his payment from her.

How long? How long must she play this game? When would she be free of him?

Never. It would never happen. She'd learned her lesson. *This* was her life.

"Easy," whispered Lesya, who tugged back Iskra's hair as she spit into the toilet.

Warmth draped Iskra's back and arms, a robe providing the only comfort she'd ever know. She stood on shaky legs, flooded by the heat of embarrassment and anger.

Lesya handed her a glass of water. "Clean up and shower. Perhaps you will feel better."

No. She wouldn't. At the sink, Iskra bent over and spit again. Rinsed. Lifted the glass and gulped. Covering her mouth, she stared at the porcelain. At . . . nothing. The emptiness of her soul.

"Bodhan sent another message."

Bodhan. A code name for Bogdashka. The only chance Iskra had for freedom.

"They are close."

"*Close* is not good enough." Iskra slammed down the glass. "I must find that book. It is the only way he . . ."

Spinning the knobs for the shower, Lesya came to her. "Why? Why do you—"

Iskra silenced her assistant with a look.

"You have killed . . . many. Done things everyone said could not be done. You are known worldwide. And yet . . ." Lesya shook her head.

Iskra shed the robe and stepped beneath the jetted sprays of water. She knew the question Lesya asked without asking. The confusion and yet understanding of many staffing this home. They were all the best at their various skills. Yet they were all prisoners. Not one dared cross Hristoff.

Hot water pelted her face, and she embraced it.

She had tried to change her course. Many times. The first time not long after Hristoff brought her to the estate. Desperation drove her to idiocy, and he'd beaten her unconscious as punishment. There had been other, smaller attempts. Most he didn't know about, times she'd been able to conceal her failure. But that last time . . . Valery.

Hands against the slick tiles, Iskra closed her eyes. Refused the memory. The pain. Breathed in and out. In. Out.

The book. She *must* find the book. Buy freedom.

Why? You don't deserve anything better than what you have.

Streams pounded her body. Washed away every sign of him. She scrubbed and rinsed. Scrubbed some more. But she could never erase the memory of him. His breath. His cruel words. Liquor-reeking breath.

The water had run cold—so had her heart—by the time she emerged, skin puckered. After dressing in athletic pants and a tank, she went out into the sunshine for some relaxing yoga. Tried to re-center herself. Find the core that allowed her to fight when she had no fight left.

Frustration and aches won the battle, so she went to the gym and shifted to martial arts. Going through the forms. Physically exerting herself.

"Focus," Ruslan growled as he held the practice pad. "Again!"

Jumping up and spinning around, she aiimed a roundhouse at his head. He deflected.

"*Da! Da!*" He grunted a laugh. He knew—they all did—what Hristoff did to her. What it took out of her. But Ruslan was unrelenting as well. Which worked fine. It helped her drown the pain with fire in every muscle. Until her limbs shook for another reason.

After a long swim, she rinsed off again and dressed. Feeling moderately composed, she sat on the sofa with a mug of hot tea and her laptop, watching an American spy-romance movie.

"I love that ending," Lesya said, sniffling as she lifted a pan from the oven in her small kitchen.

"I hope you're not dripping snot on our dinner," Iskra said, then considered the film. "Besides, it is unrealistic."

"How can you say that? Things like that happened all the time in World War II! And the last scene? When he's carrying her past the checkpoint and is shot in the back? Swoon!"

Iskra scoffed. "That woman would have been dead long before she had a chance to escape or fall in love, because she was careless."

"One day you will find a man and fall in love."

The words plucked at a raw nerve. "I have no desire for a man or love." What man would want Hristoff's leftovers, anyway? No. The only thing she wanted was freedom.

About to close her laptop, she saw an email in her inbox. Her breath backed into her throat, the pain of the previous hours vanishing. "Bodhan."

Lesya stilled from her meal preparations. "It is located?"

Iskra opened the email and found a series of numbers. A tremulous laugh escaped her. Tears threatened.

It seemed freedom called.

NASSAU, BAHAMAS

Pass. Set. *Crush!*

Mercy watched as Leif sprang upward, right hand aiming for the volleyball. Fine sand sprayed the air. He spiked, slamming the ball into the sand on the other side of the net.

"Yeah!" Mercy shouted, high-fiving him, then Adam Lawe. Again she threw her enthusiasm at Leif. "Sweet!"

He patted his buddies, and they prepped for the next serve. Gulls and waves competed with laughter on the beach. The sun blazed unhindered on UV-absorbing bodies.

Baddar palmed the ball, glancing across the net at her side. He wore a muscle shirt, which did its job of displaying his sculpted muscles.

Oh, Mercy. She sighed, watching the way his dark arms flexed.

Right. *Shouldn't be noticing this.*

"Mercy!"

She looked up. "Wha—"

A blur was enough warning for her to cringe. The ball smacked her head. Twisted her around. She stumbled to the ground.

Laughter broke out from somewhere. She tried to laugh it off, too, but it felt like a pound of humiliation.

"Are you okay?" A touch to her shoulder brought her blurry gaze to a pair of soft brown eyes beneath a khaki ball cap. Dark hair curled around his ears. Baddar crouched in front of her with a crooked grin. "You are well, Mercy?"

Just dandy. Getting smacked upside the head by the cute guy. "I'm fine." Sand defied her graceful exit, twisting her ankles and making her wobble.

Baddar steadied her. "I am sorry. I did not mean—"

"Awesome serve." She managed a smile. Lifted her hand for a high five, and he hesitantly accommodated her. She noticed everyone staring and Peyton ducking beneath the net. Great. "I think I'm going to get some water."

"Merc," Cell said, falling into step with her, "I'll join you."

"No. It's—"

"Teams are lopsided without you." He shrugged. "I'm not really a sports enthusiast anyway."

Pursing her lips, she nodded. Shot one more look at Baddar, who now stood beside Leif, his deep eyes trained on her and filled with concern. "That serve should come with an ICBM warning," she called.

Cell snorted. "Ballistic missile is right. I stopped his last one." He held out his arm where a red welt had arisen. "Dude's got some power in those guns."

"Mm," Mercy said, trying not to remember the olive-skinned biceps. The very thing that had distracted her.

They returned to the tables where the team had sat talking before hitting the sand for a game. After donning a lightweight sundress cover-up, Mercy slumped into a chair and lifted her bottled water. She guzzled it, relieved when a waitress came around with more.

"How ya doin', Merc?"

She eyed Barc and his soft, concerned tone, then drained the next water bottle before toweling the sweat from her face. He wasn't asking about the knot on her head. He was asking about Ram. "His death *wrecked* me. End of story. Nothing to say. I can't . . ." It'd been eighteen months.

"Me too." He thumbed a Perrier, staring at the green bottle. No, not *at* it. Through it.

She laid her hand on his. "Hey." She gave him a grin that she hoped conveyed the whole *I get it* message, then quirked an eyebrow. "So. Analyst?"

He sniffed. "It just got to be too much, ya know? Seeing one of the best guys I've known—" He sat back, clearly fighting back his emotion. "Ram gave his life to stop them."

Throat raw, she drew back her hand. "Yeah."

"I knew I couldn't do it anymore." He shook his head. "Couldn't go out there." He indicated the men on the sand volleyball court. "Couldn't be an operator without constantly wondering who would die next."

"So," she said, wrinkling her nose in a confused smirk, "you took a conscientious objector role of analyst."

"I'm no objector. I believe in what they're doing. I believe in them."

"But not yourself." A fracture started in her heart. "You don't believe in yourself."

He gave a one-shouldered shrug and looked like he was fifteen again. "I couldn't help Ram. Couldn't stop him." He sat forward suddenly. "If I'd had time to assess the situation. Look at all the facts—"

"Barc."

"—things might've ended differently."

"It ended the way it did because Ram made a choice, a *sacrifice*." Did he realize that his thoughts were selfish, essentially belittling Ram's noble deed? "You can't analyze it out. Don't take that heroic act away from him because you can't cope with it."

His eyes narrowed. "What about you?"

"What do you mean?"

"I've seen the way you watch Baddar, how your face went crimson when his serve struck you. Yet you barely give him the time of day."

"It's called a sunburn, *Dog*."

"You only use that nickname when you want to annoy me."

She sighed, knowing he was right—she *had* noticed Baddar. It was hard not to with his well-toned body, dark skin, and lopsided grin. "So we're both wallowing in pity." She toyed with the bottle. "Is that what you're saying?"

"I'm saying—"

A shadow fell over Mercy seconds before a warm touch came to her bare shoulder. She looked up, startled to find Baddar standing over her. Her pulse jammed, wondering if he'd heard Barc. She raised the water bottle to her lips, only to remember she'd drained it.

Baddar folded his large frame into the chair beside her. "Are you okay?"

"Yep," Cell said as if confirming something. "Going to find a drink."

She glowered, knowing full well he'd intentionally left her alone with the commando. Something she *had* been avoiding.

"Seems I gave you a knot," Baddar said.

She frowned, turning back to see his hand near her face. She froze, her heart doing that mamba thing again. His touch was feather light, despite his size, against her temple. "I have a hard head," she muttered. "I'll be okay."

"I was surprised you did not see it coming. You played so well all morning."

"College team, two years." She shrugged. "I had just looked away when you served."

His rich, dark eyes homed in on her. "You went to university? What did you study?" He shifted his chair closer, folding his arms on the table.

"Computer science."

His eyebrows rose—impressed, apparently—and pulled an unwilling smile from her. "To study that, then you are very intelligent, too."

Again she eyed him. Wondered what he meant. What he wanted. Why he had to be so Bruce-Banner-delicious with his smile and kindness. "Not so smart. Never finished the degree."

Confusion tugged at his expression. "You were bored?"

Mercy started. Then laughed. "Yeah. Good guess. Very bored."

"But you work . . ." He motioned his hand in a circle, indicating the team and the operation. "So clearly you are smart beneath that knot I gave you."

Flattery will get you everywhere, Baddar. She cleared her throat. *Insert subject change here.* "What about you? What's your story—how'd you meet Leif and the guys?" Checking over her shoulder, she saw the team now playing football closer to the water. "You worked with them before, right?" Her gaze collided with his again.

There was an eager light there. "I worked with more than two hundred American advisors in my five years with them." His accent swirled and danced around his English because of his excitement. It was lyrical and fascinating to listen to. "My last mission did not go well—the Taliban kidnapped my sister. They want me give up working with the Americans. Mister Leif and Mister Adam were on the mission. Ms. Peyton, too." The light seemed to leave his eyes. "My sister died by the Taliban."

"Your sister—I'm sorry." So he knew the grief of losing a loved one as well.

"She was like you," he said with a grin that made her a little light-headed. "She had pretty smile and laugh."

Wow. *Knock a girl off her feet, Commando.* The heat filling her cheeks had nothing to do with the sun. But it felt . . . wrong. He was a fighter. A soldier. He'd be willing to do crazy things to complete missions. Just like Ram.

No. Not again.

"I . . ." Mercy looked around. Tried to avoid the concern that returned to his expression. She stood.

Baddar hopped to his feet, his chest bumping her shoulder in his hurry to be a gentleman. "I am sorry." He steadied her by the arm. "Did I—"

"No." Mercy lifted a hand. "It's okay . . ." She ducked around him. "Excuse me."

The path to the bathroom was direct and unobstructed, thank the Lord. She shoved inside and into a stall. Flipped the lock and fell back against the door. It was stupid. *She* was stupid.

Baddar was not Ram.

Except they were both kind. Gentle and gentlemanly. Dark skin. Dark hair.

That was it—they were *so* similar, which explained her attraction to the commando. Transference. That was what the psychs called it. Problem solved. She wasn't really into Baddar. Cool. Yeah.

Gathering her wits, she exited the stall. Washed her hands for good measure, then left the bathroom.

And rammed straight into a solid mass. *Oof!*

"Oh! Sorry." Arms caught arms. Steadied each other. "I'm so—" She stared up into gold eyes. Bearded jaw. Sandy brown hair. And a face that said, *Clint Eastwood is my father*. "Hello, Gorgeous," she whispered. Holy loose tongue! She'd said that aloud. "Sorry!" She noticed a tattoo on his forearm, his pinstriped shirt having slid up in their collision.

His expression morphed from a scowl to a tiny forced smile, his gaze only then seeming to focus on her. "Excuse me." After a curt nod, he hurried off.

"Well. Feel free to knock me over any day," she said with an airy laugh.

Drawing in a breath, she headed back to the table, relieved to find the whole team there. Baddar's focus locked onto her, but she slid around to Barc and was about to take her seat when something snagged her brain. She slowed, replaying her collision with the man. Mentally repositioned herself at the bathroom door. Switched places with him. Stared as he had . . . along the bar. Out the glass wall and doors.

Right to the table with the team.

No. *You're making a mountain out of a molehill.*

"You okay?" Cell cut into her line of sight. "Mercy?"

She searched the interior of the club for Eastwood's heir. "I'm okay."

"You sure?"

Where had he gone? "Yep." She surfed past suits and platinum blondes to the far side of the outdoor seating area.

"Well, we're all heading up to change. Meet in the restaurant for dinner and dancing in an hour."

She started back inside.

"Mercy," Cell called.

She looked back at him. Realized she hadn't answered or responded. "Yeah. Sure. See you there."

Because this kind of thing, the glitching memory piece—it never left her alone until she pursued it to the end.

Game on.

"You seen Mercy?"

Leif checked his three, surprised Cell was looking for her. "Not since this afternoon when she got thumped by the volleyball."

"I can't find her."

"Maybe you should take the hint," Lawe said around a chuckle as he high-fived Klein.

"Like you?" Devine taunted. "Because you're so good with them."

Cell glanced between the two. "Ya know, if y'all need to clear the air about something—"

"Everything's crystal." Lawe stabbed a serrated knife into a medium-rare steak.

Devine stood and excused herself.

Leif's phone buzzed. So did Cell's. Saito's. Klein's. Lawe's.

"Looks like they nailed it down," Cell said.

Leif slumped with a huff, eyeing the coded text from Iliescu. "So much for a little R&R."

On his feet, Lawe smirked. "What d'ya mean? What we do is R&R. Nothing helps me unwind like unloading an M4."

Dropping cash on the table to cover the bill, Leif caught the eye of their waiter and tapped the money. He started out of the restaurant, not surprised to find Devine falling in step beside him. Her expression warned him not to ask if she was okay. Devine was tough. She held her own. And to be honest, Leif wasn't sure where the lines were when a woman and a soldier were the same person. Maybe the lines didn't even exist. He knew the soldier in her didn't want pandering.

"Lawe." Leif motioned him over and looked to Devine. "You two wait for Mercy. She's here somewhere. Meet at the rendezvous. Got it?"

The pair eyed each other but nodded. Cell, Klein, and Baddar were already leaving. Culver and Saito pulled up in a Jeep to retrieve Leif. He hopped in, and they pealed away.

Her phone had buzzed a half dozen times, but Mercy had her own self-appointed mission. Eastwood's heir was here again. And—bingo!—watching the team. Somehow he hadn't connected the dots that she was a part of said team. So when she'd caught his eye and flashed a surprised smile, he'd sauntered over with all his gorgeousness and fresh crisp scent. She'd gotten his name—Andrew.

"Recruiter," he said, grinning. "I acquire new personnel for my employer. Scout local talent and bring in the best."

"Local? You aren't American. Or Latino," she said, wrinkling her nose. "So what's 'local' for you?"

His eyebrows lifted. "How would—"

"I don't know," she said with a schoolgirl giggle. "Just the way you say some things. I knew this guy once. He was from Israel but very much American. Every now and then, I heard something in his words that told me he hadn't spent his whole life in the U.S."

Andrew folded his arms on the white linen tablecloth and leaned in. "And what about you, Lara?"

She had to admit the name Lara was cool. She'd donned it in honor of her favorite archaeologist/relic-hunter heroine. But she hated herself for picking it—she'd used it with Ram in the beginning, and now? Now it wasn't funny. "Me?" She sipped wine. "What about me?"

He grinned, his eyes pinching at the corners in a way that also pinched her stomach. "*You* are not American either."

Now her stomach ached. "Oh, I am," she said. "Quite."

"That thing you mentioned about certain words—I hear that in your speech, too." He ate the olive from his martini.

"Maybe it's that I like accents," she said, bending in, closing the gap and shortening his attention span. Most guys were putty when she turned on the charm, though it had taken a little longer to get this one distracted.

But those green-gold eyes were a sort of poison. Every now and then over the course of the last hour, she'd lost herself in them. Forgotten that she was supposed to be finding out why he was tracking the team.

He reached across the table, cupped her elbow. "How long are you here?"

She lifted a shoulder in a casual shrug. "Told the boss this was a business trip. So it'll come to an end . . . eventually. But for now I'm enjoying the sun and vibes."

He traced his thumb up and down her arm. Maddeningly, teasingly.

"So," she said, her voice catching. She laid a hand over his, stopping the caresses but allowing herself a better angle. With the small table, they were very close. She could smell the alcohol in his words.

Andrew's expression shifted at her control of his movement. She had to remedy that. She reached for his face. Dragged her fingers over the beard that lightly descended from his earlobe and thickened at the jaw, then lessened around his chin. It was an interesting look. Gave him a rough persona, but those eyes sparked with intensity.

"Most American girls aren't so bold."

She smirked. "See?"

"What?"

"You said American. An *American* wouldn't qualify that." She intentionally looked at his lips, hoping to drag his mind from her probing questions. "So—"

Tires pealed outside, snatching his attention.

He muttered something, gaze darting to his phone. "I must go." He stood.

Her heart was in her throat—not over Mr. Gorgeous, but because the team had left.

Andrew stepped away, his focus now wholly divided. He turned back to her. "I'm sorry. I'd better go. Storm's coming." He tossed a C-note on the table, nodded to her. "I hope our paths cross again, Lara."

"Hope so," she said, the pout in her words genuine. It was easy to appreciate his good looks and smooth manners. And to be disappointed she hadn't pulled more out of him.

Must be rusty. It'd been a while since she'd had to operate. She made her way out of the restaurant, catching sight of Andrew hurrying to a black sports car. No, not just a sports car. A Lamborghini Centenario. If *Andrew* was in acquisitions, what was he acquiring—beyond people—to be able to afford that beauty?

"Stay out of my head!"

Mercy jerked around to see Peyton and Lawe quibbling. She took a second to compose herself, then stalked down the path toward the lovebirds.

"You promised—"

"No," Lawe growled, "I never—"

"You are a coward! You *da*—"

"You know," Mercy interrupted, "Felicia Hardy wasn't honest with Spider-Man either."

The two blinked at her, their argument scuttled at the introduction of superheroes. It always worked. Not many people knew much about comic book characters, so their initial confusion afforded an opening.

"Felicia. Black Cat," Mercy explained, nodding to Peyton. "When Doctor Strange helped Peter, he ended up giving Felicia more superpowers, but she kept it to herself. She couldn't live with it or the secrets she kept from Peter."

Peyton's gaze slipped away from them. Touché.

Mercy pursed her lips. "She left, then when she returned years later, she was angry because Peter had married."

"I'm not married," Adam countered.

Mercy tilted her head as she started walking. "I didn't say it was a *perfect* analogy. Just similar. Besides, Black Cat lost her memories of—"

"Mercy." Peyton sliced a hand through the air. "Enough."

"It is, isn't it?" She smirked at them. "Just kiss and get it over with already. Tell him you're angry because he didn't ask you to marry him." Adam looked like he'd been on a boat too long. "Because he chose the Navy over you."

"I never—"

"And you, tell Peyton you're terrified of letting her down but also afraid that if you give up your career, you'll be less of a man. Which you won't. Because"—she squeezed his bicep, or tried—"hello! Too much man packed beneath this skin."

"Mercy," Peyton hissed.

She held up her hands and started backing away. "Middle ground. All I'm sayin'. I mean, we're on the same team, so it's not like either of you lose what you want." She clapped her hands. "Chop-chop. Get it done. We have a mission, and by the number of times my phone has buzzed, I think the director is a little peeved."

Adam and Peyton considered each other, their uncertainty blatant. Wondering if what she'd said was true. Which it was. The truth was as obvious as the blush on Peyton's face and the flush on Adam's—both ticked yet both wanting to be together. It was painful to watch.

"Middle ground," Mercy whispered.

Adam growled.

"Cute." Mercy shrugged. "But Hulk does it better."

SIX

NASSAU, BAHAMAS

"We were wrong."

Arms folded, legs shoulder-width apart, Leif stared at the live feed of Admiral Braun and three other uniforms. "About what, this time?"

Her ire and eyebrows rose, but she stayed her course. "Mr. Purcell anticipated the artifact would be detected here on the island—"

"Let's be clear," Cell interjected, hands lifting in a placating manner. "It *was* here, but by the time there was enough actionable intel—"

"It's pinging in Greece." Braun cut him short.

"Greece." Culver scoffed, pushing back in his chair and stretching out his legs. "That's the other side of the globe."

"Why didn't we hit this thing when it was here?" Lawe asked, stabbing the table. "You have those trigger words, right?"

Silence gaped through the hangar.

"Trigger words," Klein repeated, easing forward in his seat. "To have a list of trigger words you're monitoring, you'd need to have a knowledge base." He squinted at the screen. "How do we have a knowledge base to work from if we've never had the scroll itself? If this thing has been lost—"

"We're getting off track," a captain said, angling into the camera. "Let us worry about the intel, and you guys pound the ground."

Irritation skidded around the team, who were not cool with a *shut up and do the dirty work* attitude.

"Thank you, sir," Leif said firmly. "You are?"

"Leif," someone muttered.

"He's giving orders, and I can't know his name?"

"Captain Aznar."

Aznar. Aznar. Why was that familiar?

"We work with the intel handed to us," Iliescu said, his gaze straying to Leif's for a second. "And then we move."

Aznar. *Intel handed . . .*

Reimer.

Was the deputy director saying this intel came from Reimer? Or was he saying they'd intercepted it? Because those were two very different scenarios. It had to be the latter, because Iliescu wouldn't send him out on intel from Reimer. Not after the Sahara Nine.

Would he?

"The facility is Aperióristos Labs in the Port of Igoumenitsa." Admiral Braun smiled through the live feed. "Gentlemen, this is right up your gangway." Using a laser pointer, she circled a location. "The port is approximately ten klicks outside Athens. It primarily services ship docking along with passenger and vehicle traffic. Abutting the inlet," she said, slowing her explanation as she zoomed in on the satellite image, "is this lab just up the hillside from the main road that cuts through the area. You'll boat in, then dive and take props inland. You'll cross the road, then hoof it up and around the facility to come in on the back side."

Leif folded his arms as he considered the building. "Large facility. How do we know where to find the book?"

Braun nodded to another uniform, who lifted a remote.

"Bill Masters," he said in introduction. "When the trigger words were detected, we were able to narrow down the location—that facility—but we haven't been able to isolate beyond what—"

"I can," Mercy said in a demure tone.

Nobody responded, probably too stunned that she'd say she could do something CIA analysts hadn't been able to pull off.

"Look, I appreciate—"

"No, I really don't think you do," she countered.

This was why guys fell hard and fast for the hacker. From the corner of his eye, he noted her sit back and cross her legs. Throwing every bit of her femininity behind her words so the tech would discount her because she was beautiful and a woman. She'd use that to her advantage and face-plant the guy right in his own arrogance. It was cruelly effective in getting her way.

"Ms. Maddox, certain systems are locked down tight. The company knows there will be hack attempts, so they layered in redundancies."

"Really?"

It wasn't a question but probably sounded enough like one to feed her ruse. Leif tried to hide his smirk so he didn't steal her incoming thunder. He could feel static building in the air.

"Look, I know you—"

"Let's stop right there." Mercy squared off her tone and her body language. "You *don't* know me. Won't. And neither will this facility, because I'm good at what I do. Give me access. I can find the book's location."

"It's a scroll, actually," the tech snarled. "And you're out of your pretty head if you think—"

"If I *think*?" Mercy laughed—that caustic, almost lighthearted laugh. "Dude, you have no idea. Never will either. But thanks for calling me pretty. Now, get over yourself and get out of the way. Allow the big girls to do their work."

Culver and Saito barked laughs. Though Mercy had shredded this tech, Leif tried not to laugh. No need to make things worse. Because this would be remembered. It would create problems down the road if Masters didn't recover some face.

"Ms. Maddox—"

"Do you even know what a reverse port forward is?"

"Sure," Masters said. "I use Metasploit all the time."

"Why are you even worried about that?" Mercy asked. "Look, if you just Nmap their servers and probe for SQL injections, then we can gain access and move along." She huffed. "I can spend the next twenty minutes explaining, or I can spend the next twenty *doing*."

"You can use mine," Cell said, sliding his laptop to her.

"Thanks, but no." Mercy pulled a laptop from her bag.

"Ms. Maddox," Braun huffed, "just a minute." She leaned over and whispered something to Masters.

Saito glanced at the team, then the screen. "What's going on?"

Leif noted the granite-like quality of Mercy's face. On the screen, Braun and Masters were still talking, the latter making sweeping gestures with his hands, indignation marching a cadence across his jaw.

"Mercy?" Leif asked.

"They want me to use a CIA system so they can piggyback what I do," she growled. "It means they can steal my secrets, and that's so not happening."

Leif moved in front of her, nearly toe-to-toe. Not breaking eye contact, he slid her laptop between them. "Mercy," he said loudly enough to be heard through the feed but his face telegraphing a hint, "we need to work as a team."

Mischief tweaked the hard edge that had overtaken her expression. She had a silicon keyboard protector that all but silenced her typing, yet he felt the weight of her fingers as she logged on.

"For this to work," Leif said, trying to add irritation to his voice, "we all have to be willing to make sacrifices."

Her eyes lifted briefly to his.

"Yeah," Culver drawled, joining in, "it don't work for us to fight each other. We have to fall in line. Be good submissive soldiers." His chest pressed against Leif's shoulder. Another presence formed on his left, shielding Mercy from the camera. They weren't lying. The team *was* working together now. Just not in the way the upper echelon intended.

"It is good thing," Baddar added, "to work as a team. To be most effective."

"I get it," Mercy said, her fingers flying. "But sometimes . . . it's just a little much . . . asking a girl to expose herself."

"That is appreciated, but the—"

"Ms. Maddox?" Braun's voice grated from the feed, staticky but tinged with suspicion. "Ms. Maddox, we feel—"

"What's she doing?" Masters asked.

"Hey, we're just trying to talk her through it," Saito said, angling the lens more toward himself. He grinned, eyeing himself in the reverse camera, and scoffed. "I had parsley between my teeth. Sorry about that."

"Inside their servers," Mercy murmured.

"Mr. Saito!"

"*Hai.*" Classic Saito, acting like a foreign national when it suited. "I mean, yes. You gotta admit—Ms. Maddox isn't used to working within the system, so give the guys a minute to talk her down."

"We can't see her anymore," Masters complained. "What's she—we're picking up . . ."

"Mr. Purcell." Braun tried a different tactic, attempting to get their new dog on a leash. "You have a job—"

"Yes, ma'am." Cell took over the camera angle. "What can I do for you?"

"Level two o-bliterated," Mercy muttered.

"Shut her down!" someone barked. "She's hacking."

"Ms. Maddox, I insist you stop what you're doing."

"How long?" Leif didn't bother whispering.

"Few more minutes," Mercy said, her work fast and furious.

"She's running algorithms."

"Wait," Cell said. "Masters, I thought you were the expert. If you think Mercy is hacking, surely you can shut her down. But I'm starting to wonder why you're sitting in the seat of power and this beauty is kicking your—"

"This is not a game!" Braun barked. "You could seriously compromise—"

"Not a chance," Mercy bit back.

"Cease your attempts immediately, Ms. Maddox, or you will force our hand to—"

"Mercy," Leif warned.

But she wasn't listening. She was working. Flying through what she called cyberocity.

"Can you find her system?" Braun asked Masters. "Locate her signal. Backtrace her."

"It's all over the place," Masters complained.

"C'mon, c'mon," Lawe said.

"Mercy . . ." Leif said again.

"Yeah, yeah. Shush." She took the laptop and swiveled around to the table, shedding all pretense.

Leif and the guys followed her, more curious than protective about what she was doing. And if command came after her, it would be through that laptop. He hoped she had protocols to protect herself and that system.

Watching, he saw her gray screen filled with black letters. Folding an arm over his chest, he covered his mouth.

The screen went black. The text changed to turquoise.

"Hello, Masters," Mercy said, never slowing but apparently registering the breach.

"What does that mean?" Baddar swung to her right, placed a palm on the table.

"It means . . . they've detected and located my system." Her long auburn hair hung in her face as she worked. "Started countermeasures."

"That's not good, right?" Leif asked, noting a din of curses and raging on the CIA side.

Mercy continued typing out strings of commands. The screen shifted. The letters turned red. "Crap." She bobbed her head, hair swaying. She opened a nested file and scanned it. Clicked. A series of images popped up on the screen. At first, four, then six. Nine. "Bingo!" With a flurry of keystrokes, she attacked the laptop. "Tag," she murmured, then began a series of steps that closed out the multiple screens. "You're it." She straightened. Let out a breath.

"What?" Leif asked, checking her laptop, seemingly innocuous and innocent now. No nefarious coding. Yet still running.

"I planted a back door into the facility's video feeds. We can access them at will and see what's in there."

Leif smiled. "So we don't go in blind."

"Or end up dead."

He pivoted, stared at the screen into CIA HQ. At the flushed faces. The scowls. "And why couldn't your team do that?"

"We could," Masters growled. "But . . ."

"You had red tape," Leif said. "Had to get authorizations."

Culver added, "Which would've cost time."

"Time nobody had," Saito finished.

"But see? We"—Leif thumbed around—"don't exist. So accessing that from an island in the Bahamas buys us cover."

"If she used CIA servers—"

Mercy snorted.

Leif stood straighter. "Point is, ma'am, we can now surveil the facility and find what we're looking for."

Braun huffed.

"Leif," Iliescu said, "you and the team get airborne. Mercy—that back door—"

"Not really a back door," she said with a shrug.

"Is that something *we* can access?" Iliescu asked.

Mercy considered them for a moment. "No, but I could probably change that. If you ask really nice."

"You do realize I'm your boss, right?"

"Mm."

Iliescu smirked. "Get it done, Mercy." He raised his eyebrows. "*Please.*"

SEVEN

APERIÓRISTOS LABS, PORT OF IGOUMENITSA, GREECE

The chopper flew low over the dark waters, stirring up an angry wake. The bird veered around and hovered above the landing pad of the super yacht. To save time instead of landing, Marines secured the team's rucks to a line and lowered them, while Leif, Culver, and Saito fast-roped onto the deck.

Crouched against the downwash of the rotors, two men greeted them. Leif pressed into his fear and followed the guys off the deck. Boots on the rails of the steps, he slid to the lower deck. A buzz against his wrist made him angle his arm as they rounded and descended another flight. "Maps are in," he noted to Culver and Saito.

The dark-haired guy—no names would be used or given to protect both sides—stalked down a narrow passage. "We've picked up a lot of radio traffic in the area. Foreign."

"That unusual?" Culver asked.

"Not on these channels." He pushed through a door into the launch bay of the super yacht. Three diver propulsion vehicles—or DPVs—bobbed on the water like long black torpedoes with encased fans at the stern. There was a cutout for the diver to sit in and grips to control gear shifting. They quietly lapped water as if anticipating the new adventure. "I'd recommend you stay eyes out. Might have some company there."

Culver shared a long look with Leif as they geared up. He stepped into a dry suit. Strapped on the tank. KA-BAR around his thigh. Weapons in the ruck secured to the prop.

With comms pieces, they were able to connect with Cell and

Mercy, who were holed up in a CIA safe house five klicks south of the facility.

"Moby Bravo is a klick out," Cell reported.

Devine, Lawe, Klein, and Baddar were hidden in the hills on the northeastern side of the building to allow a quick exfil.

"Roger that."

Leif stepped down onto the skid, straddling the prop and testing the ruck anchored to it. He scooped water and smeared it over his face, then settled the mask over his eyes and nose. One more glance at his device told him they were tracking well. With a thumbs-up to the yacht, he tucked in his rebreather and pressed his gut to the prop's spine.

The three team members with the most water experience glided into the water. Some found being submerged frightening. Leif found it reassuring as the liquid coldness enveloped him like a glove. Reminded him this was his expertise. A thousand things could go wrong, but that was part of the thrill. Could his training save him? Maybe that was what it was about—the challenge. The ocean wasn't a gentle adversary. Without hesitation, it could choke the life from a body.

But it was also the silence. The forbiddance of noise, other than a deep sonorous sound wave that rolled through the liquid. Quiet. Serene. Vast.

Leif checked his device to verify their heading. A shadow skittered through the water, bisecting the dull glow of his headlamp. Could be a threat but was more likely a biologic.

Twenty minutes in, the ocean started to surrender its depth. A vibration against his wrist indicated it was time to dump the prop. He aimed down to the sea floor and let the prop come to a rest. Then he threaded his arms through the ruck and began the one-klick swim to shore. Culver and Saito did the same.

Invigorated by the swim, he breached the surface stealthily. Far enough out not to be noticed. Culver and Saito came up on his three. They aimed at a cluster of rocks amid craggy shrubs. When his feet hit slush sand, he waded in. Slow. Calm. Eyes out. Tracking. Listening.

The throaty whine of a diesel engine split the night.

Leif crouched in the water as a white van barreled up to the facility gate. Two guards emerged from the hut, while those walking the meter-wide wall moved toward the area to provide extra security.

With the guards distracted, Leif crawled onto the beach as if being washed ashore. Anything not to splash or draw attention. There, he checked the guards. Then sprinted to the rocks and flattened himself. Silently, he stripped out of the gear, tugging off the suit from over his pants and tactical shirt, stuffing the tank and rebreather into the bag, then started digging. He buried the gear and covered it, using rocks to mark the location for the retrieval crew.

Weapon slung crossbody, he knelt and took point. A pat to his shoulder, then another, told him the guys were ready. They used the rocky slope and crags to traverse the road to the southwest side, beyond the guard hut. Barked commands at the gate ordered the van to pull through. Which meant the guards would be returning to sentry duty.

Time to move. With hand signals, Leif sent the others across the road. As soon as they launched out, he provided cover. They cleared it, and he pushed up to follow. A shout erupted, forcing Leif behind the rocks to wait. To watch. A sentry was eyeballing his location. Demanding light.

If they lit this place up . . .

Tires pealed on the road.

Leif glanced to his six, where a small dark car tore down the hill. Fast. Too fast. What the—?

Guards hollered at each other. At the tower, the sentry was still perched, monitoring this location.

The car barreled around the corner. Tipped as its tires screamed through the curve. The driver overcorrected and flipped—right into the lap of the protected entrance. Guards shouted and ran toward the gate. Several at the wall trained their weapons on the scene, but more were concerned about the driver.

Move!

Leif pitched himself up over the hillside and sprinted until he reached the coordinates. When he slid to his knees next to the guys, he breathed easier.

"What was that?" Culver asked.

Leif double-checked the lit-up gate. Considered the car wreck. How that driver had managed not to take out the wall.

"Distraction." Saito voiced the same conclusion as Leif.

"But not ours," Leif amended.

Which meant they had company. So who else was here? Now they'd need to anticipate trouble getting into the facility. Opening comms would make it possible to detect their signal and location. Couldn't risk that.

"What's the call?" Culver asked, eyeing Leif.

"Keep moving."

The men pushed on. Picked their way through the heavily treed hillside toward the only vulnerability Mercy had discovered in the electrical fence. She'd created a time-lapse program that would sync with the internal security of the facility and their computer system to bypass locks, taking the team straight to the book.

A concrete wall abutted the sheer face of hard-packed earth that rose another klick above them. Up there somewhere, Devine covered their six with her sniper rifle and Lawe as her spotter. Klein and Baddar were positioned on the opposite cleft for a clean exfil.

Weapons up, cheeks to the stocks, they slid along the wall like the skilled operators they were. At a blind corner, they paused. Leif bobbed out for a split-second recon. More concrete. Air units. Large containers with ladders running to their domed peaks. Massive industrial units. He stepped out and hugged the wall, his shoulder lightly scratching against the concrete as he advanced to the terraced entrance. A lone door waited.

He motioned Culver forward to use the programmed access card.

As Culver came around, Leif detected movement on the other side of the glass. He snapped up a fist.

Culver dropped into a crouch.

Watching down the barrel of his M4A1, Leif eyed the group of four techs inside, laughing and talking as they strolled down the hall.

Laughing. Talking. Not running.

Maybe the internal alarms weren't blaring after that car accident at the gate. That was a classic distraction technique. They should be on full alert. Or maybe he was just jumpy.

No. He had instincts most didn't have. The ability to read a situation and process information lightning fast.

When the hall was clear and fell into darkness—sensor-activated lighting dropping back into sleep mode—he nodded to Culver, who made quick work of crossing the terrace, staying close and out of range of the cameras. Head down, shoulders hunched, he swiped the card.

Nothing. The light stayed red.

He swiped again. Same result.

Crap. Mercy . . .

A third time. Even from his position ten meters away, Leif heard the locks disengage. Which—if Mercy was right—should also disable the cameras and the motion-sensor lights, thanks to her handiwork. They had 10.5 seconds to reach the next juncture. She couldn't blitz all the cameras and locks at once, or it'd draw attention and trigger a security alert.

Leif and Saito snaked inside, wishing for night-vision but not able to risk it if someone came into the hall and unexpectedly splashed light all over and blinded them.

As the map instructed, they banked left. Then left again. Leif sighted the gray double doors. Two paces out, he heard the click of the locks. Weapon and tension up, he reached for the door handle.

Voices came from his six. Culver slid around him and palmed the door handle. Stock tucked against his shoulder, Leif gave him a curt nod. Culver tugged it open. Leif hurried through, sensing his near-silent partners follow him into the next passage. The door hissed shut. Clicked.

It was 8.7 seconds to the next lock. He angled his wrist, a move that took his gaze off the sterile halls, to check the map. *Right. Then left.*

Lights in the next corridor sprang to life, and he stilled. Voices and shadows danced along the slick white walls.

With two fingers, he sent Culver and Saito to the doorways on the right, then plastered himself into an opposite small juncture, hidden enough not to be seen if someone wasn't looking for an intruder. Most people were oblivious to threats around them. In familiar places, they saw what their minds expected to see.

A short Asian doctor in a gray lab coat came down the hall with two women. One wore a similar lab coat. The other had on a black pantsuit and nodded at something the doctor said, her attention wholly on him.

A vibration against Leif's wrist told him they'd missed the second lock timing. Although they were radio silent, Command monitored their infiltration through short bursts sent from their comms at random intervals. They'd be okay as long as Mercy reset the time.

Keep moving, keep moving, he mentally prodded the threesome.

The woman in the black suit was friendly. Enthralled. Too enthralled? She bent forward, nodding eagerly. Her dark hair was tied back from a complexion that wasn't quite olive. But it also wasn't pale against those raspberry-colored lips. Her brown eyes were amused.

Wait. Eyes? Leif's pulse jacked. The woman wasn't looking at the doc. She was looking right at him.

I'm made!

The human, natural side of him exploded with an urge to hide. But his heightened instinct and training warned any movement would seal his fate. Besides, he wasn't convinced she'd seen him in this pitch-black alcove. What made her scrutinize the shadows of the semi-darkened hall anyway? Apparently, *she* had a heightened instinct.

He didn't move. Didn't twist. Didn't take his eyes off her. He slowed his breathing, refusing to betray himself.

She touched the doctor's shoulder, laughed in a melodic way, then turned as they entered another lab. Thank God.

Once the door hissed closed, Leif twitched forward. Eyed the others with a nod. He checked the map on his device, then the door. And realized the disastrous truth.

The room the trio had just entered was where intel suggested they'd find the Book of the Wars.

EIGHT

APERIÓRISTOS LABS, GREECE

"Doctor Chowdhury, is that door locked?" Iskra glanced back, eyeing the steel frame and jamb, her heart still thudding over the shifting shadows of the hall beyond.

Just get it and get out.

She turned. Glaring white stabbed her corneas as she took in the sterile facility. They were in what looked like a reception area that fanned out into grayish-black windows accessing five additional labs. At the far side of the individual labs were floor-to-ceiling cabinets containing at least fifty drawers. Decontamination tubes stood guard between the foyer and the labs.

"It is. All doors are automatically secured when they shut."

"Good." She smiled. "And when you access the rooms and the vaults, you go through to the other side?"

"Yes, but the artifact can't go through—it must be preserved."

"Of course," Iskra said as if she agreed. "And if this outer door is unlocked, the inner door remains locked, yes?"

"Correct!" He stabbed the air, his dark complexion showing the ash of age. "We cannot risk contamination."

Iskra studied the vaults, the decon hubs, the inner doors. Then the larger ones on the far side of the preservation room. Which, according to the schematic she'd memorized, should lead her to a rear passage. She let out a shaky breath that was more real than she wanted to admit. "I am very pleased with your security measures, because I'm afraid I have very bad news."

He frowned, laughing uncertainly as he looked at his assistant, Lisa.

"In that hall, I think there were some . . . intruders." Iskra leaned in and cringed. "I think they had guns."

"Wha—?!" He spun around, staring at the door in disbelief. "I didn't see anyone."

"I think they are very dangerous." She touched fingers to her lips, doing her best to appear scared. "Maybe even deadly soldiers."

Lisa let out a strangled yelp.

"Do you think—should you notify security?"

Rattled, shifting between going to the door or the desk phone, he nodded. "Y-yes. Yes. Of course." His brow beaded with sweat.

Darkness clapped through the facility. Someone had cut the power. After a mechanical whirring, emergency protocols sounded and washed the lab in a sea of bloody light.

Iskra lifted her gaze and traced the strobing patterns. The cameras. "No," she breathed, spinning toward the lab doors. She bolted to one and yanked. Locked tight. "Those fools!"

The loss of power—compliments, no doubt, of the thugs in the hall—had locked down the bays, preventing access to the artifacts. To the book.

"We should go this way," Chowdhury said, tugging her arm. "We have emergency power, which allows only those with upper clearance to open the doors."

"Like you," Iskra said, batting away strands of hair.

"Of course," he crooned with a laugh. "I am the lead specialist. And do not worry—they often do special drills to test response times."

"I know. How do you think I got in?" Her ruse as a journalist had only worked because the guards were so distracted at the front gate that they hastily authorized what appeared to be legitimate credentials. They hadn't looked closely enough.

His smile wavered as he hesitated. "What?"

She rotated the thick ring on her finger. "I'm so sorry." She touched the doctor's neck, pressing her fingers around his throat, then stepped back.

He pulled in a sharp breath, covering the spot where the ring had punctured his skin. "What . . . what did you do?" But even as he breathed the last word, he wavered.

Lisa screamed as Iskra caught and lowered him to the ground, then checked his carotid. "Did you kill him?"

"No. But the ring only has enough sedative for one. So now you have a choice." Iskra shoved heavy threat into the look she gave Lisa. "All I want is a book you're keeping."

"DS-972," the assistant said. "You're after it, too."

Iskra hesitated. *Too?*

The assistant smiled—then flashed out a knife-hand strike.

Iskra blocked, but the swift move knocked her backward. Lisa lunged at her, taking Iskra to the floor. She cuffed Iskra's throat. She was wild. Feral. Vicious as she constricted.

With a swing of her legs, Iskra flipped them. She wasn't going to lose to this woman or leave her alive. Because that look in her eyes—Iskra knew it. Knew what drove it. She didn't just *know*. She remembered. Had felt it. This woman would never stop.

Iskra reared back to punch. To drive the woman's nose through her skull. But as she unleashed the strike, Lisa jerked aside. Iskra pulled the punch, narrowly avoiding cracking her knuckles.

A flurry of arms and legs had them wrestling. Tangling. Writhing. But one thing registered in Iskra's mind in the chaos and fury.

Behind Lisa's ear was a tiny dot.

A receiver. Communication. *She's not alone.*

Iskra switched tactics. Prayed it wasn't a mistake. She let Lisa gain the advantage. Let the woman's fist connect with her cheekbone. She slumped flat against the ground with a groan.

"Finally," Lisa mumbled as she climbed to her feet. She stood over Iskra. Kicked her in the side.

Rage seized Iskra, but she coiled it tight and stowed it. Not yet. Not yet . . .

A stream of German flew from Lisa's lips. Iskra fought the urge to groan. German. Rutger. Again! No doubt protecting his precious artifact.

"*Ja*. It's me. Restore the power to the lab," Lisa said as she walked toward the bay doors. "I'm right in front of it. *Ja* . . . Wha—she's down. No, didn't kill him—there was a woman posing as a journalist . . . I wanted to."

Iskra heard the voice aim at her, knew Lisa was looking at her again.

"Just give me power," she said, her voice bouncing on the walls again. "I've got his card, and we can get the book to another location for safekeeping."

Iskra smiled.

A distinctive *shunk* rattled through the facility. Lights hummed and bloomed.

Iskra hopped to her feet. Slid in. Struck the woman in the back of the head, pitching her into the bulletproof glass. Her forehead hit. Bounced. Lisa fell backward. Iskra snatched the card and swiped into the main bay. Inside, she endured the blast of sanitized air, itching to get into the vault, get the book, and get out. Before the operators in the hall—

Crack!

As the mist died, she looked back at the lab's main door, which bucked beneath a breach. Three men glided in, moving with precision. Smooth. They wore no insignia, but the weapons—M4A1s—were preferred by American special operators.

Leaving the sanitizing bay, she hurried into the vault. Checked over her shoulder, relieved she now had *two* doors between her and the operators. The middle guy had pale eyes that were locked on her and furious. She smirked. Then checked her escape route—an exit via a rear sanitization hub.

One of the operators eased to the main bay door. Stuck something on the glass.

Heart in her throat, Iskra realized it was a charge. A small one but enough to erase the protection she'd just gloated over. "Wait!" She lurched toward the clear barrier. "Don't!"

Pale Eyes held a hand up to the others.

"If you blow that door," she shouted, no idea if they could hear her, "this door"—she tapped the barrier in front of her—"won't open." Neither would the one behind her, which she needed for her escape.

He hesitated. Wariness guarded his face as the other operators shouldered closer, their mouths moving, probably voicing their reluctance to trust her. But their gazes betrayed uncertainty, too.

Good. Time to find the box! She pivoted and scanned the rows of vault boxes. Fingers tracing the labels, she finally found the one marked DS-972. She tucked Chowdhury's card in the slot. The door hissed open. A black box the size of a legal letter lay there for the taking.

Thwack. Thump.

Lifting the box, she glanced over her shoulder—right as claxons sounded. The team was through the first door and stood in the decontamination hub, the sanitation spray hissing.

Iskra darted to the exit on the other side. She couldn't get through the decontamination hub if the inner door they were working on opened first.

Pale Eyes was shouting. A charge was on the window.

She swiped the card. It didn't work.

"No." She checked the team as she reswiped. Heart thundering, she whimpered when it failed again. Then she noticed she held the card wrong.

Thwack!

She swiped.

Thump!

The door started opening—then stopped.

"No!" Iskra threw herself at the inches-wide gap. Wedged herself sideways into the sliver of a space, thrusting the box ahead of her to be sure—in case she got stuck—that the soldiers couldn't get it. She shoved, pushed.

Shouts reached her, followed by a gust of air.

Right shoulder through, she wiggled against the crushing door. Rocked back and forth, trying to squeeze through.

Something caught her leg. She cried out. As if responding to her pleas, the door gave—apparently released because the operators' door had closed and sealed, thereby freeing the rear hub doors. She stumbled into the chamber, stunned. As the pelting decontamination spray started, she realized the new dilemma facing her: after the spray ended, whichever door opened first would automatically seal the other door. Therefore, they could trap her if she was even a microsecond slower. They'd win. Take the book.

The operators were working hard and fast—like her heart.

The hissing air slowed. She reached for the handle.

Pale Eyes held her in a visual standoff, talking to the side, to his teammate.

The door finally unlocked, and she yanked it open—but it froze. She glanced back to see what had happened, why it had only given her a couple of inches. The operators were facing the same predicament. The power had somehow failed. But their brute strength was widening their gap.

Panicking, Iskra shoved the box through the opening, refusing to fail or be stopped. She couldn't let freedom be ripped away.

"Stop! Stop or we'll shoot." His voice was deep, filled with threat.

It pulled her around, her nose skimming the wall. She leaned toward escape, but he held her upper arm. She wrestled. Writhed. Then slipped free—but was still wedged. She glared at him through the door that provided the only available protection. Kept the box from his reach. Wished she'd brought a weapon.

The ring.

Using her thumb, she twisted it around her finger. There might not be any paralytic left, but it would sting. Cut.

He reached through the gap. Like a cat with claws, she slapped him. Dragged the ring down his hand.

But he kept coming. As if the cut hadn't even fazed him. It must've been sharp enough not to register. Had she missed? She did it again.

Same. No response. That wasn't possible. She looked at his hand. Two angry thin red lines. He eyed them too, then glanced back up at her. Apathetic about her attempt to harm him.

"Clear!" The guy behind him was backing away.

What was clear?

Pale Eyes held her gaze for a second. She inched back, and her periphery snagged on something. A gray brick stuck to the door.

C-4! They'd set a charge. She bounced back to his gaze. "You'll kill us all."

He gave a cockeyed nod. "Only you."

Only? Iskra checked the charge and found he was right. It was attached to her side of the decontamination hub. It'd blow her and the door. In all her fighting with him, she hadn't noticed his buddy working the odds in their favor. "You blow that door, the outer one won't open."

This time, he smirked. "We can handle it." He thumbed over his shoulder, indicating the inner door they'd somehow bypassed without damaging.

Think! How did she stop them? "You'll damage the book."

"Box is fireproof. Blast won't touch the book." He grinned. "But nice try."

She cursed him and herself. Tried to wiggle free, but he held here there. With everything she had, she backfisted him. Felt her knuckles connect with hard cartilage. He stumbled back, releasing her with a muttered oath.

The charge was counting down. And she was still stuck. She thrashed. Jolted. Kicked to free her left ankle.

Without warning, she was falling out of the decontamination hub. She thudded hard against the floor. She tensed, expecting a blast of superheated air. The concussive punch. But then she realized the detonation wasn't why she'd fallen. Her foot had broken free. She stared down at the small gray charge—now on the other side of the door. She'd somehow kicked it loose.

The operators were diving away.

She did the same. Rotated and pitched herself toward cover. The detonation hit. With a jumble of sounds, the concussion streaked through the small space. Slammed her into the ground. Heat seared her leg. Had the exterior door not been there, she'd have been blown to bits.

Disoriented, she forced herself to move. *Go! Now!* The team would be on her soon. They'd get the book.

She rolled over. Groaned. The door was cracked and hung crooked—that was how the heat had escaped.

The pale-eyed operator was on his feet. Blood streaked his temple as he lunged at the door. Not wanting to get captured by him, she clambered upright. Her ankle screamed in protest. She dragged herself around. Spotted the box a half dozen feet away. She lunged at it. Cradled it. Glanced through the dusty fog and glass door.

Crack-crack!

Using his weapon as a battering ram, he was making quick work of the now-flimsy barrier. Iskra swallowed at his determination. The same kind spiraled through her, mixing with adrenaline and the taunt of victory.

Pain radiated through her leg. Crying out, she used the wall to steady herself. Braved one more look at the door. After a glower in her direction, Pale Eyes threw his shoulder into it. The frame gave but then popped back into place. She had time. A chance to get out. Their eyes met again.

Fury tangling his features, he unleashed a roar that crossed the barrier. He punched the door in frustration.

He couldn't get through. Couldn't stop her. And she had the book.

Iskra smiled as she left the lab, babying her injured leg. Though it slowed her, she kept hobbling. Shouts and gunshots pervaded the halls ahead. She had to get to the stairs. One more junction.

She hobble-hurried to the next secure door. Swiped Chowdhury's card. It opened.

"Stop!" his deep voice commanded.

Not looking back, she shoved forward.

Crack! Pop! Ping!

She ducked, startled that he'd fired at her. But why should she be surprised? She'd just tried to blow him and his men to pieces. She hadn't really wanted to *kill* them. However, she also didn't want them killing *her*. But considering they had weapons and she had an aching ankle and a heavy box containing a scroll, things weren't looking good.

Palming the walls helped her move. She scrabbled along. Found the satchel she'd prearranged with a contact to leave. Bribing people shouldn't be that easy, but most were glad for the money and rationalized something as innocuous as an abandoned satchel didn't make them complicit. She tucked the box in the bag and rolled around the corner.

Their backs to her, a group of security personnel stalked away from her down the corridor.

Iskra froze. Eyed the door across from her. Stairs. She had to get there. But first she'd have to swipe the card. It'd chirrup, giving her away. Could she do it surrepti—

The hefty thud of a security door came from behind. The operators, no doubt. She was out of time. She leapt across the hall, aiming Chowdhury's badge at the strip as she did. Swiped. Shouldered through into the stairwell, hearing the door slam shut behind her. The weight of the box pulled her down. She tripped. Nearly face-planted against the concrete steps. She dragged herself up.

Shouts. Shots. Thuds. Running.

She held her breath, listening. There was no sliver or window through which to watch the unfolding drama. She expected them to burst into the stairwell at any moment.

One breath. Two. Heavy steps pounded past the door.

Silence fell.

Go. Go, Iskra.

The guards must have encountered the Americans and given chase. She took pleasure in thinking Pale Eyes had unwittingly *aided* her escape.

Iskra hobbled the steps. All the way up three excruciating floors to the roof. She pushed through a final door and tumbled into the crisp, cool predawn morning. Into the embrace of darkness and anonymity. She hurried to AC unit number three and dropped to her knees, but not before checking the northeast corner. The triangular shape there gave her the slightest glimmer of hope that this might work out.

Feeling around in the gravel at the concrete base, she kept watch on the door. The operators were skilled. Quick. Determined.

So was she.

Which could make things interesting.

She set down the satchel and dug a little harder. Where was it? Her pulse skipped a beat. What if her bribed contact hadn't left it?

She swiveled around to the other unit, its motor cranking and rattling. She squinted across the darkness, tracing that base, too, then scooted over and searched the area. On the side facing the front of the building, dirt, tar, and gravel revealed something smooth and long. "Yes!" She brushed away the dirt and rocks, then shook it out.

Thwack!

The noise came from behind.

Crouching behind the unit, she peered through a jungle of steel and iron to the area illuminated by a lone floodlight. The stairwell door had belched two operators onto the roof. How had they figured out she was up here?

Too good. They were *too* good.

The sharp edges of relief struck as they veered west, away from her. Gave her time. Not much, but maybe enough. Propped up against the unit, she shed the business jacket and stuffed her injured leg into the wind suit. Grimacing as she put her weight on the sore ankle, she threaded the other leg, then her arms. Zipped up the suit. Turned for the satchel and—

Oh no. She looked from the AC unit beside her to the first one she'd checked. She'd left the satchel there. A mere four feet separated her from it, but that was four feet of exposure. She muttered an oath. Eyed the operators bringing their sweep from the south. With a quick breath, she crouch-ran to the north side of the other unit.

For at least a few seconds, she was hidden. Back to the vibrating unit, she rolled her head to the left. Locked onto the satchel. She stretched out an arm, trying to keep the movements small.

Oh, forget this. It was too far and taking too long. Knowing the danger, she sprang across the gap and snatched up the bag. Dropped back behind cover.

"Over here," one called, his voice strangely close and yet distant beneath the powerful growl of the AC units.

She tucked the satchel strap over her head and shoulder so it lay crossbody, then eyed the triangular shape hugging the northeast corner. Two meters. If she stayed low, she could make it. Probably.

It was enough of a chance to seize. She stretched onto her belly and slunk toward it, dragging her injured foot noisily. She cringed.

"Runt, I see movement."

"Hit it!"

So much for stealth. Iskra pitched herself at the triangle and ducked under it. Grabbed the crossbar. Shoved to her feet with a growl of pain, grit, and determination. She spun around and lumbered onto the foot-wide roof ledge. Wobbled and nearly yelped before catching her balance.

"Stop! Stop!"

Hoisting up the bar, she didn't look. Her precarious position on the precipice worked in her favor. They wanted the book. If they shot her, she'd fall. The book would fall with her.

Hands shaking, she secured the carabiners into the hang glider. Slid her gaze slightly to the right, assessing the men advancing, weapons up and tension taut.

Pale Eyes stalked into view. His eyes were like the moon on a dark night—with a tinge of swelling. "I don't want to end you, but—"

"Don't be stupid," Iskra hissed, clipping the last carabiner onto her suit harness. "Shoot me and you lose the book."

He inched closer, the predawn light exposing his muscular forearms and the edge of a tattoo. He slightly lowered the M4 as he considered her. Or maybe he was considering options. "I let you fly off, I lose the book altogether. But if I take the shot now, the *book* won't die of high-impact trauma." He shrugged, once more lifting his weapon.

"Perhaps." She tested her weight, feeling the searing fire in her ankle as well as the heavy pull of the wind itching to yank her off the building. "But if you hit the book, it's destroyed."

His confidence faltered.

Iskra took advantage of his hesitation and hopped, felt the air catch the nylon wings, and then shot forward, sprinting the length of the ledge, peripherally aware he'd snapped up his weapon again.

A shot cracked and echoed.

She didn't care. She went flying, tasting the only freedom she'd ever know.

NINE

APERIÓRISTOS LABS, GREECE

Curses sailed into the air after the woman. Leif rushed the ledge, trying to take aim, but the wind jerked and tugged her. He fired a warning shot. They needed her alive. As she swooped down, an air current caught and carried her out over the water. He couldn't take another shot, but if that book drowned, they all did. "Augh!"

"Runt, let's move!"

Crack. Plunk! Plunk!

The sharp gust of air made Leif twitch. A shiny blur thudded almost into his feet.

Plunk!

He swung aside. Glared at the hills. "A bit *close*," he growled into his comms as he stared at the grappling hook that had nearly punched a hole in his boot, a quick exfil assist by Devine and Lawe on the hill.

"I missed," Devine said. "Aiming for the mountain beside me."

"Be nice," Lawe responded.

Leif's attention was focused on the woman gliding away with the scroll. Should he be impressed or ticked?

Ticked. She had the book. He didn't. And she'd *smirked* at him, knowing she'd won.

Culver slapped his shoulder. "Company."

Stressed guards spilled from the stairwell onto the tarred roof. Stressed meant shaky trigger fingers. Reactive shooting rather than strategic, logical. Klein and Baddar kept them busy.

After one more look out to sea, her shadow fading from view, Leif lowered himself, placed the cable trolley on the rope, and shoved off. The air snatched at him, assaulting him with an acrid scent. Was there a treatment plant nearby?

The rope's incline wasn't steep enough, forcing Leif to use his body weight to propel himself out of range. They zip-lined a half klick, then dropped into the trees. After fast-roping to the ground, they set out at a quick jog, moving through the unfamiliar territory to the rendezvous point. The hike proved rigorous, each thud of his boots making his head ache. And the woman's wicked backfist had bloodied his nose and made it swell. It wasn't broken but painful all the same.

"What're you thinking?" Saito asked.

"That I need to work out more," Leif grunted as he shoved aside a branch and side-slid down an incline.

Saito scoffed. "Always were soft."

Leif snorted. That had never been true. He'd regularly buffeted his body. Not for vanity, but for this very reason—so he'd be ready, no matter what.

"Might want to hurry," the throaty voice of Lawe said. "Got a storm brewing off the coast."

"What?" Slowing, Leif glanced at the sky but saw only a dark canopy of leaves. "Radar was clear before we launched." Part of their prep was to know weather conditions.

"Roger that," Lawe said. "But it's coming."

As if on cue, a wind gust slapped the branches. A dull roar through the trees, swirling and snaking, as if surrounding them. It reminded him of—

Leaves. It's just the leaves. Keep moving.

"That's not creepy at all," Saito said as they fell into a steady lope.

The air sizzled. Crackled.

Leif picked up his pace, but this time, Culver and Saito had trouble keeping up. They weren't out of shape. The PT this team regularly went through bordered on insane. Hauling tractor tires and towing rigs with nothing but brute strength built up their core so they could face whatever got thrown at them. Holding their breath underwater for minutes at a time bettered their chances of not drowning. But since the desert over five years ago, most people were slower than Leif.

Ten more minutes delivered him to a hillside. Down and to their six, a tunnel had been carved through the island for uninterrupted travel. On a knee, he eyed the gaping maw that birthed and swallowed vehicles heading into or leaving the city. He scanned the sky. Dark clouds to their west. They didn't have much time. Dawn would soon break, and that storm would hit about the same time, eliminating their chance for a safe extraction. He drew out his night-vision binoculars and aimed them out to sea.

Though Culver and Saito were quiet, their movements—weighted by exhaustion—reached his ears before they did.

"It's obscene that you aren't out of breath." Saito knelt beside Leif.

Answering that in any respect would only breed contempt. If he said he'd been out of breath, that would imply having enough time to recover before they caught up. If he said he wasn't out of breath, well, they'd punch him.

No sign of the woman. He rotated to the tunnel and spotted the right front corner of a vehicle's bumper. "They're there." He keyed his mic. "Guardian in position."

"Roger that," Cell replied from the van.

"Let's go."

They hustled down the hill and strolled into the tunnel as casually as possible, even though the early morning twilight hopefully shielded them. At the van, Leif dropped into a side-facing seat. The others piled in, and the vehicle merged into traffic, heading to the safe house.

Leif's thoughts turned back to the woman. When she'd slipped out of his grasp, beaten him, she'd smiled. She *smiled*. Lip and cheek bleeding, face dusted with smoke and ash, she'd stood there and smiled because he'd failed.

Leif thumped the back of the driver's seat.

"Where'd Viorica come from?" Cell asked.

Viorica. It made sense. The reports of her ferocity, the reverence when people spoke of her. The fear.

"As far as we can tell, straight through the front door," Saito said. "Had a cover as a journalist or something. Staff seemed to cater to her, giving her the grand tour, especially considering that wreck by the gate."

Cell's gaze bounced to the rearview mirror and met Leif's.

"Thought it was your job to find out who was in that facility so we'd be ready," Leif said. "To feed us intel to protect our mission from being a total cluster—"

"I'm good but not perfect," Cell replied, gripping the steering wheel tight and hunching forward. "We knew she was after it and still didn't see her until it was too late."

"You look like you're going to blow chunks, Barc," Mercy said.

"I just . . . I've seen enough connected to Viorica to know we have no hope of getting that book back."

THE *TAISSIA*, MEDITERRANEAN SEA

"I want to know who those men were!" Iskra punched the hull of the yacht.

Gentle hands tightened a neoprene wrap around her leg. "The twist is swelling your ankle, but the bone's not broken." Vasily Kuznetsov shook a finger at her. "You must rest. It will only heal if you do. And you need it."

"I *need* answers, not rest!" She hobbled to her feet and tried to pace, the itch of annoyance too great to sit still. "How did they know about the scroll and where it was?"

"Iskra." Vasily was calm as he leaned on the table, eyeing her. But there was no petulance or patronization. Not in those brown eyes, so like his twin's. Valery had been her staunchest supporter. "Let me get this scanned, then we can talk." He nodded to the gangway that led below. "Go. Shower, eat, *rest*. This will take a while."

Survival instinct made her snort, but arguing with Vasily would be futile. He was ten times as stubborn as Valery. With a huff, she left the upper deck, heading down into the yacht. She made her way to the end of the narrow gangway and into a stateroom, where she shed the glider suit and her clothes. A shower kneaded the kinks from her muscles but stung the knot on her cheek. Rubbing her shoulder, she remembered the pale blue eyes, the man who'd nearly destroyed her one chance.

His gaze had seemed . . . hyperfocused. Intense. Fathomless. Beautiful. Like the sky over the sea after a storm.

After drying off, she dressed in a pair of black jeans and a light sweater. Iskra considered the bed as she towel-dried her hair, listening for the first time to the many aches, including the bruises from fighting off Rutger's minion, Lisa, pulsing through her muscles. She touched the soft comforter. Sat on it as she tied up her hair. Just for a minute. Lying down, she stared up at the ceiling and let out a contented moan.

A creak above drew her attention to Vasily. The scroll.

She swallowed, then shook off the temptation to rest and headed topside. As she rounded the corner, Iskra noted dawn creeping into the sky . . . with a storm. Her breath backed into her throat. She vaulted up the stairs, her wet ponytail slapping her face. She dove into the wheel deck.

Vasily jerked up, reaching for a weapon she hadn't noticed before.

"A storm," she breathed.

He scowled. "No. It's clear—"

"There!" She stabbed her hand out the door. "It's a storm."

Vasily's placid expression fell away. He skirted the table where the scroll was secured beneath a glass plate and a large, very powerful camera was stealing its image. He moved past her, out to the railing.

"It's him." She hated to sound so desperate, afraid. "Isn't it?"

"It can't be," he said, but even she heard his uncertainty. "He cannot know we are here."

Her thought bounced to the men she'd disabled, to Lisa. "There was another, besides the three who chased me at the end. A woman with the doctor—she worked there, maybe. But I think she was Hermanns'. I neutralized her."

Vasily's scowl grew. "What nationality?"

"She spoke German and was talking to Rutger."

He skipped his attention back to the dark cloud circling the mainland's southern tip.

The smell had been in the air, but she'd ignored it, too focused on escaping the facility. "It's the same, isn't it? How can it not be him?" She slunk back, heart pounding. "He knows I'm here." She strangled the urge to panic.

"He doesn't." Vasily faced her. "Iskra, you're safe here. I promise." He looked at the facility, fading in the distance. "The woman you neutralized must be tied to the storm—Hristoff isn't the only one with a Meteoroi. Perhaps Rutger has one, too. It's effective for creating distractions and diversions."

"Don't be a fool. What are the chances *we* encounter two?" She shook her head. "One lightning strike could've destroyed the facility and the scroll!"

"I'm not being foolish. There are people who want this and are clearly not as clever or as efficient as our Wild Rose."

She tensed, feeling sick and angry. "Do not call me that."

Following him back inside, she gave the storm one last glance. Concern tugged at her insides. *Please don't be . . . just let me finish this. Get the answers . . .*

A light table illuminated the old scroll from underneath, seeming to lift the words from the centuries in which it had hidden. So much lay within those words—hope, destruction, truth, danger.

Iskra nodded to it. "Tell me that's the right one." Just one piece of good news, for once in her life. Was that too much to ask?

Vasily stood at a small monitor that magnified the images. Another larger computer hummed to his right. He tapped its monitor, which was suspended from the ceiling. "I think . . ."

She moved behind him, peering over his shoulder at the screen. The words weren't known to her. The script she guessed to be Hebrew or something. "Can you read or understand it?"

"I will need to work on the translation, call in some favors, but yes." He glanced at her and smiled. "Yes, Iskra. I think you did it."

At his words, something foreign leapt in her breast. She wanted to believe him. Wanted to believe this book would help her buy freedom. "I only retrieved it."

Vasily laughed, angling around to face her. "Only retrieved it? You walked into that facility and convinced the entire security detail you were supposed to be there. You convinced Chowdhury to take you straight to its vault. That's not 'only' retrieving it."

It was true, but she deflected his flattery because she'd seen the same glint in his twin brother's eyes, and it had gotten him killed. "I couldn't have done that if you and Bogdashka hadn't found where it was being hidden in the first place." She wanted to ask how they'd learned of its location, but she didn't care. Not anymore—not now that they had it.

"Speaking of the Empress," he said with a roll of his eyes, "she'll want to know you've succeeded."

Indeed. She would. Iskra chewed her lower lip, wondering what Bogdashka would say about the men. "While I was cleaning up, did you have a chance to retrieve the facility's security footage?"

Vasily held her gaze for a moment, then slowly nodded.

"And?"

More hesitation, but he would relent. Vasily always did when it came to her. He felt he owed his brother.

"Who was he?" she asked.

His eyebrow winged up. "American, I think."

"Their weapons told me that. But who? How did they know to come to Greece?"

Wariness crowded his handsome features that so resembled his twin's. Valery had been much like Vasily, but with a streak of intensity found in few men. "They are very skilled."

She pointed to the knot on her temple. "And have no hesitation in fighting a woman to stop her."

Menace swirled through the planes of his face, much like that storm off the island, which was, thankfully, farther away with each passing second. "Coldhearted."

"Mm," she said, thinking, "I don't believe so. Just determined."

"Men who are willing to do that have probably seen a lot."

"Like war—combat."

He nodded. "Someplace where women are as likely to attack as men."

"Suicide bombers. Middle East." She spun back to the table, where she noticed a bowl of mangoes. Her favorite. She freed her knife from its sheath on her belt and cut into one.

Vasily was staring at the screen again. "Mm, likely."

"So, Special Forces, SEALs, black ops—"

"*Da*. Most likely that," Vasily said, holding a pen toward the scroll. "They knew where the book was stored, and that was a very well-guarded secret."

Pinning a chunk of mango between the blade and her thumb, she pointed its tip at him. "So, intelligence operators?"

"Their military has those as well."

"So does the CIA."

A phone buzzed, and she glanced at the device, only then realizing it was hers. She chewed the mango and moved closer, inwardly cringing at the number. Bogdashka. The Empress calling to make sure she had succeeded.

Swallowing and savoring the fruit, she pocketed the phone, not surprised to find Vasily watching her. "Can you get facial recs on them—no." She cut off another slice. "On the leader." She tapped her knife against the small video image of Pale Eyes. "You can find him, *da*?"

"Eventually," Vasily said, peering at her over his glasses, then indicated the scroll. "But the translation is more important, no?"

With a sigh, she relented. "Yes." She tucked another wedge of fruit into her mouth. "Definitely."

"Is that why you are not talking to the Empress?"

"We're talking."

"Just not right now."

She held up her palm. "'As you see,'" she said, quoting one of her favorite movies.

He grinned. Shook his head. "For a woman who kills for a living, you have strange taste in movies."

"It is because I long for civility and decency again."

"And you take your cues from *Pride & Prejudice*?"

"Careful." There was a time when men treated women with respect, acted in honor. Those days had vanished. Valery had shown her some respect, but in the end, he had used her just as Hristoff did, something she'd never admit to Vasily, who thought the world of his brother. Valery's usage had been just as damaging, even though it was less violent. It was why—

"No." Vasily wrote on a tablet, studied the screen, then again recorded his thoughts on the device. "You long for *romance*."

She coughed a laugh. "Romance is archaic and dead."

"It's not, actually," he said, again staring over his glasses at her. "It's beautiful and very much alive."

Iskra set aside the mango and went to a small sink, where she rinsed her blade. "If you think it so beautiful and alive, why are you out here on a boat, alone?"

Vasily shrugged. "I am always saving you. When do I have time for romance?"

True—he'd become integral to her missions. She depended on him heavily. But that happened because he was the only person with breath still in their lungs that she trusted. "That's sad."

"When it is time," he said with a nod, "I will find someone."

"Here?" she said around a laugh, sheathing her knife. "Or in the afterlife?"

"Does it matter?"

Now she really laughed.

"Ahh," he said, straightening and closing his eyes as he smiled. "There's a sound I haven't heard in a while."

Though he shot a glance in her direction, Vasily knew better than to meet her gaze. He'd find a scowl. A mask for the wound of that truth. There was not much to laugh about, not with Hristoff in control.

Iskra looked at the mango, guilt somehow weighing her. It wasn't her fault, this life that had stolen her existence. Valery had seemed to hate her stolen life as much as she did. In fact, he'd even made a plan to help her escape Hristoff. It was the last thing he'd planned.

When Vasily did not try to bridge the awkward silence, she turned to him. He hunkered over the equipment. Intent. He stilled. Frowned. Adjusted the high-powered camera. His brows climbed into his hairline.

When he rose from the eyepiece, what she saw closed her throat. That look—elated but splashed with caution—pulled her around the light table. "What?" She tucked her hands in her back pockets.

"This . . ." His head bobbed.

Anticipation gripped her. "Is it—"

"Yes," he said, nodding again, his breath mixed with laughter and near-reverence. "I'm sure. This is it." A nervous chuckle rumbled through his chest. "This is the Book of the Wars of the Lord."

Iskra stared at the document beneath the glass, her breath trapped behind the barest thread of hope. Giddiness speared her, and even though she wasn't an archaeologist, she could appreciate the significance of the scroll. The beauty. Someone thousands of years ago had touched this, written on it. But the real source of her excitement was what this would mean for her.

But before she let herself get truly excited . . . "Why do you think this is it? What convinced you?"

But he was already distracted again and muttered an oath. Tossed his tablet and pen to the table. He drew the massive ceiling-mounted camera down to another spot on the scroll, then hurried back to the monitor, where the new location came into focus.

Anxious as he worked, her question unanswered, Iskra dared to let the specter of hope creep closer. She hugged herself, watching. Waiting. If it was the Book of the Wars, she could use it to buy a favor from ArC. A life for a life.

No. No, don't go there yet. Just wait.

Minutes ticked by with Vasily engrossed. He retrieved his tablet without looking and scribbled, though his eyes almost never left the enhanced image. He swore another oath. Hissed.

"Vasily?"

He pressed a hand against his face, muttering fast and frenetic in Russian. To see this slower, calmer half of Valery so enlivened frightened her. And still he gave no response, no explanation.

"Vasily!"

He flinched.

Iskra took a step back at what now lurked in his face. How he'd gone pale. His shoulders sagged.

He'd been wrong. It wasn't the book.

She'd known it. This whole thing was too good to be true. All that work, risking her life against Rutger. Against those American operators. Mentally, she flung up the defensive perimeter that doused hope in cruel reality. She would *never* be free.

But even as she held Vasily's gaze, she also vowed never to give up. It was not about her. She would take this defeat as she had all others—head on.

"What?"

He wavered as he slumped back even more, something deep and aching in his expression.

"*What?!*" she snapped.

"It mentions them."

Cold dread poured into the pit of her stomach as she pulled up straight. Stared at him, disbelieving. Unable to process. *Unwilling* to process. "Them." A chill raced around her shoulders and snaked down her spine.

Sorrow threaded his blanched features. "I cannot be sure, Iskra. The text *is* ancient, the language . . . difficult to interpret and translate in some places, but—" His gaze hit the monitor again and pulled hers there as well.

Tears burned as she fixed her eyes, her very soul, on the brittle piece of history she'd retrieved. If Vasily was right, then all these years, all she had endured . . . would be worth the payoff.

"It speaks of them, Iskra. Those set to guard the world."

She'd find him. Finally. "The Neiothen."

TEN

CIA SAFE HOUSE, GREECE

"*What* is with this weather?" Culver complained as they slumped into chairs at a CIA safe house. He shook the rainwater from his high-and-tight. "We have storms like this back home, but *in season*. With twisters 'n' all."

"Agreed. This wasn't even on radar." Mercy nodded to her computer, as if that'd tell them something. "Radar was clear when we set out. Nothing coming. Then *boom!*" She flicked her fingers from fists to splayed palms. "Thunder and lightning."

"Reminds me of Florida," Klein said. "Wait a few minutes and the weather will change."

"Seriously?" Leif huffed. "You're talking *weather*?" He stabbed a hand toward the wall. "On our first real mission, we lost a major artifact to that . . . that woman!"

"That woman," Lawe said, pointing a pen at him, "turned your nose into a goose egg."

"Hey," Saito said, "go easy. What she did wasn't a lucky hit. She was all ferocity and elegance. Confidence oozed out of her."

Hating the reverence in Saito's voice, Leif glowered around his swollen septum. "Cell, I need the 411 on this chick. We need answers on how to take her down, but more than that"—he rapped the table—"how did she know where it was? Who's her source? How'd she get in? I want *everything* on her."

"I've tapped in Iliescu and Braun, because this is big Cheez-Its." Cell indicated the wall screens that went live with the two team sponsors.

"Well, seems Mr. Purcell has landed a big one," Iliescu said in a way that sounded like cursing. "We knew this woman was interested in the book, but we didn't anticipate she'd be ahead of us on the location."

"Let's run down what you should know about her," Braun said. "She was born Iskra Todorova, but in the last ten years, she's simply been called Viorica."

"Viorica? Why?" Klein asked.

"Means 'wild rose,'" Cell said with a shrug.

Baddar coughed. "She is known well in my country." His words were weighted. "For what she can do. Has done." He did not look impressed or pleased. "She is . . . bad."

"And there's not much she hasn't done." Iliescu resumed control. "She's part spy, part assassin."

Leif stared at an image of Viorica on the screen. Brown eyes. Black hair. Olive complexion. Roiling in intensity, ferocity. Coldhearted.

"Basically," Braun said, leaning in, "she does whatever she's told."

Leif folded his arms, his gaze snapping to Braun in the lower left corner of the screen. "Told by Hristoff Peychinovich, yeah?"

This time, Culver nearly cursed. "You gotta be kidding me. The Russian steel magnate?"

"Steel, diamonds, drugs, gold, skin," Iliescu explained. "You name it, ol' Hristoff is involved, and the control he wields in eastern and southeastern Europe is phenomenal."

"Ghastly, is more like it," Braun said. "This is not a man to mess around with. And we are very concerned that Viorica now has the scroll. If she has it, then we must assume Hristoff has it."

"I'm missing something." Leif angled in to the conversation and a better view of the live feed. "Why are they interested in some ancient text? And why do we care?"

"We've already told you—"

"Right—you told me you can't tell me much." It wouldn't help to get angry, but Leif was already there. "But the stakes are upping, and the intel needs to match that progression. We aren't dealing with everyday treasure hunters. That woman is not a run-of-the-mill assassin or thief. She is resourceful and determined." The look in her eyes as he held her by the cuff, her frantic desperation, warned him to tread carefully.

"Someone put a hang glider on the roof for her," Saito said. "Can we look into that?"

"We'd just be chasing our butts and wasting time. She probably paid some low-level employee to plant it there, along with that satchel," Leif said.

Culver scowled. "She had a satchel?"

"That's what I asked myself when she stood on the ledge with it across her body," Saito said.

Leif shrugged. "The only explanation is another plant. She had enough resources, enough time in the area, to scout it and figure out who to buy off. It'd take days, if not weeks, to track that intel, and that's time we don't have if we're going to chase down the book."

"Are we?" Lawe sounded excited.

"You mean chase *her* down," Saito corrected, looking at Leif again for direction.

"We are." The thump in Leif's chest surprised him. "First we need sat footage from the area surrounding that facility. Where'd she land with that glider? Did she have someone waiting? Was she working alone?"

"We'll get that unlocked for you," Iliescu said. "I'm also trying to reach an asset on the ground to keep tabs on Peychinovich, see if he goes to Viorica or she to him."

Cell and Mercy both burrowed into their systems, working through various feeds.

"Lawe, call and get some birds scrambled," Leif ordered. "I want to be out of here and en route within minutes of finding where she landed or is headed."

"Roger that." Lawe stood and left the room.

"Klein, Saito, and I will get the gear prepped and ready," Culver said.

"Light and fast," Leif said.

That left Baddar and Devine. He turned to the latter, recalling that she was a cultural support team member and spoke several languages. "You know Russian?"

"*Ya nemnogo govoryu po russki*," Devine said with a rueful smile. "Emphasis on '*little*.'"

"Just as long as you know it." Leif nodded. "You might have to take point when we find her."

Lips parted, Devine hesitated.

"Don't worry." He offered a smile. "You won't be alone."

"Guess I need to earn my keep somehow."

Leif smirked. "You more than do, but annoying Lawe is the cherry on the top."

"Well." Devine had a smile that could level most guys. "In that case, I will always accommodate."

Yet everyone who met the two knew they were hot for each other. And for the same reason, guys veered away from Devine. It wasn't a territorial thing, though some wanted to say that. It was about respect. Leif had seen enough trouble in that regard to not even approach that incendiary line. Besides, there were too many holes in the black box of his life. He wasn't sure what was hiding there, but there'd always been this vague foreboding that haunted the gaps. No need to unwittingly place a woman in the crosshairs.

His thoughts snapped back to the facility. To Viorica. Iskra Todorova.

"You'll kill us all."

Fear. He'd seen fear in her eyes when she noticed the charge. Not anger, which he'd expected. She didn't want to die. Most people didn't, but there was a desperation there. He couldn't explain it, but it hung in the back of his mind like an annoying itch he couldn't reach. What was it?

Why did he even care?

Know your enemy. It was the only way to catch her. Get the book back.

The way she'd looked at him on that ledge when he had a bead on her, wind shredding her, slapping dark strands in her face . . .

Why hadn't he taken that shot? It would have solved everything. They'd have the book. She'd be dead.

Screwed that one up.

"Leif."

He glanced over his shoulder at Baddar, whose accent shaded the name more like *layf* than the typical pronunciation of *leaf*. The Afghan hunched close to Mercy, who had a screen lit. "See this."

Leif rounded the table and shouldered in. "What am—"

"We couldn't find anything on government satellites," Cell muttered from the side.

"While he was using legit channels," Mercy said quietly, "I decided to Bruce Wayne it and tap into cameras around the city to spy on the local populace."

"Wait, Ms. Marvel, did you just use a DC reference?" Leif teased.

"While I'm no Carol Danvers—"

Leif grunted his disgust. "Forgot about her."

"—you'll notice I made the reference in regard to a *theft* of private security, what most would call invasion of privacy and a criminal act. Which fits Wayne and his superpower-less self."

"His superpower is that he's rich." He smirked. "What'd you find?"

"I *found* your girl." Mercy's mouse pointer grabbed a map and swiveled it around, tilting the topography as she zoomed. "And here we see . . ." Her shoulders moved as if she were physically adjusting the cameras. "Ba-da-bing, ba-da-boom." She folded her arms and sat back, giving Baddar a coy look. "Mercy saves the day. Again."

Leif frowned, eyeing the image. The water and the sky. "I'm not—" Then he did. "Yacht." His heart thumped against his ribs. "Could be any yacht . . ."

Mercy swiped her touchpad, and the image zoomed in more. "Look what's on the rear deck."

A smile filtered into Leif's mood. "Hang glider." He tapped the screen. "I need the name of that yacht."

"Wait wait wait," Cell muttered, working frenetically on his system. "That . . ." Bent over his computer, he was murmuring and shaking his head. Scowling. Trying one thing. Then another. "What in the conspiracy theory is going on?"

"What's eating your lunch?" Saito asked as he rejoined them.

"Look." Cell clicked and sent his image onto the big screen. "The yacht is in the feed, but zoom in, and that glider is not there." He fast-framed the feed. "Not ever."

Mercy pointed at her system. "But it's right there."

"The images are exactly the same, except the glider," Cell said.

They watched it over and over. Same result. Yacht. No glider. But on Mercy's laptop, it was clear as day.

"What's this mean?" Devine asked quietly.

"Means someone high up doesn't want us tracking down this book." Leif's thoughts rampaged through the revelation.

"Or Viorica," Mercy countered.

"Same thing," he said. "Find her, find the book. Bugs me, though, that someone was informed and aware enough to already alter that image, which means they could've saved us some trouble at Aperióristos."

"Maybe the same people who know why this book needs to be found but won't tell us or our supes?" Lawe stood behind Devine, shoulders squared. "Birds are winding up now."

"Maybe," Leif said. "Whoever altered the sat feeds wants to bury the path of that book. Doesn't make sense that our side is doing it."

But then who? Someone didn't want him to find it. Which made him want to nail it down even more. Like the Sahara Nine. He'd get answers. Eventually.

Leif grunted. "Their fault for putting us up against this."

Culver grinned. "Hooah."

"Okay," Cell announced, pulling their attention back to him. "It's a super yacht, the *Taissia*, once owned by a Saudi prince."

"Pretty sure most super yachts are owned by Saudi princes," Klein added.

"It was sold to"—Cell clicked through a few more links, then barked a laugh—"Vasily Kuznetsov, owner of Black Tides, a Russian company responsible for recovery of oceanic artifacts."

"He tied to Peych?" Leif asked.

"Peych?" Cell repeated with a nod. "I like it."

"Brings the guy down to size," Leif muttered.

"Yep," Cell said, eyes on the data again. "Valery Kuznetsov is listed as—"

"*Vasily*," Leif corrected.

"What?"

"You said *Vasily* Kuznetsov owns the boat. Not Valery."

"I . . ." Hesitating, glancing between the information tabs he had open, Cell harrumphed. "Sure enough. But . . ."

"So is the intel wrong?"

"Twins," Mercy interrupted, swiveling her screen around, displaying a picture of two men in front of a yacht, their visages identical. "Vasily and Valery Kuznetsov are twins. Intel has Valery as Peychinovich's chief of staff three years ago, but then his body washed up in the Moscow River—a retaliatory strike by one of Peychinovich's enemies. The twin ran one of Peychinovich's companies as CFO until two years ago, then retired and started Black Tides."

"Retired. Yet he's on that boat with Viorica." Leif didn't care about the twins. He looked to Cell. "Where's the *Taissia* now?" All he cared about was finding enemy number one: Viorica.

"The global ship tracking on the *Taissia* isn't working," Cell said.

"Convenient."

"But we can find her via satellite, now that we know what we're looking for. And it seems like we're heading up the Aegean to . . ." He craned his neck. Another scowl. Then he sat back. "I can't find her now."

"Me either. They know," Mercy breathed.

"Of course they do," Leif said. "I practically ran her off the roof. She'd know we'd come hunting for her."

"They also know how to stay out of sight," Mercy continued.

"Maybe they have mirroring tech that makes them look like more of the same water."

"That exists?" Saito asked.

Mercy shrugged. "Why not? Russians are working with reactive armor."

"Really starting to feel outgunned," Klein mumbled.

"There!" Cell barked. "Sea of Marmara, heading . . . looks like . . ."

Mercy twisted up her face. "Istanbul."

How did that make sense? "She's Bulgarian. Peych's Russian."

"Wait," Saito asked, swatting Leif's arm. "How do you know she's Bulgarian?"

"It's in the dossier we were given." He shifted to the screens, not surprised to find Braun still listening. "What's there? Why would she go to Istanbul?"

Annoyance pinched the admiral's weathered face. "We aren't sure, but we're looking into it. Iliescu has an asset on the ground."

"I want to know what kind of trouble we'll be walking into."

"Walking into?" Braun scoffed. "I didn't say you'd be going, Mr. Metcalfe."

Leif pivoted to the others and jutted his jaw. Culver, Saito, and Lawe took the signal and cued the others in. They started toward the doors. "Sorry, Admiral. You're breaking up."

"Mr. Metcalfe!"

Leif eyed Cell. "Did we lose them?" he asked, knowing full well they hadn't.

"Uh . . ."

"Screen's hazy," Leif lied, motioning to the wall monitor, where Braun was shouting that her connection was fine, then asking those around her if they'd lost communication and to find out what was wrong. It was hard not to smile. "No sense in you wasting your efforts here." He waved at Cell, who killed the feed. "Let's find an assassin!"

Hustling, Cell muttered, "That's really not as enticing as you might think."

ELEVEN

GOLDEN HORN, ISTANBUL, TURKEY

There was a glory to her father's homeland that stirred something deep in Iskra as the yacht made its way up Haliç, the Golden Horn. Vasily guided them past Galata Bridge and docked parallel to the stretch of green grass and paths that hugged Abdülezelpaşa Caddesi. Cars packed the busy street.

"Think about it."

Iskra turned to him, wary. "You did notify Veratti, yes?"

"I did. But I"—he shook his head—"I think the Americans are your best chance for what you seek."

"No. Veratti wants the book. I give it to him, he can take care of Hristoff for me." It sounded so coldhearted. But she must be that way if things were to change.

"Please. Veratti is too dangerous." Vasily sagged. "Use the Americans. At least think about it. Promise me."

"I did!" For two seconds. Using the Americans might speed things up, but it would bring about her end faster, too. Freedom would never come. "I can't. I can't risk it. There are too many unknowns—"

"And there's not with Veratti? With the very organization that could do severe damage to you and this world with that book?"

"They want the book, and I have it. So they'll help me." At least, that was what she told herself. "Now, enough of this. I've made my decision." She shrugged into the satchel that held her laptop, phone, and the book.

Vasily sighed. "You know what to do, *da*?"

Iskra flicked a frown at him. "I have been doing this longer than you've been helping."

He hung his head. Nodded. "*Da.*" His gaze came back. "But it does not mean I worry less. I do this for Valery, but also because I care for you, Iskra."

She managed a smile, but this felt too much like Hristoff's smothering. "I learned long ago how to read a situation and be quick on my feet."

"But that was before Bi—"

"Enough!" she snapped, not wanting to hear the name poised on his tongue. "I do not need you to remind me what I'm fighting for."

"*Nyet,*" he said softly, "but perhaps to remind you of what you're *living* for."

Heart thudding, Iskra snatched up her worn leather jacket and limped off the boat without another word.

"Stay in the city, Iskra," he called. "Around people. Call Bodhan."

Her irritation burned as she strolled up through the park toward the busy street. She hustled, ignoring the honk of annoyed cars and the pedestrians heading to mosques. She made her way to Atatürk Köprüsü, the bridge spanning the same waters they had ridden into the city. She made quick work of getting off the main streets and let herself get lost in the crowds of the smaller streets.

Why? Why must men think she needed handling? Why did they tell her every step to take? She had been traveling the world, doing one dirty deed for Hristoff or another, for nearly a decade. All without babying or minding.

Yes, this was different because Hristoff didn't know where she was or what she was doing, nor that she had the book already. She'd hidden her mission's purpose until she'd been sure. Until Vasily verified it. Bogdashka had promised it would lead to Mitre. Iskra hadn't believed her at first, but the ardency, the fervor in the old woman's eyes had been unmistakable.

As she hiked up Yolcu Hamam Sokok, she coiled her fist around the USB drive that held a copy of the scroll. Because eventually the book would go to Veratti. She'd gladly give up the book and the questions in her mind about what Bogdashka knew as long as she found Mitre.

Being in the city where her father—curse the man and his other children—once lived and worked felt oddly like coming home. More so than Russia, where she'd spent most of her life. The smells, the sights. The call to prayer, which stirred nothing in her. She respected them, appreciated that Muslims were so devout to their faith and practices, but she felt no desire to join them.

A brisk walk down Yanikkapi Sokok delivered her to Eski Banka, which then got her onto Galata Kulesi. The narrow street and its graffiti-streaked buildings hovered close as she climbed the steadily sloping street toward the infamous Galata Tower. Defiant trees shot up, scraggly and staked for protection from vehicles jockeying for the sliver of road. A compact sedan, parked on what served as a sidewalk, forced its way onto the anemic street. Iskra stepped around it and barely avoided a white van, its horn pealing a shrill objection to her intrusion.

Another three meters brought her to a junction where three roads converged. It felt kilometers wide, as if the streets could finally breathe. Flowering vines adorned a knee-high wall to her left, a bit of vegetation in this concrete jungle. Up ahead waited the hotel, where she could rest and sort things. And yet the sight of this hotel tugged on her heart. Her memories.

He used you. That's all. It wasn't special.

She ventured past it, up the incline of the hill, and turned down a narrow alley. Glancing around to make sure she was alone, Iskra tucked herself into a tiny space behind a shop. An exterior, long-forgotten storage room. She'd walked past it the last time she was here and noted it because an orange cat had been curled in the corner. She slipped inside the space and stuffed the box on a high ledge that formed the frame of the door. Whispering a prayer that probably went nowhere, she scanned the alley and exited.

As a taxi waited for someone near the valet parking of the restaurant with the flowering vines, Iskra seized the chance to dart across the street unencumbered. She swept past the soda machine and candy stands, eyeing the green sign dangling from the hotel building. The Misyon.

Breathing a sigh, she leaned into the door. It was a strange mixture of European and Turkish décor, but the lobby welcomed her with air conditioning that wafted spicy scents from the café. She strode to the desk and produced her passport and ID.

"Welcome to the Misyon," the host said. "Room for one?"

"Two." Though a lie, it kept her safe. Presented a front that she was not alone, which was important in this male-dominated environment. "One night. Please."

As the clerk worked, Iskra took in the hotel. Its guests. The café patrons. Doors that led onto the street. The back entrance that wasn't known to most guests. But then, she wasn't—

"Ms. Tolson." A deep, resonating voice thumped through the din of the hotel.

She turned, her gaze alighting on a handsome olive-skinned man emerging from a side door, hands behind his back as he strolled toward the counter. "Mr. Aksoy, nice to see you again."

"It is a pleasure to have you return to the Misyon." He angled to the clerk, who looked distinctly pale. "The presidential suite."

"Oh." Iskra touched her throat at his generosity. "No, please. No special treatment."

"I insist."

He always did. Because of Valery, who had thrown around a lot of money when she'd mixed business with some pleasure, extending her trip by a couple of days due to "delays," as she explained to Hristoff later. "You are too kind."

In her suite, she stared out the windows overlooking the beautiful bustling city. Eyed the balconies. Her ankle ached, and she knew she should rest it. On the bed, she lifted her leg and found immediate relief from the throbbing.

She removed her laptop and phone from her bag, noting several messages. Two texts from Vasily, encouraging her to be open to it. Using the Americans was better than dying. "Not by much," she muttered, reading the next text.

Why have you not called? You make me worry, *kotyonok*.

Iskra groaned at the message from Bogdashka. "I am nobody's kitten. More like a lioness protecting her cub." She tossed aside the phone, hating what the older woman brought out in her. And she also hated what Bogdashka reminded her of—the past. That Iskra had been sold like a stock negotiation between two companies. But it hadn't been companies. It had been two men. Her father and Hristoff. Bogdashka was a safe haven in that—not a participant. Some said she was a saint because she rescued so many girls from trafficking, but there was something about the old woman that made Iskra unwilling to give her more room than she must. Or perhaps that was just her approach to anyone she met.

But now she could not talk to her. For the first time that she could remember, the forbidden fruit of hope teased that something good might happen. That she could bring life to a very dead part of her soul.

On the bed, she pulled over her laptop and checked her email. Every time she opened this blasted computer, she ached to put her connections to use. But she wasn't savvy enough to search for Mitre and conceal her tracks from Hristoff, who monitored her technology. But there was somewhere she didn't have to worry about being tracked. First . . .

She lifted the phone Vasily had given her. Dialed the lone number he'd programmed into it.

"*Chi è questo?*" a voice demanded in Italian.

In an eruption of panic and uncertainty, Iskra froze. What if Vasily was right? She dropped back against the bed, staring at the ceiling.

". . . the Americans are your best chance for what you seek . . ."

But the Americans were too big of a risk. Veratti knew who she was. What she'd done.

"Who is it?" he demanded again.

Iskra took a measuring breath. She could hang up. He'd never know it was her. But she would be walking away from more than freedom for herself. It was bigger than that. More dangerous. "Viorica."

"What do you think you're—"

"Meet me in Istanbul at midnight."

"Why would I soil my name and reputation meeting with *you*?"

"Because you want what I have."

"You have it?" he hissed.

"Tonight. Agreed?" When he gave his consent, she drew a leaden breath. "And if you betray me, if you contact a certain acquaintance of ours, the book will meet with a fiery end. Understood?"

THE *TAISSIA*, SEA OF MARMARA

"She has it."

"You're sure?"

"Yes." Vasily shifted the phone and glanced at the images he'd printed off, but for his own safety, he chose not to mention them. "I saw it and made scans."

"Send it to me."

"I'm not—"

"Do it if you want to stay hidden."

Vasily gritted his teeth. Defiance wasn't an option. He needed her help to stay under Hristoff's radar. "If she ever finds out I—"

"That's on your own head."

"You can't stay ahead of her forever," Vasily warned.

"Not forever. Just long enough. Send me what you have on the book. You planted the tracker in her phone?"

Vasily guided the yacht back across the blue-green waters, leaving Istanbul and wishing he could leave his guilt, too. His brother would kill him, were he still alive. "*Da*. Before she returned."

"Good. It's for her own good."

"You don't believe that, Bogdashka."

"*I* don't have to."

If Iskra were not so bullheaded, so driven to find Mitre, he would not have to protect her from herself. "What about her?"

"I'm sending friends as we speak."

Thunder rattled in the distance, and Vasily looked to the skies, half expecting another conjured storm. Instead, a black helicopter was alighting on the yacht's helipad.

A storm had come, all right. One he probably would not escape.

ISTANBUL, TURKEY

Iskra awoke to a rumbling stomach. She freshened up, surprised but grateful the rest had helped her ankle. Vasily, dear man that he was, had been right. She grabbed her purse, placed the laptop in the safe, then headed out. She took the rear stairs to conceal her movements from Mr. Aksoy. This location should be safe, but she'd learned a hard, painful lesson with Valery about trusting the wrong people. Well, trusting anyone, really. Hristoff could find a diamond speck in a sea of white sand. He always did.

She checked her messages, and her stomach squeezed when she found one from Vasily.

> Interesting. Found mention of "Pearl of the Antilles." Could be significant. Suggest you look into it.

Pearl of the Antilles—what was that? It must be significant for Vasily to mention it. She lifted her phone to Google it, but as she did, it rang. Bogdashka. She might as well answer. She couldn't ignore her forever.

"Hello." She left the hotel and stepped into the bustling nightlife of Istanbul.

"*Kotyonok!*" boomed the ebullient Bogdashka. "How you make me wait, *kotyonok*."

"I've been busy."

"How are you? How did the facility go?"

Annoyance plucked at Iskra, knowing the only reason Bogdashka was contacting her was to find out about the artifact. "Well."

"Then you have it?" Excitement laced her words. Clever Bogdashka, trying to pry information. "No, don't answer that. If you do, keep it safe."

"Do not worry." Iskra cringed at the pinch in her ankle. Just a little farther.

"I understand. Just stay safe."

"As best I can."

"You sound worried."

"Always." Iskra's phone buzzed, signaling another call. She glanced at the screen and her stomach plummeted. "I must go. He's calling."

"Step into a building, *kotyonok*. I can hear too much."

Iskra drew up short, startled at the truth, that the noises around her could betray her location. Good thing Bogdashka wasn't a threat. "*Poka*."

She decided to take the call, only because it had been too long since she'd spoken to him. Too long since she'd given him an update on her work. His profits.

She stepped into a small shop and tucked herself in a corner. Steadying her breathing, she answered. "Hristoff."

"It has been a while, *malysh*."

She winced at the *baby* endearment. "I know. I am sorry." Would she ever stop telling people that? "This mission has been . . . tough. I have one more thing to tie up."

"Good. Where are you? You have it?"

When a man rounded the row of shelves and scowled at her, she lifted a book and opened it. "I had some trouble. They may be following me."

"*Who* is after you? I will send Ruslan!"

"Not necessary," she said quickly, eyeing the back of the retreating clerk. "I plan to catch a flight in the morning."

"Then you have it—brilliant. I will send the jet."

She cringed, staring at words on a page that made no sense as she scrambled for a plausible way out of this nightmare. "It'll draw too much attention. I can do this. Trust me, Hristoff."

"You screw this up, and it is my head, Iskra. Fail me and I will make sure you never forget this. It will cost you dearly, if you understand my meaning."

Dread wormed through her. She had to lighten his mood. Convince him she wasn't worried. "I said tomorrow, and it will be then. I swear."

"Do you?"

She winced at the familiar tone. Waited for him to toss out a threat. Tear open her shredded heart again.

The line went dead. She glanced at the phone, confused. He'd never—

When a video call came through, Iskra drew in a breath, knowing what he was going to do. With trembling hands, she swiped to accept it and turned down the volume so the other customers wouldn't hear.

Hristoff's face came into view, vengeful spite in his eyes.

She squirmed. "Hris—"

"I thought perhaps you might need a reminder, *da*?"

"No. I told you. Just one more—"

"So I want you to see my face. To see that I am not happy." The camera blurred black, but the audio worked fine. "Come here, you little"—a grunt, then a laugh—"*zaika*."

No. Please. She curled into the corner of the bookstore, trying to hide from those in the shop but also from this nightmare. "Hristoff, this isn't—"

A scream from the phone severed her words. She sucked in a breath. *This* was why she didn't believe in God or hope.

Small and cherubic, a little girl's cheek smooshed against Hristoff's slammed the door on any objection or defiance Iskra might feel.

"It's okay," Iskra murmured, desperate for the child not to know this man. Not to know his cruelty. She gritted her teeth so hard that her jaw ached. Pain pulsed up into her temple.

The girl whimpered.

"We are clear?" Hristoff asked, his question leaden.

Staring at that face, those brown eyes with innocence still intact . . . "Yes."

"Tomorrow morning." Hristoff released the little girl and held the phone in front of his face again. "Say it."

"Tomorrow morning."

"Or you know—"

"Tomorrow morning."

When she ended the call, Iskra stared at the screen. Pocketed the phone and pulled the burner from her pocket. If Hristoff discovered she'd called Veratti . . . her fate was sealed.

TWELVE

ISTANBUL, TURKEY

Splitting up was the only way to reduce the chance of discovery. So they'd gone in different directions in various modes of transportation—a civilian airliner, a ferry, and a car. They descended on the ancient city, knowing that somewhere within its chaos was a slippery operative.

"Runt," Cell commed, "an asset there put eyes on and verified a positive ID on your target in the city."

"Give it to me." Leif memorized the provided coordinates.

"It's a club on the city's outskirts. Out of the way. Old. Quiet. Its approval rating is two-point-three stars," Cell explained, "so don't expect much."

Culver, Klein, and Saito headed up from the west ahead of Mercy and Baddar, who were strolling from the north as tourists. Leif and Lawe exited a ferry, knowing that Cell and Devine were on the same ferry but taking a slightly different route.

"A Marine instructor in chemical warfare—" Leif said as the ferry bumped up against the dock.

"Seriously? You're going to start that crap now?"

"—asks soldiers in his class, 'Anyone know the formula for water?' One recruit says, 'That's easy, sir.'" Leif scanned their surroundings as they disembarked. "'Then what is it?' he demands of the recruit, who grins and answers, '*H, I, J, K, L, M, N, O*.'" He loved the confusion on Lawe's face—a departure from the smug expression usually parked there. "'What the heck is that?' the instructor demands, and the recruit explains, 'It's *H* to *O*, sir.'"

A long, pained groan. "Man, that was so bad I should kill you," Lawe complained as they hoofed it up a path into the cramped, bustling city. "But since you made it about a Marine, I'll let you live."

Leif laughed.

"What is it with you and the jokes, anyway?"

That was a loaded question. Leif took the short way out and shrugged. "Just a way to bring some levity."

Lawe shook his head, scratching his dark beard as they cut through a slog of cars waiting to turn against oncoming traffic onto a street barely wide enough for one car. Somehow, the Turks managed to make it a two-way street.

"That how you deal with stress?" Lawe asked.

He was hitting a little too close there. "Did the joke upset you that much?"

"Just trying to figure you out, man." Lawe pointed to a street vendor with meat dangling from a rack. "No rat problem here, I guess."

"Sick." Leif's stomach protested the idea. "And you grill *me* over jokes?"

Lawe chuckled at the lame pun.

Two more streets, and they should find the squat building matching the coordinates. "What's with you and Devine?"

Lawe's grin fell, and silence encased the clogged street. He looked upset. "Can't figure her out either."

"Guess you need a course refresher on reading body language."

"I can spot trouble from a mile away except when it comes with curves."

Leif snorted. "But what happened?" he asked as they wound up a slight incline. "The mission a few years back—you two hit it off. I expected you to come home, make it legal, and start popping out kids." When Lawe's hands balled into fists, Leif guessed that was a little too much truth.

"She wouldn't give up the CST."

Peyton Devine stood out among the Army's cultural support team members, a select program that gave women the opportunity to participate in the combat theater, entering homes and talking to the wives and daughters, a setting where men weren't allowed. The women were tough, smart, and invaluable to the success of operations. And it was part of why Leif had tapped her for the team. She'd earned respect among the brass and with the operators because she wasn't looking for or needing help. She was providing it. And her skill behind the scope? Wicked.

"And you weren't walking away from the Rangers," Leif said.

"Heck no." Lawe shoved up his sleeve, revealing the *RLTW* inked in broad, confident lettering across his bicep. "We *lead* the way. We don't sit on our butts." After a few minutes of silence punctuated only by Lawe's huffed breaths, he glanced at Leif. "Think we can stop this chick and get that book?"

Bravado tempted Leif to say *of course*. "I hope so. Don't want to get my derriere handed to me again."

Freedom was a siren's lethal lure. A goal she could never attain, no matter how hard she tried.

"A little blue?" Emir slid a glass of vodka across the table to her. He was built like a hundred-year-old tree and was as solid in character as he was in brawn.

Iskra took a sip, grateful for the familiarity of the bar and the company. "A little," she conceded.

"Want some food to help?"

She couldn't eat. Not right now. "Thank you, no." Managing a smile took effort. "I'll be okay."

"If you say so." Emir adjusted the empty chair at the table, then went about tidying up the vacant tables in his small club that featured local musicians.

Hristoff had threatened Bisera. Threatened her. Not for the first time, Iskra considered what Vasily had suggested—going to the Americans.

Yes, and kill any chance of success.

She turned the glass in her fingers, watching the liquid slosh inside. There had to be an answer. A way out. But what?

A large shape loomed over her.

"Emir, I—" She snapped her mouth closed when she realized the figure above her wore an unfamiliar face.

The meaty, oily-haired man spun the empty chair around. Straddled it. Folded his arms on the table. "Viorica." His grin was lecherous as he produced a knife, twirled it, then slammed it into the wood table. "Mr. Veratti has a message for you."

Her pulse sped up.

"He says if you really have what you promised, then whatever you want in exchange will come at a cost—"

"A cost?" She lurched forward, snatching the knife from the table and tipping it beneath his chin before he could blink.

He chuckled. "I would check your surroundings before doing that."

"Three men," she growled. "Armed. But not fast enough to stop me from gutting you."

"Pretty stupid," the man said, "considering who I answer to. Who *you* answer to. Mr. Veratti is not a man to anger, Viorica." He patted the table and lifted his eyebrows. "Now. Are you ready to listen?"

"I promised him what he wants in exchange for what I want."

Another chuckle. "I'm afraid before we can move to that, you must placate his anger."

"Anger?"

"You called his private number. You put demands on him. You hung up on him. Treated him like you were in charge." He clicked his tongue. "I'm afraid that was very unfortunate—for you. It comes at a cost."

Iskra swallowed.

"I wanted to kill the bartender. You know him, yes?"

She refused to look at Emir, who was behind the counter now amid the glass bottles of liquor.

The man lifted a shoulder in an apathetic gesture. "But Veratti said no. He said you would cooperate."

Fisting her hands, she glowered at this coward.

"He said he knows what is important to you." He cocked his head to the side. "But he would not tell me. But you know, yes?"

"I'm falling asleep. Is there a point?"

"You want Bisera alive, yes?"

The chilling words froze Iskra. He could not— "How dare you!"

"Me?" He snorted. Shook his head. "No, Viorica. It's Veratti. Remember that. The man who makes people disappear every day."

Her breathing ragged, she struggled to keep her anger in check.

"If you want Bisera alive—"

"Do *not* threaten her, or it will be the last thing—"

"Then listen closely, Wild Rose."

Leif identified the small, squat building that matched their coordinates and thumped Lawe's arm. Scattered up and down the street, the rest of the team had already fallen into position, a strategic insertion so that when Leif and Lawe showed, they could be confident their backs were covered.

They entered the club, which also could have been called a defunct café with a bar. Dimly lit, its dark wood reeking of—

"Cigars." Lawe inhaled deeply and grinned. He slapped Leif's back. "Feels like home."

"Feels like pain," Leif countered, stretching his back, which afforded him time to take in their surroundings.

To his nine, the long bar stretched the length of the room. Mirrors threw scant light across the paneled walls of the restaurant, which was a generous word, considering there could only be a dozen tables and the dance floor wasn't more than twenty by thirty. What the patrons lacked in numbers they made up in stale cigar smoke and the smell of liquor. Three men barreled past them toward the exit, knocking Leif's shoulder. Probably drunk.

Lawe was right. This felt like home. Like they were back at an FOB, chilling before their next assignment sent them outside the wire.

Leif went to the bar and ordered a Moscow mule.

"A girl drink?" Lawe snorted then turned to the bartender. "Whiskey neat."

Leif snorted. With their drinks, they negotiated the tables and headed to the rear. They sat, backs against the wall, monitoring the activity of the so-called club. But as Leif nursed the mule, assessing their infiltration of the club, something buzzed his brain. His gaze hit the team. Then the patrons.

His team was too obvious. Too American. All in one location.

Would Viorica notice? But more importantly—what would *she* be doing at a hole-in-the-wall place like this?

"So, your friend actually put eyes on the queen?" Lawe asked.

Leif wanted to know the same thing. If Iliescu's asset had seen Viorica here, where was she? "That's what he said." He lifted his drink.

"What happened to your hand?" Lawe asked.

Leif glanced down, remembering the standoff with Viorica in Greece. "She did."

Lawe puffed a cigar. "Come again?"

"When she got caught in the door, she used a ring to slice it up, trying to force me to let go."

"So that's how she got past you. Spy gadgets."

"Think I'd let her get away because of a couple scratches?" A strange trill scampered up his neck. "You know better." Was she here—was that why he had this feeling? Had they been made? He searched the sidewalk outside the dank club through the windows. Then scanned the interior.

"Yeah, but what about a pair of pretty blue eyes?"

"Brown, and I never said they were pretty."

Smirking, Lawe let a lazy curl of smoke fill the air, looking far too proud of himself. "You never mentioned them, period." He grinned. "But apparently you took note."

"Taking note is my job. Yours too." Yet even as he said it, something snagged in his mind. He rewound the mental film. The shifting shadows. Signs on the dingy walls. Laughter—Baddar and Mercy chatting at a corner table. But there. Beyond them . . .

"Well, I'd just like to know when she's going to show, or if I'm out twenty for a bad drink and bad company." Lawe pushed to his feet. "Going to hit the head."

"Uh-huh." Leif saw the brown eyes he'd just mentioned to Lawe. Sitting right there. Son of a . . . Though he was looking in her direction, he also took in his periphery. Lawe walking to the back bathroom. Devine and Klein talking football. Nobody else had spotted her. How long had she been there, monitoring them?

Glass in hand, he made his way over to her corner. Pulled out a chair, fighting the shadows and dim lighting to gauge her response to his approach.

"That seat is taken." A Russian accent dripped from her words.

"Yes." He parked himself on it. "It is. Glad you noticed." He folded his arms on the table and leaned forward conspiratorially. "So, tell me, are you following me?"

"It is hard to *follow* someone who arrives *after* you."

So he'd been right. She'd been here awhile, watching and assessing. There was no sense in playing dumb. Not with the woman who'd sliced his hand and leapt off a building. Extreme measures warranted extreme directness. "You have something I want."

Her hard and steadfast expression didn't change. "You're not the first man to say that to me."

Leif knew that was probably her tactic. Embarrass him, get him off-kilter. "I'm not going to go away, Viorica."

She tilted her snifter, which held ice and a clear liquid, in a toast. "Score one for the American and his tenacity." After a sip, she squinted at him, then looked at each team member one by one. How had she picked them out? "You feel threatened by me."

"I could say the same about you."

She arched her eyebrow.

"The man behind the bar has stayed to the far right since I sat down." Leif nudged aside his glass. "Near a weapon."

Swimming in confidence, she pulled forward and condensed the gap between them to inches. Black fabric hugged her arms and torso, accenting her jet-black hair. "What I have that you want"—she was nearly smirking—"will *not* change hands."

"That's a mistake."

Amusement mixed with indignation and intrigue. "Who are you?"

"It doesn't matter."

"Of course it does." She angled in with a sidelong glance, shoulder and chin nearly touching. "You know my name, and by the way you said it, it has meaning. Inference. Someone says 'God,' and people feel a need to be reverent. 'Paris' conjures the Eiffel Tower in that quick little brain of yours."

"*Little?*" He angled in, too, accepting the challenge in her words.

"When you contact one of your people, you use their name so they know who's being addressed. Names not only matter, they're imperative for clear conversation."

Leif lifted both brows. "Is that what we're doing, conversing?" It felt like she had him right where she wanted him.

"The bigger point is that you want something I have, but you won't give me your name." She shrugged. "It's a small thing to provide, a sign of respect."

Respect. After stealing the artifact out from under him at the facility, she was playing verbal chess. This was all about toying with Leif as a distraction. But from what?

Gaze never leaving hers, he took a sip. A discordant realization—her eyes were not brown as he'd been so convinced two minutes ago—sent a tremor of strange nerves through his muscles. Was it the lighting? Because now they were . . . green? Gold? Amber? A mesmerizing hazel that left him guessing which color to name.

Olive skin betrayed her heritage, which had to be from this side of the world. She wet lips that were bare, not smothered in artificial color, and he felt another twang.

Back on track, he chided himself, toes too close to the swirling vortex that was Viorica. "Respect is earned and requires more than a conversation," he made himself say. "The book is all I care about right now."

"Is it?" Another wry smile as she relaxed, looking all ease and confidence. She knew she was in control. That she had the advantage, which he intended to flip. "I suppose you expect me to hand it over." She lifted a shoulder. "Just like that."

"Better than you handing it over to your lover, Hristoff Peychinovich."

Something flashed through those hazel irises. When she gave another casual shrug, her hair slid over her shoulder and traced her jaw. "Is it?" There was irritation in her words.

"It is," he said, more convinced than before that she was taking it back to Peych. He had to prevent that.

A fire flared through her expression, threatening to burn him. "Why are you so convinced I will take it to him—and what makes you better than him? What's one thug over another?"

Leif took a moment to gauge what he'd seen. Assess her reaction and words. The way she'd shown no hesitation in openly talking with him about the book. Behind the beauty, the intelligence, and the formidable operator, a mental picture formed of a large wall. Gray and covered in slippery vines. A burden. Grief. And the way she hovered over it . . . "You're protecting something."

She sniffed. "The scroll—"

"So it's a scroll." He pointed out the information she'd revealed and was rewarded with hesitation in her face and body language. "But no, not the scroll." He'd been called a pit bull before because of the way he chomped into something and didn't let go. But if he pushed, if he pursued what he'd read in her—which made no sense weighed against the notorious Viorica—would he lose? Jeopardize this? But they couldn't just sit here in a verbal sparring match, trying to outwit each other.

Call it.

"The scroll is a means to an end—you don't care about the scroll. You want what it brings."

"And what's that?"

"I don't know," he allowed. "But whatever it gets you—that's why you want to take it back to him. As to why I'm better?" He lifted his arms with a cocky grin. "Thought that was obvious."

Wariness guarded her secret. "That is true of everyone searching for it. I want it for my sources. You want it for your government." She was probing for intel. "I bring it to Hristoff"—her expression went dark—"and get what I want."

"There." Leif craned his neck forward, hearing the slight hitch in her breath. "That's what you're protecting." The quick intake, her blink, and the way her smile faltered told him he was on the right course. "That's sadness. Why? What did he promise you?"

"Sadness?" Her voice changed. Went hard as granite. Her wariness vanished, and confidence and fury roared to the fore.

He'd made the wrong call.

The assault of his deftly spoken words on her heart made Iskra falter. "I'm a-afraid, Mr. Soldier"—why was it so hard to speak?—"that you are *sadly* mistaken." She caught the slippery reins of control and buried the mental claxon. There was no way he could know. It was impossible.

But he did. Somehow he did.

Just as Veratti had known the Americans would come. She had always considered herself a skilled operative, but the events of the last couple of weeks made her feel inept.

She straightened, thumbing the length of her glass. *He knows who you are.*

Easy enough to know Viorica. Her reputation preceded her in many countries due to her effectiveness and sheer determination to see her mission completed. Sometimes with flourish. The very name often alarmed people, inducing mistakes. But this man was so dangerously close to her guarded vault. She needed him focused on her persona, so *he'd* start making errors. Having engaged Veratti, she knew her stakes had never been higher. One did not cross the founder and leader of the Armageddon Coalition and live.

"You sure?" His voice was silk, gentle and soft against the harsh reality of her life.

"Are *you*, Mr. Nameless?" He was far too confident. Besides his eyes—nearly impossible to ignore—he had a lot going on in his expression. Jaw littered with stubble and mouth parked in a smirk, his face could easily be on billboards, and his physique belonged on fitness magazines. That was what she didn't like about him—he was too pretty.

But there was a brawn about him that wasn't tied to his appearance. It filled up all the uncertain places of her thoughts, an invasion that made her hesitate. Pull her punches.

Which was a problem. What was she doing, sitting here with him, thinking about his body? An ignition source, he could burn down all she'd meticulously assembled. Complying with Veratti's instructions meant flying with this fire.

Her gaze drifted to the door, though she knew she shouldn't leave. Couldn't leave. Not if she had a chance to get Veratti to solve a problem.

". . . the Americans are your best chance . . ."

Yes, exactly.

"Runt."

Iskra blinked. "What?"

He looked around the small bar. "My name—you asked for my name. That's it."

She gave an incredulous laugh, but his expression didn't change. Was he serious? Why would he give her a name, albeit phony, now?

Why barrel ahead, regardless of the danger she presented? Or did he not take her seriously? Not understand the danger he toyed with?

His problem. She wouldn't make this easy on him, though. He had to think this was his idea. "You think making up a silly name means I'll just beli—"

"You're deflecting."

Iskra masked her reaction, but if he could see how closely that arrow had come to hitting the mark . . . How could he read her so easily? He seemed to open the book of her life and read from its tattered pages.

Annoyance stretched the planes of his face toward his now-tight lips. "Earlier you mentioned respect. I had a modicum of that for you because of your name, but now?" He shook his head. "Now that I see you're more about games, less about action? Well, that respect took a hike. Gone." He tapped the wood surface of the table. "I thought Viorica would be the type to call it as she saw it. A tenacious fighter."

"You know nothing about me."

"Apparently not." His words were sharp, true. "How about we stop diverting the conversation and get down to business?" Fire sparked in his expression with surprising strength and anger.

Until then, she'd only seen the exterior. The pretty boy with the nice smile and easy manners. This man seizing control from her was formidable. Swift. Confidence and arrogance weren't the same thing, but he had them both.

But his gaze . . . the way he stared at her, waiting, patient. Focused. *Why are you staring back?*

"Maybe you can use them." Vasily's haunting words took root in the intensity of the man before her. She must. If only to satisfy Veratti. But playing this game, entering the arena of this man's world . . . could she ever regain the upper hand? Using them meant putting him in control, even if it was an illusion. She'd have to play the lapdog.

"Look." He shifted against the table, zeroing in on her. "We can do this the hard way." Experience lurked behind his words.

"Threatening me is not your best hand."

"No threat. A promise, because you're ready to run." He squinted, the dim light of the club playing along the hard lines of his cheeks and jaw. "In Greece, when you leapt away with the book—the boat you flew to? The man who helped you?"

Her heart tripped over the reference to Vasily.

"We'll hunt him down. And through him, we'll find you."

"Find *me*? But you already know my lover. Why would you need to *find* me if you know about Hristoff?" Valery had been killed because of her, but she would not be responsible for the death of his twin, too. "Why bother with a sailor who prefers water to land? Go after the big fish."

The muscle below his left eye twitched. "That big fish isn't the one you fled to after the facility, which says something." He tossed back his drink. "That, and this lame attempt to downplay the sailor's importance."

"What you should think about," she said, furious that she had let this go on so long, "is what my *lover*"—saying that word in relation to Hristoff made her want to vomit—"will do if he finds you with me. What he will do when word gets back about this ambush by your team."

He smirked. Shook his head, rubbing his jaw—strong hands. She recalled scratching his hand with her ring. He hadn't flinched. Then or now. "I'm disappointed."

"In yourself?" She arched her brow at him and scoffed, reaching for her purse, needing to give him the idea she was uninterested. "So am I."

"Disappointed," he hissed, "that you are supposed to be this notorious operative, but you haven't read me. Haven't read that this is legit."

"What exactly is 'this'?"

"Work with us."

It took several heartbeats for those words to push past all her barriers. But when they did, her heart rate ramped up. This was too good to be true. God was on her side. Or the devil. She wasn't sure which, but one of them had handed her a gold chalice.

Too easy. If this man figured out why she was suddenly working with him . . .

Okay, so she'd have to play hard to get.

Still, what would happen when he found out she was playing him?

Worry about that later.

"The way you operated in Greece and your presence here tells me you have a plan for the book."

"Not terribly hard to figure that out. My boss wants that book." *I want the book.*

"But you didn't go back to Peych, which means something."

This was a fast-rope to death. "It means you're trying to find a way to convince me." She lifted her drink and took a sip. "It's not working. You're wasting your time."

He shifted. "I'm not asking you to give up the book altogether."

She sniffed. He had no idea what he was suggesting, the price she'd pay if caught. She visually traced his scars—one etching out from his left eye and down to his cheek. The other just below his hairline. A small rise in his otherwise straight nose could be a break. His hair was sun-bleached blond, cut sharp and flat. She'd bought the tantalizing lies of a handsome man once before . . .

"What makes you think I'd give it up at all?" Veratti would kill her if she turned up without it.

"Because you're still talking to me."

"Maybe it's your good looks keeping me here."

"Well," he said with a cocky grin, "clearly."

Iskra rolled her eyes, the teasing edge of a laugh crawling up her throat.

"But beyond that . . ." His fingers closed gently around her wrist. His touch was warm.

Iskra realized her mistake. She'd been so caught up in his banter and figuring out how to lure him in that she hadn't noticed him erasing the gap between them. It set off a nuke inside her. She punched to her feet, heart hammering, and panicked when he came with her, that grip firmer but gentle.

She could've broken his grip, could've snapped his wrist. But she didn't. Instead, she braved his gaze. "If you want to keep that hand, release me."

His shoulder pressed into hers as they stared at each other. He was truly gorgeous. And intense. He meant what he said. That she could trust him—he wasn't playing her.

"I need the book." His breath was a whisper against her cheek. His touch hot but not harsh. Yet too much like Hristoff.

"Then you should've gotten there first."

She had just lifted her arm to wrest free when movement by the front door told her this man's proximity wasn't the only thing she'd missed.

Hristoff's men. Tension snapped through her veins, snatching her breath. No. No, he couldn't know. Shouldn't know. First Veratti, now Hristoff? When had she gotten so sloppy? They had come for her—she was dead. And if this man touched her, he was dead.

He started to look over his shoulder.

"No," she hissed, snapping his blue eyes back to her. He might be cocky, but she didn't want his death on her conscience. "Let go," she said in a low, controlled voice. When his brow furrowed in confusion, she hurried on. "Now. Or they'll kill you."

As his fingers fell away, leaving her wrist strangely cold, he narrowed his eyes. "Peychinovich."

Good guess. She skidded a sidelong look at the door. No time for dialogue. She'd used up the few seconds it would take for the men to assess the situation and determine if this man standing too close to Hristoff's favorite toy needed a lesson. If that happened, the task set by Veratti would be undone. That meant Bisera would be in danger. The best thing she could do for this American and herself would be to walk out.

"Hey," he said, moving to intercept her again.

"I'm not for hire," she said loudly, then slapped him.

He jerked, startled. His cheek bore the imprint of her palm—but his look said he understood that she was covering for him. That she'd just protected him.

"There a problem here?" Emir demanded.

Unshakable, he didn't flinch at the voice of the bartender.

Don't do or say anything. Please. "We're good, Emir." She huffed and turned toward him. "Just an American acting like he owns the place."

"Thinking about another drink." The soldier watched, telegraphing too much through those pale eyes. "Thought the lady might join me."

She wished she could.

Emir grunted. "Bar's closed."

THIRTEEN

ISTANBUL, TURKEY

Read between the lines.

Between the disparate women he'd just interacted with: the one who moments ago seemed on the verge of opening up to him, and the one now walking away. Her face had lost its color, her fight its flush.

Leif mustered every ounce of control, forcing himself to stay put. To avoid engaging his skills or team.

The way the atmosphere shifted, the way she changed—subtly but notably—at the appearance of those men gave a strong indication that they had a leash on her. Whether out of loyalty or fear, it didn't matter—same result. And disgusting.

Fists clenched, he watched as the bartender steered her to the counter. To the thugs.

Culver was moving closer, and Leif gave a slight shake of his head, telling him to stand down. He tracked the rest of the team as they left the bar. Good. Too much tension here. He skipped back to Lawe, still at the counter. Head down.

C'mon. Roll out. If Viorica was nervous with the newcomers . . .

Why wasn't Lawe moving? He seemed lost in his cups, but that man was never lost. When he looked up, he was focused on something. Forced Leif to search the bar.

And spot the problem: Viorica. Coming straight at him. His chest ached with expectation.

"Next time," she snapped at him, "perhaps check out your competition"—she lifted her forgotten purse from the chair, then swung around very close, breathing into his face—"before you abandon the top *mission*."

Top mission? Leif wanted to react. Wanted to catch her arm and tell her to come with them. To stay. Give him the book. They could work together to sort out what it meant. But the thugs by the door warned that if he did, he'd leave this club on a stretcher or in a bag.

One heavyweight broke from the group and pounded toward Leif.

Fight or flight? Fight or flight?

Neither.

"What are you doing here?" the man barked, waving a gun he no doubt would use. "Touch a prized jewel and get your hand cut off."

"Whoa-ho." Leif put a wobble into his step and a slur into his speech. "Ain't doing no harm." Maybe that was too much. "Just having a nice chat with a pretty lady."

A fist flew at his face.

He let it connect. Fling him backward. His ribs collided with the table. With a grunt—the pain was legit—he stumbled. Rolled around and collapsed into the chair, then fell over it, relieved to find the big guy thudding toward the front door. Shoving Viorica ahead.

She met his gaze. Then put her nose in the air. But the look she gave him in between tripped him up. Had him wondering what he was supposed to do. What message did she intend to telegraph through her hazel eyes? Because he read a whole lot of *help me.*

You always do.

But what if it wasn't just him reading that? What if it was real trouble?

"Bathroom that way," the bartender growled in broken English. "Go. Get out." He probably didn't want someone getting killed in his club.

Leif considered the beefy man and realized the irritation in his words wasn't irritation. It was . . . concern?

Had he read the situation, too? *He knew her long before you did.* So maybe Leif should listen to the guy. Or maybe he should help her. Like, now. He glanced to the front of the room again.

Lawe slipped out of the bar. Two guards lingered, watching Leif as if itching to use their weapons. They were also buying time for the other guy to get away with Viorica. Leif had just lost the primary target and the primary objective. He bit back a curse.

"If you want her live," the bartender hissed as he bumped Leif's shoulder, "out the back."

The words hit a soft spot. Speared Leif with worry and alarm. But he couldn't show that. Stowing his surprise, he again faked drunkenness and stumbled through the narrow corridor. Banked left and found the door. Indecision gripped him. If he went out this way, he'd definitely lose her and the book. But if he didn't, he could lose his life.

A flurry of Russian climbed down the passage after him—a thug.

"They'll kill you." Her warning told Leif to shake off his hesitation. His failure. Get moving. He had to trust the bartender, who said leaving this way would keep Viorica alive for him to find later. Had to trust that his team, who'd left before the operative, might have the chance to tail her. But him? He was out of luck.

Teeth gritted, he punched open the door and pushed into the cool evening. A shout from behind urged him into a jog.

Metal slammed against concrete as the thugs emerged from the club. They were coming after him. A loose end to tie up.

Bullets chomped into concrete walls beside him. There was no polite Hollywood-like order to stop. Just a promise of pain or death. Possibly both.

Feet pounded behind him.

Leif broke into a sprint. Veered hard left, using the wall to swing around the corner. Wood splintered off a fence, nicking his face.

He ducked but kept running. Avoided parked cars. Mangy cats. Garbage and a rank puddle. Twenty meters ahead, he spotted another alley. Pitched himself into it. It bottlenecked but left enough room for a person to dart through its innards. The same space provided a perfect shooting range. Narrowed the field of vision. Gave him less room to escape.

So don't get shot.

At the crack of a weapon, he dove into a roll, then came up running. A searing trail hit his shoulder as the sonic boom of another bullet leaving the chamber reached his ears. "Augh!" He threw himself out of the confined space and into the open. Banked right.

Shouts and thudding steps pursued him.

The panicked blare of a truck's horn screeched through the street. *"Ahtars, majnun!"*

"Hey!" came from behind.

"Get out of the way!" the truck driver shouted in Arabic.

That voice gave Leif the courage to keep running. To get out of sight and make his way to the rendezvous. But it wasn't *just* a truck driver. Leif's mind caught up to the fact that the voice belonged to Baddar, driving the van that probably held Cell and Mercy.

He started to slow, then changed his mind. The thumping of his pursuer's feet warned him to steer clear. If they saw him get into the van, they were all compromised.

Reassured he'd given the guards the slip, Leif slowed to a fast walk to put as much distance between himself and them as possible. He navigated the crowded city with its white-plastered buildings and tangled streets. His thoughts drifted back through his conversation with the operative. The myriad details he would add to the intel profile on Iskra Todorova. Viorica.

Why had they named her the Wild Rose? She wasn't wild. Not the woman he'd met. She was dogged. Decisive. Used to being in control. Though he might've seen a lot, only one thing badgered him—the undercurrent beneath her cold façade that weighted her responses, held her captive. It was so familiar. It reminded him of the first time he'd met Danielle, his sister-in-law. She'd been traumatized in captivity by the brutality of a Venezuelan guerilla general.

Something in Leif twisted at that memory. He wasn't sure what, but it made him furious.

Head back in the game, Runt.

He took out his phone and used the navigation to steer north out of the city as agreed. The system isolated his location, labeling nearby buildings. Yeah, yeah. Butcher, baker—

Leif stopped in his tracks. Stared his screen, disbelieving what he saw. What he had heard. "*. . . before you abandon the top mission.*"

But that last word . . .

He quickened his pace and darted across the street, heading up and over a block, thinking about the way she'd said *mission*. More like a French word, with the *see-on* ending. It had bugged him then. Even more now that his mind was trying to blur two words into one meaning.

He followed the map around the block and stared up the street at a green sign hanging above a suited bellhop. A black SUV idled in the street. *The Misyon*.

Mission.

His heart thumped. He *hadn't* misheard her. It had been a message. A hint. A plea.

Back up, Chief. Leaping without looking got soldiers killed. Rubbing his chin, he eyed the building. Trap? Probably.

He needed to rethink everything about the operative. Her words, her motives. First, he had to be stealthy. Figure this out—had she been giving a hint about where to find her?

Her goons spot you, you're dead.

But if she'd been giving him a hint, luring him to her hotel . . . why? Though she was beautiful and their attraction crackled, he was sure the hint hadn't been to invite a fling. Things were too hot right now, and not just between them. Besides, that black SUV warned she had no carnal intentions.

So. She needed . . . help?

Letting the shadows of an alcove absorb him, he studied the multistoried structure. Traced its height. Where was her room?

. . . top mission.

"Holy . . ." Had she really even dropped a clue on which floor? If she wanted to be found, it made sense to make his task easier. Right?

Quite a leap there.

Yeah, but he'd take it. Because it was that or search the whole blasted hotel.

When his phone vibrated, he backed against the wall and answered. "Yeah."

"You okay?" Culver asked.

"Yeah." Going in was stupid. Limited his exfil options. Increased his probability of being seen or captured.

But she'd dropped the hint about abandoning his mission—to get the book. *Means she wants me here. Wants me to find her.*

Right, and the black widow lured idiot males into her web.

Fist to his mouth, he came up blank. He might not have an infil plan, but leaving wasn't happening. Not yet. Not till he explored this. Found a way in. *This is really stupid.*

"Baddar said you got hit."

"Huh?" The words snapped him back to Culver on the phone and the fire in his shoulder he'd ignored. Leif checked the wound. "Yeah." A line of dark red trailed the meaty part below the joint. "Tagged me. A graze." He eyed the hotel again.

"She left in a black SUV," Culver said, bouncing Leif's attention to the black armored Suburban at the curb and the waiting thugs. "Cell's tracking her. Or trying. He's a bit slow."

"It's called triangulation, and it takes time," explained Cell in the background, eliciting chuckles from the team.

"Forget it. Waste of resources," Leif muttered, scanning doors and steps up the street. Could he go around the back? Have less chance of being seen that way? "Get to the rendezvous. I'll be there by"—he checked his watch—"twenty hundred."

"Copy that."

He ended the call and stalked up the street, gaze sliding and mapping the threats he would encounter. Two front guards. Another two in the lobby. Possibly a couple by the elevator. Likely more at the rear entrance, if the hotel had one.

Six to one. Not impossible . . .

Who was he kidding? Too many.

There had to be a garage, right? For a building this tall and luxurious and with that many rooms—definitely. They wouldn't let their ultra-rich customers hoof it through the elements. Then again, most filthy rich people had staff to assist.

So. Garage—yes or no?

Lights flashed in his eyes, seemingly from belowground—then leveled out. A car swung onto the street and headed away. Bingo! Leif shot between two cars jockeying around the black SUV and hustled up the walk to the gaping mouth of the parking structure. Alert, he descended the ramp into the lower section, scanning for the stairs or elevator or more thugs.

His phone vibrated again. With a huff, he answered. "What?"

"Uh . . . hey, man." Cell sounded distracted or hesitant. Maybe both.

"What's up? Kind of busy not getting killed," Leif muttered, spotting the sign for the elevator. He dove between two cars.

"Yeah, um, thought I might help with that."

He stepped into the elevator. "How's that?" He checked the number panel. The floors went to twenty-four, so he selected twenty-three. It was probably better to ride most of the way up, then hit the stairs. Avoid getting riddled by bullets when he stepped out.

"If you're near a certain hotel, then—"

Leif's pulse skipped a beat, wondering how Cell knew his location. Were they tracking him?

"—just know. He's there."

The doors slid shut.

"Who?" The gilt-mirrored box glided upward.

"Just . . . —ful . . . there."

Frustration coiled as the elevator choked the signal. Visually tracing the doors, Leif felt his stomach tighten. He wanted to shake off Cell's alarmist message, but he wouldn't call without due cause. Only one person would arouse that much alarm in his buddy in light of the situation.

"P—*crackle*—vich."

Peychinovich.

Crap. He was walking into a trap.

FOURTEEN

SECURE LOCATION OUTSIDE ISTANBUL, TURKEY

Mercy lurched from her seat and tapped one of Barc's screens. "That—who was that?" When he rewound the recording feed, she tapped it. "There! Right there."

The team hunched around them, staring hard at what she pointed to. They glanced at her in question, but she knew she was right. "That man was at the beach club in the Bahamas. That's Andrew."

Culver's face darkened. "You sure about that?"

"Absolutely. Something about him"—she shook her head, remembering—"felt off, wrong. So I tried to ingratiate myself into his time, see what I could pull out of him after some liquor. We had a couple of drinks—"

"That's why we couldn't find you."

"—but I got nothing except a fake name: Andrew. He was locked tight, and then he bolted after y'all left."

Lawe rubbed his jaw. "You're sure they're the same?"

Irritation clawed at her patience. "I didn't do a DNA test, but yes. I don't forget a face. I realized he'd been watching you guys. This is not a coincidence that he's in Istanbul at the same time." Mercy put a hand on Cell's shoulder. "Can you run a facial rec on him?"

"Roger that," Cell muttered.

"What about Runt?" Klein asked. "If that guy's been in both places, maybe Leif is walking into trouble."

HOTEL MISYON, ISTANBUL, TURKEY

"Elevator's coming up," Ruslan announced, looking out the open door of the suite.

The American. Could it be? Had he really figured it out? Iskra's heart thundered, both wanting him to show and not wanting him to show. He could get killed being here, but then again, Bisera could get killed if he didn't come.

"It should stop before reaching this floor," Hristoff said. "Mikhail and Sergey have the ground floor and orders to allow no one to enter. If it comes up, you know what to do."

"Someone from a lower level could simply be coming up to their room," Iskra offered, trying to make her tone playful, but the panic drumming in her chest made it hard. "There's more than one penthouse, and the garden atrium is a favorite spot." She gestured up to the terraced garden. "Perhaps give them a chance to explain before you kill them?"

"You're a pacifist," Hristoff taunted.

Iskra sniffed. "Hardly." Straightening the top she'd changed into after the smoky club, she made her way across the suite to the stocked bar and crystal stemware. "But I like the Misyon and Aksoy. It'd be a shame to get banned." At the small bar, she lifted a snifter and tipped it toward him. "Brandy?"

"No time." Hristoff's face was a façade of irritation and intention—all business. "Pack your things. We're leaving." He moved to the far window, where he slid a hand over that stupid goatee.

It stung that he assumed she hadn't gotten the book. That he hadn't even asked. Why was he here? Unless . . .

She eyed him. Years ago, he had resembled the Irish actor who'd played a German hero during WWII, then a science-fiction icon. But Hristoff had aged a lot in the last few years, lines scratching gray shadows beneath his eyes that matched the streaks at his temples and in his facial hair. Though in his early fifties, he had lost none of his ferocity. In fact, she believed he'd become more short-tempered.

More willing to do violence. His stance might seem casual to most observers, but the way he rubbed his thumb and middle finger together indicated he was stressed. Or angry.

Biting her lower lip, she set down her glass, sensing that though he'd told her to pack, he wasn't done with her yet. Not with the way he strangled her with his silence.

Tell him. Tell him you found the book.

Hristoff's anger would go away, and his favor would return. He'd be pleased. Maybe relent in whatever he'd dreamed up as punishment for making him come after her. It probably had to do with Bisera.

No. She couldn't. Because then she couldn't give it to Veratti. Or the American, who could be in the elevator even now with no idea the trouble he would walk into.

But he had to expect that, right? He seemed smart, a thinker. So that begged the question—why *would* he come? To talk? What other explanation? She glanced to the bedroom, the bed meticulously made up. Unless he was like Hristoff in that respect, too.

Annoyance flickered through Hristoff's pale complexion. His Roman nose always made the ridge of his brow appear tangled in a knot of anger. The longer his silence lingered, the further back in time she wandered to find some sin that had brought him here. Because there was no way he could know that Veratti had set a demand on her life.

"I had thought," he began, his voice gravelly, devoid of emotion, "that showing you Bisera on the phone would be a reminder of where you belong. Where you should be. What you have to protect."

Desperation laced a heady cocktail in her veins. She swallowed, resting her hands on the cool marble of the liquor bar, but told herself there was a reason she'd become his most prized asset: she was very good at deception.

"And it worked. I planned to check out in the morning and return home. Just as we agreed." The bar formed a barrier, and he was notoriously sensitive to blocking, so she moved around it and forced herself to cross the room. "My reservation ends tomorrow. If you don't believe me, ask Mr. Aksoy."

Brow tight, he peered down at her. "I have." His expression held something she could not peg. Something she hadn't seen before. If she didn't know better, she'd say it was sadness. Grief.

Her heart tripped. *Veratti*. Hristoff knew she'd betrayed him. But how? And how had he gotten here so fast?

Head down, he returned to the window like he was wrestling with this. He shifted and angled a shoulder at her, a dark smugness taking over his face. Antipathy. "He is dead."

Numb, breath stolen, Iskra shut down her heart. "Who?" Pale blue eyes barged past her barriers. Somehow, standing here with Hristoff and death hovering so near, she realized how much hope she had allowed to seep into her pores at the club. The American seemed so capable. Smart. Clearly she'd been desperate, thinking he could help her. And that had killed him.

"So you care now, *da*?" He sneered over his shoulder. "Go. Pack your bags." His words were barely restrained.

"Who?" she insisted. "Who is dead? What have I done that you would kill someone to punish me?"

Lightning sparked through his expression. "You want to do this *now*?" His brows rose in challenge, and he looked around the suite. "Here?"

She recoiled.

"Go! Pack!"

"Who—"

"*Go!*" he roared.

Withdrawing, she stared at him. He might have killed a man, but he hadn't harmed Bisera. That alone turned her toward the bedroom.

"Elevator's empty," Ludak murmured from the door.

Iskra entered the room to find her clothing-strewn suitcase perched precariously on the bed. They'd already started packing for her. Most likely to conceal that they'd rummaged through her things, searching for . . . what? Evidence that she'd been unfaithful?

She breathed a snort as she finished what they'd started. To be unfaithful required faithfulness, which relied on a promise or agreement between two consenting parties. There had been neither. Except that she agreed she did not want to be bloodied and broken or dead.

Broken couldn't be helped. But bruised and bloodied . . .

"What happened with the book?" Hristoff demanded from the doorway.

Folding the black T-shirt she'd worn beneath her suit jacket the night she'd escaped the facility, she remembered the way Pale Eyes hadn't taken the shot. The way he'd punched the doors when she'd fled. And the way his eyes twinkled in that club. "Nothing," she said, unwilling to divulge that she had the book. Veratti was a better option.

"It's imperative, Iskra. Veratti will kill every one of us if you fail."

She did not care about her own life. It was as good as forfeit, no matter which path she took. She dropped the shirt in the case, grabbed a pair of jeans from the bed.

"Did you sleep with him?"

A bolt of heat shot down Iskra's neck and spine. "No."

"I thought you didn't know who I killed," he growled. "I'll ask again. Did you sleep with him?"

"No." She snapped the suitcase closed. "No no no *no*!" She twisted to face him. "I haven't slept with anyone. I don't want to sleep with anyone. I don't need to know who you killed to know I haven't slept with anyone. There's no one I have interest in. How much plainer can I—"

Hristoff grabbed her shoulders. Glowered. "That's a lot of anger for someone with no interest."

She wrested away and straightened her shirt. "I am not playing to your jealousies!"

His hand flew. Struck her cheek, spinning her across the bed. The suitcase caught her side, and she yelped. He grabbed her by the hair and jerked her face close as he leaned over her. "My jealousies? This isn't *jealousy*." He sneered. "I own you. Paid for you. Trained you. I feed you. Fund you. You give *nothing* to any man. Not money. Not sex. Not anything! Everything you are—I own."

Iskra gasped through the pain in her ribs.

"You have a job to do. Everything depends on it. Your life and B—"

"Yes, I know!" She winced at the pinch on her hair. At the pinch of *him* on her life.

Hristoff shoved her against the soft mattress. "I see you need more lessons when we get back." He straightened his scarf. Ran a hand through his hair. "You bring out the worst in me. But that's what it will take to be sure you do your job."

He stalked out, muttering to Ruslan to get her suitcase and for Ludak to call the elevator and notify the car they were coming down.

Trembling with fury, Iskra dug her fingernails into the comforter and coiled it into her fist. She would not kill him. She would endure it. She would be smart. Compliant. Bisera needed her to think past the anger. Freedom for Bisera demanded obeisance just a little longer.

"Iskra," Ruslan said in a mixture of rough and gentle. "Now."

She pushed off the bed. Gathered her pride and courage, then lifted the makeup case and her long cream jacket. "A moment. I need to fix my face." She could feel the heat where his hand had stung her cheek. Drawing attention would also draw his anger. She touched up the spot with base, blush, and a highlighter, but she worried about the welt that was rising. Though she tried a cold cloth, it was useless. He'd worn that accursed ring again.

A large shape loomed behind her, and she glanced at Ruslan as she repacked the travel case. "Who did he kill?"

"Vasily."

"Va—" Iskra sucked in a breath.

"It wasn't pretty."

She fumbled the case, her hands shaking. Merciful Mother . . . How had he found out about Vasily? About the yacht? And so quickly? Impossible. It was impossible to learn so much . . .

Vasily was dead. Because of her. Aches bloomed through her breast. Tears threatened.

"After Valery, to find you'd been with Vasily—"

"I wasn't *with* him," she spat.

But it didn't matter now. She wasn't sure even the ancient book would be enough to stave off Hristoff's rage, especially since he thought she'd been sleeping with the brother of the one man she'd given herself to.

And Hristoff had killed both brothers.

Oh, Vasily. Pozhaluysta, prosti menya.

Asking forgiveness of the dead marked a new low for Iskra, because he could neither grant nor deny it. However, she knew Vasily would grant it if he could. She hadn't been blind to his attraction, but she hadn't needed or wanted that from him. Just his assistance. He was the only person she had trusted. And now, because of her, he was gone.

"It's a mistake," Ruslan warned. "Grieve later. He's too angry."

He is not alone in that. Taking the cue, she eyed her cheek in the mirror, refusing to meet her own gaze. Threading her arm through her satchel, she followed Ruslan out of the bedroom.

Hristoff again stood by the windows, a formidable brooding presence.

The ding of the elevator rang outside the suite. "No. Back in," Ludak barked from the corridor. "Go down."

"No." Hristoff swiveled from the windows, tossing back the tails of his long black trench coat. "Hold it."

"We can call another," Ludak said.

"No time." Without acknowledging her or Ruslan, Hristoff stormed into the hall and entered the elevator.

She turned to it and saw Pale Eyes. Her breath hitched, but she did not slow or stop as she joined Hristoff. Enough men had died for her today. Ruslan barged in, pushing Iskra closer to Hristoff and taking up position behind her. Ludak crowded in.

It was hard not to glance back at the American. Her eyes skidded to the side but stopped when they hit Ruslan's plainly visible sidearm. She couldn't risk the American saying anything or stepping into this situation, or he'd die. So how did she let him know that? How would they reconnect later?

"The artifact you sent me after," she said to Hristoff in Russian, adding a hefty dose of irritation, "*that* is why I was with Vasily."

"Later," Hristoff growled.

"He was helping me find it. He *wasn't* a love interest."

Nostrils flaring, Hristoff gripped the soft flesh of her arm. "I said *later*." He looked over her shoulder at the American.

Wincing, she drew up. Silenced herself. Hoped the display she'd created between herself and Hristoff was enough to warn off the American. He might be a soldier, but he wasn't prepared for Hristoff.

"She's quite beautiful, isn't she?" Hristoff's expression billowed with possession and challenge.

"Sorry?"

The voice was so strange and nasally, it sounded like a different person than the American she'd met in Emir's club. Iskra turned to verify who had spoken but felt another pinch under her arm. With a whimper, she jerked back, furious that Hristoff was treating her like this in front of Pale Eyes.

"Yes, sir," came the nasally voice again, "this here hotel is something else. Never seen nothin' like it."

Hristoff's glower deepened, and she caught his nearly imperceptible signal to Ruslan. Ludak's chest bumped her spine as he wedged past, then his presence faded. He'd probably stepped back, forcing the American farther into the corner. Away from Iskra.

The shift of balance as the elevator came to rest warned Iskra that the doors would soon open. And she had no way to find the American again. Which meant Bisera would die.

FIFTEEN

HOTEL MISYON, ISTANBUL, TURKEY

Shoving aside his irritation over the way Peychinovich manhandled Viorica, Leif stepped out of the elevator. He was smart enough to recognize when the odds were against him. When a fight meant inevitable failure. He detested men like Peychinovich, who treated women like property, and competition like body counts. They were cowards. And those thugs who'd pinned him to the back of the elevator . . .

Leif watched Peych drag Viorica across the hotel foyer, which smelled of trouble. Buzzed a dozen different alarms in his tactical brain. He had no time to slow, but he took in his surroundings. Particularly the guy in jeans and a hoodie who tucked his chin and lifted his wrist to his mouth, moving away fast. Two shifting shadows beneath the lamplight across the street took off in opposite directions.

Clerks out of sight. Empty lobby.

Then came the growl of an engine. Screams outside.

Guards lurched, bringing Peych to a dead stop. The steel magnate angled toward—but didn't look at—Viorica, his attention still on the commotion.

The hollow *thwack* of metal impacting metal deafened the world to anything else.

Familiar faces appeared in the uproar, and a gallon of stress whooshed out as Leif spotted his team engaging Peych's. Shattering glass and the report of weapon fire joined the chaos. He silently thanked the guys for being on top of things. For giving him an out. A chance to do what he must. He was moving toward her before his brain caught up.

As Peych sought cover, Viorica spun, her hair splintering across her face as she snapped around. Her gaze was shot through with painful desperation. Apology. Fear.

So much fear.

He knew that look, because he'd lived it.

Instinct took over. He extended his hand. Didn't breathe a word. Didn't betray their collusion. She latched on, her grip like a vise.

Somehow they both knew what to do. Where to go. They sprinted to the right, down the narrow hall to the garage. At shouts from the lobby, he drew his weapon as he propelled her ahead, then whipped around to face the direction they'd come. Waiting. Expecting to be discovered.

A guard broke into the corridor.

Viorica slipped in front of him. "Hold me," she breathed.

Realizing her intent, he hauled her back against himself like a shield and aimed at the guard. She screamed. Bare feet—she'd kicked off her shoes?—toed the wall as she shoved. Thrust both of them backward. What was she doing?

He stumbled over a threshold. Swung out an arm to steady himself and found the steel door to the garage. He shifted back, falling through it. Spun her around.

She landed on both feet and vaulted off the steps into the garage well.

Disbelief—she'd done that on purpose, guided them into the garage while playing the victim—choked Leif as he slammed the door shut and heard the slap of her feet against the concrete. She was leaving. He sprinted after her.

She looked back. Not out of fear. But for direction.

"Go! Up and right."

Viorica surged ahead, moving fast for someone with bare feet. Like the pro she was, she darted up to the garage exit and pressed herself against the concrete wall. With stealth, she did a quick recon. Checked the street.

Leif itched to do the same. Didn't trust her to lead him into the open safely. What if this was an ambush? He leaned forward.

Her arm slapped his chest, pushing him back with a huffed, "Wait." She rolled out of point and slid to his other side.

A second later, two men rushed past the opening.

Crap. He'd nearly gotten them caught. He checked the street. "Go go go," he breathed, motioning her forward.

She hugged the wall, scurrying up the street. Following, Leif monitored their six, three, and nine as he walked backward. He wanted to cut through the anorexic alleys, but in the seconds he'd taken to ensure their safety, she'd covered thirty feet.

Shouts from the garage were almost swallowed by howls of outrage loud and distinct enough to force Leif into a lope. He glanced back. One of the guards swiveled toward him.

Leif abandoned stealth for speed.

A woman emerged from a shop. He whirled around her, stealing a glimpse of the two—no, three—guards barreling after him. One lifted a weapon.

Stupid. The shot would go wild. No telling where it would hit.

He pushed himself, gaining on Viorica as she burned up the distance. Crossed the street. Rounded a corner.

When he did the same, he found nothing but an empty sidewalk. A beat-up white sedan lumbered down the steep incline. Leif cursed. He'd lost her. Or had she done this on—

An olive face peered from the shadows of a small alcove.

His heart thudded as he leapt after her. His shoulder collided with a wall. Head smacked it. "Au—"

"Quiet," she whispered as a wood-slat door in front of him eased closed. "Here, back." She tugged his shirt, and he allowed her lead. Trusting. Which was strange because he barely trusted his team. But he had his weapon. He mentally touched the tactical knife strapped to his ankle.

The musty smell of the dark space made the walls close in on him. A sliver in the door slats allowed a line of sight on the alley. Behind him, Viorica placed her palms on his shoulder blades to give herself room. Warmth radiated through his shirt. Her breaths were quick and shallow. It awakened something in him, the need to protect. The desire to give her the safety she sought.

He swallowed, listening, monitoring the corner where the door met plaster and light brazenly pushed into the space. But as feet pounded the pavement, he realized if they were discovered, he didn't have enough room to take a shot. He shifted his right boot back.

She gave a strangled whimper when he crunched her bare foot.

"Sorry," he whispered. He adjusted and so did she, allowing him to watch that sliver and cradle the gun at chest level, pointing down and out. The repositioning put his shoulder roughly center mass to her chest, but he tried not to think about that.

Her pale pink top grabbed the light, and he couldn't help but notice the rise and fall of her chest—each breath dousing him with her smell. Light, floral, with a sweetness of fruit. *Eyes out*, he chided himself.

Shapes moved up and down the street. The tenacious buggers weren't branching out but were instead clustering where they'd lost their prize.

Her hand came to his shoulder. Probably, again, to keep him from crowding her.

A stream of Russian flew outside, a command to search the shop.

Viorica's other hand grabbed his forearm. Tightened.

Understanding, he wanted to nod and allay her fear. Reassure her they'd be okay. But he couldn't, because there was very little chance they'd get out of this intact.

Iskra clutched the book she'd retrieved from its hiding place, relief flooding her veins. Quickly, she tucked it in her satchel.

Braced behind the American, she tried to vanquish her smothering fear. Running from Hristoff would not work. Never had. Yet some piece of her trusted the man crushed against her. He'd known. In the hotel, when she had looked at him—that instant when Viorica fell away and Iskra lay bare her soul—she did not have to utter a single word. Then, in the corridor, she had moved in front of him to pose as a hostage, and he seized the idea. And it had worked, making Ruslan pull his weapon.

Now, more than ever, she had to side with the Americans, or Veratti would kill her. And if he did not, Hristoff would. But dread tightened her stomach as she imagined Hristoff returning to the Volga District, to Bisera. At the thought, panic threatened to overwhelm her.

What have I done?

The American shifted, looking up and around. Each move allowed the light to scrape his face. Intensity radiated from him. He was handsome. He was also an operator, always looking for an opportunity. Who was he? How did he know her thoughts as if they were his own?

When he glanced over her head and around her shoulders, she had one thought: *Hristoff will kill you. Brutally. Furiously. Because of me.* A part of her wanted to warn him. Tell him to break out of here and run as fast and far as he could. Before it was too late.

His eyes traced the wall behind them and then came to rest on her. Something about him seemed to wrap around her like a warm blanket. Embedded in her wounded soul, vulnerability skated out and attached to him.

He had gone still, too. Watching. His gaze bouncing around her . . .

Wait. Not around you, idiot. Behind *you*. "What?" It was more air than word.

"I think it's a door."

"Find them!" Ruslan barked outside.

She couldn't see faces through the gap in the door. Only legs below the knee. Shoes. Coming closer, then wandering away. A breath staggered from her.

"Hey." His word huffed against her cheek. "It's okay." More of that confidence. "Don't move."

She froze, wondering what he'd seen. What worried him.

Without a sound, he rotated. Though he only covered half her body with his own, it was too much. She could feel the rocks and dirt beneath her feet and worried the crunching would alert Ruslan or that she'd step on something sharp. Already, stickiness slushed between her toes. She'd cut her foot somehow, and she cursed that she'd had to ditch her pumps in the lobby. They would have slowed her down, so she'd kicked them off and fled.

The American's focus and hand drifted to the ceiling. He tracked where the ceiling met the wall. Both arms came up and his chest pressed toward her face. His shirt tickled her nose. She looked away, but the scent of him encircled her mind.

"Found a handle," he grunted. "Be ready."

"For what?"

"Light. Trouble. Dunno. Just be ready."

She gave a nod. Neither could know what was behind this wall. "Wait." She touched his side, and his abs jumped. "Are you sure?"

He eyed her. "Never." Then he smirked. "That's half the fun."

Fun? This was his idea of fun?

Click.

Iskra sucked in a breath as the door popped. Though prepared, she still lost her balance and tumbled backward.

He caught her, his hand slipping to her waist. "You okay?"

Irritated—with herself or with him, she wasn't sure—Iskra shouldered into the exit. She eased aside and peered through the two-inch gap. "Dark. Can't see . . . wait."

Aisles sat in silence, stocked and clean.

She nudged the door a little farther, palming its cold surface. She inspected one aisle. Peered around a freezer case. "I think it's clear."

"Nice and easy," he muttered and widened the opening.

Slipping out and using the end of the aisle for protection, she checked the windows littered with flyers and advertisements. Beyond them, night owls clubbing and partying sauntered down the street. But the figure who made her want to jump back into the cramped space had broad shoulders and an ominous stature.

A shadow spirited across the windows. Her breath caught, then released as she realized it was her partner in this crime. How he'd gotten to the front of the store without a sound, she couldn't fathom. But he was there, hunkering behind a rack of crisps.

He crouch-ran back to her and straightened in the shadows. "No good." They stood close, warily scanning the activity on the street. "Too exposed."

Ruslan jogged by. "He will not stop until I'm found."

"Especially since he thinks I kidnapped you."

Guilt hung from Iskra's shoulders like an anchor. It would be nice to think he cared about her, but this was about the book. Her hand fell to her satchel.

He frowned, eyeing her bag. And in his gaze she saw that he knew what she had. "Where'd you get that?"

Iskra stared at him, unwilling to divulge her secrets.

With a nod and a huff, he headed back down the aisle. "C'mon."

She hurried to catch up. "Where?"

"Stairs." He snaked through the shop. "If we can get to the roof, we might have options."

Most places like this didn't have access to the upper levels through the shop. Only through a separate, inner hall. They should have just stayed in the storeroom.

"Here." Hands working the knob, he winced and grimaced. A stream of light from a car stabbed through the glass and slid over his face.

Click. Snick.

He flicked open the door and motioned her into a dank, well-lit stairwell. She hesitated at the cast-iron steps. The iron traction nubs would be painful against her cut and chewed-up feet.

"Hang on." He vanished back into the shop.

"I—" Iskra watched him go, a new fear tearing through her. What if he left and she got caught? She'd be beaten, but maybe she should make that happen. At least that way, he'd live.

Like a specter, he reappeared. "Here." He handed her a pair of cheap canvas shoes and a black T-shirt.

She frowned. "I have a shirt."

"It's pink, and everyone can see it. You need camouflage."

Surprised she hadn't thought of that, she threaded her arms into the shirt. The shoes were too small, but beggars couldn't be choosers. Leaning against the wall, she mashed her toes into them. She started climbing.

They made it to the roof, and she remembered the last time she'd encountered this man—on the roof of the Greek facility.

He gave her a cocky grin. "Like old times, eh?" He glanced around but frowned.

"What?"

"I was hoping you had a hang glider up here, too."

She couldn't resist the retort on her tongue. "It's invisible. Trust me. Just hold out your arms and jump."

"Sounds deadly."

A rumble of laughter in her stomach startled her. She swallowed it. "Can we get out of here? I don't want to die."

"Booyah," he muttered, then nodded behind her. "That way. Alley's narrow enough for us to jump to the other side."

They made the first leap without incident. Then the second. The third trapped her breath into her throat, because it wasn't an alley. It was a road, if a small one. She visually measured the distance and backed up.

"Well," she said, bouncing on her cramped toes, "if this kills me, Hristoff will never stop looking for you, and that will be my revenge."

With a hop, she sprinted toward the edge. Toed it, then launched into the air. She wanted to scream. Wanted to shriek. As she hung in the air, she had the morbid realization that she wasn't going to clear it. She landed, her left shin whacking the edge. She rolled, pain blinding her. Slid across the tarred roof. Arched her back against the pain, knowing if she let that cry escape, Hristoff would hear. Somehow he would.

A soft thump, and the American was scrambling to her side. "You okay?"

Pride forced her to peel herself off the rooftop. She reached for her leg.

"Let me see." His hands were warm against her cold ones. He slid up her pant leg and hissed. "That's going to be wicked painful, but I don't think anything is broken."

Except her pride.

"Can you walk?"

"Yes."

His lips pulled up on one side, and he eased off. "Hang tight." Crouched, he slunk around the perimeter of the roof. And one by one, she recognized the buildings. Alarm hit her—they were right across from the Misyon now! They would see him!

She wanted to call his name but still didn't know it. He knelt at the corner, head seemingly plastered to the surface. Then he pulled back and returned. Slumped against the wall.

"Are you an idiot?" She glowered.

"Most times," he said with an unrepentant grin. "He's still there. Last chance."

Iskra eyed him, her heart agitated. She thought not of the abuse, the rapes, the psychological torture. Only of one—

"Okay. We'll head north a few more buildings, then I'll contact my team."

She was doing this. Really doing this.

Bisera.

Her stomach squirmed.

"Ready?"

Before she could change her mind, Iskra nodded. As she came

to her feet and her shin throbbed in protest, she knew it would be the least of what she'd endure. Flee with him and obey Veratti. Or face Hristoff's reprisal for defying him. She would not even let herself think of Bisera. Not right now.

This was the only way. She must risk herself to buy the freedom she desperately wanted. She limped across the roof.

"You able to jump still?"

"Yes," she bit out.

"Hey," he said quietly, hovering close. "It's not a challenge, just a question. If you're in pain, we find another way."

Could they? "We need what is fastest, *da*?"

Though he hesitated, he nodded.

"And that is?"

He looked across the city roofs.

"Then we go that way." She lined herself up to make the leap to the next northern building.

"Why?"

Iskra scowled at him. "You said it was—"

"No," he said, closing the gap between them. "Why'd you come with me? Why are you leaving him?"

She dropped her gaze. *Just make the jump*. She turned to the roof.

"I'm not going any farther until you tell me."

"You want me to lay it all out, but you will not even tell me your name." She hopped, shutting off the stab of fire in her shin, then sprinted at the ledge. Sailed into the air and over to the next building.

He landed almost simultaneously with her. "Runt." He didn't even sound winded. "I told you before—they call me Runt."

She curled a lip. "Like a rat?"

"No," he said, drawing it out in confusion. "Like a *runt*, you know—smallest of the litter."

Hobbling to the other side of the roof, she said, "You don't look small."

He grinned. "Feel free to keep those compliments coming."

Iskra felt another smile coming on, so she forced herself to make the next jump. With each one, it seemed her leg improved. Or maybe it was so injured that it had gone numb. She really didn't care, as long as she was able to put distance between herself and Hristoff.

"Two more, then we climb down," he said, indicating a narrow building that lined the river.

Exhaustion taunted her, threatening to yank her down each time. But she wasn't going to quit. They made the jumps. He hustled to the edge of the final building and stepped over the ledge, gripping the fire escape handles. It looked as if he were walking on air.

He gave her a wink. "See you on the ground."

He dropped out of sight. His hands sliding along the rails, his booted feet toeing them and slowing his descent. She smiled. Though she could easily do the same, she knew that final landing would wrack her shin. So she took hold of the first rung, glanced down, and released. She plummeted, free-falling, then grabbed the rung a half dozen feet below. The escape rattled and jarred her shoulder, but it held. She did it again. Her canvas shoes hung just over his head now.

She caught the last rung and eased herself down, landing softly. Perfectly.

He wore an all-out wide smile, and his eyes glittered. "Crazy awesome."

A trill of victory rang through her, a strange giddy feeling. Dusting off her hands, she felt weird. Light. She smiled.

He touched her back. "How's the leg?"

"Oddly, I can't feel any pain."

"Normal—it's swollen and fluid's protecting it," he said, already moving away from the city. "Between that and adrenaline, you'll be okay for a while. When we get there, Saito will check it." He tugged a phone from his pocket. Though it activated, the screen remained black. He keyed in a number and lifted it to his ear as they wound up a street and crossed into a vineyard. "Hey . . . yeah. No, about a klick out." He nodded. "Yeah . . . cool. See you in ten."

The softer ground helped with the heaviness of her leg. "You did not tell them I was coming."

"They saw us on satellite," he said.

Which meant Hristoff could do the same. He'd be furious, fighting to get her back. He'd put all his resources to use. It was more important than ever to get out of here.

"Don't worry. They're cleaning up the feed. Altering it."

She eyed him, wondering who they were to have access to satellites. That spoke of a large entity. Yet despite her attempts, she hadn't been able to dig any information out of him. And who was he, that he read her so well? Anticipated her needs and concerns? Why did she trust him?

"I can't do it."

He glanced back, his face damp with sweat and concern. "Why? I thought—"

"I can't call you Runt."

His consternation shifted, morphed into a smirk.

"It's too much like *rat*."

"I told you—not rat, *Runt*," he said slowly. "Besides, I think we're both stuck with code names we don't like, *Viorica*."

How did he know she didn't like that name?

"What do you want to call me?" he asked.

"I think *idiot* would not go over well with your men."

"Psh. They use it all the—" His hand flung out toward her. "Down!"

Only as she instinctively followed his command and searched for a threat did she feel the vibration rumbling the soft dirt of the vineyard beneath her hands. Helicopter.

He scanned the air. "Stay below the vines. Keep moving."

She did as he instructed. About thirty paces later, with the thunder of the chopper closing in, she saw its spotlight. Clinging to the vine, she silently thanked him for the dark shirt. Her pale blouse would have been a big white surrender flag beneath that explosion of light.

In the sparse gaps between the *thwump-thwump-thwump* of the rotors, the air carried his voice to her. He was on his phone again. Calling in reinforcements, she hoped. But even as the thought entered her mind, the fields to her right flared brighter and brighter. The sound grew deafening. Her fear terrorizing.

Runt looked back at her. Something in his expression slowed Iskra. Uncertainty darkened his eyes. Then determination as his gaze shifted to her left. She turned. Another incoming helo. He straightened, shoulders and head above the vines as he moved past her. He would be seen!

"No!" Her shout was drowned out by the rotors.

The spotlight homed in on him. And in that moment, he pivoted behind her. His arms encircled her throat.

"Stop." She gripped his arm, then relaxed—he was playing the part again, *da*?

His forearms flexed, squeezing her throat between the corded muscles and his chest. He forced her head forward, cutting off her oxygen.

Air seeped from her lungs, but she could pull no more in. Her chest ached. "Stop!" She couldn't breathe. She slapped at him. Pawed. Thrashed.

His chest was a wall of muscle, crushing her. Forbidding her from moving, from getting away. From breathing.

No. No no no.

Why had she trusted him? Why had she thought him different?

Bisera! She'd hoped for freedom. Now Bisera would be alone with Hristoff.

Her vision ghosted. The spotlight arced away.

Faded. Fade . . .

SIXTEEN

UNDISCLOSED LOCATION NEAR CUBA

Hand over his fist, Leif bent forward in his chair and pressed his knuckles to his lips, staring at the gurney where she lay strapped. Padded restraints cuffed her wrists. Wider straps held her chest, hips, and ankles.

What he'd done made him sick. But the order had been given to bring her in—unconscious. Never would he forget the way she'd screamed. Thrashed. That moment when her trust in him collapsed into sheer panic. It had ripped into him, gutted him.

Is this what I've become?

Whatever it was about him that she'd latched on to, that made her decide he wasn't an enemy, he would take it. But he felt like instead of biting off more than he could chew, he'd stolen the whole freakin' cow.

It had to be done, though. Peychinovich thought Leif had kidnapped her. Even Viorica had said that if she died, the steel magnate would never stop looking for Leif. Besides, the local police chopper likely had cameras. If it had captured her fleeing the city with Leif, whatever ruse she was playing would have been destroyed.

And it *was* a ruse. She said one thing, but her eyes and actions said another. She was tough and quick, but he was sure that behind her tough façade lurked a mischievous imp. When she'd mouthed off to him on the rooftop about the invisible glider, then when she'd fast-roped without the rope at the edge of the city, he'd seen her struggle to hide a smile. Which had a nuke blast yield of . . . well, enough to obliterate rational thought.

That moment stuck in the storage room, though. Her shallow

breaths. The way she nervously watched his face. When he'd itched to kiss her. But he'd detected fear swimming beneath her desire, too. It warned him to behave. To save the passion for later. If there ever was a later.

Probably not. She'd hate him after—

"You strangled me."

Leif came to his feet, conscience thudding at the sound of her hoarse words. "Sleeper hold." He gripped the safety bars of the bed and peered down at her. "Couldn't let you know where we were headed."

Hurt seeped through her gaze, which rested on the ceiling, not on him.

"The chopper was local. Might've had cameras."

She blinked. Processed that with a shake of her head. "Hristoff could have seen the video."

He hated that she used his first name. It was too . . . personal. "I guess I could've knocked you in the head with my weapon." Since she'd plucked his heartstrings somehow, he'd taken a less violent approach. It was slower and nearly got him killed. But she was alive. And here.

"And mess up my makeup?"

Leif snorted, surprised yet glad she didn't hate his guts. "You're welcome."

She shifted, and the restraints resisted. Her hazel-brown eyes flashed.

"Command's orders." Ones he'd vehemently argued against. Viorica had come willingly. She wasn't trying to get away. But Iliescu and Braun countered with a stiff reminder that she was a skilled operative and assassin. Allowing her to move freely about a military base was not an option. He saw their point and agreed they had to play this smart. But she had trusted him. Which was why he'd insisted on being here when she came to.

Lips tight, emotion roiling through her olive features, Viorica glowered. "I trusted you."

He leaned down, elbow on the bar, and scratched his jaw. "Yeah. That part's bugging me."

Her brows lifted into a pinched expression. "You think . . ." She sagged. Looked back at the ceiling. "You think I'm working you."

"Don't we all? I'm using you to get the book."

Her eyes, now a strange yellow-green, struck his. Panicked. "Where is it?"

His statement had been a test to gauge her reaction. Figure out what on the planet she was doing leaving Peychinovich. Her lover. Her funding. It made zero sense.

She wrestled the cuffs.

"I'd go easy," he suggested. "They tighten the more you strain. Sort of like those Chinese finger traps I hated as a kid. Still convinced they're a torture device."

"Being here with you is torture enough."

"Ouch," he said with a laugh he didn't feel.

"Where are we? Where are my things?"

"A secure location, and your things are here, along with your satchel."

A glint hit her expression. "Secure location? Where?"

Now, why had that gotten such a response from her? "If I told you, it wouldn't be secure."

The door hissed open, the security override releasing. He peered over his shoulder and found two guards and a female doctor.

"I will break free, I always do," Viorica growled. "And I'll find that book, and you will never see me again." The words were filled with hurt. But was it more?

Holding off the medical staff, he leaned closer. "V, put that vendetta on ice. This isn't what it seems. I'll get you out of these restraints."

"I trusted you once. I won't make that mistake—"

"If I release you, can we talk?"

Wariness punctured her anger. "About what?" she gritted.

"The whys, mostly."

She considered him, mouth in a tight line.

"Agreed?"

"Mostly."

Leif liked that she threw his words back at him.

"Chief?" the doctor insisted.

He nodded to the medical team, not looking away from her. "I'll be back. Don't go anywhere, okay?"

"Not funny."

"Yeah," he said with a grin, "it kind of was." He touched her shoulder—a strange thing, but he did it. Why he felt protective, why he even thought he could convince her, work her . . .

At the door, he stopped the doctor. "Who do I talk to about the restraints?"

"Colonel Brust."

"Where can I find him?"

"Right here," a uniform growled as he stormed past the room. "Walk with me."

After one last glance at Viorica and a signal for the doc to wait, Leif caught up. "I—"

Brust lifted a hand. "Save it. Not happening."

"What's not happening?"

"Her unchained, in any respect."

"But—"

"Son, I get you." The colonel hadn't looked up from the OD-green file folder he was flipping through as he stalked down the dull corridor. "In the city, you had an experience. You trusted each other." He swiped his badge and shouldered them around a checkpoint. "But there are things you don't know about her."

"And things you don't know about me."

Brust gave him an appraising look as they trudged through the bustling command center that was like something out of a thriller movie with its black walls, ominous lighting, and hushed voices. "I know enough."

Not even close. And Leif kept it that way, an agreement with

Iliescu and his brother, and the Army chief of staff. "I need the restraints off. I'm working an assignment—"

"Maybe you didn't hear me the first time," Brust said, dropping the folder on the table and turning. "It's not happening. She's wanted in thirteen countries. She's killed dozens of people. Purported to have killed twice that. Don't think she wants anything from you other than to snap your neck. That's all the Wild Rose ever wants. And those she meets end up dead. Including that guy on the yacht we tracked her from."

"What man?"

Brust lifted a stack of papers and rifled through them. Spun one across his desk. "Kuznetsov, Vasily. Age forty. Twin brother to Valery Kuznetsov, right hand of Peychinovich, also found dead and floating in the Moscow River." He glowered. "See? Dead. They're all dead, and I know you might go a little weak in the knees at the pretty brown eyes she bats at you, but I'm not going to be the one notifying Iliescu or Braun you're belly up because you had a thing for the Russian operative. Capiche?"

"Sir, with all due respect, this isn't about attraction. She has an artifact—"

"Actually, we have it now." The colonel's glower turned to a gloat. "And now we don't need anything from her save information, which we plan to extract from her in one pain-filled second after another."

"No." Leif heard the bark in his voice and didn't care. "You touch her, and I promise you will have a nightmare breathing down your neck—after I'm done with you."

Face crimson, the colonel bellowed, "You threatening me, son?"

"Check your facts. Check my mission, and you'll find you're on the wrong end of this, Colonel."

Storming out of the command bunker, Leif balled his fists and stalked back to where they were holding Viorica.

"Holeeee crap," Barclay muttered.

"What?" Mercy dropped her feet to the ground and straightened in her chair, glancing at him. His whitewashed face gaped at his monitor and forced her to look, too. The security feed of the base showed a fight in one of the hallways. She sucked in a breath. Stood, leaning in closer.

A confrontation with two MPs and— "Runt."

Barc lifted his phone. "Lawe, get to the med bay. Now. Before Runt—"

Leif slid into the two MPs. Dropped one with a half dozen strikes that were violence in motion. He snatched his weapon from its holster before the soldier even hit the ground and aimed it at the second, who lifted his hands and backed away. With no sound, the silence added an ominous feel.

"Too late," Barc corrected. "Just get down there."

"Don't shoot," Mercy willed Leif. That would be a mistake he couldn't come back from. "What is wrong with him?" Phone in hand, she ran out of the communications center and toward the medical wing. "Sir, we've made the trip from Incirlik. Arrived a couple of hours ago, but something's wrong with Runt. You won't believe this."

"Hang on." The clattering of keys made it through the line before Iliescu issued a long-suffering sigh. "For the love of . . ."

"Sir?"

"Director." Through the connection came Culver Brown's voice—had the director called him up, too? "I heard what's happening."

"Get down to Metcalfe. Tell him I'm involved now."

Shelving the confusion, Mercy huffed. "What's wrong with him?"

"Nothing's *wrong* with him," Dru said. "He's doing what his training demands."

"You kidding me?" Culver's objection was deep. "We have the same training—"

"You don't, in fact," Iliescu said. "Get there. Tell him."

"With what I'm seeing, that won't be enough—"

"Do it!"

When the line went dead, Mercy stared at her phone. Leif had different training from Culver? Did Dru mean specialization? Something niggling at the base of her brain said he was referencing something else. She jogged to the medical wing and rounded the corner.

Runt snapped his Glock at her. "Far enough, Maddox!"

She skidded to a stop, hands raised. "Easy, Runt." Where was Culver? "Let's talk. What's going on here?"

Two more MPs entered the fray. She half expected Runt to look wild-eyed, crazy. Manic—in a rage, like Banner when he Hulked. But Runt was the epitome of calm. Focused.

A uniform rushed him.

Runt didn't look or turn. He simply responded. And before Mercy could twitch a muscle, the MP was on the ground, unconscious. The lightning-fast reflexes had come out of nowhere and vanished just as quick, Runt sliding back into a ready stance with his weapon targeting the remaining MPs.

Where in the 'verse was Culver?

"Stand down, or I will put you down," Runt warned in a preternaturally even voice. It seemed so wrong and menacing.

"Leif," she said, advancing a step.

"Mercy, stay there," he growled, not looking at her. "Do not make me hurt you."

She balked, stunned at the threat. "Iliescu—I talked to him."

He hesitated.

A team of doctors approached with more MPs, crowding the already too-small hallway. "Please"—a female doctor held a hand toward the window—"we need to take her to—"

"No." Runt eyed them. His hesitation hung rank and loud. "Nobody's taking her anywhere." He positioned himself in the doorway.

That was what this was about? The female assassin? Surprise pushed Mercy's gaze to the room, where the dark-haired woman lay chained to a bed, watching the showdown.

Leif homed in on Mercy again. "You talked to Iliescu?"

Her heart thudded. "Yes." *Get him to talk. Get him distracted.* "You know he's always got your six, right?" What was it Dru had said to tell Leif? Adrenaline had her botching this.

Leif didn't answer, his focus shifting to an MP closing in.

"Easy there, buddy. Iliescu sent a message," came Culver's booming voice as he rounded the corner. "He's involved. Just give it a minute."

Leif wavered. "Brust threatened to torture her." His jaw muscle flexed. "That's not happening."

"Nobody's going to torture her," a young male doctor said, gaping. "I have no idea what you and the colonel talked about, but we want to run an MRI, make sure—"

Runt snapped his weapon toward the chatty doctor.

"Easy," Culver warned. "Let's not add to the body count."

Body count? Add to it?

Oh. The confrontation at the hotel. She skirted a look at Runt. Did he know what the team had done? How they'd gone in, put their lives in harm's way so he could get out?

Radios squawked. The MPs tentatively reached for them but didn't take their eyes off Runt. From this end of the hall, Mercy couldn't understand what was being said, but their postures shifted. The MPs nodded to each other, then backed away.

Lawe rounded the corner. "Stand down, Runt. It's good. Colonel Brust understands he's no longer in authority over our prisoner."

As the MPs lowered their weapons and eased back, Runt did the same. He eyed the doctors. "She doesn't leave this room unless I or someone on my team is with her. Understood?"

The female doctor seethed. "This is—"

"Not your problem," he finished. "I brought her in, and *I* am responsible for her." Weapon still at the ready, he motioned Mercy closer. "Inside. Remove the restraints."

Uh . . . Mercy eyed Culver, very uncomfortable with entering the room of a notorious assassin and setting her free. It was sort of like trying to pet the pretty pattern on a cobra without expecting to get bitten or die.

"I'll help," Culver said, giving Mercy the courage to enter the room.

Still unsettled, she eyed the female assassin who'd somehow convinced Leif to protect her, and moved to the left side of the bed, reaching for the buckle on a wrist cuff.

"What're you doing?" the assassin asked, her gaze darting between them.

"Making it easier for you to kill us, apparently," Mercy muttered. "Keep still."

"I hope you realize what he just did for you," Culver growled as he worked the straps on the other side.

"I have no reason to hurt you," Viorica said.

"Yeah, didn't know assassins needed a *reason*. Just a target," Mercy countered.

"You don't trust me."

"Wow, Culver, she's got brains after all."

Good job, Mercy. Tick off the murdering operative. When she shifted to the hip and chest restraints, the woman lifted her hands. Mercy flinched. And hated herself for being so smart-mouthed and jumpy. The woman was only rubbing the red welts on her wrists.

"You realize," Mercy said, feeling insanely protective of the guys she worked with, "he could've been killed just now. For you." When their eyes locked, a cold violent streak slithered through her. "If anything happens to him because of you . . ." She unbuckled the final strap and stepped back as Culver assisted the assassin to an upright position.

Viorica touched her fingers to her temples. "I'm dizzy."

"I can knock you unconscious again," Mercy offered with a shrug. "Might resolve that issue."

"Mercy," Culver chided.

She had no idea why she didn't like this woman—well, besides the cold-blooded killer thing—but she didn't. Like royally. Like archnemesis.

Viorica lifted her jaw. An arrogant, coldhearted villain.

Then Mercy remembered the woman spoke Russian. Mercy could do that and knew that the guys wouldn't understand. "I may not be Lara Croft," she said in the assassin's language, "but I'm her cousin, Trinity—you know, brilliant hacker. If you hurt him, I'll find your enemies and relay your location to them. To every one of them."

Viorica's brow rippled, both in surprise and confusion. "I do not want to hurt him."

"What you *want* and what you *do* aren't always the same thing," Mercy said.

"Okay." Runt let himself into the room, acting as if he hadn't just had an armed standoff with the staff of a military installation. "They want you downstairs for an MRI."

Viorica hesitated. "Why?"

"Need to verify no tracking devices." He handed over her laundered clothes. "I told them you needed to freshen your makeup."

Viorica took the clothes, hesitated, then gazed up at Runt, her lips parted. Was she going to pledge her undying love? Kiss him?

"Where's the book?" the assassin asked.

Mercy snorted. "Of course. No thank-you for putting your life on the line. No acknowledgment for what you protected her from. Just 'where is the book?'"

Runt scowled. "Show her the bathroom."

"Right. Because I'm now reduced from hacker to lady's maid."

Viorica walked over to the chair where her satchel sat. She peered inside, almost as if she didn't believe the book was gone. With a huff, she turned to them.

Gliding dramatically to the door, Mercy pointed. "Bathroom."

The woman looked uncertainly at Leif.

"It's secure." He nodded toward the restroom. "Go on. I'll wait."

SEVENTEEN

CIA HEADQUARTERS, MARYLAND

"I'm sending you something."

"Okay."

"We might have a problem." Dru eyed the still image of Leif turning a weapon on their own soldiers. "Check it out. I'll wait." He hit SEND and then let the video replay.

"Must be serious."

What he hadn't sent was the video of Leif and Brust. That was EYES ONLY.

A curse hit the line.

"Now you see my problem."

"Think he's cracked?"

"I . . . I don't know." That would be worst case. "I know so little about what happened to him. There are things I suspect but can't prove. He's done so well. I really expected it to take more. The one medical file I scrounged up indicates 'extreme heightened factors' is the only primer, but AARs from the team don't show that's happened. He was never in that level of danger."

"But if he's regressing . . ."

"Yeah." Iliescu roughed a hand over his face. "We have a ton of trouble. We should meet. Make a plan."

"Think it's that bad?"

"I . . ." Dru moused over to the other file. Pulled up the dossier on Viorica. Then he eyed the video again. "I'm worried about someone he seems to have paired up with."

"Paired up?"

"An assignment. He's acting as protector."

"Female?"

"Yes."

"That's your problem right there. The protective instinct is one of the strongest, especially in a soldier—maybe the primer's heightened factor isn't limited to danger to himself but also applies to this woman. I can speak from experience that a soldier's definitely in a state of vigilance when protecting an innocent child or woman."

"This woman doesn't meet the 'innocent' qualifier." Dru huffed. "Meet me at the tarmac. We can figure out how to handle this en route."

"To where?"

"Cuba."

"Seriously?"

"It's that or . . . you know what I have to do if he goes active."

UNDISCLOSED LOCATION NEAR CUBA

Wearing sweatpants and a blue long-sleeved shirt with the American Air Force logo on it, Iskra knew her time and options were limited. She sat quietly at a table in a conference room with a tray of cafeteria food. Though she'd tried to read the patches on the security team, she hadn't been able to figure out what secure location they'd come to.

"How's your leg?" the pale-eyed American asked, sitting in the chair facing her. He'd showered, too, and wore a black shirt and tactical pants.

"Fine." She had bigger concerns now. "I'm worried."

"I won't let anything happen to you."

"Noble words." She smiled, toying with the edge of a napkin. She cleared her throat, mind pinging since she'd lain in that MRI tube, wondering, thinking. "If I have a tracking device"—it galled her that Hristoff would microchip her the way people did their pets—"you have to leave it alone."

He cocked his head to the side, brows knotted. "What?"

"It is for the best." She scooted the sloppy potatoes around the tray with a spork. They must really be worried she was a threat to give her useless plastic utensils. She was tired. Of running. Of doing horrible things to survive. Of fighting for freedom.

"Is that what you want? To stay tagged?"

"If you don't leave it alone, he'll follow the signal to where it stopped. He'll come. He'll kill everyone in this facility."

"Let him come—if it was there, it's already been neutralized. He won't find this place. It doesn't exist. And besides—don't you think he's already en route, after I took you from him?" His voice was hard-edged as he shifted closer. "V, what's the relationship between you and Peychinovich?"

"You called him my lover."

"And you can't say that without recoiling." He leaned in. "The way he roughed you up—I saw his manhandling in the elevator." He studied her. "You aren't his lover."

She folded her arms, wishing she could bury herself in the clothes that were too big. "It does not matter, R—" She grunted and touched her temple. "I refuse to call you that." Amused by the word that popped into her mind, she asked, "Do you know Russian?"

"*Nemnogo*."

She sat back, surprised that he knew how to say "a little" in her language.

He shrugged. "I asked a friend. Read a book."

She laughed at the absurdity of learning a language by reading a book, but then realized which of his friends had probably taught him the words. "The woman in the room."

He nodded.

"She does not like me."

"She's been through a lot and wants to protect her team. We all do."

What would it be like to have people who looked after her not because she was a possession but out of loyalty or friendship? He cared about the people he worked with. Understood their history. Their wants.

"As do I." Lesya, her assistant in Russia. More than anything—even her own life—Bisera. "The book, where is it?"

"Secure."

"Are you sure?"

"V, I—"

"Why do you call me that?" She needed a rapport with him, one that built trust. That convinced him he could share secrets with her.

He eased back with a sigh, probably noticing the way she detoured the conversation. "*Viorica* is an assassin who works for Peychinovich." He narrowed his pale eyes at her. "The woman sitting in front of me is not that person."

Her throat tightened as she wondered—was it possible someone saw her? The real *her*? No. It was a job, just like her using him now. "I am that person," she said, the ache within churning. "Do not think anything can happen here."

He sat forward again. "Happen? Like what?" He traced her jaw.

At his soft touch, Iskra drew up, breath snatched from her lungs.

"Like that?"

She smacked his hand away. Shoved to her feet. He didn't move, just smiled up at her, and Iskra noted the way the guards outside the room jerked to the ready.

He came and stood in front of her. "I apologize. That was out of line. I knew better."

"Then why do it?"

"Because . . ." He ran a hand down the back of his neck. "Look, maybe things are crazy beyond recognition here. We can't be . . . open. But . . ."

Of course they couldn't. It'd get them killed or betrayed.

He shrugged. "We're here. Together." His eyes widened and he looked down. "We both . . ." He seemed to swallow words that had gotten ahead of him.

Weirdly enough, she could taste what he didn't speak. Sweet words of temptation. But right now she had to draw him to her side. "Why was your team after the book?"

"Honestly?" He leaned back against the table. "I'm not sure." Palm on the table, he considered her. "They said it needed to be found, that it was dangerous in the wrong hands—Peych's. Yours. That we had to stop you from getting it."

"So . . ." She tried to make the two sides of this man align. He'd been told to stop her, yet he was helping her. "Why did you . . . ?" It had been startling to watch him protect the entrance to her room. She'd never seen anyone do that. Most took aim *at* her, not *for* her. "In the medical room, you stopped them. Why?"

"Had my orders." His answer seemed to bother even him. Like he didn't believe it or used it to mask the real one. "I made a promise to protect you."

"You"—she shook her head slowly—"never made me a promise."

"To myself." He folded his arms, biceps straining the shirt. "Not real sure why. Maybe it was the way you outsmarted me in Greece. I had to one-up you."

"By protecting me?"

"If you died here, how could I one-up you later?"

She couldn't tell if he was serious. But did it matter? Nobody had ever protected her, unless under Hristoff's orders.

"Why did you go after the book?" he asked.

"I was ordered to."

"Peychinovich."

She shrugged. "Control of an artifact that holds great secrets. A contact said it was worth a lot. Hristoff insisted I find it." Lies were built on truths, *da*?

"That why he was at the hotel? To see if you had it?"

It struck Iskra that despite the threats from Veratti, despite the rage Hristoff felt when she'd failed the Cellini mission . . . he wasn't worried about the book. He'd asked about it, *da*, but he did not press her. He wasn't concerned. "He already knew I had it."

Vasily. Was that why Hristoff had killed him, besides thinking she'd slept with him? That was how Hristoff knew she was in Istanbul. The poor, weak fool.

"You okay?"

Pulled back to the moment, she shook off the weight of those thoughts. "You don't know anything about the book? I'm supposed to believe that? Or is it like this 'secure' location, and you just won't name what you know?"

He spread his arms wide. "I've told you what I know about the book—its name and that it might contain information about some wars. It's rumored to list the outcomes."

"But you won't tell me what you know about this facility."

He squinted. "How is that important to the book?"

"Just exploring what level of trust we have." She cleared her throat, deciding to give him more information in the hope of buying more points with him. "The Book of the Wars is believed to be a holy text, so it includes other things."

"Like?"

"I've heard"—*careful, Iskra*—"it is even said to have writings from Saint John."

Face screwed tight in confusion, he repeated the name. "John?"

"The apostle who wrote Revelation."

He grunted. Cocked his head in thought. "Guess that makes sense. Our team thinks there are wars in it that haven't happened yet."

"Wait—so you *do* know more than you've told me," she challenged.

Smirking, he huffed.

"What?"

"There is no way I believe you'd go after this thing just to make Peych happy. You said you aren't his lover, so what makes you risk life and limb to secure this thing for *him*?" He shook his head, scratching his jaw. "Doesn't add up. There's more."

"I went after it because it's an artifact that will . . . buy me time." She could admit that, right? Now to distract him. "Look, I cannot read the text—it's in multiple languages—but what I've told you is true."

"Now who knows more than they're admitting? So, what else?" He crossed his arms. "I'm not budging till you come clean."

Anger churned through her that he could figure her out so easily.

It scared her. And yet drew her in. Nobody knew about Mitre. She'd kept it that way on purpose. "There's this"—fear clogged her, shutting out the threat by Veratti's man—"my friend"—liars went to hell, didn't they?—"told me that what John wrote . . ."

Nerves cramped her stomach. How could she make this not sound ridiculous? What Veratti's man had told her, what he'd ordered her to find out, it bordered on absurd. How could she tell the American in a way that convinced him when *she* wasn't convinced?

"What are you nervous about?" he asked.

Iskra pivoted, only then realizing she'd started pacing. She returned to the table. "You'll think me crazy."

"I already do." He laughed. "You escaped across the rooftops of Istanbul with me."

"Okay." She had everything to lose, but here went nothing. "Before Vasily died, he told me the book mentions a place," she muttered, twisting the cords of this revelation tightly, "called the Pearl of the Antilles. It hides the location of a secret organization that creates a super-army."

His expression darkened.

Did he not believe her? "Makes sense"—she again threw his words at him—"since Saint John had revelations about Armageddon."

He unfolded his arms, intensity radiating from his expression.

"What?" Her heart raced.

He rapped the table. "This information about the location and the super-army—that's in the book?" He looked like he'd had a revelation of his own

"I believe so. As I said, Vasily told this to me." She touched his hand. "Why?" Why did he look like that meant something to him?

He pushed to his feet.

"Please!" Iskra stood as well, relieved when he stopped, but she didn't dare scare him off by rounding the table. "What did you figure out? I gave you what I know. I crossed a line I shouldn't have. Will you now do the same?"

His jaw muscle popped. He tapped the table again. "Pearl of the Antilles?"

"Yes." Her heart tripped over the way he said it.

He tugged out his phone. Thumbed something into it. Then turned it to her.

Iskra drew closer. Saw the image of a blue and gold sign that read *U.S. Naval Station, Guantanamo Bay, Cuba*, and below it, *Pearl of the Antilles*.

Unable to breathe, she waited for an explanation.

"It's here—not this facility, but across the water. Not twenty minutes."

Dumbstruck, she almost didn't register him heading for the door. "Where are you going?"

"To get the book."

"They'll let you have it?"

"I won't give them a choice."

"Runt!"

He gripped the handle. Glanced at her. "You know," he said, "I don't like that name when you say it either." He winked. "I'll be right back."

Her worlds were slipping and colliding into one another, like continental plates shaking her to the core. Vasily had said the book mentioned the Pearl of the Antilles. Then Veratti's man gave her the word *pearl* in connection with the facility. What were the chances all that would explode into one massive coincidence called this nearby base?

U.S. Naval Station, Guantanamo Bay. The umbrella base that shielded a more nefarious one. The same one Vasily and Bogdashka said housed a treacherous organization called Netherwood, an entity with answers about her brother. And the Neiothen, that superarmy. It all linked back to the Pearl of the Antilles. The scroll.

How had Veratti known the facility's name?

Vasily had warned her to stay under the radar. Said that if Netherwood learned she was looking for them, she'd end up dead. And now she sat in the belly of the beast. With the book! And Veratti awaiting her word. Bisera's life in the balance.

She let out a strangled cry.

I have to get out of here.

Spork in hand, she carved a line into her arm, drawing blood. "Hello?" She waited for the guards to turn. "I . . . I think I need help."

There was no freakin' way this was happening. A super-army?

His thoughts crashed and burned at that term, but a buzzing in his head said this had to be *something*. No way Iskra could know where they were. And for this place to be mentioned in the Book of the Wars?

He used his secure phone. Made the call.

"Leif," Iliescu said, sounding relieved—and nervous.

"You said you found stuff about my missing six months, right?"

The silence on the other end gaped.

"Stuff you suspected but couldn't prove. About me and my team. You said everyone died except me and Guerrero."

"I didn't tell you that, Leif," Dru said quietly. "You brought Guerrero back. He died on the surgery table. Remember?"

Why was it all so confusing? Didn't matter. Back on track. "What you've found, does it entail a super-army?"

"Why would you think that?"

There was no conviction in the question. Dread pooled in Leif's gut. He pinched the bridge of his nose "Dru. Why did you want the book?"

"I didn't. I was told to put a team together to locate and retrieve it." A nervous laugh. "Where is this coming from? It sounds a lot like the third degree. Why are you interrogating me?"

Because there were still too many questions. "We'll talk later." Still too much uncertainty in the director's answers. More than ever, Leif needed that book. Needed to see what was in it. Find out if Iskra was telling the truth.

He made his way into the quarters where his team had been bunked and found them grabbing rack time.

Mercy came to her feet. "What's wrong?"

"Nothing. Where's Cell?"

"In the communications tower," Baddar said.

"Yeah, he's apparently too good to hang with enlisted now," Culver drawled, his arm hooked over his eyes. He lifted it and craned his neck to see Leif. "Why? We done being bored yet?"

"Anyone know where that book is?"

"Heard they were keeping it in an airtight container in the research lab," Mercy said.

"Where's that?"

"I'll show you," she volunteered.

Saito sat up. "They give you the report on her MRI?"

Leif shook his head.

"She's chipped," Saito said. "Several healed fractures, too."

Neither intel piece surprised him. "Why's that important?"

"Maybe speaks to her mind." Baddar shrugged. "I have many break in my leg and arm. Because I not give up easy."

Leif nodded.

"Runt." Baddar rose and stood near Mercy. "I am concerned for this woman." He placed both hands on his chest. "She is dangerous. I see what she do to some men once. Her heart is dark. Very dark."

The dossier on Viorica proved that. But the experience he'd had with the woman locked in that conference room didn't. And his instincts were raging when it came to her and this book.

Though a quick visual scan of the guys provided the pulse on this situation, he nodded. "Noted."

He trailed Mercy out through the corridors, well aware of how personnel gave him a wide berth. Crazy, what he'd done. Staring down that Glock at his own band of brothers. He'd never done that before. Then again, he'd never had to protect a target like that. But something was off about the whole thing.

The super-army she'd mentioned . . . it was a long shot. A leap. One he couldn't get to coalesce in his mind yet. It was like having all the specs on a bomb about to detonate and not knowing what order they should go in. Maybe that was why he'd been so focused on her.

There were things happening in him that he couldn't explain.

Too many. Like the vehement conviction to protect her. Or the way he'd seemed to step back into himself only when Culver entered the hall and said Iliescu was involved.

Mercy pivoted and stopped.

Leif checked their surroundings. No door. No lab. "What—"

Hands on her hips, auburn hair curled around her shoulders, she touched her forehead. "Okay." She shuffled. "I know this isn't my place—"

"You don't like her." Could they get past this already? He really needed that book.

"That's an understatement." She gave a shaky laugh. "Have you read her full dossier?"

Leif let his irritation bleed into his expression. "Would you like me to recite it?"

"I'm not talking about the one Braun sent us." Mercy quieted as an airman slipped past them. "I'm talking about the one Iliescu has on her."

Iliescu had a separate file? "I want to know, but not right now."

"Leif, listen. She's"—Mercy closed her eyes, head shaking—"there are no words. If I were to guess, I'd say she's soulless. But I really think she's more like Storm. That makes sense because—"

"Merc." He motioned to the hall. "More walk, less talk."

"How about talk *and* walk?" She compromised, settling into a slower pace, angling back so she could look at him. "Listen, I'm not big on grudges, but I don't want to see you or any other team member get hurt."

He kept walking, refusing to engage in this convo.

"But Viorica—or more accurately, Iskra Todorova—is a very damaged woman. She does not hesitate to kill. She does not fail to finish her mission. Dru has videos of her kills." She'd stopped walking.

"Which way?" he asked, looking up the hall.

"Are you even listening?" She groaned and started moving again. "She's Peychinovich's lover. They've never married, but she goes back to him. Every time. Steals for him. Kills for him. And I know you have intel on that man. He's as crooked and slimy as they come, yet she's *his*."

Which bugged him. Not because she was going back for a roll in the hay—which he didn't believe for a second—but because *something* drew her back. Over and over. There was no way she went back just to be with that piece of dirt. So what was it?

"She came with me." He didn't know why he'd said that.

Mercy gave him a questioning look, and only then did he realize he'd stopped on his own.

"Iskra ran out of that hotel lobby with me. Put her life in danger. Saved my butt when I lost visual."

Though she considered his words, Leif found himself looking back in the direction they'd come. Yes, Iskra had escaped with him, but what did that mean? *Did* it mean anything? Was it enough to keep her here?

"Why do you think she did that?"

"I . . ." He lifted his shoulders in a shrug, thinking about the book. The supposed super-army. "I just know she did."

"A trick? To gain your loyalty?"

He narrowed an eye, thinking. Assessing his conversations with V. "No. She was afraid—I could see it in her eyes that she feared being found." He recalled it clearly.

"How do you know it wasn't faked?"

"That level of fear can't be faked."

"How do you know? She's a skilled—"

"I *lived* it. I know!" Leif reined himself in, feeling the torrential heat of the Sahara, the way that nightmare had slaughtered his life. He'd thought he was rescued and back on safe soil, but that was when things really imploded. "She tried to hide that fear from me."

"Maybe she's just really good at what she does."

Of course she's good. I wouldn't be interested otherwise. His anger bubbled up, but Mercy had a point. He'd be stupid not to consider it. But he'd done that in the hours alone in the hospital room while she was sedated. Had V—Iskra, he liked that better—worked him to get what she wanted? Entirely possible.

So. *What* did she want?

"Before this facility," Leif said, gaze on the near past, "I had nothing to offer. She had the book. The advantage. If she was going to leave Istanbul and go back to Russia, Peychinovich was her ticket."

Mercy stared at him.

"Instead she ran with me."

"And that was a nice ego stroke, wasn't it? That she picked you over that steel magnate?"

"No," Leif said. "Not really. She tipped me off about which hotel she'd be at. What floor."

Questions lingered in the silence. "Why would she do that?" Now Mercy looked just as confused as he was. "Ambushing you?"

"Yeah, maybe." But— "No. Augh!" He ran a hand over his head. "Look, I can't explain it, but my instincts tell me to trust her."

"Which makes no sense."

"With *this* instinct, sense rarely comes into play."

"For your sake, I hope you're right."

So did he. Leif gestured down the hall. "Where's the lab?"

Mercy gave him a cockeyed nod, relenting. "Right behind you."

He pivoted and found the door marked *Laboratory*. On the access panel, he entered his code. Pushed the door open, knocking something across the room. It rolled, clanking to a stop against an overturned stool. The glass that separated the biometrically sealed area from the main lab was covered in spider-web cracks. It looked so much like Greece.

"My spidey senses are tingling, Bruce."

Leif scowled at her, inching closer. Nerves buzzing. "Thought Banner was—"

"*Wayne*. Bruce Wayne. Never confuse a reference to Banner with you. No comparison," she scoffed. "Though by the look of this place, maybe Banner has been here."

He nearly smiled—until he saw bodies on the floor in the containment area. "They're down." He hurried to the keypad, entering his code as he eyed the techs on the other side of the glass. No visible blood.

The panel rejected his code. He tried again with the same results.

"Let me work my magic." Mercy slid in and hovered over the door.

Leif rapped on the glass, afraid too hard of a tap would break it. Release who-knew-what contagion they kept on reserve here, if they even did that. He wasn't taking a risk. "Hey! Hello, can you hear me?"

"Why do people do that to unconscious people?" Mercy asked.

"Because hearing my voice could lure them back to consciousness."

"*Your* voice?"

"Not—" He groaned. "Are you fixing that or not?" When one of the techs moved an arm, Leif tapped and called out again. "See? It's working."

"Bruce Wayne always did have a way with echolocation."

Dressed in head-to-toe green, a tech lumbered to all fours, then to the window, touching her temple.

"What happened?" Leif shouted.

The tech shook her head. Keyed a mic. "Don't know. Someone came . . . I can't . . ."

Alarm rang through him. He thought back to Greece. How she'd gotten into the lab. Stolen the book. She wouldn't have done it again, would she? "I'm looking for a book I brought in. Ancient."

She lifted a finger. "Just a second."

"No! Let us in," Mercy cried out.

The woman turned back to the microphone. "Can't. You aren't suited. Hang on." She shuffled to a wall of steel drawers, entered a code—55239—and one hissed open.

Revealing an empty drawer.

The sight pushed him back. He cursed. Swiped a hand over his mouth.

"Looks like the assassin has struck again," Mercy said.

"I was just with her."

"Sorry, but we stood in the hall talking long enough for her to do this," Mercy countered. "Besides, nobody knew about it except us and her."

Leif shook his head. Stepped back again. Couldn't—wouldn't believe it.

But she'd asked. V had asked about the book's location. More than once. Desperate. Determined.

"You're not the first good-looking hunk brought to his knees by a beauty. I mean, she is Storm after all, right?"

My instincts are never wrong. Never.

Fingers threaded, he planted his palms on his head. Stared at the empty box. Why hadn't he seen it? Why had he bought her story?

No, no. Don't jump to—

But he'd sure jumped onto her bandwagon fast, hadn't he?

No, something wasn't right.

Claxons rang through the base. The floor vibrated beneath the grating alarm, sending tremors through Leif's feet. Lights whirled, splashing the walls in a macabre red.

Hands pawed at him. He turned, saw Mercy yelling, but he couldn't hear her. Couldn't work past the disbelief that he'd been such a fool. That Viorica could've gotten here in time to neutralize the techs, access the vault, steal the book, and then make her exit. It meant she'd escaped right after he left the conference room.

He punched the wall with a growl. She would not get away again. Not from him. Not this time.

"Exit." The word swallowed his shock as he pushed into the hall, determined to intercept Viorica.

The door thumped against him as dozens of personnel ran through the halls.

"What's happened?" Mercy shouted to one of the hurrying soldiers, her voice like a distant echo.

"Massive storm and a perimeter breach!"

PART TWO

EIGHTEEN

UNDISCLOSED LOCATION NEAR CUBA

It had come full circle.

She had dared hope. And it defied her.

This. *This* was why she didn't do hope. Why she refused to buy into the shameful idea that someone could control their future. It was a nice sentiment, but it wasn't realistic.

At least not for her.

Cursing herself for getting caught up in a pair of blue eyes, Iskra blended in with everyone else rushing through the halls. But even as her feet carried her away from where she'd talked with Runt—she'd use that name now, relegating him to the least of the men she'd known—guilt harangued her. Told her to find him. Ask him to explain why they had come to this location. Of all places, why *here*?

She didn't need to ask. There was only one plausible explanation. He knew of the super-army. So . . . was he complicit? The abhorrent thought seized her stomach.

You assume too much, thinking he had a choice in where to bring you.

But if he didn't want to come, he wouldn't have. She'd seen what Runt could do when he was diametrically opposed to something. The way he'd stood guard at her door.

If he stood guard, why would he leave you to be taken?

Because earlier didn't suit the plan? Because maybe they'd given her some drug that hadn't taken effect yet?

Iskra slowed, glancing at the spot on her hand where they'd

driven the IV port. She rubbed the bruise, thinking through everything she felt. The possible side effects of sedatives and poisons.

This was stupid. There were easier ways to kill her.

Then why?

"Sort it later. Get out now," she muttered, palming the wall as soldiers jogged toward the security point straight ahead. This reminded her so much of the Greece facility, trying to escape amid the alarms. Runt chasing her.

But he wasn't chasing her this time. He'd left her in that room.

She thought of the Marine who'd been tasked with guarding her. It hadn't been too difficult to convince him to open the door and help her at the sight of blood. She'd taken his access card and weapon, which she stuffed at the small of her back, then swung her satchel around to cover the imprint. The facility was kind enough to post emergency exit routes by the door with the fastest way to evacuate. She'd brought the map with her.

She needed to go out a different way, avoid the crowds and decrease her chance of being identified or stopped. She headed toward a rear side entrance that—if she read the schematic correctly—would lead her straight past the lab. The guard she'd disarmed had said the book was in the lab.

Considering the map, she confirmed that from the lab she could scurry across a small corridor to an exterior door labeled No Exit. The map was marked with several divots on the other side. Water. It had to mean water. The Guantanamo base was near water, *da*? If her bearings were right, there was no exit because the facility ended at the lip of a massive cliff that dove into the sea. She would swim out. Keep swimming. For miles, if she must.

You've never been a strong swimmer.

Not strong, but determined. And she must be. Veratti could solve all her problems now that she had what he wanted—the book and intel on the Pearl. For the first time in her young life, Bisera would be safe.

It wasn't too late, was it? Because Hristoff protected his own, he wouldn't hurt Bisera as he'd repeatedly done to Iskra. Her stomach wrenched at the thought of him striking a child, but cruelty didn't see age.

He wouldn't. The image of him squeezing Bisera's face, threatening her safety if Iskra didn't return, wrestled with the flimsy logic that enabled her to do something she'd never had the courage to do before—leave in order to find a way to free Bisera from him.

And what if he kills her?

The thought shoved her back against the wall. Unfeeling concrete dug into her shoulders. She gulped breaths, watching as personnel darted past the juncture.

No. He would not. If he did that, then he had nothing on Iskra. Nothing to hold her back from leaving. Bisera was the anchor that kept Iskra drowning in his grasp. All she had to do was get the book to Veratti. And she would never have to worry about safety or freedom again.

Shuddering, Iskra drew herself up straight. With a staggering step, she started walking. Scanning the thrumming corridors, she backstepped to the last junction and scanned in all directions. The lab waited on the other side. Confirming the halls were empty, she darted to the lab, slowing when she noticed the door was ajar.

Shouldn't it be locked? Why wouldn't a research lab on a remote military facility be locked? The darkened interior warned what she'd find—not just no lights but also no workers. Disarray.

"No," she whispered. She rushed in, even more surprised to find the seals of the inner decontamination chamber broken. Whoever had done this didn't care what or who was left behind.

The book. She couldn't leave without verifying. Working past the bent frame of the chamber, she went for the larger drawers. No use wasting time on the smallest ones, since the scroll wouldn't fit inside them. But as she delved deeper into the dark void, Iskra knew she was right. They'd taken it. Her heart sank.

Bereft, she glanced around the messy lab as if she'd find the book or an answer to who had beaten her to it.

That's what you get for trusting Runt.

"What happened here?"

Rotating, Iskra found herself facing one of the guards who'd been in a standoff with Runt outside the medical bay. She silently cursed herself. *Careless, Iskra. Way too careless.*

Eyes widening, he drew back. "*You.*" Fast as the storms Hristoff brewed, he jerked up his weapon. "Hands! Show me your hands—*now*!"

"Easy. I'm not—"

"Stop!" His gaze raked the disarray. "What'd you steal?" He patted her down visually. "Where is it?"

"It wasn't me," she snapped. "Shouldn't you be more concerned about what might have spilled? What did they keep here? Are we in danger?"

"I'm not telling you anything," he growled.

"Your stubbornness could kill us all, you idiot!" Panic always seemed to push men like this past their arrogance.

"Everything dangerous is belowground. We aren't anywhere near it."

Good to know.

"I knew we should've kept you restrained," he said, reaching to key his comms. "Se—"

"Wait!" She couldn't let him alert anyone to her location. Though she didn't want to draw the gun at her back, she would if it stopped him. "Please." When he hesitated, she rushed on. "I didn't do this. I was looking"—she had to divert from the truth a little to gain his trust—"for Runt. He came here."

"You might have him bewitched, but not me," the guard bit out. "I know what you are."

Do you? "There are two big differences between now and that moment outside my room," she said. "One, my guardian's not here."

"Metcalfe's always been full of himself."

This man's attitude was more about jealousy and wounded pride than legitimate complaint.

And . . . Metcalfe. She absorbed the name. Felt a piece inside her shift, like a crack in a bridge on which she stood. It scared her, as she sensed it splitting wider and deeper.

Two women paused outside the lab. "Edwards, storm's out of control. They're ordering an evacua . . . tion." The female soldier noticed the weapon held on Iskra. "You need help, Edwards?"

The guard glanced over his shoulder.

Like a bolt of lightning, Iskra shot forward, avoiding the debris in her path, and nailed him in the nose. His head whipped back and struck the bent metal decontamination door. He crumpled at her feet, his temple scraping the corner of a desk, leaving a bloody trail.

She winced at the rapid swelling of his nose and eyes.

When did you start caring? Caring is dangerous.

The women—she looked up and found them gone. Iskra cursed this nightmare. After a quick scan of the room, she knew she'd lost this battle. Lost the book. Veratti would be ticked. She just hoped the scans would be enough to buy her time to find out who'd taken it. Except her planned escape route involved water, which could ruin the USB.

So. Remedy that.

A few seconds rummaging around cabinets and workstations provided her with a preservation sleeve. She ripped open the corner of her satchel binding, removed the USB, tucked it inside the sleeve, then stuffed it into her boot. Eyeing the guard, she grunted. He'd be mad when he came to and would use that weapon, given the chance. She couldn't risk that. She stuffed the gun in a drawer.

Before leaving the lab, she double-checked the map. Verified her route. In the open, she made her first turn. Jogged to the next juncture, cleared it, and went right, feeling like she was leaving something of herself behind. No, she was leaving Metcalfe behind. It didn't matter. Once he found her gone, he'd figure it out. That "together" thing he'd hinted at would evaporate.

She'd told him it would never happen. Yet, looking into his face, she'd started to wonder if it could.

"Viorica!"

His voice pulled her around, slowed her as their gazes connected.

"Stop right there." His hard, icy eyes stared down the barrel of a Glock.

She came to a stop.

"Where is it?" he demanded, sidestepping closer. "Where's the book?"

Stunned at the accusation, she balked. "You think *I*—" It was okay to toy with her affections, just like Hristoff, because they had control of the book. Now that it was gone, she was suddenly the bad guy again?

Even though she had been planning to take the book, it hurt. A lot more than she would've thought. Foul gods and whoever else tricked her into thinking he was different, that with him she had a chance to get things right. She looked away, cursing the stinging in her eyes.

If you cry, I will kill you myself.

"Just give it back. I don't want to hurt you." Some of the edge had left his voice. Was he softening? Because he thought *her* soft?

Wrong again, Metcalfe. Her hand moved almost on its own to the small of her back. Felt the hard grip of—

"*Don't*," he gritted as he inched closer. "Hands!"

So. Him and her. In a standoff. She hadn't seen this coming. She had wanted things to be different. Wanted him to be different. Because she had this crazy idea she could trust him.

But trust was a fool's playground.

"Hands, V. Do it now." His voice had lost even more of its ferocity but none of its authority.

Refusing to yield, she worked through her options. Which were next to none. A bloodbath with Metcalfe. Or . . .

"Hey." He raised his eyebrows and hands, flipping the weapon so it dangled from his thumb in the trigger well, the spine against his palm. "Seriously. Let's not do this." Surrender, but not quite—or he'd have holstered that weapon. His hands came down but still controlled the gun.

Trust him. Her heart skipped a beat.

Trust him and die.

He's better than the rest of them.

He was just like the rest of them.

He helped you escape Hristoff.

He had used her to get what he wanted—the book.

A voice grated over the intercoms. "Attention, base personnel. Contaminant has been detected. Impending hurricane to reach Category 4. You are ordered to evacuate the facility immediately. Follow protocols. Stay calm."

Contaminant. Had she been infected by something in that lab? And a storm! Hristoff had tracked her!

"I see it." His voice was hoarse and hollow beneath the hammering alarm of the station. "I see in your face what *I'm* thinking and feeling. Hurt." He touched his gun-free hand to his chest. "We both feel betrayed."

She arched an eyebrow. There was no way he could know she'd used him for Veratti. And by the fates, she hated that look he mentioned—because yeah, she saw it in him, too. Why was it so hard to breathe right now?

"I brought you here." He again read her unspoken questions. "Against orders. I defended you. Against orders." He splayed his arms with a shrug.

And I *trusted you.* Let *you bring me here. Endangering* everything.

"Where is it, V? In your satchel?"

She'd never convince him she hadn't stolen the book. It was too perfect a setup, and he'd already decided her guilt. So how did she end this and remain alive?

Her gaze hit the red canister mounted on the wall halfway between them.

"V." Weapon down, he advanced another step. "Please. Give me the satchel."

Defiance fueled, she yanked it around and pitched the clothes from it onto the floor and then turned the bag upside down and shook it, knowing the secreted item wasn't there.

"What'd you do with it? Plan to come back for it later?" His eyes widened. "D'you have help? Tell me so we can get out of here with it—together. Alive."

She snorted a laugh. "Does any of what you said really make sense?" She cursed the way her voice wavered. "Do you *really* think I didn't want to work with you? I didn't want you to find me at that hotel? To what—to bring the scroll here, then steal it and try to run? Seriously? Are you that dense?" Her fingers coiled around the grip of the weapon at the small of her back. "And what do you know about that super-army? As soon as I mentioned it, you changed. Then you left. And you blame me for all this?"

He blinked.

Relief swept her. Maybe he didn't believe she'd betrayed him. But that relief only made her angry at herself. How many times would she fail her own common sense by trying to trust him? She had too much to protect.

She visually measured the distance to the canister. "I did something here I haven't done in a long time." She held his gaze for a long second. "I trusted someone." She whipped out her weapon. "You."

"No!" His Glock snapped up.

She fired.

NINETEEN

UNDISCLOSED LOCATION NEAR CUBA

Gunfire cracked. Mercy rounded the corner and stopped short. In that split second, several things happened: Runt dove to the side, the fire extinguisher on the wall exploded, and the concussion clapped her ears as flame retardant plumed into the air. Eyes stinging, she tried to recover fast.

"Runt!" Baddar darted past her.

The floor was slick, but Runt was already moving. "V, stop!"

"Something in the lab leaked into the air," Mercy called as he slipped and slid down the tunnel. "We need to clear out. Iliescu's orders."

He didn't answer. Just kept moving, finding traction as he went.

She looked helplessly at Baddar. "He has murder in his eyes."

The handsome Afghan hesitated, glancing at her, then down the hall where Leif had vanished. "I think it is worse than that."

She keyed her comms. "Dru, he went after her."

"Tell him—"

"He's *gone*. I tried to tell him."

"Mercy, listen to me." Something about the director's voice stilled the frustration and war in her. "We *cannot* lose him."

Duh?

"She will kill him if given the chance. Peychinovich has a noose around her neck, and she will do whatever it takes to complete her mission."

"I think he already knows that."

Thudding boots drew her attention. She peered over her shoulder just in time to see three men racing down the corridor. The one in the middle— "Holy resurrecting villains," she muttered. "Gotta go."

She pivoted, grabbing Baddar's arm and tugging him with her. "It's him. Again!" Darting after the mysterious Andrew, she barely heard a new order blasting over the intercom. Steel partitions slid from the ceiling, severing her pursuit. She slapped the cold metal. "No!"

"Mercy." Baddar touched her elbow. "Did you hear? The storm?"

"If you're talking about Ororo Munroe—"

His face screwed tight in confusion. "Who?"

A little embarrassed about her sarcastic reference to a comic character, she touched her forehead. "Never mind." But it fit. Ororo was an orphan who became an accomplished thief. Much like Miss Bulgarian Mafia.

"We have to leave. There is a storm coming."

Boy, is there ever. "Not without Runt." She backtracked, thinking through plausible scenarios. Possible routes Leif might take to find Viorica. The main exit—too obvious. East exits—too far. Rear—no exit because of the waterfall. She wouldn't be that stupid.

"Stupid is her specialty," Mercy mumbled, breaking into a faster clip, hearing Baddar follow.

"Lost visual on Runt," Lawe reported through the comms.

Mercy confirmed the same, as did several others.

"Runt, we've lost audio and visual on you. Can you read us? Over?" Dru's words were drenched in concern. "Runt?"

Mercy keyed her comms. "Check the waterfall terrace."

"That'd be idiotic," Culver said.

"Which is exactly why she probably went there. She wouldn't expect us to check it." Mercy grew more confident with each step she and Baddar covered toward the rear of the facility. "We're en route."

"Negative!" Iliescu said. "Lawe and Culver—find Runt. Everyone else to the helos."

"*Where's the book?*" His voice was a howl against the raging of the sea and waterfall as he pressed his arm into her throat.

Shooting the fire extinguisher had the effect she wanted—and more. The floor had been slick, making it hard to run. Yet Leif had pursued with the relentlessness of a bulldog. Chased her out to the falls. She hated that he believed she'd betrayed him—because she had. Just not in the way he thought. Her own foolish desperation made her falter. And he'd caught her.

Mist from the churning, rising storm plastered Iskra's hair to her face as she struggled to breathe beneath his fury. She cupped his elbow and wrist, trying to get a solid grip, but the retardant and water made his sleeve slick. She did not want to hurt him, but she would. Dying wasn't an option. Bisera needed her to survive. To succeed in her mission.

But Leif pressed in, doggedly determined. He shoved his shoulder into her breastbone. She felt the remnants of oxygen seeping out of her.

His gaze shifted. No doubt the comms providing a distraction.

Tightening her grip, she twisted his elbow and wrist in opposite directions.

"Augh!" He stumbled around with the thrust to avoid injury, and she shoved his back, sending him fumbling toward the chasm that ended in a pool a dozen feet below.

Last chance! Iskra threw herself toward the cleft. Her feet slipped, but she clawed into the soft earth, pulling herself onward. Up around the edge of the cave.

She whipped her satchel around and tore the front pocket away. Ripped it open and extricated the wingsuit jumper. It wasn't a whole suit, but it would provide a span the wind could catch. She shoved herself into it.

"Nothing there but the ocean, Viorica." His voice carried from below. "Give up."

Don't look, don't look.

Zipping into the suit, she looked over her shoulder, startled to find him closing in. How? How could he already be so close? Was he human?

"Or let me shoot you in the back, and the sharks dine on prime assassin."

Could he really? Shame bit at her like the needling rain and water. She had pulled her punches. Missed by fractions—close enough to make him worry—but not enough to make him think she'd give in.

Leif didn't believe her. Hristoff would brutalize her. Veratti . . . she didn't want to think about what he would do.

"The book. Give it up—tell us where it is."

Mad, she jammed her elbow into the wall of earth. She wished to the heavens she *had* stolen the book—at least hearing his vitriol, feeling it in his words, would be understandable. She wasn't sure at this point if she was more angry that she'd failed or that he thought she'd betrayed him.

"C'mon, V."

She had nowhere to go.

Frustration and defeat tremored through her limbs. Even with the modified wingsuit, this dive from the waterfall had no guarantees. With Hristoff's storm, she could be smashed into the rocks. But she could not stay here to be held by Leif's people again. Bisera was all that mattered—getting back. Freeing her. Somehow. There had to be a way. There must be.

Furious, she faced the storm rising over the waters. The angry spray spitting in her face. She'd lost. The book. Bisera's safety.

"Viorica," Leif growled. He was close. Right behind her.

Over her shoulder, she saw his eyes. Saw the pleading, but also his determination. Which mirrored her own. "Letters of Marque." She twisted her wrists, feeling the *thwap* of the wingsuit deploying.

"*Don't!*"

She bent her legs and shoved off the cliff. Lightning splintered the sky as she plummeted, arms stretched out. In Greece, she felt freedom calling. Here? Death.

And she welcomed it.

Lightning streaked and threw its electrical darts straight at Leif. Furious, he dove away from the ledge, back down the ramp to the pool, feeling the searing heat and sizzling air as the bolt narrowly missed him. The hairs on his arms stood up as he slid into the tunnel and collided with Lawe.

The big guy grabbed his arm. Hauled him on. "Move—now! Hurricane's right on us!"

They sprinted down the tunnel, noting it filling with water. Electricity buzzed Leif's nape. The storm wasn't natural. It had come out of nowhere.

They beat it to the main facility hub. Lights popped and blinked as Leif tugged on the doors. Darkness clapped hold of them, the door suddenly heavy without the hydraulic assist. But it wasn't a problem for two special operators.

"How'd she get away?" Lawe asked as they jogged through the R&D wing.

Leif didn't want to talk about it. He hated that she'd outsmarted him *again*. "Suicide dive with a glider or something."

"She had that last time, too." Lawe barked a laugh. "That demon spawn has every trick up her sleeves." They rounded the corner to the main hangar. A chopper waited, wind tearing at the rotors as they whined into action.

"Yeah, yeah!" Saito waved them on. "Let's get out of Dodge like the director suggested."

Culver stood ready, a scowl on his red-bearded mug. "'Bout time y'all showed up."

"He threatened to leave you." Peyton handed them mic'd helmets. "I said it was a good idea."

"You couldn't live without me, baby," Lawe hollered as he stuffed the helmet on his big head, then climbed in, Leif right behind him. Vibrations wormed through their boots.

Saito dropped onto the bench, and Klein took the jump seat with the gun. He looked as comfortable there as he might in a Ram pickup back home.

The helo lifted off, then wavered.

Nothing unusual. But with the electricity and winds, Leif tensed.

The bird bounced. Then lifted again.

Okay, that was different. Leif glanced at the pilot, worried. He tucked himself into the five-point harness and had three of the straps secured when the helicopter veered sharp right, swinging out as if it had been struck. Leif's stomach vaulted into his throat. He grabbed the harness, fumbling with the final lock.

Then he saw them. Fingers. White-knuckled on the gun post.

Klein was dangling out of the bird, over the churning sea.

Leif shouted his name and slid out of the straps to the deck. Wrapped the nylon harness twice around his arm and let the wind tug him to the edge. He reached—strained for Klein, who struggled to maintain a single-hand hold.

Cursing himself for not paying more attention, Leif inched toward his buddy. The others caught his shirt and belt to hold him while he saved their man.

Klein's face was etched with terror. Eyes wide. Face white. He threw a hand up toward Leif but missed. He did it again—their fingers touched, then slid away.

"Augh!" Leif strained, his muscles screaming. His mind screaming that if he didn't do this—

In a blink, Klein was gone. Ripped from the edge of the helo.

"No!" Instinct had Leif disentangling his arm. Aiming for the opening to go after his friend.

Something hit his side, and he heard someone yell his name. He felt the tug of the water and air, luring him into the livid elements. But the chopper held fast. Anchored him. He glanced down at the two carabiners tethering him to the interior hull, then turned to see Lawe climbing back into his seat.

His gaze again skipped to the waters. Gray and frothing, foaming at the mouth for more human sacrifices. Surreal. He couldn't see Klein.

There was no way. Even if he dove in with a life vest, there was no way he could find Klein in that mess.

He punched the hull. Kicked the door. Cursed the raging storm. Hung there, willing the elements to take him. To settle the score—because that was what this was about somehow: Leif had lived when the Sahara Nine hadn't.

EN ROUTE TO CUBA

Using the AWACS, Dru tried to pull up current satellite imaging of the facility in Cuba. "They mentioned a super-army."

Canyon Metcalfe sat across from him, blue eyes ablaze. "You told him?"

"Can't tell him what I don't know." Dru huffed. "It's that operative. Leif doesn't even recall that facility."

"And you're sure that's where it happened, whatever *it* is?"

"I am sure of very little right now."

Canyon stared out the window. Stretched his jaw. "And now my little brother isn't responding to comms." He frowned. "Think he remembers?"

Dru wasn't sure what he thought. "I don't think so. His silence is probably due to this storm we're waiting out, but I think if anything could push those memories to the surface, it's this situation."

"We need to make sure that doesn't happen." Roughing a hand over his jaw, Canyon stared at the water. "I don't want whoever did . . . whatever it was they did, to think he's remembering things. And I just feel like they're looking over our shoulders, waiting for it to happen. More than that, I don't want Leif to regress."

"Neither do I." Dru nodded, feeling the maelstrom circling his head. "I hear you." He tossed down a pen and shook his head. "And I don't have answers."

"But you sent him there, to that facility. With that black widow."

He held up a finger. "I sent him to Cuba—Guantanamo. With no idea that Braun would reroute them to this facility."

"And when you found out?"

He shrugged. "I assessed the situation. Deemed it too risky to relocate him without somehow drawing attention."

Fingers steepled, Canyon blew a few breaths across his fingers. "Director, if my brother opens that vault, if he connects anything to that facility . . ." He held Dru's gaze for several long seconds, then dropped back against the leather seat of the jet. "He will hunt the truth down no matter who it kills, himself included."

"I know. And I understand he's your brother and you feel the need to protect him—"

"I will do whatever it takes to protect Runt."

"Even if that means stopping him—forcibly?"

Canyon stared daggers at him, then peered out at the tempest that seemed mirrored in his forty-something face. "Whatever the cost."

"Sir!"

They both looked down the aisle, where a Marine stood.

"Chopper lifted off. They're a man down."

Letters of Marque. That was what she'd said, as if it justified everything she'd done. The betrayal she'd delivered. But it didn't. A letter of marque and reprisal granted government authorization to a privateer to attack and capture enemy vessels. But that was during the age of sail. And they hadn't been enemies. Or were they?

Beneath the vibrations of the chopper, Leif stared blankly out at the black sky and the violence it was unleashing on the facility. He recalled the way V had hit that canister and sprayed fire retardant across the gap between them. Cost him precious seconds pursuing her. Then at the terrace, she'd jumped right into the raging waters.

There was no way she could have survived that. Even with his training, it was a long shot at best.

And the book. If she'd had it going into the water, it was lost.

Crack! Boom!

Leif blinked at the electricity sparking across the big black clouds.

"I will rise."

"I will rise."

"I will rise."

The chanted words reverberated through his head like the thunder in the skies. Or maybe that *was* the thunder. What were those words from? A song? Lines from a movie?

A solid *thwat* against his chest startled him. He gripped the hand that hit him, pulled it, and snapped his elbow up—then caught himself. Startled at the instinct that had nearly destroyed Lawe's joints.

"In the water," Lawe barked over the comms. "About a klick to our nine."

Klein? Had they found him after all? Leif scanned the churning waves, dawn a hidden mistress on this dark morning. But there, amid the foamy wakes, bobbed a blip of orange with a twinkling strobe light. Viorica?

Was that a life vest? She hadn't had time to put one on. That suit—it was a BASE-jumping suit. Did it have a floatation device?

It's her!

Without hesitation, he shifted to the jump seat, hanging out of the chopper, disregarding the danger. Hands pawed at him, but he focused on her. Was she alive?

"Let her go," Lawe hollered. "We couldn't save Klein, we sure ain't risking our butts for her. We're all better off with her dead."

"Move in, move in closer!" Leif shouted to the pilot.

"Sorry, Chief," came the pilot's staticky voice. "Storm is coming fast and hard."

"*Move in!*"

"Negative," barked the pilot.

Leif scanned the ocean. Maybe they were right.

A wave crashed over the blinking light. She vanished, submerged by the angry waters. No. She'd be lost.

Jump. Go after her.

Right, and die with her? At this height, if he jumped, he could break his leg. Probable. But if he didn't help her, she'd drown. Certain.

And if you do break your leg, you'll both drown. Maybe . . . probably.

A life vest thumped against his arm. Surprise pushed his gaze to Lawe even as he stuffed himself into it. He abandoned his helmet and stepped out into the air. Wind tore at him.

Gravity snatched his legs and yanked him down.

TWENTY

U.S. NAVAL BASE, GUANTANAMO BAY, CUBA

"At least we're landing."

"About time," Canyon said.

"Sir, we have a situation," the Marine reported.

Canyon glanced at Dru.

"The chopper landed at GTMO."

"Good." Dru smiled but then noticed the tension radiating off the Marine. "What's wrong?"

"Metcalfe jumped in the water."

"You mean fell."

"Jumped, sir."

"You sure?"

The Marine nodded. "Team reported Viorica in the water. Said he went in after her."

Stunned, Dru tried to make sense of that. "Thank you, Sergeant."

The Marine nodded again and left.

Dru cursed and threw himself against his seat, the descent of their aircraft evident in his popping ears. He stood and paced. "He's activated."

Canyon stood, shoulders squared. "You don't know that."

"And we don't know that he isn't." Dru shoved a hand through his thinning hair. "We have to be prepared."

Canyon said nothing, but his facial expression screamed his objection.

This was a colossal snafu that awakened all Dru's old fears that all they had buried would find its way to the surface again. A storm rising.

CARIBBEAN SEA

Blurs of black and gray slapped and tossed her. Blinking only made her eyes sting. Iskra tried to lean back and hold her chin up, trusting the buoyancy of the wingsuit to keep her afloat. Her limbs ached from the exertion and cold water. A wave rose high overhead, and she whimpered, knowing she could do nothing but try to survive. She was at the mercy of an angry ocean. The wave rose. Up . . . up . . . up. Its maw opened and lunged.

She squeezed her eyes shut. Thought of Bisera.

The wave punched her. Carried her down deep, the ocean swallowing her whole. Though she tried to remain calm, knowing she would rise after the torrent ceased, she grew disoriented. She kicked her feet, but which direction was she going? Up or down?

Panic threaded a thick line through her lungs. Tightened. Constricted.

No! Calm down. Let the suit carry you back up.

But I'm too heavy.

Terror ripped through her. Forced her eyes open. Black. All black. She could see nothing. Just a watery tomb. She kicked. Thrashed.

No hope. She had no hope. Never had. Why had she even thought . . .

Bisera!

A sob wrenched free. Water gushed into her mouth.

A tidal force shoved her sideways and seemed to pick her up. Suddenly there was air. She coughed. Gagged.

Only to realize she was going under again. She clamped her mouth shut, but a cough shoved its way out, refilling her lungs with water. Desperation for air clawed through her. To breathe. To . . . to not. To simply stop fighting.

It would be easier. No responsibility. No fear.

She relaxed, falling into the empty hopelessness, the relief. No more fighting, just sleep. She drifted into the darkness, where she belonged. Where she no longer had to worry . . .

Bisera. Hristoff couldn't use her as a tool anymore. And he couldn't use Iskra at all. Ever again. The thought was too beautiful to ignore. It came with its own sense of hope.

Something warm and strong latched on to her leg. She flailed, jolted out of her malaise, feeling whatever had caught her attempting to snatch her life. Water rushed into her mouth again. She coughed, gagged, but emerged into the air.

Something swept her forehead. She blinked, saw a blur of gray. Heard a hollow shout.

Her lids fluttered, plunging her into the darkness. Her body rattled.

"Fight!" came a hollow shout.

A face swam before her. She blinked. "Metcalfe." And then she felt the arms. Warm, strong arms. His body supporting hers. Legs kicking. Hers tangling.

"V—c'mon!" Eyes fraught with worry and fear, he was there. Holding her. Water and rain pouring over him. Using his free arm to keep them afloat. "Stop or we'll drown!"

Suddenly aware of how she countered his moves out of natural instinct, she stilled. Relief choked her. She coughed a laugh and hooked her arms around his neck.

"That's it," he murmured against her ear.

As the terror of nearly drowning washed away, she pressed her nose into the crook of his shoulder. Sobs overtook her, riddling her with shame that she was crying and couldn't save herself. But mostly because he'd come for her. She had betrayed him, and he had still come.

"Thank you," she said around another choked sob. "I'm sorry. So sorry."

His chest rumbled with words she couldn't hear. Trembling from cold and exhaustion, she clung to him, to the body heat radiating through his chest.

Water lapped and splashed them, but they didn't fight it. Instead, they focused on staying afloat and alive. She eyed the sky, surprised at the fading surge. It was as if the storm was somehow responding to the rescue as well. How? How had Hristoff gotten here so fast? Dread curled through her.

"You could die," she breathed, arms still wrapped around him. The sea and storm quieted, but the waves continued to thrash angrily. "Why did you come?" The ache of what he'd done—the possible risk and sacrifice—made her shiver. "It was stupid."

"A soldier, a Marine, and a sailor are condemned to be executed," he said, taking shallow breaths to avoid gulping water. "Their captors say they can have a final meal before their executions—"

A joke? He was telling a joke?

"—so they ask the soldier what he wants for his last meal. 'Some pizza and beer,' he says. They give it to him, he eats it, and then they execute him. Next is the Marine, who asks for a big steak. So they bring it to him, he eats it, and then they execute him."

"If this is your way of saying we're going to drown—"

"You're ruining my joke." His arms moved around her as she clung to him, treading water. "Now it's the sailor's turn. He says, 'I want a big bowl of strawberries.' The executioners are outraged. 'Strawberries! They aren't even in season!' The sailor shrugs. 'Then I'll wait.'"

She lifted her head and looked into his eyes. "That wasn't funny."

"Hey, don't knock the comedy."

Thunder boomed through the skies.

She groaned. "Not again. Please, no more storms."

He wrapped an arm around her waist and paddled around. "I think that's our ride."

After spotting the aircraft thumping closer, she gripped his shoulder, drawing his attention back to her. "*Why?* Why did you come for me?"

He frowned, his gaze bouncing around her face. "I—"

But his words were lost in the howl of the helicopter's approach. A basket lowered.

"You first," he shouted as he held it.

She dragged herself over the side, the ocean now angry at their rescue. Swells reared and crashed as he climbed in behind her. He straddled her hips and drew her tight against him. Then he secured the straps and gave the line a tug.

The basket heaved—and they tipped downward, the weight unbalanced. His arms vised her as they rose into the air. Ocean spray threw them a few last stinging reminders of its power.

Shivering, she wondered if Hristoff knew he had almost killed her with the Meteoroi. But . . . how? Maybe it wasn't him. Did the Americans have one of their own? Had anyone else detected that strange chemical odor before the storm?

The rescue crew hauled the basket into the chopper and anchored it as the doors closed, shutting off the biting wind and rain. Thermal blankets soon cocooned them in warmth. It was a fifteen-minute flight to another base, Metcalfe informed her. Warm, safe, and relieved, she relaxed back against his chest. Stared at the arms holding her. That had held her above the water. Saved her.

I'm not worth saving.

And yet he had. But once he found out she had used him, that she only manipulated him to get the information she needed . . .

She closed her eyes, grateful for what he'd done but knowing this was where his niceness would end. Though she'd fought to escape, here she was safe. With him. That thought coupled with exhaustion to lull her into a heavy sleep.

She awoke to someone unlacing her boots. Something shifted in her—

Iskra snapped alert. The USB. "No!"

"Easy." Someone in scrubs stood at her feet. "Just removing your wet clothes to get your internal temp elevated."

"I-I've got it." Glancing around the medical bay, so unlike the secure room she'd awakened in at that facility, she eyed the empty beds, looking for Metcalfe. The lights were off. It felt cold, sanitary.

She was alone.

U.S. NAVAL STATION, GUANTANAMO BAY, CUBA

Jake Klein was gone. Drowned in a mission gone wrong. Leif had tapped him. Chosen him for the team. Now he was dead.

After a physical eval, inoculation against whatever contaminant had been released in the lab—they wouldn't be told what it was—and a debrief following his harrowing adventure in the water, Leif showered and changed into tactical pants and a thermal shirt. He had a chill that had nothing to do with their death-defying swim.

When he exited the showers, he was stunned at who stood there waiting. "Canyon."

"Runt."

He snorted and stepped into a back-slapping hug with his brother, grateful for the sibling who had anchored him. "What're you doing here?"

"Viorica."

Leif frowned as they made their way to the command center. "What about her?"

"Been tracking her through the years. So finding out my little brother is facing off with her—"

"Not facing off," Leif countered. But then it hit him. He stopped and pivoted to his brother. "It's me."

Canyon's expression hardened.

Unbelievable. "You're here because of me. Worried I'll go ape—"

"You've been under a lot of stress. Today you lost a man."

Of all the . . . "I don't need you to remind me." He started walking again, faster than necessary, but then again, it wasn't fast enough to shake his brother. "I don't need to be babysat."

"She's not—"

"Exactly." He stopped short again. Stared into blue eyes like his own. "*She's not.* She's not what anyone thinks she is."

Canyon's eyebrows rose to his high-and-tight.

How could Leif explain that she felt like part of those missing months he was trying to unearth? When she'd mentioned the Pearl of the Antilles, something resonated in him. There was no way to explain that, so diversion was best. "What about Dani?" he tossed into the silent gap. "She know you're out here?"

"My wife knows I'm doing my job."

"Job." Leif snorted, giving a cockeyed shake of his head, and resumed course for the command center. "I am *not* your job, Canyon. Not anymore. Now, let me do mine."

"Jumping out of a helicopter into a storm surge isn't exactly instilling confidence that you're in a good frame of mind." Canyon called after him, "She's not in there."

Leif slowed. He did not want to play into his brother's hands, but it made sense that Canyon knew where she was being held. And no doubt his big brother took pleasure in knowing something he didn't.

"Look." Leif turned back. "It's great, what you're doing here. Trying to support me. Checking up on me." His cheek twitched, and he felt a scab forming. "But I'm a grown man, a SEAL with an impeccable record." Minus what had been redacted and removed after the Sahara. "I lost one man to that storm. I wasn't going to lose anyone else."

"Leif—"

"I got this, Canyon. I don't need someone to wipe my butt for me." He patted his brother's chest.

"Latrines are that way if you need TP." His brother smirked as he pointed down the hall. "But the director wants to talk to you."

"In a minute. I want to find—"

"Director said now."

Leif hesitated and glanced at his brother, who had the common sense to look abashed. "Where?"

Canyon straightened and started back in the direction they'd come. The halls were dimmed and ominously quiet as their shoes squeaked on the vinyl.

This felt too familiar. Blips of the past stabbed his brain.

Long gray halls. Personnel in scrubs. Soldiers. Medical equipment.

"Where's Harcos?" he asked, shuffling with the help of an older nurse.

"You already know that answer, Chief." Her smile was wrinkled but genuine. "Remember? He didn't make it."

"And Zhanshi. He was—" His gaze tracked a dark corridor. At the far end, a light blinked. Red.

Blood. There was so much blood.

"We need immediate evac!"

"Taking fire. Two men are down."

He dragged out a med kit and extracted a tourniquet. Slid it over Kappi's stump, ignoring the squelching, suctioning sound of blood.

"This is X-ray Charlie Lima Seven Two Seven. We are under attack. Request immediate evac. Over."

"Leif?" A warm hand settled on his shoulder.

He flinched, grabbed the hand. Took in the blue eyes studying him. Canyon. He released a breath.

"You okay?"

He'd stopped walking. "Yeah." He knew that look on his big brother's face. Thought his little brother was cracking again. "That swim took more out of me than I realized. Tired, is all." Not a lie. His limbs were still trembling, his legs bruised from the drop into the water.

Canyon nodded uncertainly, then pointed to a door with light seeping out beneath it. "Almost there."

If Canyon was here, he knew what had happened to Iskra. "Any word on how she's doing?"

Without answering, Canyon flicked open the door.

The director turned in a chair behind a heavy oak desk. "Come in."

What was going on? Leif took in the roomy office, the couch, the table, and the partially hidden chair . . . that was occupied.

"V." Even with the bruising around her face, the nick on her cheek, and swollen, split lips, the sight of her invigorated him. It shouldn't. He should be ticked. She'd stolen the book. Run.

"Thank you. I'm sorry. So sorry." The words she'd whispered into his neck when they were fighting for their lives cocooned him. And then ticked him off.

"Sit down, Chief," Iliescu said. "We need to talk."

Talk? Leif slid his attention to the director and felt his fists balling. Noted the grim line of the director's mouth. Recalled Canyon's heavy silence. His instincts knew before his brain—something was wrong. "I'll stand."

"Chief, I think—"

"No." Leif gritted his teeth and slid a skewering look at the director. "Not this time."

"Son?"

Man, he hated that word. "Not this time. You aren't controlling the dialogue, Director." He forced his gaze back to V's. "Why'd you run?" No, that didn't matter. "Why steal the book?" Because if she hadn't done that, she wouldn't have run. "I guess I should clarify." The razor-sharp edge of his words couldn't be hidden. "Why did you steal it from us? I mean, you stole it from the Greeks. I guess it was our turn."

"I didn't." She scooted to the edge of her seat, earnestness in her expression. "I am not the one who stole it from the station. After you left me in the conference room, I did go to find it, but I was too late. The lab was already ransacked."

"Went to find it? Hard to do when you're under armed guard." Which she'd obviously subdued. "Guess they were too soft. Trusted you." He grunted. "I made that mistake once. And you said the lab was ransacked? Not when I was there, and the book was already gone."

She shrugged, looking to the director.

"Mercy reports she saw that operative from the beach there," Iliescu said.

"Not possible," Leif growled.

"That's what I would've thought, too," Dru agreed, "but it happened. They're reviewing the footage from the station now." He heaved a sigh as his eyes returned to Viorica.

Leif hung his head. He didn't trust himself to talk. To ask what was going on. Because he'd been here before. He was about to be handed bad news. "If you didn't steal the book, why'd you run?"

"What was I supposed to do? Stay there?"

"Yeah," he said with more growl than intended. "That would've been a good start."

"Why? To be held prisoner, then shot? Or to succumb to whatever contagion was released—"

"You've all been inoculated," Dru pointed out.

Leif didn't buy Iskra's reasoning. "You don't know that would've—"

"*You* don't know—" she protested.

"You neutralized several men—"

"I *didn't* kill anyone," Iskra hissed.

"Maybe." That could be verified. "But you did run, and you did shoot at me."

"You know very well if I had wanted to kill you, you would not be standing here now. I hit the fire extinguisher to buy time."

"To flee the one person who handed you trust on a silver platter."

"Viorica," Dru prodded, his tone anything but friendly, "get on with it."

"Wasting your time, Director. She looks out for herself." Leif cocked his head at her. "I thought we had—"

"A thing?" A hard glint in her gaze pinged with challenge.

Leif's eye twitched. "An understanding."

She swallowed. Looked away.

"But just like before, you played me!"

"I didn't."

"You leapt off the cliff rather than come with me."

Her expression was a tangle of irritation and . . . regret? Nah. She was too coldhearted for that. "You don't understand."

"No freakin' kidding."

"The night you found me in the club, I had set a plan in motion that unilaterally backfired on me. There is a man named Veratti. He's powerful—I've seen the influence he wields. I failed Hristoff on my last mission."

"Mission?"

She skirted him a glance. "It was a costly mistake and put Hristoff in a bad position with Veratti. And the man who usually sends others to handle all his affairs paid Hristoff a very personal, very threatening visit. He said if Hristoff found the Book of the Wars, he would consider all debt paid."

"So Hristoff sent you to find it."

"I had no choice. What I owed Hristoff would cost me my life, so I set out to find the book. And when I secured it, I . . . I realized that I possessed something that could buy me freedom . . ." Breath staggered through her lungs. "My friend Vasily gave me the information for Veratti. I called him. Said he had to meet me if he wanted the book. Instead, he sent his thugs. They threatened me and—" She gulped. Shook her head and stared at the vinyl floor before drawing in a breath and continuing. "They said before Veratti would even consider the trade, I must sate his anger." She shifted and cleared her throat. Sweat beaded on her upper lip.

"How?" Leif demanded, patience thin.

She cringed—which annoyed him. She was stronger, better than that. "Veratti wanted to know about the location of the facility."

Leif lowered his hands to his sides. Slid his gaze to Dru and back to her. "What facility?"

"The one we were just at. He was convinced if I"—she licked her lips—"worked with you, eventually I would be taken to that station."

"Why on earth would he assume that?"

"He saw the footage from Greece, knew—just as I did—that you were Americans. He said if you were looking for the Book of the Wars, then you would know the name of a secret facility."

"What made him think that?"

"I don't know," Iskra said. "But he was adamant that I learn the name of the facility before he would even talk about the book and a trade with me."

"So the lives of all those people at the facility—you just traded your life for theirs. Was that worth it?"

She was on her feet. "I didn't do anything at that facility except escape. When the sirens went off, I knew there was trouble."

She had used Leif. Lied to him. Lured him in with trust and pretty hazel eyes. And like a stooge, he'd fallen for it. And yet . . . "What else?"

Iskra blinked. "What do you mean?"

"I mean that's just a mission. But there's a whole lot of fear and trepidation happening in you, and as much as I wish that were about my reaction to your betrayal, there's something else you aren't giving up."

She brushed aside her ocean-stringy hair. "He swore that he would own me if I did not succeed." With a sigh, she tried to smile. Failed. Tried to look at him. Failed.

No, there was still more.

Leif fisted his hands. This was as futile as trying to find his own answers about those missing six months of his life. But this time he'd get to the bottom of whatever she was hiding. "Look, I risked my life—"

"I never asked you to."

"Yeah," he said, "you did." When confusion tugged her brows down, he pointed to the nick on his cheek. "With this and every other time you've failed to kill me—which I now see wasn't about anything but using me to serve another master. Man, how many men are you groveling at the feet of?"

Iskra went rigid. Her face darkened.

He had to push those buttons. Had to find out what she was hiding. "I mean—you're Hristoff's lover. Are you this Veratti's, too?"

She launched at him. Nailed him in the gut. Her momentum carried Leif backward, and he tripped over a small table. They both went down. She punched at his face, but he deflected. Managed to flip her. He drove his arm up under her chin, locking down her limbs.

"What'd you sell your soul for, V? What was worth this?"

He was hauled backward. Leif stumbled but found his feet. And his brain. He turned away, furious with himself. Palming his head, he let out several calming breaths.

"Get her out of here," Dru ordered Canyon.

Leif set his hands on the waist of his tactical pants, eyes closed as she was removed from the room. Leashing the beast back up inside. After the roar of his pulse abated, the silence felt deafening.

"Veratti does exist," Iliescu said, "but we have no intel that corroborates what she's claiming. Ciro Veratti is Italy's prime minister, the most revered one they've had in decades. We even try to touch him, and we'll go down in flames."

"Maybe she's lying."

"Using big bait to lure us away from her." Dru nodded. "Could be."

With a huff, Leif dropped into a chair and cradled his head. "Why didn't I see it?" He clenched his teeth. "I fell right into her trap."

"That is Viorica."

Leif shoved to his feet and went to the door. "I . . ." He didn't know what to say. Or what he was going to do, except get out of this office.

"Debrief in twenty, down the hall." Dru held his gaze for a long minute.

With a nod, Leif punched open the door and strode out, determined to discover what Viorica was hiding.

TWENTY-ONE

U.S. NAVAL STATION, GUANTANAMO BAY, CUBA

"What'd you sell your soul for?"

His words haunted Iskra all the way back to her room, where the blond man who so strongly resembled Metcalfe locked her in after reassurances it would only be short-term. Despite being a prisoner—again—she was glad for the solitude.

She sagged on the gray mattress, the springs creaking. She'd lied to men around the world. Burned them. Killed some, though she hated that. Hated what she'd done in life. But nothing more than she hated seeing that look on Metcalfe's face. He'd held the anger in well. Better than she had.

But man, had he infuriated her.

Why? Why was he able to draw out that anger?

Because he hit the nerve. The one she thought she'd buried. Yes, she had been used by Hristoff. For years of her life and centuries of her mind. But never once had she been his *lover*. And the cruelty of his accusation that she'd had sex with Veratti, too.

It hurt. Because it was the one thing in life she could not change. Could not alter. Could not control. She'd tried fighting when she was younger. Those broken bones had healed. Her broken spirit hadn't.

And Leif believed it of her. Believed she used sex to get what she wanted. Hollywood tramped up spies. Insisted they sold their souls for their countries. For peace. She had nothing so noble but everything more precious: Bisera.

She pressed a hand over her heart and clutched her shirt. Fought tears. It was over now. If it hadn't been before, telling the Americans about Veratti had sealed her fate. She was as good as dead. Bisera . . .

Iskra cupped a hand over her mouth, hearing in her mind the girl's melodic laughter. So innocent. Untouched at this point by Hristoff.

All hope was gone. Everything had changed in that raging sea. That near-death moment.

Maybe it was better if Hristoff and Veratti believed her dead. But then . . . how would she get Bisera?

She strangled a cry. Why did God hate her so much?

Keys jangled in the door and startled her. Shoved Iskra to her feet as she wiped at the tears that had escaped. Even if she returned to Hristoff, he would kill her.

"Debrief, ma'am."

Following a security officer and the man who looked like Metcalfe, Iskra realized they were marching her to a room where he would be present. The thought made her sick. She must find a way to vanish. From here. From existence. Jitters danced and collided at the thought.

They stepped from the sterile corridor into a briefing room with a long brown table surrounded by personnel. Her betraying eyes scanned the uniforms and suits, searching for him. Dru Iliescu, who stood about her five-nine height, was at the head of the long table, hands on his belt. "Miss Todorova, have a seat."

Fear nudged her back, but training made Iskra present that tough façade. She accepted the seat he offered, and when she lifted her gaze, it rammed right into Metcalfe. He was directly across from her. His pale eyes looked like silver in this light. No, like steel. Cold, hard steel.

"To my right," Director Iliescu went on, "is Admiral Braun with the Defense Intelligence Agency, and next to her is Colonel Dom Wolsey, who recently joined the DIA as an artifacts expert. Beside him is one of our most senior intelligence analysts, Charlie Harden, who will fill . . . since Klein . . ." He cleared his throat.

A brief look at Metcalfe and the men gathered around the table, who were avoiding her—though some glowered openly—had already made it clear to Iskra that something was wrong.

"There's tension in the room," Iliescu said, "due to the loss of one of our operatives. Jake Klein."

Iskra frowned. "I . . . I'm sorry."

"Unless you control the weather and the storm that tore him from the chopper," a red-bearded man said, "it ain't your fault." She remembered him from Leif's standoff back in the facility. Culver.

"Then again," an Asian man added, "we wouldn't be here if it weren't for her."

"Not true. She was only part of what brought us here," countered the hacker woman who did not like her. Culver had called her Mercy in the medbay.

"Right, the book did," Culver said. "And it's gone."

"Okay, reel it in." Iliescu rubbed his brow as he gave Iskra a look. "As you can imagine, the loss is hard. But we should get down to business."

"The sooner the better," Metcalfe muttered.

"Anything you'd like to offer?" Admiral Braun asked Iskra.

"If we were in Russia, perhaps drinks and biscuits." She regretted her sarcastic tone as soon as the words were out. "Forgive me. I'm sharp-tongued when I'm nervous."

"Tell us about the book," Iliescu, clearly the more reasonable of the two in charge, requested.

It was strange, as she'd already had a long conversation with Iliescu about this, but he must have a reason. She would play the game. "I know little, save what a friend shared with me." And even that knowledge from Vasily was in fragments. Would the USB change that? She couldn't give it to them. Though if she did get out of here, maybe she could convince Veratti that the Americans had forced her to give up the information. For Bisera's sake, she must get him to take care of Hristoff. The thought made her feel like a cold-blooded killer, but with Bisera's life in the mix, she had no choice.

Other than the USB, she had little intel, so giving up what she knew wasn't a problem. Except the information about the Neiothen. Her intent regarding those ultra-secretive guardians had to remain a lesser priority. For now, her focus must be on freedom.

"Please share what you have on the book," Iliescu said, his gaze already tracking to a tablet as he leaned toward the admiral, who was whispering something.

She worked up a smile. "Of course, I'm not an archaeologist. What I do know, I've already shared with Mr. Metcalfe."

"Metcalfe?" barked the admiral.

Still ignoring Iskra, he nodded. "One of the guards at the facility let my identity slip."

Iliescu motioned to her. "You know little, but you did know to go after it at the salt mines. Want to tell us how you knew of its existence and its location?"

"Like any operative, I work under intel that is both delivered to me and acquired through my own reconnaissance and careful verification. I was told about this book and its possible location by an asset." She shrugged. "I verified it was true and went after it."

"Who was the asset?" Braun asked.

"I—"

"I'll interject here," the deputy director said, "to say Miss Todorova shared a name with me, and I feel it's best not to reveal it until we have definitive or actionable intel."

"So, are you saying her assertion is questioned?" Braun asked.

"I am saying we'll investigate," Iliescu said.

Charlie Harden gave Iskra a wry smile. "You failed at the salt mines."

"Unfortunately, yes. The tunnels collapsed, forcing everyone to evacuate, but Rutger Hermanns escaped with the book."

With a knowing smile, Harden nodded to Iliescu.

The deputy director tapped something into his tablet, then stared down the length of the table at her. "What about Greece? You retrieved the book from the lab there. What can you tell us about that?"

"One, I didn't break in. I was invited in." Perhaps she was feeling a little smug about that. "Second—again, I will not betray my source—but having clearly beaten your team to it, yes, I *was* aware of its location."

Charlie Harden sat forward, his light brown hair trimmed short, as was his beard. "So the source who provided this intel is someone you trust."

Was that a trick question?

"Trusted enough," he amended, "to enter two foreign locations in an attempt to retrieve this artifact."

"That or whoever gave her the intel had something on her, forcing her to act," Metcalfe said.

Maintaining her cool façade was impossible with Metcalfe and his seeming ability to read her mind, though she knew he was just a very shrewd operative who could read a situation. Read *her*. "Nobody forces me to do anything."

"Noted," Metcalfe snapped.

She'd never convince him she meant no harm. That she went to Iliescu with the truth because something in that ocean with him had irrevocably changed her.

"So where is the book now?" Braun asked.

"I'm sorry," Iskra said, "I thought you were aware. It was stolen from the facility we just left."

"So you didn't steal it back?"

Mercy lifted her hand. "Ma'am, we have been reviewing footage from the facility. I believe another party is responsible for the theft of the book."

"Show me," Braun barked, the lines of her face severe.

Mercy nodded as she worked her laptop, then pointed to a wall screen. "There. No sound, but this is the camera right outside the lab." Her gaze bounced between her screen and the wall. "Annnd there we have John Stewart, Guy Gardner, and Simon Baz—"

"Wait, you have identities?" Braun asked.

"Low, Maddox. Low," Metcalfe said, a tease in his voice as the admiral continued her objection.

Mercy cleared her throat. "No. No names yet, but Cell's working on that," she said, winking at a lanky guy near the director. Then she smirked at Metcalfe. "The names were sarcasm meant for Leif—he looks a bit under the weather, so I dubbed these three part of the Green Lantern Corps."

Someone groaned. Iskra was too distracted by learning Metcalfe's first name—Leif. She mouthed it, trying it out.

"And here they so expertly break into the lab." Mercy clicked again, then tapped a button. "Now we are in the lab."

The three men on the screen moved through the chambers without hesitation. Bypassed protocols. Opened a drawer and removed the book. Two of them headed out. A third set a device on the floor.

"And they leave. Head down the hall, and bam! Newcomer is like Nick Fury—slick as snot at avoiding revealing his face to the cameras as he takes down the others with ease. This is the guy I saw in the Bahamas, but we've got no visual or facial rec. It's like he doesn't exist—yet. But he goes in, then he and the book vanish." Mercy frowned at the screen, then squinted.

"Something wrong, Merc?" Leif asked, and it annoyed Iskra how close they seemed. The way they teased each other.

"Yeah, no." She looked at him. "No. I'm good." She turned back to the screen again.

Who had taken it? Iskra stared at the wall, where the footage had frozen on the three Lanterns, as Mercy had called them.

"Maddox, can you put together a file for me to send to my contacts, see if we can identify them?" Iliescu asked.

"Good luck—yes." This Mercy had spunk. "I'll work it up immediately after the debrief."

"So you don't have the book," Braun continued, once more glaring at Iskra.

"Where could I have possibly hidden it? It would have been ruined. Recall that I nearly drowned."

"Yeah," the Asian said, "our guy did that for you."

Iskra choked on regret.

"Then the chief there extracted you," Culver added.

She lowered her chin. Remembered the smacking waves. The saltwater burning her eyes and mouth. The scruff of his jaw as she hung on to him.

"Colonel Wolsey," Iliescu said, shifting the conversation away from her, "what can you tell us about the book?"

"Much," said the man seated beside Admiral Braun, "and sadly, little. I haven't yet had the privilege of seeing it, but my research has unearthed a few key facts. First"—he sent a smarmy smile down to Iskra—"tell me, Miss Todorova, you saw it, yes?"

Did he not recall?

"Silly question." He dismissed his own words with a fake laugh. "We know you did. But . . . was it in one piece?"

"For something that old, it was remarkably preserved," she admitted, "thanks to the salt mines, although there were pieces that had disintegrated or torn off."

"Yes!" Wolsey laughed, and there was something maniacal and unbalanced about him, though she couldn't say why she thought that. "Of course. Good, good."

"Wolsey?" Braun asked.

"Ah yes. See, about a year ago, a fragment was found by treasure hunters. That is how the full book was most likely found—they knew it was in the area, so they were searching all the caves." He nodded to her. "By asking Miss Todorova if it was intact, I could verify—loosely—its legitimacy."

"Unless she knew about the piece found earlier."

Wolsey's smile faltered. "Well, yes. Perhaps. But it is unlikely she would know of that fragment. It was a well-kept secret as the team hunted for the rest of the book."

"Negative." Leif leaned forward. "Well-kept secrets don't have multiple countries hunting them down."

Braun grunted. "Tell us about this book, Wolsey, before I die of old age."

"Of course," Wolsey said, stealing back the conversation. "It is a lost-to-humanity book mentioned in the Hebrew Bible. Numbers 21 says the information contained in it resolves a dispute about borders between the Moabites and Amorites. It calls it the Book of the Wars of the Lord, or the Book of Yahweh's Battles, which is more accurate and—elegant, if I might say so. Verses fourteen and fifteen are supposedly a quote, 'That is why the Book of the Wars of the Lord says, ". . . Zahab in Suphah and the ravines, the Arnon and the slopes of the ravines that lead to the settlement of Ar and lie along the border of Moab."'"

"Dude, was that even supposed to make sense?" a younger man asked.

"Well," Wolsey explained, "like many books of poetry, the Book of the Wars was written in Hebrew, some Aramaic, although not much, and later Greek. It opens with a 'Come to' invitation, which happens in the Book of Jasher and the Song of the Well, etc. That's really all that is known about it, though there are many and varied beliefs about it and its existence. Some scholars aren't sure it's even a distinct book."

"What are the other books you mentioned?" another female operator asked.

"Well, the only pertinent one is the Book of Jasher, which is another ancient Israelite collection of poems the Bible often quotes. It's in the Book of Jasher that the mention of the sun and moon standing still is found." Wolsey wiped his nostril. "Actually, some scholars suggest the Book of the Wars is the same text as the Book of Jasher. You see, most ancient books weren't given titles—most were simply known by the first line of the text. For example, *Bemidbar* is the Hebrew name for the book of Numbers and simply means 'in the wilderness.' Obviously 'in the wilderness' tells us almost nothing of what is found in the book, but this naming practice was used across cultures—the Akkadians and the Babylonians did the same."

"Obviously it's a legit book," Leif said. "*She* found it."

Was he defending her? Iskra drew in a breath. No, he was defending the book.

"And lost it," Wolsey added.

The cur—implying the theft was her fault! "I was—"

"If you want to be technical," Leif asserted, "Uncle Sam lost it, because the book was in our custody at the time it was stolen."

"Okay, wait. Time-out." The big guy with a bigger chest and thick forearms formed a *T* with his hands. "Let's back up." He tossed a look at his buddies. "Am I the only one hearing this?" He craned forward. "Tell me I'm not risking my assets to find a book of . . . *poetry*."

"Hey," Culver muttered, "songs are poetry. Nothing to mock."

"This isn't about your failed singing career." The Asian man huffed. "I'm with Lawe. Where's my exfil?"

Leif nodded. "Agreed—this isn't adding up." He adjusted in his chair, glancing around. "This is a lot of manpower and government mobility for *poetry*. Can anyone tell us why everyone's chasing this thing across the globe, including us?"

His gaze struck hers, and Iskra wondered if he was thinking the same thing she was—the super-army mentioned in the text.

The Neiothen. Beyond the guardians, she could not fathom anything else worth pursuing in that text other than its historical and cultural value. But nobody here had even brought up the Neiothen. Did they not know?

Plausible, she supposed, but it seemed farfetched that elite military leaders like this had no knowledge of the faithful guardians said to fulfill the wars. Granted, even she had a hard time believing they were truly mentioned in the ancient text, but Vasily had promised they were there. Leif seemed to know about the super-army. When she'd mentioned it at the facility, he'd leapt up and left.

"But wait," the big guy—Lawe—said again, his irritation plain as he focused on the deputy director. "You told us this thing could be prophetic." He turned to Iskra. "That right?"

"I . . ." She hadn't really thought of it that way.

Wolsey laughed. "That's ludicrous! This text is significant because it's the find of the decade, but there's nothing predictive or amazing about it. It hasn't even been verified by scholars. I think the pursuit of this artifact is about someone wanting to put their name to the discovery."

Iskra blinked. How could he say that and claim to be a scholar?

"It won't matter anyway," he continued, "because once it's recovered and publicly verified, Israel will claim ownership, since it was found there. Which means it will be returned to them, just as many artifacts have been returned to Syria and Iraq."

"Which will stir the hornet's nest in the Levant," Harden said.

"True," Wolsey agreed. He subtly shifted his eyes to Iskra. "I mean, look what happened at the salt mines. Women and children hurt and killed in the pursuit of this thing."

Those expertly delivered words were a message. There was no doubt in Iskra's mind, nor amid the thundering of her heart, that a threat had been delivered against Bisera. She must not let this man know his words had an impact, but his message was received. Loud and clear.

"A man who hurts a woman or child is not a man," Leif said. "He's a monster."

"So." Lawe palmed the ball cap sitting on his knee. "If this thing doesn't tell us about coming wars—although, I have to say, I'd go to war if someone started reading me poetry—are we aborting this mission?"

Wolsey shrugged. "Yeah, I don't see the point. It'll surface eventually."

They could not! She had to save Bisera. It had been part of her plan: tell them the truth and trust their consciences to do the right thing. She must convince them to keep looking. Iskra looked at Metcalfe, and her heart thumped to find him watching her.

Then he sighed. "We've come this far. Be a shame to put fresh intel to waste."

"But what do we do? Who do we go after?" Lawe asked.

Frustrated silence seeped through the pores of the room. Surely they must see this book was important. But if she betrayed the Neiothen intel, she betrayed someone else. Someone she wasn't even sure was still alive.

"We are acting on a lot of instinct and guessing," Cell muttered. "Maybe a break would be smart."

Iskra's heart skittered across her doubts. *You have a way to convince them to keep looking.* The USB. If she told them, there would be chaos and anger. Accusations would build a deep case against her, fill Metcalfe with more doubts and uncertainty. What little trust she'd convinced him to yield would be shattered.

Wait. Their expert—she glanced at Wolsey, his sweaty upper lip sparking her wariness—had denied the book was of use. So Wolsey wouldn't be in on the game plan. She'd find a way to deliver the intel away from him. But how?

"Miss Todorova," Leif said, his tone all business, "what do you think? I mean, you saw the book, right?"

Play it cool, Iskra. "I recovered it, yes." Would he understand her surreptitious attempt to let him know something was wrong?

"But you saw the text—"

"I'm no archaeologist, Mr. Metcalfe. I just hunt what I'm told to hunt."

Confusion teased the pale blue eyes that seemed to probe her soul. And she let them. Wanted them to see that she needed to talk to him. But doing it overtly could alert the man she now didn't believe to be on the same side.

"It seems," Iliescu said with a frustrated huff, "that unless we have more information, we call off the mission until we know where to look or—"

"Sir." Leif thumped the table. "I might have an idea, but I need to do some research. Can we just call a break?"

Iliescu frowned as his gaze started a dangerous trek to Iskra, then aborted. "Okay. We'll reconvene in the morning." He nodded to a Marine. "Escort Miss Todorova to her room, please."

On any other occasion, she would object to being a prisoner, but this worked because it meant she'd have an assigned room. It meant, assuming her subtle hints were enough, that Leif would know where to find her.

TWENTY-TWO

U.S. NAVAL STATION, GUANTANAMO BAY, CUBA

As the room emptied, Leif started for the director. "Sir."

Iliescu turned as Todorova and her security detail exited the briefing room. "What is it?"

"Sir." Leif double-checked his six to make sure they were alone. "What do we know about Wolsey?"

"That the brass sent him to brief and assist us," Iliescu said, brow furrowing. "Why?"

Leif roughed a hand over his jaw. "He seemed pretty insistent we give up the chase."

"I noticed that." A nod. "Funding is tight for our missions." Iliescu's words lacked conviction. "How are you with what she came clean on? Thought you said—"

"I did."

"Can we trust her?"

"You're asking me?"

"I'm asking those instincts of yours."

In the last half of the briefing, Leif had seen a reaction from her that he couldn't explain. He didn't know what happened or why she went all high and dry. "I'm about to find out. If her armed guards will let me in."

After a lengthy pause, Iliescu nodded. "They will."

"Thank you, sir." Leif smirked and pivoted, heading out into the hall. He followed it to the second right and spotted the security detail hovering outside a room.

As he approached, the Marine stepped forward and extended

a hand. "Sorry, sir—" Glancing down the hall, he hesitated. The objection fell from his tongue, and he resumed his position.

Leif looked over his shoulder and saw a blur that had been the deputy director disappear, then moved to the door. The guard used a key to unlock it.

Leaning against the wall, Iskra waited on the other side of the bed, an obvious barrier between her and whoever was entering. Expression tight, she pushed away from the concrete but said nothing.

Leif shut the door, registering the way she eyed the lock as it clicked behind him.

"I'm surprised you're talking to me," she said.

"You and me both." He rubbed the back of his neck. "I'm not quite sure what I figured out or what happened in the debrief." He tucked his hands under his armpits. "There at the end, you clammed up."

She stood unmoving.

"I have this crazy sense you want to tell me why."

No hesitation, all business. "The man brought in to tell you about the Book of the Wars," she began, "is he trusted among your people?"

"Never met him before."

"Not what I asked."

"It really is." He itched to move closer but planted himself near the door. Since things had changed between them, the distance seemed appropriate. "Can't trust someone you don't know."

She considered him. "So, what? Did everything I divulged to your director erase the little trust we'd built?"

"Pretty much."

Quiet for a second, she slowly gave an acknowledging nod and stepped around the bed. "You're right not to trust me. I don't even trust myself at the moment. Not with you." She blinked and shook her head fast. "I mean—I . . . don't know why, and honestly I don't want to, but I *do* trust you."

"That trust is one-sided."

She breathed raggedly, her shoulders drawing up, then releasing. "I understand." She worried her lower lip, then winced—probably at the cut she had apparently forgotten about. Hands on the back of her hips, she sighed. "Well, I went quiet because I do not trust Wolsey."

"We have that in common."

A pound of tension seemed to drop from her shoulders, and a near-smile touched her eyes. "I am glad to hear that."

"Now tell me why you don't."

"Two things he said—well, one direct thing, the other more implied. Wolsey was intent on convincing everyone in the room that the Book of the Wars has no value."

God had a funny sense of humor, making their minds so equally matched. "I mentioned that to Iliescu."

"Which does not make sense when you look at the forces converging to find it."

"Agreed." Waiting for her to talk was tough, but he needed to tread carefully here. Her confession to Iliescu had angered him—being used did that to a person. But she had come forth on her own.

When her gaze drifted to the scuffed floor, he wondered if he'd lost her. "And the second?"

She blinked. "He said the text was in Hebrew and Greek."

Leif shrugged. "So?"

"Ancient Israeli texts were almost always Hebrew—sometimes later on, Aramaic. But Greek wasn't typical until after the New Testament. Especially not in a text as old as Numbers."

"Not an archaeologist, huh?"

"I'm not. But I know about this book because I've researched it, since lives depended on me finding it. And remember, I have seen it."

"Okay, so what did you see?"

"There is a section very different from the rest." She lifted her shoulders. "And it *is* written in Greek—which Wolsey couldn't have known unless someone who had seen it told him or he'd seen it himself." She hugged herself. "Either way, he has intel he shouldn't have. He's lying to your team."

He believed her, but this did them no good. "We can't prove it."

Again, she worried her lip. "I am sorry, Leif. Nearly dying . . . changed my thinking. I can't explain it, but I couldn't go on—"

"Using me?"

Her lips quivered. "No. I couldn't. Not after . . . the water."

"I'm sure you've been in deadly situations before."

"I have."

"Why did this time matter?"

Shaking her head, she shrugged. "I don't know."

That was a whole lot of heavy right there that he did not know what to do with. And he hated that it tugged on something deep in his core. "You coming clean"—man, it hurt to own up—"I appreciate that." He held her gaze. "The damage your actions did—I can't promise that will change. Especially since we're now back to ground zero on this mission."

"I'm not to blame for that, though." She sounded defensive. Frustrated.

Balling up the angst he felt at the way her expression went all soft, he said, "I hear you, but it's the truth of the situation. Good intel on Wolsey—thank you. But again, we can't prove it, so we're back to ground zero."

"Actually, we can."

She has the book. Or knows who does. He bit back the ideas. Because there was something more . . . devious in her eyes as she bent toward her boots. Messed with the laces. Getting undressed?

"*What* are you doing? Are those the boots you had on in the water? Are you crazy?"

She straightened, flipping dark hair from her face. A nearly exultant flush filled her cheeks. With a smile, she held out a small, plastic-wrapped object. "This is a USB drive with scans of the scroll."

Stunned, Leif took a step back. Enraged and amazed all at once. "You've had that. This whole time."

Iskra neither moved nor spoke.

"Holy . . ." Anger wound tightly around his chest. "What else are you hiding from me? What else is there, Iskra?"

Hazel-green eyes flicked to his, molten with anger. "Why do you see everything as for or against you? This is much bigger than you!" She considered him for several long seconds, withdrawing her hand and the device. "And this device may not seem like much, but it represents my *only* chance for freedom."

"The trade."

She reluctantly nodded.

But this seriously made no sense. Why would she hand it over and give up the one thing she wanted? "I am getting some seriously confused signals here, Iskra. I think you're trusting me, but you run. Then we make good on that, and supposedly we're working out this trust thing, only to find out you've been working me from the start. Now this? How am I supposed to believe anything you say?"

She smirked, and the shrewd Viorica returned. "Don't overthink it, Mr. Metcalfe. I am out of resources now that I have fled Hristoff, and I believe the Book of the Wars to be very dangerous, especially in the wrong hands. My friend who scanned it said the information in the book was phenomenal. Life- and world-altering. I told you about the super-army. You asked how I knew about the facility—the Pearl of the Antilles." She nodded to the drive, which she extended again. "He said it's in there."

Leif reached for it, but she tightened her fingers around it.

"Of course." He sniffed. Why had he thought—

"I would prefer to stay with it. To be sure it's returned to me." She gave an apologetic shrug. "Sorry, but now that the book is missing, it's all I have left if Veratti or Hristoff find me."

Leif wrapped his hand around hers and moved in.

Iskra straightened, lips parting as she looked up at him. Though she didn't step away, didn't yield ground, it was clear standing so close to him made her uncomfortable. It mirrored his own struggle at being so near her, noticing the way her breath quickened. How the rise and fall of her chest pushed against his own.

"It seems this USB says you'll trust me. Or, at the least, buy my trust."

"The former."

Yeah, he wasn't that stupid. "Trust me a little more."

Wariness crouched at the edges of her expression.

Taking in her features—strong cheekbones that betrayed her Bulgarian heritage, pale pink lips, mesmerizing hazel-green-gold eyes—he realized how fast he could fall down the rabbit hole with her. It was like standing on wet ground with electricity crackling around them. Binding them together.

Maybe he *was* that stupid. "What is the trade?"

She frowned at first, then realization flooded her expression. Twitching as if to step back, she broke eye contact. Then seemed to swim the depths of uncertainty away from him, away from this moment of truce he was trying to establish, before she met his eyes once more. "Freedom."

"From Peychinovich?"

When she hesitated this time, it felt like it lingered for years. "Yes," she finally whispered.

No. That was a lie. Or a half lie.

"Wherever this USB leads, will your director let me work with you?" she asked.

Leif frowned. "Yeah. My team—"

"I do not know your team."

So me. She wants to work with me. Did she expect him to get careless again, give her an advantage? "I guess I look really dumb to you."

"No. You are the only one who has shown me respect." She shifted. "Even when I haven't earned it."

"False humility."

"Will you ever believe me?"

He shrugged. "Doubtful. Let's find out what Iliescu says." He moved toward the door.

She caught his wrist. "Leif. Wait."

Man, just when he thought he had these idiotic feelings tied down, she touched him, used his name, and they sprang free again. Irritated, he glanced at the vise on his wrist and then to her. She must've taken a step, because there was an unrespectable lack of space between them.

"I . . ." Again, her gaze skipped around his face for a few seconds until a pink glow rose on those wide cheekbones. She released him. Stepped back. "I think Wolsey may work for Hristoff. He can't find out about the USB."

He started but couldn't afford to ignore that accusation. "Okay . . ." But if she wanted the book to buy freedom, why would she care if word got back to the crime lord about the USB? "What am I missing?"

"A lot," she said, looking grieved. "But that's the way it must stay. For now."

Message delivered. He cocked a nod. So be it. "Understood." He started for the door.

"Leif."

He gritted his teeth. Paused, hand on the doorknob. When she didn't say anything, he yanked it open. "Let's find out what's worth dying for."

Things were getting mixed up, her priorities confused, her focus diluted.

All by a pair of blue eyes. Why was she so determined to win his confidence back?

Seeing the way Leif stalked out of her prison cell had made her call out. Want to spill everything. Tell him that what she did wasn't for her. That she saw his intent to help, to free her. But that wasn't the name of this game. Or his call.

He had some serious morals. He was way too good for her, and when he'd found out how she had used him for Veratti—no, for Bisera—the little connection that had grown between them shattered. He regretted fighting for her. Which was twice as devastating, because no one had ever fought for her before.

Withdrawing her heart was prudent—vital. She could not afford to mess this one up. Because even if Leif Metcalfe could move past her betrayal and then see beyond her terrible life, it only meant he'd end up dead. Like everyone else. Help was futile. A waste of time and lives. She must rely on herself. Only herself.

Two hours after she handed over the drive, the team sat in angry silence as Harden pored over the documents. Noticeably absent was Wolsey.

"First," Harden said, "we're having trouble retrieving some of the data—well, a lot of the data." He bobbed his head side to side, then smiled at Iskra. "Not surprisingly, with all you put it through, the data is corrupted."

She scowled. "Are you sure?"

"Yes," Cell said. "Very. But we're still working on it."

"However, what is there is pretty amazing." Harden slid through screenshots. "And you really had no idea what you had?"

"I know *what* I had." Iskra forbade herself from looking at Leif. "But I am not a linguist, so I did not know specific details."

"The person who gave you these scans . . ." Harden began, clearly wanting her to fill in the blanks. But there were too many to fill—and others she refused to touch—so she offered nothing. He raised his eyebrows, smiling like a kid on the playground with a new ball. "Did he tell you what it said?"

Her and Vasily's concern had been solely about the Neiothen, which she wouldn't share here, and Vasily—God rest his soul—had promised those clues were hidden. Hopefully well enough that those here wouldn't find them. At least not right away, because she was pretty sure they'd take extreme measures to stop the guardians. She couldn't let that happen to Mitre.

"We were short on time," Iskra said.

"Well." Harden's smile grew bigger. "I think I understand why everyone is after this."

Her heart skipped a beat.

"I read through the decipherable scans—very quickly, obviously—and I'm amazed. There are odd things in it—"

"Like?" Leif asked.

Harden shrugged. "Odd grammar, out-of-place letters or symbols. That sort of thing. Again, what I'm working with is preliminary. I'll have and know more as I spend more time with it."

Iskra frowned, confused. "How do you have the training to read an ancient text? I thought you were an intelligence analyst."

"One of my specialties is antiquities."

"He's modest," Iliescu added. "Harden has multiple degrees in linguistics and studied intensively with the University of Israel."

"I wouldn't say *studied intensively*. It's more like a morbid fascination that keeps me up into the wee hours, reading and studying the Levant and its languages, as well as its history. What gaming is to some, this is to me." He had no remorse, but neither had he pride. This was pure passion. "And this—wow! Incredible find. Granted, I can't guarantee what I'm seeing, since we're only dealing with scans at this point. The fascinating thing is that the majority of this scroll was written in one language and possibly even the same hand over decades, but the last of it is in a totally different hand, and of all things, Greek!"

Iskra felt Leif's stare but kept her attention on the analyst.

"So how about we get down to business instead of jabbering?" Lawe said.

Harden swiped through the images. "Try this one. Where . . ." His gaze slid over the illuminated screen. "Ah. Here. Just a small quote. '. . . In what will be known as the largest and bloodiest battle of human warfare, a battle against the great army of the bent cross that continued for five months, one week, and three days . . .'" He looked up at the team. "Any guess—"

"Sounds like the Battle of Stalingrad," Leif offered, his tone awestruck. "It lasted five months, one week, and three days."

"And you know that how?" the Asian guy asked.

"I like history," Leif groused.

"He's more like a human encyclopedia on military history," Iliescu muttered.

Harden laughed. "Listen to this one: 'There will come the Unknown War—'"

"That's helpful," someone grunted.

"'—in which a nation will split in two, each with its own governments. The ensuing battles will . . .'" Harden hesitated, frowning. "Not sure about this word, but maybe—gain, garner?—'the help of multiple countries and in time, due to greater conflicts, will be forgotten.'"

"Korean War. My grandfather fought in that." Culver looked confused. "How—"

"Hold up," Lawe bit out. "So that thing *is* prophe—"

"One more," Harden insisted with glee. "'. . . years, in the Land of Shinar and Mesopotamia'"—he seemed to chew over the words—"'a cruel leader fell in the square, his bronze image beaten to defeat by those oppressed at his hand—'"

"Holy freakin' cow," the kid behind the computers said. "Saddam Hussein. Our guys helped the Iraqis knock down his bronze statue."

"You see?" Harden's eyes glowed. "This Book of the Wars not only describes wars of ancient times, but it foretold wars that would not happen for centuries."

"Isn't it more likely that someone found it and added to it?" the Asian guy asked.

"I can't prove that definitively wrong, but I would argue that's not the case, because trying to alter a scroll like this centuries later would do more damage than anything. Also, the Greek syntax seems older."

"Okay." Leif rubbed his lower lip, thinking. "So it told about these wars. Which is amazing, but—"

"Don't discount it yet." Harden held up a finger as he stared at the tablet again, shaking his head. Frowning. Squinting as if that would make the words clearer. "There's a lot here, but we've only managed to scratch the surface. The encryption on the USB is pretty advanced, according to Cell, and the transliteration is a slow, painstaking process to make sure we read it correctly. So far, we've only managed to piece together the first part of the first scan. I read it briefly, but the latter columns become more vague, indecipherable. Or . . ." He pursed his lips and bobbed his head in thought.

"Or?" Leif prompted.

"Or it doesn't make sense because it's talking about wars that haven't happened yet."

TWENTY-THREE

U.S NAVAL STATION, GUANTANAMO BAY, CUBA

A thunder of protests punched through the briefing room.

"I told you lugheads it was prophetic," Dru objected.

"The Bible has prophecies, but they're already fulfilled," Leif said and heard the guys agree. "But prophecies about what hasn't happened still, in our time?" He shook his head. "That's a different brick of C4."

That would explain why people were hunting this book as if their lives depended on it. It was one thing to read about wars they hadn't been involved in—'Nam and Korea were big, but no one in this room had been a part of those conflicts. Reading about wars they would be involved in, wars that *would* happen—it was a game changer.

The commotion receded.

"Imagine," Leif said suddenly, sitting forward. "Knowing what wars are coming. What outcomes are going to happen." He could hardly breathe.

"That's too much power for anyone to have," Baddar said.

"But someone does have it," Lawe argued. "And I'm starting to see why sitting here on our butts is a bad idea. We need to get this book back."

Leif noted a wave of relief wash over Iskra.

"Think the brass knew about this, and that's why they sent us after it but didn't want us looking too deeply into it?" Peyton asked, her voice quavering. "Why would they hold that back from us, though?"

"I believe they were relying on the fact that we had no experts"—

Iliescu glanced at Harden—"or thought we didn't, and would just do as we were told."

"So what's in that thing?" Saito indicated the scans splashed on the wall. "What upcoming wars are mentioned?"

Harden's face shifted into a serious, determined mode. "Well," he began slowly, hand over his chin, "the first thing to note is that the earliest mentioned wars appear to be recorded in order of occurrence."

"That would make sense," Iskra said, "since they were recorded by a Hebrew as they happened. That is also how John wrote Revelation."

"True," Harden murmured, "but the Greek sections were written much later. Give me a second while I get these scans printed." He tapped the glass, and a few seconds later, the machine in the corner rattled to life. It spit out a couple dozen copies of stained, torn text, some parts still blurred.

"So we assume they're in chronological order, too?" Iliescu asked.

"Oh, I'd be careful assuming anything, Director," Culver said. "You know what happens when you assume. Makes an a—"

"Got it, Brown." Iliescu returned his attention to the manuscript. "Either way, best to start at the beginning. Give us the breakdown on these wars."

Harden nodded. "I sure wish we had the actual scroll, but okay." He spread pages over the table. "These are the ones in Greek, and the more I look at them, the more convinced I grow that John wrote these, as Miss Todorova mentioned."

On his feet, Leif bent over the table, looking at the images but not able to read them. Could he find a book on the language online? "Why's that?"

"Well, the apostle John wrote Revelation, and what he recounted was revealed—according to his own words—by an angel of the Lord. And these passages of the Book of the Wars are not only in Greek as John's writings were, but they reference a revelation sent by Jesus through an angel."

"You're saying an angel showed him these?" Peyton's eyes were wide.

Harden scoffed. "Not me. *He*'s saying that." He pointed to the scans. "I'm reading what the author—who may or may not have been John—wrote." He palmed the table. "I think there are three, maybe four . . . situations mentioned in the text. I can't guarantee these are actual wars, but they read as isolated events—at least, I'm pretty sure. When I can review these with a real scholar, I could have more confidence saying that."

He slid three pages together, then grouped four more, then another three. After a sniff, he took one page from the second group and added it to the third. His gaze traced the words, but then he shook his head.

"Problem?" Leif asked, watching curiously.

"I . . . the wording is . . . unique. There's a section in here that really has nothing to do with either scenario, but it's placed here, right in the middle. Which is why I can't tell if there are four or if it belongs as a segue between two of the three." He let out a sigh and moved the papers around again.

"Start at the top," Iliescu instructed. "Maybe once we're all on the same page, we can figure it out."

"Exactly," Leif said. "Read it."

"Right. Okay." Harden indicated the first three. "I'm not an expert, so some of this wording might be wrong."

"Just go. We need the gist."

> "'Then another angel came to me and said, "Come, I will show you what is to come. Those who would attempt to thwart what God has ordained instead hasten their own kingdom end and Armageddon." And he lifted me into the sky, and there we watched the violence induced by soldiers of the Devil. In the land east of India arose the acrid scent of destruction that breathed black clouds, which vomited rain and ruin. Though those—'"

Harden muttered, his voice and brows lowering as he squinted at the page, shaking his head. "I'm not sure about this one, but perhaps it's, 'from below came, they could not stand—'"

"What part aren't you sure of?" Leif asked, logging every word, every nuance.

"There's no reference for the *those* he's mentioning. And *from below* makes me wonder." He shrugged. "There's nothing below India but a sea."

"Bangladesh is below India," Leif corrected. "But you read 'land east of India.'" He recalled the verbiage perfectly.

"Mm, yes."

"That's Burma," Leif continued. "And there isn't anything below it, save the Bay of Bengal and the Adaman Sea. Maybe Thailand, but that's more east than south."

"Walking encyclopedia is right." Harden eyed him speculatively. "Well, I don't claim to be a geography expert."

"Neither do I." Leif simply had most maps memorized because he'd looked at them. "Perhaps he meant a people group subordinate to India."

"Then why mention the location?"

"Good point."

Harden shrugged. "Let's come back to that." With a nod, Harden resumed translating.

> "'Though those from below arose, they could not stand against the deluge of fury birthed. With those came the squall of desolation and ruin. Wrought not by the heavens nor by the hand of God, the great black clouds that covered the earth were wrought at the hands of men. Hands meant for evil. Hands meant for harm. Hands that could not control that which they created. And so the rains came upon the terraces of land that produced where none had produced before. Wealth and health had become theirs. But their success grew not only produce and profit—it bred jealousy, as their enemies of kings looked upon the lands and coveted it. So they plotted with the great council who would seize the horn of victory before Babylon the Great fell. And upon the innocent and profitable land they delivered rains and ruin. The terraces broke apart and slid into the sea

and were no more, burying the people, cities, and the lands they had tended.'"

Harden lowered the page and glanced around the room.

"Storms," Culver mumbled. "Been seeing a lot of those."

"And didn't it say a scent of destruction?" Saito rubbed his knuckles as he worked through his thoughts. "Anyone besides me notice that strange smell before the storm hit the station?"

"Coincidence," Lawe suggested, but he didn't sound convinced. "I mean, whoever wrote that didn't mean it literally." He skated Leif and Saito a look. "Right?"

"That's the question," Harden said.

"That'd be why I asked it."

"The book of Revelation has long been argued and debated," Harden explained. "Some believe it's literal. Some believe it to be allegorical. Then, if it's not allegorical, there's the whole argument of when the Rapture will happen."

Peyton lifted a hand. "Did anyone else cringe inwardly when the scroll mentioned the fall of Babylon?" She sat forward. "I remember being in church youth group as a kid and hearing about how Babylon would fall, the mark of the beast, and all that."

"You freakin' kidding me? End times?" Lawe scoffed, but when nobody argued, his smile and demeanor fell. He cursed. Loudly.

Iliescu spoke up. "We don't know for sure about any of this. That's just it—we *don't* know what we're dealing with."

"Seems like a repeating pattern," Culver said. "Something I'd like to flip on its head."

Braun finally spoke, her words turning the conversation. "There's an organization that we—the DIA, DoD, CIA, FBI, and every other intelligence branch you can imagine—have been monitoring for a number of years. I'd hoped the dots wouldn't connect to them, but it seems inevitable."

Leif saw Iskra jolt, but she neither met his eyes nor changed her expression. Maybe he'd imagined it.

"What group?" Peyton asked.

"In the intelligence community they're known as the Armageddon Coalition. They're not an officially recognized entity like ISIS or ISIL, but that is only because they operate so far below the radar that they've hidden their activities very well. The things we believe they're responsible for aren't far from the efforts of ISIS," Braun continued without answering Peyton. "ArC is just as vicious, just as rigidly focused on advancing their caliphate—but they also want to advance Armageddon in the hopes of thwarting biblical prophecy and seizing control."

Iskra's hand moved to her stomach. Had her face lost color, too? Probably because of that guy she'd mentioned—Veratti.

"If they're doing what ISIS is doing," Lawe said, his voice notably more irritated now, "why a new name? They want new attention?"

"Because," Iliescu said, "their scope is broader. So is their reach. And they're not—at least not all of them—tied to a religious ideal like ISIL. They just want to destroy the West and rule the world."

"Through storms." Saito snickered. "I mean, that's what he read"—he indicated Harden—"that storms are coming to some land with terraces."

"Terraced land," Peyton corrected. "It's a method of farming for areas with unstable soil. Usually hillsides or mountains where soil erosion is a problem and makes building impossible without reinforcing the land with walls. Think Machu Picchu."

Sitting and staring at the printed images of the scroll, Leif thought through the intel written in an ancient hand. Storms. Terraces. East of India. Burma. His gaze flicked to Mercy. "Burma—any strange storms happening in-country anywhere?"

Her eyebrows rose.

Iliescu considered him. "What're you thinking?"

"It's dry season there—so storms coming up would be notable. And if that's where it's happening, we head there."

"Hold up." Saito waved a hand. "What am I missing? How can people create storms?"

"Hristoff can." The soft cadence of Iskra's voice crackled, silencing the room. She bounced a nervous glance around. "I do not know how he does it." Quick words. So maybe she hadn't meant to say anything. "But it has happened. One of his men helped me in Israel. After the Greece facility, I . . . I knew he was there because of the storm that arose."

"She's right." Leif recalled it. "It came out of nowhere. Forced us to ground."

Cell snapped his fingers. "And there was that smell in the air."

"I smelled that at the facility," Saito added.

Iskra nodded.

"Tell me about this." Iliescu homed in on her. "About the storms. You said he can cause them?"

"I do not know the science of it. Once I was in Italy for a celebration with friends. He was jealous that I did not come back immediately. Told me he could rain on my parade. Next thing I knew, there was a massive storm with hail and winds. The pilot could not take off for several hours afterward, which made Hristoff even more furious." And yet, she was smiling. Nice. It seemed to fuel her motivation.

"So you're saying he *can* control the weather," Iliescu commented.

"Hey, Merc—he's right up your alley, since he's got superpowers," Cell taunted, eliciting laughter from the team.

"Hristoff's superpower," Iskra bit out, "is that he has a way of making people do his bidding."

"Iliescu has that ability, too," Culver jibed.

Shoving back her hair, Iskra grew irritated. Her face reddened. Lips thinned. "I came here because I thought, here is a chance to stop him. These people are determined and focused. With their help, I can stop him. Stop this madness." She huffed, eyes glossing. "Clearly I was wrong."

"Wait." Lawe frowned. "You didn't come here. We brought you here."

Iskra blinked. Darted a look around. "Obviously."

"Nah," Leif said, "this is where she admits she's been playing us to get what she wants."

"Just as you have played me into your plans," she said, her tone quivering.

Cell lifted his eyebrows. "She has a point."

"Miss Todorova," Iliescu said calmly, firmly, "you said you don't know the science of how he's controlling the storms. But what *do* you know?"

After a few ragged breaths, she pulled herself together. Sat there for a moment, as if debating with herself about trusting the people in this room. And Leif didn't offer any encouragement, because he was still stuck on her words.

"I came here . . ."

"I thought . . ."

"With their help, I can . . ."

He swiped the pad of his thumb over the corner of his mouth. *She* came here. That was an interesting thought. Did that—

"I'm not sure what it is, but I've heard them mention a machine. They call it the Meteoroi." Hesitation guarded her shaking head. "I don't know much more than that. It thrills him, fills his ego with too much power, stirring up these storms."

"There was a storm at the facility," Leif said.

Iskra sagged. Gave a faint nod.

"So we disabled that tracker on you too late." He filled in the blanks. "Peych sent that storm to kill us all for stealing you away."

"But how does he abracadabra the weather?" Cell asked, looking skeptical. "Nobody has that power."

"He does." Leif rubbed his jaw. "How can he generate them without becoming a victim of them like the rest of us?"

"Whatever Hristoff uses, I am not sure he owns it," Iskra said. "He was very frustrated in a conversation I overheard. Someone has a part of this program or machine that they would not release. It seemed he has a piece but needs a mechanism? I do not know much, except that when this person would not obey him, he was very angry."

"Is he ever *not*?" Saito asked. "I mean, you're a smart, classy chick. What're you doing with this guy anyway?"

Saito's words bothered Leif. A lot. What did his friend think this was? A flirting session? He'd probably have punched him if he had said *pretty*. For now, he'd let it go.

"So. It sounds like," Mercy said, her words soft around her thinking, "this storm generator probably has a component that must be on the ground—that would be the cause of the odor, maybe? But if that's true, then there has to be a central command or control elsewhere."

"Makes sense." Culver sat forward, hands on the table. "I mean, whoever is controlling the storm wouldn't want to be *in* it, because these are some pretty vicious storms."

"Right," Leif agreed. "So two parts—something that acts as a homing beacon, and another to control it."

Iskra inclined her head.

"So Hristoff must only have the origination device."

She smiled. "Yes, that would make him angry, because then he would have to get their help each time he wanted to use it."

Lawe cursed again. "That means we have two problems—this Peych guy with his piece and whoever actually has the technology."

"Hey," Mercy said from the side, "Leif, you nailed that on the head." She flashed one of her no-harm-flirting grins. "Showing that brain of yours again, friend."

Baddar's ever-present smile vanished as he looked between them, but Leif was lost on what she meant, so he couldn't defend himself.

Mercy lifted her eyebrows, nodding to her laptop. "Burma?"

Right. "Yeah?" A twinge of excitement hit—the call of duty. He was ready to act.

"There's been a series of unexpected storms in a northern province, a site that has been under heavy pressure by government officials to relocate. The government says they're causing crime to rise and creating a loss of revenue due to their agricultural success."

"Okay . . ." Not enough to call it, but . . .

"The land—they built terraces."

"So this order to vacate—let me guess," Leif said with a smirk. "They refused."

"To put it mildly."

"Just like in the book," Peyton murmured.

"Give us a minute." Iliescu stood, and with him went Harden, Braun, and Cell.

"Arma-freakin'-geddon," Cell muttered as he left the room.

Lawe raised his arms over his head and stretched in his chair. "I thought all that stuff was in the Bible to scare people into being good Christians."

"Clearly it didn't work on you," Saito said.

"Which is why," Lawe said with a laugh, "I don't believe in it. I stick to things I can see and verify."

"Like satellites in space," Saito challenged.

"Hey, they come down. They can be seen."

"Not when our lives depend on them. And then there's oxgyen."

"That's different." Lawe slapped their combat medic's arm. "And since when did you become a Bible-thumper?"

"So, you're Bulgarian?" Across the table, Culver had leaned closer to Iskra.

The question snatched Leif's attention. Why did Culver care?

"Yes." She smiled appreciatively, and a thermal blast hit Leif's gut.

"Culver," he said.

With a smirk, the redhead turned. "Yeah—" His gaze snapped to something behind Leif, and he straightened.

"Okay." Iliescu held the door as he returned with Braun and Harden. "I think the excerpt from the Book of the Wars *is* referencing this location Mercy identified. Northern Chin, a western state of Burma, has been struggling. Six villages have benefitted from a UN resolution to help terrace the land, which some say is sacred and holy ground. So even certain locals aren't in favor of what's happening. It's a strange situation. Agriculture is a key resource in Burma, and with the help of a big charity, the area has flourished, ticking off government-backed producers. One side says they want the land because it's sacred, but the locals aren't budging. And the government wants the land because they say these Chin locals are stealing profit from them. Neither has convinced the locals to leave." He huffed and tossed a page on the table. "Now these storms are putting the entire effort and region at risk. Why it hasn't hit the wire is . . . interesting."

"Sounds like those Armageddon peeps interfering," Lawe suggested.

"Perhaps," Iliescu said. "ArC is spreading its influence daily, despite our efforts to the contrary. We don't need another group like ISIS to put people into a panic or, worse, feed the frenzy of opposition."

Braun indicated the team. "You'll head in under the ruse of delivering supplies—the rains have flooded their fields, and they're in need of food and potable water. Get in there and find out what's going on. See if our theory is right, if some device is stirring up the storms."

"Any unfriendlies in the area?" Leif asked.

"It's an unstable location, period," Braun said. "But if these storms are man-made, then it's probable."

Leif eyed the map on the wall. "Six villages. Where do we start?"

"In the northwest near the Chin Hills," Braun said. "Near Burma's western border with the Indian state of Mizoram, there's a town called Falam. Our loci of focus is between Falam and the Manipur River, maybe up to Lumbang. Seems most of the storm activity has been there. Mountainous."

"An asset will meet you on the ground and act as translator," Iliescu said.

"And our ROE?" Lawe asked.

"You're going in as a supply convoy. Keep things as neutral as possible unless you find definitive proof of"—he glanced at Iskra—"this Meteoroi thing."

"And if we do?" Leif asked.

"Bring it back. At all costs. We need to know what they're doing, how they're using it, and if possible—their end game."

"So we're cleared to engage hostiles."

"Only if forced to do so." Hands on his belt, Iliescu lifted his shoulders and sighed. "If this is ArC as we suspect and they discover we're on to them, it's a game changer. Right now, they're operating freely and without fear. If they figure out what we know, they won't hesitate to kill you. Then they'll up their game, and God only knows what we'll face. Our advantage right now is their ignorance. If we can get in there and retrieve this device, then we might level the playing field. We might be able to stop this."

"That's a lot of mights." Leif's gaze skidded to Iskra, who seemed pale.

"It's as good as it's going to get," Iliescu said with a definitive nod. "Now, gear up and head to the tarmac. Purcell is working with logistics on your tactical plan. You'll have it en route. Good hunting and good luck."

Leif stood and started toward Iskra.

"Metcalfe." The director lifted his chin. "A word, please."

Meeting Iskra's eyes, Leif tried to telegraph that he'd be right there. He wasn't sure why she would need or want that assurance, but he gave it anyway. Then he aimed for the director and found him entering an office just outside the briefing hub.

"Shut the door," Iliescu said.

Leif did so and turned.

"I'm sending her down with the team."

Leif stiffened. "So she can betray me again?"

"She wouldn't have come clean—"

"Unless she was trying to earn brownie points."

"Exactly."

Leif started. "What?"

Iliescu's lips thinned. "I don't want her out of our sight or control. She has picked you—whether for trust or target, we don't know. Until we do, stick close and see if you can turn her."

"*Turn* her?"

"She's the favorite lover of Hristoff Peychinovich, someone we've been trying to bury for years, and she's an operative we've wanted to turn for just as long." The director shook his head. "We can't afford to lose her, especially if he gets away with this."

"If he does, I'm thinking we won't have to worry, because it'll mean we're dead." Leif hated the frustration coiling through him. "You seriously think she'll help you?"

"No." Iliescu tapped the table, his gaze never leaving Leif's. "But she'll help *you*."

Surprise pushed him back a step. "You want me to use her." It was fair play, wasn't it? So why did that thought tick him off?

"I want you to do your job. She's responding to that. She came to me because she said she couldn't keep lying to you."

Leif drew up, surprised. "She said that?"

"And you're the one she gave the USB to. You're the one she—"

"*Played*."

"And the only way she could do that was because you two are the same breed of operator. She trusted what she knew of you. And I see the way she watches you, so use that. Get what we need, Leif. Every time a new intel piece got discussed, she looked to you. I see what's happening, even if you don't. Be careful. But use it and get everything out of her that you can. It's a job. *She's* a job."

The whole thing ticked him off. "And the second reason?"

"Watch her. She's moving *too* willingly." Iliescu rubbed his jaw. "What's she after? What's she hiding? What's convincing her to play nice with the enemy?"

"My rugged good looks?"

"She's dangerous, and that's not something I say about many people, because most can be bought or turned," Iliescu said. "While I do think there's something there to work with, this woman *is* lethal. If she suspects you're reaching for her secret, she'll chop off your hand."

TWENTY-FOUR

NEAR FALAM, CHIN STATE, BURMA

Having downloaded articles on Burmese traditions and greetings, Leif used the flight to prepare himself, get familiar with the language. The rest of the team grabbed rack time, but a buzzing brain wouldn't let Leif rest. He headed to the tight quarters of the small debrief room and laid out the intel on the grease board. Got a game plan in mind. He leaned back against the table and folded his arms, staring at the board. His thoughts vanished into the white space, where he drew a mental Venn diagram to sort out the fiasco that was Viorica. Her betrayal had a blast radius of a couple hundred miles. His trust had been too close to the origin point to survive. But . . .

As an operative, she'd failed her master—a safer term than *lover*, which conjured some pretty terrible images—so she had to pay the piper. Along came Veratti—or so she said—offering a chance to save her butt and her master's. If she hadn't agreed to take the mission, they both might be dead. So she went along with it.

Okay, cool. Well, not cool, but understandable.

Then she wanted to change the game. That was what he didn't get. She had an out, so why the change? He ran a hand over his mouth and the back of his neck. What was at the center of that invisible diagram? What tethered her?

Hang it all.

He punched to his feet and shoved a chair out of the way. Paced the ten feet of the room. By exploring this, he was condoning her betrayal. And that was unacceptable.

Why? You weren't much good to humanity after the Sahara. He'd been so ruthless about pursuing answers then that he'd destroyed every connection and friendship. Except with his brother and Dru. He'd lied. Done things he'd never thought he'd do. All in the pursuit of answers. In the end, he had also nearly destroyed himself, hating the things he'd done, the people he'd hurt.

There. Leif drew in a breath. Bent forward and palmed the table. There was the thing that wouldn't let him walk away when common sense said it was the smartest thing he could do. Sometimes, smart wasn't right. It was thinking with the head, not with the heart. Which was crazy psychology, but whatever worked.

He couldn't—wouldn't—walk away from Iskra because he saw in her eyes, in every action, the very desperation that drove him.

He lifted his gaze and stared over the slick surface of the table at the board imprinted with his mental diagram. Okay. He could do this—not condone her betrayal, but categorize it as "understandable considering the context." He churned that phrase over in his mind, then nodded. Yeah. That would work.

It still left him with the empty middle circle. What belonged there, serving as anchor for everything else? Hristoff?

His gut roiled at the thought. If that was the situation—

No. Not with the way she said his name. Not with the way she went to another, more dangerous man. Bypassing Peych. *Avoiding* him.

Footfalls near the door snagged his attention. His heart thudded at the blur that passed by. Iskra.

There was work to be done. Lies to be excavated from the foundation of her mission.

"Landing in ten," the pilot announced over the speakers.

Leif returned to the main cabin and planted himself in a seat, his head still buzzing. Once they were wheels-down, he and the team made quick work of loading up and heading toward the village.

A hardened dirt road wound up the hillside, its edges littered with buildings that jutted out over it. A sea of green fell away behind them, the sight deceptively lush. The ruts thrashed them as the truck lumbered into Falam along a stone wall that looked centuries old and barely did its job of holding back the earth and homes sitting on its incline. The buildings along the left side weren't much of an improvement with their corrugated steel walls and rooftops. Locals shuffled past with barely a nod.

Their translator should be at the top of the hill in the market. But to get there, they had to conquer the road's violent switchbacks about every hundred meters. Baddar frowned as he navigated around a bend, glancing in the rearview mirror.

"What's up?" Leif asked, noting the unease in their Afghan friend.

"They are not surprised to see strangers enter their town, and they are not pleased to see supplies either." His frown deepened.

Leif understood, daunted by the realization. "We aren't the first to come."

"Or maybe," Peyton said, nodding to the Chin Hills, "they're more concerned about the large black cloud forming overhead."

"Perhaps both," Iskra said from the back. "If the storm is from the Meteoroi, then whoever generated the storm might not be far ahead of us."

"Which means eyes out." Leif visually roved the streets, making sure the villagers were villagers, not disguised enemy combatants.

"I'm more concerned about covering ground before that thing unleashes its payload," Lawe grumbled, nodding to the sky. "The supplies are slowing us down."

"Easy," Leif said. "We meet the translator, then split up as agreed."

"I'm with Lawe. This is making me tense." Saito squinted at the storm cloud. "I was thinking we should find the center, but I'm not seeing one."

"Yeah, it seems all over the map," Culver agreed.

"There's the market," Peyton whispered.

Squat structures lined both sides of a wide footpath, with steps leading up to their façades and iron bars over oddly placed windows that were open for bartering. But nobody was bartering. The rains had demolished the harvest. Men, women, and children sat around, bereft.

Baddar guided the truck to the side of the road. Even before the engine was cut, the team was climbing out. Leif turned to Iskra. "Stay close."

Surprise leapt through her features, which then darkened. "I—"

"Hello!" a voice called, chipper and thickly accented. Waving, a man crossed the road. Wide-legged pants that didn't reach his ankles hung below a dingy tunic that might have been white once. His hair was longer than Leif's short crop but stopped above his shoulders. "Hello. I help you." His smile could light a village. "My name Thet. It means quiet." An ironic name, considering his ebullient self. Obviously, he was their translator.

Ignoring Iskra's near-objection, Leif pressed his palms together and inclined his head toward their translator. "*Nei kaurn thala*," he said, offering the traditional greeting.

Thet's eyes widened. "Very good! *Sa pi bi la?*"

"No." The question about whether they had eaten was a standard greeting of respect, and the team hadn't eaten anything since the dry meal on the plane.

"Come, come!" Thet motioned them up a side path that wound crookedly around homes and through alleys. "You eat. We talk."

The uphill walk brought them to a long gray building that jutted off the road like most of the other buildings. Thet led them into a home lined with paneling. A table, no taller than Leif's shins, devoured the bulk of a corner. A few small stools sat askew around it. A short, thin woman smiled and nodded as her room filled with bodies. Thet introduced his mom too quickly for them to catch her name.

Iskra nodded and pressed her palms together, just as Leif had with Thet. It won major points with Thet's mom, who motioned them toward the table. She left and returned a moment later with a heavy pot.

Broad-chested and tall, Lawe had to bend down to enter the

home. When he spied the squat arrangements, he stilled. "You gotta be—"

Leif silenced him with a glower. It was funny, really, thinking of the big guy seated at the table, probably hugging his knees. Even cross-legged, he wouldn't fit.

Beyond the room that served as both the dining and living room, a large open balcony gave an awe-inspiring view of the valley that spread below them. Had to admit—it stole his breath. Leif thanked the host and moved to sit down, relieved when Iskra followed him. That she was complying with his brusque *stay close* said a lot. Convinced him even more that the middle circle in his Venn diagram was the key.

"Chief." Lawe stood staring out at the valley. "I don't think we have time to chow."

After a shared look of concern with Iskra and the team, Leif joined him. "It's rude not to accept the meal."

"Yeah, and it's kind of rude to die, too."

Leif's gaze struck the hillside that he and Iskra would trek out to. Satellite imaging had shown it to be covered with trees. The image must have been old, because it was now just a streak of brown.

"Holy Mother," Iskra breathed beside him.

At her Catholic phrase, Leif eyed her.

She nodded toward the hill. "That's where we're going, but it . . ." She peered up at the clouds. "Oh no."

He saw the danger, too. It was time to bug out. Leif returned to their host. "Thet, storms are coming. We have to go."

The man's smile never wavered. "Eat first."

"Sorry, we—"

"My brother bring motorbikes." Thet gave an enthusiastic nod. "They help you go fast. You wait, yes?"

Motorcycles? Was he kidding?

"It *would* be faster," Saito said. "If the bikes come soon, we might beat the storm."

"Yes, soon." Thet gave Leif a bowl of *mohinga*, rice noodles covered in a fish-based soup and topped with fried fritters.

Leif's stomach growled, and his mouth watered.

Thet laughed, as did his mother. "See? You eat."

"Might as well wait for the bikes." Culver's eyes were wide in anticipation of food, which Thet's mother happily supplied.

"Could be our last meal," Saito offered.

Culver glared at him. "Morbid."

"I agree—dying on an empty stomach is a travesty." Saito parked himself at the low table.

Despite a few grumblings about losing time, the team sat on the floor and enjoyed a bowl of steaming mohinga—albeit quickly. It was nice to have a warm meal before heading out into who-knew-what. Leif finished first and handed over the chipped bowl, its pottery a swirl of blues, and wandered to the windows again. The storm had grown, its circumference nearly covering the mountain. The center, though, seemed to be about two klicks northwest of their location. That was where he wanted to go, where he was sure he'd find . . . something.

What was the Meteoroi? How were they supposed to disable something when they didn't even know what it looked like or actually did?

Outside, a vehicle rumbled to a stop in front of the house. Through the gap where the door hung crookedly, he spotted an old rusted truck. He started outside, then paused to press his palms together again in the Thai *wai* and utter his thanks. "*Kyay zu tin bar del.*"

After everyone offered their thanks as well, they regrouped outside. By the truck, Thet stood with a man—his brother, presumably. In its badly dented bed stood four bikes. Beat-up. Old. Rusted. But as long as they worked . . .

"Four bikes. Six operators," Lawe noted.

There was no way they would hand Iskra her own bike. "Viorica and I will use one—our route is shortest."

"I'm riding my own," Devine snapped, then tucked her chin. "Our route is longest, and if something goes wrong, we might need two."

Lawe considered her. "Uh-huh."

"Guess Culver and I are piggybacking," Saito said.

After the obligatory thanks and offering a monetary gift for the bikes—which was soundly refused—the team put their plan into motion using the DoD intel on the local weather patterns. Which, thanks to the Meteoroi, Leif no longer trusted, but what other choice did they have?

"Okay," Leif said, studying the radar. "Storm's pretty big, but not as large as expected. Culver and Saito head north, but let's shrink the ten-klick radius. Stay within five klicks of the river. If you don't see anything, turn back."

"Roger," they agreed.

"Lawe and Devine, take the smaller village just south of the river—it's still within the zone of impact. Check it out. See if anyone's been there. If you can't beat the storm, wait it out. Radio and let us know."

"Baddar and Mercy, stay here with Thet. As you unload the supplies, ask around. See if the locals know anything. Viorica and I will head west, see what's happening on that stripped spine."

Stomach pressed to Leif's back, Iskra clung to him as they sped through the lush vegetation of the Chin Hills. This clearly wasn't his first time on a bike or racing through jungle terrain, because he handled it with precision and speed. But the bike seat dug into her hips and pulsed aches through her lower back. Of course, she didn't really mind. It was nice—probably much more than she should admit—holding on to his taut, trim frame.

The terrain roughened, nearly upending them. They rebalanced and started again, only to have the bike's back end swing around. Another near face-plant, and Leif slowed to a stop. "Probably need to go on foot."

"If the storm generators are still here, then it is safer that way, *da*?"

Shouldering into his ruck, which had been secured on the back of the bike, Leif grinned. "I like the way you do a lot of things, V, but the way you think is a beauty all its own."

Surprised at his flirting and generous words, she tried to stem the heat crawling up her neck. She'd seen him in the plane's conference room. He'd been bent over, staring at the table. He seemed . . . frustrated. When he'd nearly spotted her, she slipped away. She had no doubt that angsty look was about her. But when he emerged and they landed, he had seemed extremely focused—on keeping her close.

The area darkened, drawing her gaze up. The clouds beyond the canopy revealed that the darkest part of the large storm was directly overhead. Wisps churned and tumbled over one another as if fighting for the best position. The effect was so deep and terrible, she felt it beneath her feet.

Whenever the storm finally chose to dump its contents, it would drench them. Oddly, she didn't care. It had been a long time since she had hiked mountains. The last time was an op for Hristoff. Before that, running for her life. How strange that being here, fronds slapping her shoulders and tugging at her clothes, filled her with a sense of . . . rightness. Why? Was it the mountains? The sense of freedom, being on top of things? Or . . . she eyed Leif as he worked to hide the bike.

With that ever-ready smile in his eyes, he straightened. "Ready?"

A witty, flirty response hung on her tongue, but she choked it back. Nodded.

He started hiking, unfazed by the taxing incline. Neither did he seem achy from the bike ride. Leif was tall—maybe six foot or six one. His shoulders weren't broad like the other guy on his team, but they were squared. His arms showed regular weight lifting with their beautiful curves that were hard not to notice. While he had the muscles and good looks, it was the strength pouring out of him that drew her. The leader in him that urged her to be better and do more. Convinced her to hand over that USB.

"I saw you talking to Culver," he said.

Iskra slowed, confused. "Who?"

"The guy on my team, red hair and beard."

"Oh." She picked her way around a cluster of shrubs, wondering why—of all topics—he brought up her talking with his teammate. "Am I not supposed to?"

He threw a scowl over his shoulder. "Never said that."

"He wanted to know if I had a boyfriend. If I liked Chinese food." That was what Americans did, right? Go out for Chinese?

Leif stopped short, and she stumbled to avoid colliding with him. At the scowl on his face, she laughed.

He realized she was teasing and resumed the hike. "Not funny," he growled.

She'd really broken his trust, hadn't she? She skipped a step, trying to catch up. "He was telling me that I could trust you."

Again, he stopped.

"I wish—" No. She shouldn't say that.

"What?"

Though she tried to avoid his gaze, it was impossible. Especially if she wanted him to believe her. "I wish there was someone to tell you that you could trust me."

Something pinched his expression. He grunted. "Me too." He resumed the climb. "Why did Culver think you needed reassurance about trusting me?"

"He noticed I was concerned about coming here."

"You were? Why?"

"That would be telling."

"But you told Culver."

No, this wasn't just broken trust. A thought stole into her mind. "Why are you jealous of him?"

"I'm not," he barked.

She laughed. Couldn't help it. He snorted and shook his head, and she saw the disappointment he wouldn't voice.

"Look, I don't really have a lot of secrets," she said. "And I don't like you thinking I'm weak or a failure."

He glanced at her. "Not a lot of secrets, huh?"

What did that mean? But she wouldn't be diverted. She had decided to win back his trust, so she'd start with some vulnerability. "Coming out here, chasing this storm, puts me far from what I thought I'd be doing right now."

"Yeah?" he asked as they climbed. "What's that?"

"Meeting a contact. Returning to Russia."

"To Peychinovich."

"To *Russia*," she insisted. "Hristoff is just in the same place."

"Does that work for you? Saying things like that?"

"It has to," Iskra said firmly, thinking of Bisera.

"You use his first name. That implies intimacy."

"No, it implies familiarity. After living in the same mansion with him for the last twelve years," she huffed, hating even talking about him, "yeah, I'm familiar with him."

He stepped over a fallen trunk, his pace rigorous and unrelenting, but he said nothing. Was he listening? Did he care?

She scooted around a tree. "I—"

The sight before her was startling. A clearing. Stumps no taller than two feet dotted the ridge, as if the hillside had gotten a crew cut. The land had been stripped of its vegetation and dignity. Tucked against the gaping openness, a grass-roofed hut that had probably housed a family at some point sat empty and forlorn.

Leif grunted and moved into the open. He went to one of the stumps and ran his hand over it. Rubbed his fingers together. "The culling is recent. The wood hasn't even discolored."

They walked the shredded hillside to the far end where the trees began again and looked back. "Why would they do this?" It grieved her to see the trees and greenness gone, but she smiled at the heights. "I did not realize we were this high up."

Leif joined her, standing slightly behind her as he took in the view. "Incredible," he said quietly.

"Explains why someone built their hut here. It's perfect."

"Agreed."

Iskra smiled up at him, and his gaze lowered to hers.

Something altered in the planes of his face. The anger seemed to step aside, allowing civility a turn around their rocky relationship. "You're beautiful, you know that?"

She was used to men saying this, but to have *him* say it, to see in his eyes that his words implied more than something superficial . . . it made her feel a little giddy and queasy. Earlier, he'd said her beauty was about more than looks, that he liked the way she thought. Why was he saying these things? To make her feel worse about using him for Veratti?

"You been here before?"

Somehow she knew he didn't mean Burma but the tenuous, shifting sand of trusting a man who used people and situations as easily as she did. Either way, her answer was the same. "No."

The corners of his lips pulled up, not into his usual smirk but a partial smile. Then he shifted. Stepped around her. "Let's keep moving. The storm is."

Curse him—he was adept at tying her mind in knots. With the things at stake in her life, she had to step up her game. *Clear your debt, then see what's left of you afterward.*

She took a step, but her boot stuck, then slid sideways. With a yelp, she flung out her hand for balance.

A vise tightened around her wrist. Jerked her up straight. She looked at Leif, who'd achored himself to steady her. "Careful. It's getting slick."

She slipped and swished up to where he stood on a rock. "The ground changed so suddenly."

When he reached toward her cheek, Iskra froze. His touch was feather-soft and quick against her cheek. "Mud on your face."

"Not the first time," she rued.

"Another thing we have in common, then." He indicated behind her. "I think there was a rockslide recently. Probably from the tree harvesting." He motioned in the direction she'd nearly fallen. A mound of rocks lay partially buried.

"Think it's safe?"

"Probably not. Area's saturated, unstable." He glanced at the sky. "I think we're about out of time, Meteoroi or not."

As if to echo this thought, a great thunderclap rattled the air and hurt her ears. She wobbled but caught his shoulder and shot him a nervous smile. "Sorry."

"I'm not sure we'd find anything here, even if we knew where to look. Or what we were looking for. It could be under all the muck. Let's head back."

She warily considered the sky. "We'll get drenched."

"Like rats." He stepped from the boulder, and his legs whooshed out from under him. Lightning-fast, he snagged a branch and caught himself. With a grunt, forearms straining and bulging, he struggled not to slide away.

She hooked an arm around a thin sapling and leaned toward him. "Leif, here!"

Once steadied, he stretched out a hand. Not close enough. Mustering her courage in the ultimate game of trust, Iskra eased from the rock. Mud sluiced around her ankle and gripped it, refusing her stability. She strained toward him—still not close enough. She took another step. He gripped her hand, and together they hauled him off the edge.

As if someone had opened the floodgates of heaven, rain dumped from the sky. Blinking through the blanket of water, she felt the ground loosening. Iskra sucked in a breath and snapped her gaze to his. Understanding lit his silvery eyes just as the earth shoved her at him.

"Oof!" Leif clasped arms with her, then tightened his hold as he considered their route. He nodded toward the trees below. "Quick and safe."

Together, they stepped and slipped. Hurried down the hillside, their steps sliding as they put distance between them and that boulder. The deluge made it hard to see where to step. Her vision was blurred by hair and mud. She wiped her face and fought her way down.

When they reached the clearing of stumps, the ground was softer without trees to thwart some of the rain. But with the deluge right over them and not moving out, the hillside didn't have a chance. Neither did they.

"Not going to make it," Leif shouted over the elements.

She sidestepped, descending the sloping spine. Booming thunder chased her. Lightning dodging her steps. Wind whipped and punched. Sight blurred, she picked her way down. Her boot struck something, and she pitched forward. Her hands sloughed across the slick surface, and her face nearly kissed the mud. Arching her head and neck backward, she slid. A long thin root brushed her fingers. She grabbed it, bark biting into her palms, but she didn't care. She held on. Muck and rain splashed her mouth. Dirt gritted against her teeth. She spit but couldn't erase the taste.

Hands pulled her up. The root came with her.

"The hut," Leif shouted, his words reaching her ears like a distant roar. "The hut!"

She nodded, and together they negotiated the churning terrain, slick and precarious. They had to descend a few feet to where the hut was embedded in the side of the hill. Leif slipped, flailing for purchase. Iskra caught his shirt and held on tight. He flipped around, then somehow snagged the edge of the hut, startling her—she hadn't realized they were that close already. With a growl, he found the strength to drag her closer.

"Go!" he shouted.

She climbed up the plank ramp, and he shoved her over the edge. She swung around and grasped his arms as he clambered inside. She scrabbled to the back, where the elements did not invade. Most of the interior was wet from the lashing rain. Covered in mud, she huddled against the rear wall, hugging herself. Shaken. Trembling. It was cold, and the storm was far more powerful than she could've imagined.

"You okay?" Leif's words were hot and still distant against her ear.

Muddy, chilled, sodden. But safe. She nodded. "This book"—she gulped air but tasted mud and swiped it away—"has put me in salt mines and mud baths. I should be the picture of health, but I'm like an art project gone wrong."

He snorted as he settled next to her. He sagged, his head tipped back against the wood slats. But her mind whirred—how long should they stay here? If the rains continued, what would happen to the already shifting hills? Could the hut break loose? The thought was too terrible to consider.

"See it?" Mercy glanced at Baddar, who stood behind her. "The rain has started. It's like a gray blanket."

"Runt is there." His brow furrowed with concern as he set the final crate of fruit on the stack. Villagers gathered what they needed into baskets.

"I'm sure he's okay." This was why Dru had never allowed her to be a covert operative—she was a terrible liar, and her first and only op in Russia had proven that. Never again. But she had skills on the keyboard, which she wanted to use to find Andrew. Such an innocuous name. "I need to get on my laptop and locate that guy. I bet if we do that, we also get answers."

"You will find him," Baddar said without an ounce of fakeness.

"You almost sound convinced."

"I am," he said. "You are the best. Leif say so." He keyed his comms. "Six, come in. This is Four."

Static crinkled through the connection.

Baddar repeated his message. He wiped his hands, eyeing the western ridge. Tried again. Same.

"This is Five," came Lawe's voice. "What's the situation?"

"Heavy rains and concern for Six," Baddar replied calmly, but there was nothing calm about the shadow in his face.

"Copy that," Lawe said. "Six will do his job. Let's do ours and regroup."

Baddar's lips pressed into a straight line. "Roger."

Mercy touched his arm. "Leif really is one of the best."

His brown eyes fell on her. Kindness and gentlessness oozed from him like a soothing balm. "I know. But he is also my friend."

Thus the reason for his concern. It was beautiful. "You two are like Bucky and the Captain. Well, except that Bucky had some serious things wrong with him after the experiments." She wrinkled her nose.

"So not a very good analogy."

She appreciated his playfulness. "No. But you are a *very good* man, Baddar Amir Nawabi."

"That is high praise from you."

"Just the truth." She nodded to the truck, and out of the corner of her eye, she saw— Her heart jolted. "Him!"

Baddar's expression darkened as he turned.

Mercy darted around the supply truck to the front end. Nobody. Around the other side. Nobody. She spun a circle, searching, heart racing.

"What is it?"

"That man I told you about—Andrew. I just saw him!"

"Got that Leupold on you?"

"Oh. You wanted me to bring that?"

Adam pivoted, scowling at the smirk he wanted to kiss off Peyton's face. "Can I see it for a sec?" Though a beast of a scope, the Tracker's thermal sensor had a range of 750 yards. That should get him close enough to maybe see what was happening.

Waiting for her to pass it over, he eyed the ridge south of their location where a thick cloud shelf loomed. Chief wouldn't be able to answer—too much interference. He was probably fine. He had more lives than a cat on crack.

"You seriously want me to hand over my $1,300 brand-new Tracker HD scope?"

Adam glared at her. "I just—"

"*Only* because you bought it for me." She slapped it into his hand.

Man, she was holding a wicked grudge. He'd win her back eventually. Or die trying.

He put the scope to his eye and scanned.

"Anything?" Peyton shouldered in.

"Negative," he said, searching. "Rain's like a freakin' blanket."

A soft pressure on the scope opened his eyes to find her long fingers easing from a button—the thermals. He slid her a glance. "Aren't you supposed to be scanning the area, Miss Sniper?"

"Someone has my scope, Mr. Genius."

"I liked it better when you called me Sexy."

"I liked it better when you were."

He grunted a laugh but fell quiet as his brain registered a heat signature. Then another close by. "I fou—" Then another. Two more.

What the . . . ? And another. The pattern . . . converging.

Choosing not to panic—*yet*—he keyed his comms. "Six, this is Five. Come in. Over." He waited, hoping for a break in the storm's interference. "Six, come in."

Nothing. His pulse jacked.

"What's wrong?" Peyton asked.

He checked the count again with the thermals. A flurry of panicked curses flew from his mouth.

"Lawe," Peyton said, "answer or give me the scope."

"Here." He tugged her in front of him so she faced the same direction, and set the device before her. "Our one o'clock. Tell me you can hit that."

It took a second, but he heard her suck in a breath. Then, shifting and settling behind her rifle, Peyton did what she did best. Lined up the shot while he made calculations for her.

She shook her head. "He's too far."

Adam cursed again.

She glared.

"Don't look at me like that. We have to move."

"What—"

Adam keyed his comms. "Runt's got six unfriendlies converging on him!"

TWENTY-FIVE

NEAR FALAM, CHIN STATE, BURMA

"We'll have to wait out the rain."

Leif and Iskra huddled close, the driving winds and rain chilling them to their bones. Body heat was precious, so they had to conserve and trap it. Wrapping his arm around her, their backs to the wall, was most effective, and he liked it. That was the betrayal. He wanted to be mad. Wanted to hold a grudge.

Which had zero effectiveness except to breed more anger. And that would massacre the mission.

Besides, he'd told her to stay close, and this was close. It also might work on her the same way, and maybe she'd open up. Fill in that middle circle on the diagram.

She peered over her shoulder at him, concern in those eyes that were now hazel-gold, as if reflecting their wood shelter and its thatched roof. "Do we have time to hide out for long?"

"If we want to stay alive, yeah." He smirked. "We could end up in the sea with the way it's coming down." Fleeting warmth seeped between his right shoulder and her left, which jitterbugged from the dampness of her clothes.

She leaned her head back, her ear and chin angled away from him, baring that long neck. Elegant. Tempting. He couldn't deny the thoughts taunting him. But they had a mission.

"If the Meteoroi created this," he said slowly, "can we predict how long it'll last?"

"I don't know," she said. "Hristoff had his men operating it. The storm covered me a couple of times as I went in, but once I left, I have no idea how long it lasted or how the device even worked."

He nodded. "Well, as soon as the rain lets up enough, we'll run for the bikes."

"Bikes in mud?"

"Some handle it better than others, but we'll try." He hiked up a leg and propped his arm over it. "So, Peych uses the storms against you?"

"Against me, for me." She shrugged. "He uses anything and anyone to get what he wants."

Rolling his gaze toward her, he noted the curl in her lips that matched her tone. "Is that what the yacht was about?"

Pain spirited through her expression. "Killing Vasily was personal."

Something on the wood floor caught his attention. "Personal how?" He toed it closer. Lifted it. A cable of some kind. He searched the walls and ceiling. No outlets or switches. Weird.

"Vasily's brother also worked for Hristoff." She seemed to struggle against some thought. "Betrayed him."

"So Peych goes after the family members of everyone who betrays him?"

"Not usually, but Vasily was helping me. I didn't report in about the book right away but instead took it to Vasily first to have him give me a heads-up on what I'd secured. I knew if Veratti wanted it, then it was important. I needed leverage," she said, then fell quiet before adding, "So that was another betrayal."

"How . . ." It felt wrong to ask how she'd become such a prize to Peychinovich. But it bugged him. Maybe because there was a question in that quagmire that he really didn't want the answer to, and yet he did. "You're important to him . . ."

"He's invested a lot of money in me."

Invested money. That sounded . . . disturbing. Ideas and implications exploded and left him nauseated, especially the more intimate implication. "He pays you?"

"No, not really. I have an account with an allowance. Just enough to keep me from bugging him for money when I need a dress for an event he insists I attend. Or for me to secure necessary items while on a mission—though that's another account. But it's also so he can track me and my movements."

Leif shook his head. "He controls you."

Her brow furrowed, and she looked down.

"I want to understand you . . . and him."

She shifted, her shoulder slipping beneath his as she raised her head. "There is no me and him."

He stared into eyes so like an abyss, luring him in, closer. "Then why do you go back?"

"I have to."

"Why?" he asked, frustrated. What was in that middle circle? "Please—help me understand what makes you so loyal to him, when I see a very different message in your face when you look at me."

Her mouth parted slightly. "Why I go back has nothing to do with him."

"And yet there is no conviction behind your words."

A scowl touched her brow but then vanished. She ducked.

"What did you do that's so terrible? What is he holding over you?"

"Why would you ask those things?"

"Because for the life of me, I can't make sense of this. You're an amazing woman. Fierce. A fighter. You find ways out—you escaped an impenetrable facility, outdid me—twice."

"And nearly died, but a man saved me."

He cupped her face. "What is it, Iskra? Let me in. Tell me. Let me help."

Her chin quivered. She shook her head. "I wish you could. I really do."

He tugged her to his chest and held her, enlivened when her hand rested on his abs. He sighed and leaned his head back. What was he supposed to do? How did he draw her out? God always threw the life preserver that messed-up, selfish humans desperately needed, right when they needed it. Right at the point of breaking, when they'd actually grab on.

Help me be that for her, God.

You are that, a whispered reply assured.

Yeah, that made zero sense.

"Why aren't you mad at me?" she asked.

Leif drew his chin back to peer down at her. "What?"

She pushed more firmly against him, as if she was hiding. "I betrayed you. Used you. You have every right to hate me." Finally, she lifted her head. "Why don't you?"

You are that.

She really was beautiful. His words earlier had slipped past his guard. But her eyes were round and bright. A sprinkle of freckles on her olive complexion leant her a mischeivious look—which was partially hidden beneath mud splatters. Stringy, mud-caked strands of hair plastered her cheek.

"We are more than the sum total of our actions." He brushed the hair from her face, tracing her jawline. He swiped his thumb around her chin, her lower lip. He saw what he wanted, ached to test those lips. Test this electricity between them. What would she do? Her eyelids were hooded with the same ache, the same curiosity roiling through him.

Peering into those hazel-gold wells, he warned himself to tread softly, carefully. "For every negative I encounter about you, I see two positives." Was she leaning closer or was he?

The line of her brows, relaxed and dark. Her gaze danced around his face.

"We're the . . . same." A tightening in his chest sent charges through his neck and gut.

Her lips, a deep pink, parted in expectation. And . . . permission. Or an invitation. He wasn't sure which. Maybe both.

He angled in slowly, not wanting to scare her off or alert her defenses that they were down. He didn't break eye contact until their lips touched. Softly, tentatively. He repeated it, lingering a fraction longer. Her fingers gently scraped his side. Leif caught her mouth more firmly, noticing the distinct smell of earth, mud.

He cupped her face, feeling himself sinking further. His shirt tugged against his abs, her long fingers curling into the fabric. He guessed she wasn't going to object.

It was like an adrenaline high from combat. A dangerous situation, but the addiction made him repeat it. And again. Kissing more. Deeper.

He pays her.

The thought struck him, unbidden. He slowed, needing to know the details of that relationship. Needing to understand. She was, after all, kissing a man who had been her enemy two weeks ago.

He eased off, liking that her eyes were heavy-lidded. Despite his own intention, he stole another kiss. Smirked at her. "Wow."

She snorted and lowered her forehead to his shoulder. But the tension of her hands balled in his shirt didn't release.

"After a kiss—"

"One?"

"Okay, after *a moment* like that," he corrected, laughing, "why do you go back to him?"

Her sultriness slipped away. She freed his shirt and straightened. "You think I want to?"

He was convinced she wanted to be here with him, but he also had no doubt that she'd leave. For . . . what? "I don't know. My guess is you have a reason. You're . . . tethered to something."

She seemed to want him to know the truth, because she wasn't moving away. Wasn't turning vicious. Iskra curled against him. Threaded her fingers with his. "Why do you think I'm tethered?" She adjusted to face him, her knee pressing into his thigh.

"Besides that you haven't killed him yet?" When she nearly smiled, he barged ahead. "When you talk about him, your tone and expression change." He stared out the opening of the hut, watching rain dump on the green vegetation, blurring the world into a wall of gray. "But you keep returning. You're out here"—he motioned to the hills—"free."

"Free is relative."

"But he has no way to find you now that the tracker has been neutralized. And I see how much you want to be here—with me."

She studied her tactical pants. Rubbed the mud off, as if she could clean the soaked fabric.

Something in Russia kept Iskra from securing her own freedom. It was driving him crazy that she wouldn't tell him, because he wanted her to say it wasn't Hristoff. That there was something else, someone else. Well, no. He didn't want it to be a *someone*. He stood, walked to the edge of the hut, and felt the needling of the deluge. "If we gave you the USB, you'd return. Right?"

She lifted her chin. Came unsteadily to her feet. "Yes, I'll return. But not to him."

He fisted his hand. "Then to what? You're not afraid of anything but Peychinovich." He shrugged. "Or maybe kissing me."

"What?"

"You had my shirt in a fisthold, and as much as I'd like to believe it was passion, I think something more primal drove that—fear." He narrowed his eyes at her. "What are you afraid of, Iskra? What are you afraid I'll find out or say or do?"

She scoffed. "I'm not afraid of you."

"Then what? You want freedom?" He flicked his hands at the hills. "It's there, waiting for you to seize it. I'll help—do whatever you need me to do."

"No," she growled, stalking to the other end of the shelter. "Don't do that."

"What?"

"Hand me hope on a silver platter." Her voice had a new edge to it. "It's not that easy."

"Easy?" He shook his head. "Nothing worth having is easy or free." His words seemed to hit home. "Let me help you. Take the

USB home and trade it—whatever that means. I'll help. Make sure you come back out."

"Don't make promises like that."

"On my life, I will."

Her brows rose in disbelief as she searched his face. "Why? Why would you do that?" She flapped a hand in the air. "Never mind." A breath struggled through her. "It doesn't matter why. You have no stake in this, and Hristoff kills those who help me. I will not let that happen to you. And now that I've upset Veratti—the price is too high. And you don't know—" Her face paled, and she turned away.

Leif stepped closer. Leaned in. "What? What don't I know? End the games. No more. What don't I know?"

She hugged herself, as if that would keep her secrets captive.

"For the love of—" Groaning, Leif spun in a circle. Lifted his hands. "Why won't you let me in? We just kissed—and it was pretty darn good. Was that fake? Trying to burn off some energy—"

Tears glossed her eyes as she growled a no.

"Then stop shutting me out. Why won't you—"

"Because it doesn't work! And when you know—" She staggered around a breath. "When you know . . ." She gave a sorrowful swing of her head. "I can't salvage this, Leif. It's beyond repair. I'm . . ."

Something in that anguish hauled him to her side. "What?" He softened his tone. "Tell me."

She pushed him away and wandered to the middle of the hut again. "I love that you think telling you will solve everything, but it won't. I will not put anyone else in danger." Her mind seemed to catch on something, a memory or a face, because she wilted.

"How has he so convinced you that things are that hopeless?" Leif grunted, disbelieving. No—furious.

"Do not pity me. I dug this grave."

"How?"

"I—" She strangled the words. Turned, shaking her head. Crying.

"Iskra, this is killing me. You have the skills. The strength and wit. You have what you need to beat him, but you won't even try!"

She glowered. "You have no idea what I've done."

"You're right! I don't. Because you won't let me in. I give up." He turned to the storm. "I can't con—"

She caught his hand.

It silenced him. He wouldn't look, just clenched his jaw. Because the curse of this was that he'd cave. He'd do anything for her. Why? He had no freakin' idea. She'd sunk her hooks into him the first time they'd encountered each other in Greece. He'd been outdone by her. That was amazing and beautiful, especially how she'd done it. And it had knocked every lick of good sense from his skull.

Why hadn't he figured that out sooner? She must have. She'd been working him.

"Please." She kissed his hand.

"You do not play fair."

Her breaths fell across his knuckles as she stared up at him with wide, glossy eyes.

"No tears." He peered back out again. "No waterworks. Cut it straight. Don't work me."

Holding his wrist, she stared at him. So much danced through her features. Ache. Desperation. Longing. Her mouth parted again.

But then she sagged against him. Into him. She wouldn't talk, wouldn't open up, but falling on his chest, clinging to it . . . that said a lot. Told him she wanted to. But she wouldn't tell him.

He released a breath. Scanned the hills again. "The rain has slowed." He shifted away from her. Took a couple of steps, feeling . . . empty. "We should go. While we—"

"Hristoff bought me—literally bought me in a business transaction." Her words were fast. Sharp. "From my father."

Leif pivoted. Gaped in shock.

"He took me back to his estate in Russia, where I didn't speak the language or know anyone. For most of my teen years, he raped me whenever he wanted—sometimes as punishment, other times just because." Anticipation crouched in her expression, waiting for his rejection. "Over and over."

Leif steeled himself. Refused to flinch. He couldn't react and show her the disgust she expected. But the fury at what she'd endured—he couldn't fathom it—balled his fists.

"I ran. And he caught me. I ran again and again. More than once, I escaped his security detail. Escaped the estate." Her voice cracked. "And every single time, he found me. Dragged me back. Raped me again, mostly to remind me that I belonged to him. I was—am—nothing but property."

"Iskra, you don't have—"

"I do!" She studied his feet. "You think you're different, you're enough to help me? Then let's see how big of a man you are when you hear the whole story." A tear slid down her cheek. "Because I haven't met anyone in a *very*"—that word was breathed and weighted with grief—"long time who could get past *who* I am to want to hear what happened to me. What I've become in order to survive."

He stood there, fists coiled, heart pounding. Anger churning as he fought not to imagine the terror of her life. Fought not to want to rip Peychinovich limb from limb.

She stepped forward and threaded her fingers with his, as if she was afraid he'd leave. "Before my seventeenth birthday, I attempted another escape. I'd gotten word my brother was in the city, so I slipped out to see him. It was then," she said around a ragged breath, "after raping me again, that Hristoff realized that because I was so good at escaping, maybe he could use me in a more profitable way."

She went quiet, worrying her fingers over his hand. "He sent me to someone who owed him a favor—a man from the Kremlin. He trained me, using torture to correct every little thing I did wrong until I stopped making mistakes. All of them." She lifted her chin. "It was this man who gave me the name Viorica—to him, I was Hristoff's Wild Rose." She sniffed, her nostrils flaring. "The generals loved the nickname. So did he. It was a joke. *I* was a joke. But I let it fuel my anger, my determination to someday find a way to get out—permanently. Hristoff sent me on missions, and I celebrated every one of them because I was away from him. I was free. Until I realized I wasn't."

It was a lot to take in. A lot to believe. But it still didn't explain what she was trading. And that meant she was distracting him again. "It's a good story." He nodded. Ran a hand over his hair. "Sob story, really."

"It's real," she bit out.

"But it's not what I asked you."

"To understand one, you have to know the other. I knew you would—"

"Quiet." Movement to his left froze Leif. A heartbeat later, his right arm swept Iskra away from the entry. "Back. Silent." He brought his weapon up, stepping back. He'd been stupid. Careless. He keyed his comms. "Six to—"

His gaze hit the cable on the floor again. He narrowed his eyes, realizing it snaked under the hut. Oh no . . .

Crack! Crack!

Shadows peeled from the left of the hut. But Leif was looking in the other direction.

"Eleven," Iskra hissed, wondering who was here. Who was firing at them.

Seamlessly, he swiveled to the left. Fired several short bursts as he backstepped to her. When the gap closed, she touched his side to let him know.

"Gear," he grunted. "Get the ruck."

She dove for the pack. Ripped it open and pulled out the two vests. She zipped it back up and threaded her arms through one of them. Dragging the ruck and clutching the other vest, she skidded back up to Leif, who had taken a knee, defending their position. "Here."

He spared a passing glance. Reached for the vest.

She slid it over one of his arms, then the other, with him only removing his focus for a split second. Once it was on, he pushed to his feet. Backed up more, pressing them into the wall. Wood splintered, chewed up by bullets.

Iskra peered through one of the new holes and spied a guy advancing up that side. With a hop, she sprinted at the wall. Gripped the edge and flung her legs out and around. Her feet pounded into the man's chest. He flew sideways, his weapon sliding off.

She leapt to avoid landing on him and spun. He shook his head as he came up, stunned. Disoriented. That gave her the opportunity to deliver a round kick to his head. He flipped backward, and she softened her landing, slipping in the muck a little. But not enough to put her out of reach of his weapon. She snatched it up and fired at him. He didn't get up again.

Wood splintered. A trail of fire seared her arm. She snapped to the left and sighted the next attacker. She released a short burst as she hustled sideways, stealing a glimpse at Leif, who'd leapt out of the hut and run to her.

"To the trees!"

She started running. Slipping. Scrabbling. Down the next knoll.

A weight plowed into her back. Smacked her into the mud on all fours. Smothered by the mud, she struggled against Leif's weight. Heard his weapon's fire mingling with the crack of thunder.

"Go! Go!" he grunted, continuously engaging the advancing men.

She pushed up, gasping. Stumbled on. Ran, looking back to see Leif on a knee, still covering their flank. She slowed, checking him, and tripped. Flopped into the muck. She shoved up—and froze.

A man towered over her.

Her split-second assessment of his gear provided her with three options. She snapped her foot up between his legs. When he doubled, she snatched his knife. Hamstrung him. Stabbed the blade into his gut.

His howling preceded the smack of his body into the mud.

She flipped onto all fours, seeing Leif advancing down the line. How many were there?

"You okay?" When he saw her nod, he sidestepped. "Keep moving."

Iskra pushed up, but her boot slipped behind her. She face-planted, her heart rate jackhammering against the thunder of the skies and the guns of those attacking them. But she fought. Thought of his words—that she was tough and intelligent. Thought of his kisses. The promise to be there for her. Was it real? It was too good to be true. He was too good. For her.

She scrambled up the hillside, not really worrying about having her head shot off because she couldn't get enough traction to stand. On hands and knees, she crawled—trying in vain to grab earth that slushed through her hands. Sinking with each move, but still moving. It was enough. It had to be.

Her hand scraped something hard. She swatted away the mud and saw black and silver. Her heart thudded as recognition hit. "Leif." It looked like a charge. "Leif!"

He glanced back at the hut. "They wired it to blow." He stilled, but an urgency snapped into him. "Go." He waved her on. "*Move.*"

She obeyed. Putting distance between them and the explosives. Slowly, the ground firmed. Shots pursued them, but she reached the trees. Iskra pushed and shoved. A branch poked her knee, letting her know the soggy terrain wasn't going to win. Gripping a tree, she wrenched free of the mud and wrapped her arms around the trunk, amazed that Leif's back had never left hers. She pulled him closer and led him to safety.

"Have to go deeper," she called back to him.

"Go," he huffed against her cheek as she rounded and used the tree for cover. "I'm right behind you."

"I hadn't noticed," she muttered.

"I'm the muddy Bigfoot following you."

"It was all that camouflage."

He chuckled.

Using a side-to-side gait, she clambered down the spine, catching low branches to avoid slipping and sliding down the hill. It would be faster but more painful. Probably even deadly.

An eruption of gunshots slowed her. She turned, caught sight of Leif's frame coated in mud and dirt but upright. Fighting. Protecting. How had they gotten separated? And so far apart?

She pivoted—and found herself facing the business end of a weapon. The attacker, face covered in a mask, brought his Kalashnikov to bear. Without a thought, she gripped the end of the weapon. Yanked it toward herself as she sidestepped and drove a fist into his face.

He stumbled but came back up—with a Ruger.

Iskra clapped a knife-hand on either side of him—one on his wrist, forcing it to bend, and the other on the weapon.

Boom! Crack!

She froze. Convinced she'd been shot. Her mind registered the warmth. The blood.

The man collapsed, his weapon in her hands.

Riddled with shock and his gray matter, Iskra couldn't move. She stared at his lifeless form. The part of his skull that was missing. That wasn't the work of Leif's M4 or a Kalashnikov. Who had shot him?

Leif pounded toward her. Shoved into her. They both barreled away, putting as much distance between them and the attackers as possible. They ran. Slipped. Slid. Terror gripped Iskra as she canted backward. She could not go down. It could kill her.

Leif caught a tree—and she caught him with a relieved huff. He pressed his spine to the trunk as he held her.

"Who are they?" she asked between gulping breaths.

He shrugged. "No clue."

She looked back toward the fallen attacker. "Who shot him?"

"Us, I hope."

"Us?"

"Devine—sniper."

That would explain why half his skull was missing.

Leif eyed the way they'd just come. Then went still. Glanced in the direction of the bikes. Back up the hill. He cursed.

She didn't like the way it stole what little courage she had. "What?"

His keen, perceptive gaze traced their surroundings again. "What do you see right below us?"

Trees. A deforested section. More trees. Beyond that . . . "The village. I-I don't understand."

Leif pivoted and peered up the slope. "They cleared the woods, set charges to the hut—that was the cable I noticed—and you found another charge down the hill. Then they added the storm."

She was missing something and felt really stupid.

The ground rumbled. More thunder meant more rain. But then the rumble turned violent.

Crack!

The ground shifted beneath her feet. Iskra swung out a hand to steady herself.

"They're forcing a landslide!"

TWENTY-SIX

NEAR FALAM, CHIN STATE, BURMA

"Something isn't right." Mercy eyed her timepiece as she waited with Baddar, Culver, and Saito for the others to return. "They should've been back. And now they're not responding to comms."

"We'll keep trying," Saito said. "They know what they're doing. They'll be fine."

"I've heard that before," Mercy muttered.

Baddar touched her arm, but she waved him off. She moved to the front of the truck and paced. She appreciated his gentleness and concern, but she just . . . couldn't. Not right now. This was too much like when Ram went missing in Moscow. She didn't want to lose anyone she cared about. Not again.

"Six, Five, this is Three," Culver radioed. "Come in."

"*—hiss, crack—*ive."

Culver stopped short. "Five?" He cocked his head closer, as if that would help. "Repeat."

"Five to Base," came Lawe's voice, louder, clearer. "We are . . . *hissss . . . crack*!"

Seconds later, a distant crack echoed the first.

Culver shared a look with Saito and Baddar.

"That was not thunder," Baddar said.

"Devine intervention," Saito laughed.

Right. Like Mercy needed more to worry about. So who was Peyton shooting at?

"I need high ground." Culver spun, searching the village.

"The truck," Baddar suggested.

"—in trouble. Repeat, unfriendlies converging on Six," Lawe said.

Culver threw himself on top of the truck. Legs spread for balance, he used his binocs to peer to the west. The way Leif and Viorica had gone. "Rain's a sheet up there. Can't see—"

When he didn't finish his sentence, Mercy looked up at him.

"Gunfire. I see multiple sources." And then he swung out his hands, his balance apparently shifted.

That was when she realized *she* was swaying. No, the *buildings* were swaying. Wait, no, the street—

Her phone rang. Recognizing the ringtone, she answered. "Dru."

"Chopper's inbound, Mercy. Get in the truck and drive east. We're—"

Crack! Boom!

She pitched forward. Caught her balance. "What on earth?" She glanced around. "Leif and the assassin aren't back. Neither are Lawe and Devine, and—"

At the edge of the village, a river of mud crashed past the huts, slashing the structural supports out from under them.

She stilled, searching for the source. "What was that?"

"I heard from Leif," Dru barked in her ear. "He said someone set charges in the mountain to create a landslide."

Her gaze rose to the Chin Hills, though she couldn't decipher where Leif would be at the moment.

"Get in the truck and leave," Dru ordered. "Now! We're sending evac choppers, but they're at least twenty mikes out."

Twenty minutes. Did they have that long?

"Sir, there are hundreds of people here," she said. "We can't just—"

"*Get in the truck!* Or we won't have to worry about *anyone*. Clear?"

"Yes, sir."

"I'll call back in ten. Make sure you're heading east."

The line went dead, and she stared dumbly at it.

"Mercy?" Baddar's voice was calm but firm. He nodded to her right.

Thet was trotting toward them from between the buildings, his face carved with worry. "The rain too much." His black hair was plastered to his forehead. "All the food—wasted. So sad."

Inspiration struck. That was it! Mercy darted to him. "Tell the people to come to the truck. We have to leave now. There's a landslide coming! We must leave now."

Crack-creeack-crack!

They both spun and watched as the terraced hillside canted and collapsed.

Thet held his head, crying out.

Mercy shoved him. "Go! Get the people to the truck." She darted back to the guys. "Get the truck turned around. We have to be ready to leave."

Culver's face darkened. "I'm not leaving my team."

"Lawe is north of the ridge. Norther of the gunfire, right?"

"*Norther?*" Culver blinked, but his twisted-up features smoothed out. He nodded. "Yeah."

"He'll be fine." Probably. "Leif can't hear us. Can't reach us in time. He's on his own." With the operative, but that was a moot point. "Here there are hundreds of people—"

"They won't all fit in the truck," Saito pointed out.

"They have to fit," Mercy barked. "Now get it moved!"

Culver smirked. "Ma'am." He pinched the bill of his ball cap with a finger and thumb, then jogged to the truck cab. He climbed in and started it up. The throaty rattle of the diesel engine echoed through the small street.

Thet had made quick work of spreading the word, because people were spilling into the street. Women carrying children. Men dragging belongings. They waited as Culver repositioned the truck, and then Baddar set down a crate as a step stool, and villagers clambered inside.

But there was a lot of room left and no more villagers coming. Mercy spied Thet rounding the corner, alone. "Where is your mom? The others?"

"They not come." Tears streaked down his face. "I stay too."

"No!" Panic squeezed her heart as she stumbled toward him. "You can't! There are men trying to destroy the village. They have explosives. When those go off, there will be a landslide. Everything here will be buried!"

The ground rumbled, churned. The road growled around them, and Mercy staggered back. A line formed in the muck near Thet and splintered down the road.

"Mercyyy!" Culver hollered, his gaze on the hills.

She dared to glance that way and could not comprehend at first what was happening. Trees tilting back. Green turning brown. Oh no. She grabbed Thet's collar, but he shoved her away. She stumbled. Slipped in the mud and rain. Nearly fell.

Hands caught her. Baddar.

But her focus was on their translator. "Thet, please!" she called as he vanished around the corner. Heading home. To his mother.

Grief clawed at her. She couldn't let this happen. She had to intervene. "Thet!" Mercy started after him, but a strong arm hooked her waist. Hauled her off her feet.

Baddar's breath was warm against her ear. He twisted and angled her into the bed of the truck.

She growled at him and slapped his chest. Then dropped, defeated, on the wood floor of the truck. Sagging, she buried her face in her hands, feeling Baddar at her side. He banged the hull of the truck, which lurched into motion in response.

As Culver navigated the winding, switchback roads that were costing them precious time, Mercy watched the village's defiant last stand. And it *was* the last. Because as a peal of thunder and the din of explosions rattled the mountain, the earth surrendered. Mud slid and thrashed as if racing for shelter.

She prayed Leif made it out alive. It would be good to hear that Lawe and Devine were alive, but she would trust Iliescu's intel on that.

Baddar yanked the door closed, leaving her to imagine the worst.

The village would be wiped away. What if the landslide was too big? What if it out-sprinted them? She hugged her legs to her chest.

The truck jerked and bounced. The people—maybe seventy of the hundreds who'd occupied the village—grunted and yelped as they were tossed about. Mercy clung to a support brace and Baddar, who was sandwiched between her and the closed door.

Minutes took on the life of hours as they rocked in the hot truck, knowing that out there raged a tempest. She dug her fingers into her hair and fisted her hands. Blocked the fatal thoughts, the hopelessness. So awful.

No more. She couldn't take this kind of stuff anymore. It was time to get out. Stop seeing people die. Normal people worried about espresso shots dying, not the person next to them. It would be good to have a First World problem instead of this. That was what she got for having a thing for superheroes.

Superheroes who died, apparently.

Baddar touched his comms piece and lowered his chin, brow knotting. Without a word, he stood. Tied a rope to the brace of the wall.

Mercy rose. "What?"

He reached for the door and thrust it upward.

Alarm seized her at the sea of mud rushing the tailgate. "What're you doing?" The landslide was furious. Hungry. Ravenous. "Are you crazy?"

Baddar was searching. Intent.

And then she saw it. A blip just barely in front of the raging, writhing earth. A blip of light—a headlamp from a motorbike.

"Leif."

The *twang* of the motorbike was lost in the roar of the mountain crashing down behind them. They'd had nearly a mile lead when he'd first hit the road. Now they were down to seventy-five yards at best.

Iskra gripped his sides like a vise, and he was glad, because this would be close. If they made it. He wasn't sure they could, but he wouldn't give up. Not when he'd made it down a mountain he'd expected to die on.

The rear door of the white supply truck rolled up, and a figure stood braced in the opening. Leif wanted to accelerate, but the throttle was already wide open. And losing. Frustration tightened around his gut. He hadn't felt this helpless since the desert.

But then they were gaining on the truck.

His heart tripped. No—the truck was slowing. Probably to help Leif and Iskra catch them, but that was a mistake.

Yet he was relieved. If he snagged the chance, maybe they could get away from the landslide before it was too late.

Mud splashed his face. Cold dampness slapped his leg. Forced by the road's switchbacks, the truck swung away.

Leif whipped the bike left, tearing into the brush and aiming east, where the road would arc back. But the terrain was unforgiving, not caring if they survived. Ahead, a wall of shrubs formed a barrier. A drop-off on the right. The vicious displaced earth raced at them from the left.

Iskra's arms tightened. So did her thighs around his hips, mirroring his own tension. They had about a twenty-percent chance of survival.

But it was twenty percent. He'd take it.

Gaze bouncing between the truck and the terrain, Leif lined them up. Sighted an overhang.

He sailed off a small ridge, the bike airborne. And for one second, Leif could swear he heard the thunder of his own heart. The fear of being mortal in a supernatural battle against Mother Nature. Who'd had an assist.

The bike hit hard. Jounced. The rear tire swung out. He straightened, grinning like a fool when the truck made a hard turn, just as he'd expected.

Leif throttled hard. Gained on the truck. There was a line about a klick ahead where mud had failed to overtake the land. But how long would that last?

Baddar stood in the back, a half dozen guys holding him by a rope as he balanced on the bumper. Leif revved and caught up, monitoring the terrain, the truck. He glanced over his shoulder at Iskra. Nodded to the truck, indicating for her to go first. She pulled up her legs. Her hands slid along his back to his shoulders, where she gripped tight for balance and brought her feet to the seat.

Leif met Culver's eyes in the side mirror, then focused on aligning with the truck so Iskra could jump. Her launch shoved the bike sideways. The front tire veered dangerously close to the truck's left rear wheel. Bounced off the hull. He nearly lost control, dirt and rocks merging.

Mud slapped his face and slicked his tires. He growled at it, warning it to back off. Focused on reaching the truck.

Shouts blended with the throaty growl of the engine. He needed better alignment, but the bike fought him hard. His grip slipped.

Mud punched him, shoving the bike into the truck. It crushed his leg between the bike and the bumper. Agony demanded attention, but survival needed it more.

Hands latched onto him. Hauled him to safety, scraping his spine along the metal floor. Mud ripped away the bike and thrashed it down the hillside until it was smothered beneath the fury of the landslide.

Relieved, exhausted, Leif slumped to the floor. Closed his eyes, adrenaline dumping and leaving his limbs trembling as darkness descended, the rear door sliding shut. He felt weak. Very weak.

"Chief, you okay?"

"Yeah," he said through a dry throat.

"Because you're shot."

"What?" Leif looked at the large hands that palmed his shoulder. "Huh." He dropped back against the floor and laughed. He wasn't sure why. It wasn't funny. "That explains a lot."

"I . . . I didn't know." Iskra's voice was soft. Worried.

"It's just a graze," he lied. He had no idea. He couldn't feel it because of the adrenaline.

The truck jounced, silencing any arguments as a chorus of yelps shot out.

Leif slid—thumping against Iskra and Mercy, their expressions startled. "Guess we aren't out of danger yet," he said. The truck groaned and creaked, then . . . near silence. Pulling himself upright, he ignored the protests to keep still. It was too quiet. "Why aren't we moving?"

Scraping and groaning along the hull continued but eventually quieted.

Baddar touched his comms. He nodded, his gaze hitting Leif. "Mudslide drove us down. We're stuck. The mud is splitting around us. We should be okay."

Leif shifted against the wall, and pain throbbed in his shoulder. But pain didn't hit him like it did most people. This was the worst he'd feel.

"How'd you two escape?" Mercy asked. "You were much farther out."

"We had a head start," Leif said. "I saw the charges, realized what they were doing. We fought our way down the mountain, then rode as hard as we could. I lost my comms piece, so we stopped every five klicks to look for a cell signal to call Iliescu."

The back of the truck rolled up, and Culver stood in thigh-high muck. "Choppers are inbound. We have to hike out to reach them." He scowled. "Chief, you hit?"

"Just a graze."

"Graze my hairy backside," Culver growled.

Saito climbed in and inspected the injury. "Entrance and exit wound. That's good, but—"

"It'll heal."

"—you're out of commission."

Leif glowered. "Try that again."

"Debate later," Culver said as the *thwump-thwump* of helos approached.

Leif allowed Saito to sling up his arm to prevent further injury, and then they focused on getting the survivors to the four choppers. Three ferried the locals to a UN camp, but the fourth held a surprise—Lawe and Devine.

Lawe shook his head in disbelief at Leif. "You're one lucky—"

"No luck about it," Leif shouted, then nodded to Devine. "Nice shooting."

She smiled. "Thanks. Not my best, but sniping through a curtain of rain is a challenge."

They boarded the chopper, which delivered them to an airstrip and a waiting jet. Used to a C-130 transport, Saito muttered his appreciation for the bit of luxury. Showers and fresh gear waited in the plane. While the team cleaned up, Leif had his wounds stitched, then did the same before joining them in a small conference room.

Applause broke out.

"There's Evel Knievel himself," Lawe said, clapping.

Leif snorted.

"Where's that sling?" Saito demanded. "You need to keep that shoulder immobile for at least a week."

"Yes, *Mom*." Leif eyed the Styrofoam boxes of food on the table. "Any news about who was on the mountain shooting at us?" Grabbing a box, he eyed the only empty chair, right next to Iskra. Hair wet and face clean, she wore tactical gear like the team. It was nice. Weird, but nice. He sat and dug in.

"Negative," Lawe said.

Chewing his food, Leif dug a wire from his pocket. "This is what they used for the charges."

"Unless it's custom," Devine said, "I doubt it'll tell us much. Looks standard."

"Let's hope you're wrong," Leif said.

"There's a first time for everything, I guess," Lawe said.

"Wait." Devine shifted toward the big guy. "Are you saying I'm right? That I'm *usually* right?"

"Careful," Culver warned with a chuckle. "Sounds like you just stepped in something."

Devine had homed in on Lawe and wasn't letting go. "Because recall the whole thing you said about—"

"Can we *not* do this now?" Lawe looked like a kid caught raiding his brother's candy stash.

"You mean, not ever? Because that's when you do talk about things, Adam."

Culver snorted. "I think you're dead meat, *Adam*."

The team broke into laughter.

"Anyone else find strange stuff in your zones?" Leif asked, hoping to shift away from the trouble Lawe had found. On his own, but still. Never leave a man down.

"Actually," Mercy said quietly from the other end. She lifted something from her lap and set it on the table.

"What's that?" Leif asked.

She angled it toward him, and it gutted him. He ran a hand over his head, suddenly losing his appetite. A pottery shard. Blue swirls against a brown exterior. Like the bowl he'd eaten from at Thet's house. The house that, thanks to the landslide, no longer existed. The unstable conditions made it impossible for recovery efforts to start yet.

"I found it when we were sludging out to the choppers." Mercy's chin puckered with restrained tears. She shrugged. "I tried to get him to come with us."

"It was a matter of honor." Baddar touched her hand. "He would not leave his family or his home."

"And now," Mercy said, her lips flat, "neither exist. Makes so much sense."

Grief hung heavy, diverting their attention.

"But that's not all I found." Mercy shuddered a breath. "Remember that guy in Cuba, Andrew? Who popped up in the facility where the book was stolen?" Her gaze hit Iskra, but she said nothing to her. "He was at the village."

Leif scowled. "You kidding me?"

"Wish I was."

"Who is he?"

"Wish I knew." Mercy huffed. "I tried to find him, but he vanished"—she snapped her fingers—"like that."

"I'd like to know why you're the only one who keeps seeing him," Lawe said.

Devine slapped his arm.

"What?"

"Are you insinuating that she's unstable?" Devine's expression was malicious.

"What? No!" Lawe's eyes widened, then looked stricken. "I swear on my mom's grave. I never intended that."

"He makes a good point," Leif agreed. "Nobody has seen this guy except Mercy, so that could be intentional on his part or not. Either way, we need to get facial rec. Ask Iliescu, since he was aiming sats at that village while we were onsite."

"That might also tell us who to pay back for the chunk they took out of your shoulder," Lawe said, pointing his fork.

"Hey." Cell jogged into the cabin and hit a switch on the wall. A white screen scrolled down from the ceiling. "Director's on the line."

Leif scowled. "Where'd you come from?"

"Communications center." Cell shrugged as if this were common knowledge. "The—at the front of the plane. A communications hub." He tapped into a panel on the wall. The screen went black, then cycled through a "waiting" icon. He glanced at the mostly uneaten trays of food. "I'd finish eating, then rest up. You're going to be busy." With that, he left.

Gaping at the now-empty doorway, Leif grunted. "That guy is getting weirder every day."

"Barc has always been weird," Mercy said, her tone lazy and happy. "That's what makes him so great."

"Gentlemen—and ladies," the director's voice boomed from a speaker. "Mr. Metcalfe, how're you?"

"Hungry but good, sir." Leif snagged a slice of bread from his tray.

"Doc says you're healing."

"Healing?" Saito blinked. "He just got shot and stitched in the last two hours."

"We've got some new intel I need you to follow up on," Iliescu continued.

"Storms?" Leif asked, his instincts buzzing.

"It's crazy how you know these things. Someday you'll be after my job."

"Can't sit behind a desk. Too boring."

"I think you mean too safe," Iliescu said. "Anyway, you're now en route to the African continent."

The last two words snagged Leif's attention. "Africa." He hadn't been back there since he'd first met Tox Russell's team and helped them navigate the locals. Even then, it had taken an act of God to get him to lead Wraith out there. When a guy lost nine men in a desert, he wasn't real anxious to go back. And he could tell by the look on Iliescu's face which country they were headed into. "Egypt."

"You'll land at El Gorah before heading out." The director telegraphed Leif an apology that didn't make it into his words. "There's been some serious abnormal weather activity. Word's been filtering back about an unusual acrid odor making people sick."

"Storm smell," Iskra said. "I noticed it at the village, too."

Iliescu nodded. "When we ran imaging, we were surprised at what we found." He looked to the side and told someone to put the image on the screen. A swath of brown stretched wide, as far as the eye could see.

"Where is this?" Leif asked, frowning.

"Just north of Aswan," Iliescu said.

"Aswan?" Leif barked a laugh. "I think you need new analysts. Aswan is an hour from the Nile. That area is—"

"There's a drought. Nobody thought anything of it until we put two and two together." Somber-faced, Iliescu hesitated. "I'm not sure what you'll find in the villages, but I can't stress enough after the fiasco in Burma how much we can't let whoever's behind this succeed again."

"Director," Leif said, "Mercy has seen this Andrew person in multiple places where the team has been. I think we need to follow up on that—she saw him in the village right before the landslide. You were sat-watching us. Can you run that back and do facial recs on him?"

Iliescu pointed to someone offscreen and nodded. "We'll get on it."

Leif swiveled his chair. "Any progress identifying the guys with Andrew at the facility or which route they took?"

"No luck at all—we have a clear shot on one, but it's like he doesn't exist."

"Which means someone doesn't want him found."

"Exactly," Iliescu said. "We're also trying to reverse-track using Peychinovich, check who he's been with, who visited him, who he visited."

Iskra sat forward, arms resting around her plate. "Pay particular attention to his German and Chinese contacts."

"You know something, Miss Todorova?"

She didn't shift or retreat. "Hristoff has spent a lot of time with both in the last year, and considering I encountered Rutger Hermanns in the salt mines and his lackey in Greece, I would say it's a safe bet."

Iliescu considered her for a moment, then bobbed his head. "Thanks for the tip. If you think of anything else, we'd appreciate the help. You saw what they're doing. They nearly took your life."

The words had an impact. She shrank against her seat.

"Metcalfe, once you're there, you'll have a SEAL team at your disposal, should you need it, as well as weapons and supplies necessary to find this Meteoroi and destroy it." Iliescu's tone was hard. "Understood?"

"Hooah," Lawe said.

"That's all for now." He met Leif's gaze. "Metcalfe, in private in five."

Nodding, Leif came out of his chair. He skirted the table and exited the conference room to find Cell coming toward him with a phone. "You missed a killer mud bath."

"That isn't as enticing as you'd think."

"Seriously? You like being the director's lapdog?"

"I am not a lapdog, but yes, I like what I do." Cell pivoted and started back to the comms center. He turned. "Private room is second on the left."

Leif headed that way, let himself in, and closed the door. The phone rang. "I'm here."

"We'll need to be careful with your rapid healing."

"Agreed." Leif touched his shoulder and detected no pain, just a dull ache. No loss in range of motion. He couldn't explain it, but it had been proven time and again that his body had a phenomenal healing rate. Even as a kid he'd healed fast, but since the Sahara Nine, the speed had been insane.

"How's Viorica? She do okay out there earlier?"

"She did." Leif sat in a chair in the corner, facing the door.

"Learning anything new about her?"

Besides that she was a good kisser? "Sibling—a brother. She last saw him a decade ago. Peychinovich bought V from her father when she was young. Kept her for himself, rapes her often. Then had a Kremlin agent train and torture her."

"She loyal to them? Should we question it?"

"Question it, yes. But *because* of him? Negative." Leif scratched his jaw. "I'm not sure what keeps her going back—she deftly avoided telling me why, but it's not him. She can't stand Peych. She's afraid to leave. Never succeeded before. Said that yacht incident with Vasily Kuznetsov was personal. That he betrayed Hristoff, too."

"With her?"

Leif hesitated. Why hadn't he thought of that? "I . . . I don't think so."

"Well, I've got a team investigating her history, digging deeper than before. Keeping her on the move is a good thing, I think. But if Peychinovich learns her whereabouts, things will get complicated."

"Agreed."

"You sure learned a lot in a short time."

"It's why you hired me, sir."

Iliescu grunted. "Just keep it clean, Metcalfe. If we can turn her, she'll be the most valuable asset we have."

"I think I'm offended, sir."

"Look." Iliescu's quieter tone made Leif's defenses slam up. "You okay going back to El Gorah?"

At least it's not Hurghada. "It makes sense—I know the people. They trust me. We might gather more intel there than in Burma for that reason."

"That's why I want you there." Iliescu huffed. "Look, I know it's not ideal, with the way Egypt affects you."

"I'm good."

Iliescu hesitated. "Okay. I trust you to keep it together, Leif. The team and I are depending on you to get ahead of this so we can stop chasing our butts and get the book back."

"Understood."

"Stay in touch."

"Roger that."

He ended the call and sat in the darkened room, alone with his thoughts. His misgivings. Not about the mission but . . . himself. In Egypt.

The mountain. The heat. The royal snafu in heading west instead of east. They'd had no idea of their location. Nobody could remember how they'd gotten there. Or what had caused the chopper to crash.

He roughed a hand over his face and sat back with a sigh. Leaned his head against the wall. Stared at the hull.

". . . Egypt affects you."

It did. Because he'd searched for answers and found none. Ten of them had fought their way out of the Shaiyb al-Banat mountains, fleeing into the Sahara Desert. He'd nearly died. Had it not been for the pararescue team doing training ops, he would've been buried in the sand with the great pharaohs. Nine of his team were.

Surviving that tortured him. Drove him nearly into the ground. Suicide had seemed a good option. But Canyon had convinced him that God wasn't through with him yet. Got him reinstated and assigned to El Gorah for cultural support. It was the first sign that maybe he should keep his feet this side of the grave. So he'd accepted the assignment. Kept his head down, despite the nightmares and paranoia. During his off hours, he trekked out to the desert. Searched for answers, for any sign of the missing pieces.

Because that was the bugger of it all. He never forgot anything. Except six months of his life.

TWENTY-SEVEN

NORTH BASE CAMP, EL GORAH, EGYPT

The wind was different here. Iskra followed the team off the jet, also noticing that more than the weather was different—so was Leif. They'd had an hour of downtime while the base arranged a van for their use. Quieter and withdrawn, Leif radiated an intensity she hadn't expected, even considering he was already one of the most intense men she'd met. One might not think so, when introduced to the gregarious, joke-telling sailor. But beneath his calm surface lurked a rip current. The team must have noticed, too, because nobody talked as they piled into a white unmarked van.

Leif climbed behind the wheel and adjusted the mirrors. No smile. No lighthearted banter. "We'll check the village, then RTB."

The van shot across the base, Leif negotiating the buildings and vehicles with the precision and skill of someone familiar with the area. The director had implied that in the briefing. Was that what all this anxiety was about?

Leif's credentials cleared them through the security checkpoint.

"How long were you out here?" Lawe asked from the front passenger seat.

"This was my duty station till two years ago. Spent the better part of three years out here."

"Why would anyone want to be here that long? It's too hot," Saito complained from the seat next to her as the topography shifted from a busy, thriving city to an angry desert.

"It's quiet," Leif said, his attention never leaving the road. "Gives you time to think."

Iskra eyed the brown-on-brown terrain that waited beyond the clutter of buildings and multistoried hotels. She thought of where she lived now, the estate that overlooked the river. Posh by most standards. Lush grounds. Looking at the desert, she couldn't help but wonder if she'd grown soft, spoiled, living in luxury.

It was a hard thought, considering *why* she lived there. And *lived* was a loose term. More like survived. Existed.

Regardless, the desert terrified her. The emptiness and heat. The lack of water, vegetation. Granted, the phenomenal history left her agape. Years ago, she'd visited the Valley of the Kings. Luxor. But . . . the barrenness was forbidding and cruel.

"So, I'm trying to understand." Culver squinted out the window. "We're worrying about a drought. In a desert."

"Most of Egypt is consumed by the Sahara Desert." Leif picked their way down a road that had more holes than concrete. "But there are cities and villages along the Nile that are lush and extremely profitable. It's really amazing what they produce here—you'd be surprised. And the seasons dictate what's produced.

"Main export is natural gas," he continued, hitting the wipers to wash a yellow film—pollen?—from the windshield. "But non-petroleum products like clothes, cotton textiles, and medical are also big. Then there's citrus fruits, rice . . ."

So was *this* home to Leif? "Sounds like you are fond of the area," Iskra said.

"I get stoked when people overcome adversity and thrive." And for the first time in the hour since they left the security of the base, his gaze drifted to the rearview mirror and met hers. She had adversity. Now if she could just conquer the "thrive" part.

They lumbered up over a rise, and what spread before them seemed like more of what they'd seen. But apparently not to Leif. The van coasted down a slight incline. Though the team chatted and laughed, Leif's silence felt deafening.

He veered to the side of the road and set the brake. Killed the engine. Climbed out, his mood weighted.

"We're here." Lawe shot them all a warning look. "Nice and easy."

Iskra left the safety and coolness of the van to join Leif.

He walked to a depression in the earth fifty feet to their left and squatted, scooping up the dirt. He smelled it. Dusted it off his hands. Elbows on his knees, he stared vacantly at the cracked earth. It spread outward in a streak of tan, reaching toward the shrubs and trees as if to siphon away whatever drop of water remained. Some of the greenery was wilting, smothered by the heat and lack of rain. An endless sea of sand and dirt. Tan everywhere.

Rubbing his fingers over his palm, Leif squinted across the open plain. This felt very private, his assessment of the land, so Iskra waited at the ridge and shielded her eyes from the sun.

"Talk to us, Chief." Lawe's voice was deep and concerned as he trudged over, the others circling up around him. Strange—they looked like a ragtag bunch until you considered the weapons and readiness in their stances. Their training didn't let them relax.

"This"—Leif pushed upright and raised his arm over the parched depression—"was a lake fed from a natural spring. It supplied the villages with potable water and irrigation for crops."

Shocked, Iskra scanned the area again, distressed for the people who had lost their water source. What had become of them?

"Doesn't bode well," Saito said quietly.

"No." Leif's jaw muscle jounced. "It doesn't." He focused on a spot in the distance.

"I get how they cloud seed to start rain, like in Burma," Peyton said, "but how do you *stop* rain?"

"Cloud seed in a nearby location to draw away the moisture," Mercy said. "That film on the windshield—"

"Silver iodide," Saito said. "China and Russia have been experimenting with it for years."

A plume of dust churned toward them. Sun glinted on something—metal. Maybe a windshield.

"Weapons," Leif instructed, his expression flipping from grieved to concerned. "Keep them close but out of sight." Next, he turned to Iskra, and a storm had taken up residence where she'd normally found confidence and lightheartedness. "Stay close."

She nodded, because this time his words felt more protective than controlling. "Trouble?"

The truck raced closer. Who was coming?

"Never can tell," he murmured.

"Army?" Lawe asked under his breath.

Shouts assailed the late afternoon, showering the team with uncertainty and tension, especially hearing the Arabic language.

"This doesn't look good," Saito said.

"It isn't," Leif replied. "Stay calm. Be ready. But let me handle this."

The truck vaulted over a slight incline. It landed violently, but the men poised in the back with AK-47s weren't fazed. When the old vehicle swept up to them, it spewed dust and dirt. Tiny grains of sand prickled Iskra's eyes and cheeks. She protected her face but heard the telltale thud of feet as the men bailed out of the back. Angry shouts drew closer.

Hands up as he moved in front of the team, Leif joined the din, repeating some phrase to the . . . soldiers? Rebels? They wore dingy clothes. No uniforms. But that didn't matter out here.

Two lanky shapes stormed toward Iskra.

"No," Leif barked, stepping between them and her, rattling off something in their tongue.

The darker of the men attempted to shove Leif aside. A bad move.

Leif was a flurry of motion. He caught the man's wrist, twisted it up and behind his arm, forcing the taller man to his knees with a shout. And in that split second, Leif had also disarmed him. He held up his weapon, his knee at the back of the man's neck. He shouted to the others, his expression implacable.

After a nod, he pushed up, freeing the man. Stepped back. Disassembled the weapon, dropping the pieces on the ground. He held up his palms again, talking much quieter but no less firmly.

He'd made a point. That he could defend his own, but he had no intention to cause harm. But he would if provoked. If his people were threatened. Leif knew the power he possessed. The abilities he had honed. Knew what he could successfully oppose. And he showed them, too.

Rifles snapped in Leif's direction, but he stared hard at a man who didn't even reach Iskra's five-nine height.

The shorter man jutted his jaw. "You think you big man?" he said in stilted English. "Leave and others like you come, destroy our lands. This—*this* is what you do?"

Leif kept his hands raised. "I didn't have anything to do with this."

They knew each other, but the association was an uneasy one.

"Come." The man motioned to the truck. "Chibale will deal with you."

Leif started. "Where is Ausar?"

The man curled a lip, then shouted to his men, waving them back to the vehicles.

Blunt force pitched Iskra forward. She stumbled, startled. Spun around.

Leif appeared between her and the tall lanky man, who drew back in surprise. The presence of two more people created a buffer around Iskra as Culver and Lawe herded Peyton and Mercy into protective custody as well.

"Easy, easy," Leif murmured, motioning with his hands.

The leader shouted something, and the man who'd started the confrontation trudged away, his attention leaving them only when distance forced it.

"Thought you knew these people," Mercy said as they returned to their vehicle, an escort of armed locals encircling the old van.

"I do." Leif glanced in the rearview mirror as they took an extremely leisurely pace into the village.

"Guess you forgot to mention they don't like you," Saito added.

Leif scanned their escort, weapons propped casually on their shoulders. "Not all of them."

On edge after the encounter by the dried lake, Leif slowly made his way up the road to the dozen or so mud homes circling a great pit. Dealing with Bes warned him things were worse than he'd expected. With the loss of a water source, he'd anticipated bad, but this—if Ausar wasn't the village chief anymore, then this was about to get interesting.

Thick-bellied Chibale sauntered out of the larger, more central hut, surrounded by a half dozen men and as many women. Children were shooed off to the fields.

Leif met each gaze, searching for not just familiarity but acceptance. Finding none, he focused on the apparent leader. He extended his hand in the customary greeting reserved for those not family or friends. Because he was definitely no longer a friend here. "*Salaam aleikum*, Chibale." He broke protocol by using the leader's first name, but he wasn't a stranger.

It would look poorly on Chibale if he did not return the greeting. Through tight lips, he said, "*Wa-aleikum salaam*." He gave the team a lengthy visual assessment, clearly denoting his displeasure. "You come without gifts," he continued in Arabic.

That was all leadership meant to Chibale—money, power—even when Ausar had been alive. "My gift," Leif countered, not cowed by this man, "is my presence. To find out what happened here."

"What happened is, men like you came. Made promises to Ausar."

"What about your brother?" Leif asked, noticing Baddar quietly translating for the team.

"Do you question me?" Chibale asked, squaring his shoulders and narrowing his eyes. He took a menacing step forward. "I am the one you deal with now. I—"

"Yes." Leif inclined his head, offering deference he did not feel. "I asked after Ausar because he was my friend."

"Where were you when these men come?" Chibale demanded,

motioning wildly with his arms. “When they say they have miracle for the soil? When they put this thing in the ground that drained our water?”

Heart thudding at the words, the intelligence Chibale unwittingly divulged, Leif let him finish. Let him speak his mind while Leif formulated his thoughts. He sensed the team’s restlessness as they picked up on the information, too, and what it meant.

“. . . Ausar is ill, and now you come back.” Chibale stomped, snapping out his hands. “For what? What good are you now?”

Leif started. “Ausar’s ill?” The words jarred him forward. “Is he ill because of what these men did?”

Chibale stared down his long, broad nose at him. “I will not speak—”

“Leif.” Iskra’s voice was soft, nearly a whisper on the wind that came louder than the accusations and assertions flooding the air.

He met her hazel-green gaze and was surprised when she nodded toward a hut. There stood a wraith-thin woman in faded cotton that hung to her ankles.

“Habiba.” But even as Leif moved forward, he knew his mistake.

Chibale leapt in front of him. Shoved Leif backward. “This is not your home! You have no place here. Go, leave—”

“He asks for him,” Habiba called over the shouting.

He? Leif’s hope surged. “Ausar?”

“Let him come.” Habiba lifted an achingly thin child into her arms.

Leif’s brain lagged, realizing the little one she now held was the baby she’d been pregnant with when he’d left.

When hands and objections fell away, Leif crossed the path and climbed the wooden stairs of the hut. Each step, however, pounded into him a dread that whatever the condition of his friend, it wasn’t good. What would he find?

Black-as-obsidian eyes met his as he reached Habiba.

“He’s alive?” he repeated in Arabic.

Her shift in expression warned him that his friend was alive, but not well.

He touched the child's back, smiling at Habiba. "You carried her in your belly when I was last here. What is her name?"

"Farid," Habiba said. "Ausar is very happy about her."

Leif smiled, but it faded as he angled toward the darkened interior of the one-room hut. A mattress hugged the far wall, away from the window. On it lay a stick-figure of a man, drawn, broken. Shriveled amid a sheet of white.

"You are jealous," came a raspy, dry voice from the shadows. It had aged, grown weaker, but the voice of his friend was undeniable and forced Leif closer as his vision adjusted to the dimness.

"You were always the better-looking one." Leif went to a knee. Light left a scant impression of his friend that shocked him. Leif ordered himself not to react, not to convey that Ausar was a ghost of the man he once knew. "You need to get up." He heard the grief in his voice and neutralized it. "Your brother is anxious to seize power."

"I fear," Ausar mumbled, his breath snatched by the effort of those two words, "he will get his wish . . . soon."

Silence padded the emptiness between them. Though it had been years since he'd left, there was no distance in their friendship. And it angered Leif that he hadn't been here. That he'd had no idea what was happening. That he had not protected them. "What happened, Ausar? Who came?"

"They come—" He seized, hunching his shoulders as he grabbed his side. A spot there glittered.

Glittered? Leif angled for more light. Not glittered—wet. Blood! A bloody wound caught the light of the lamp. He pitched forward and yanked back the blanket. "What happened?" he demanded as his friend let his hand fall away, revealing clothes soaked with blood. And merciful God—the stench! "Saito! Now!" he hollered over his shoulder to the team medic. He glanced at Habiba. "Who shot him?"

"No," Ausar breathed. "Leave her . . ."

Leif knelt again. "Tell me—is this from a gunshot?"

"They come. Insist we let them test our water." A sheen coated his face in the struggling light.

"Chief?" Saito asked cautiously.

Swiveling, Leif nodded to the injury, his hand resting on Ausar's arm. "Gunshot—infected. Possibly septic."

Saito shouldered out of his ruck, lowered to the ground, and went to work.

"We'll get you fixed up." Leif inched closer to the head of the cot. "Who was it, Ausar? Who were they?"

His friend grunted. Drew up his chin, arching away from Saito's initial prodding. "Soldiers. American."

The pronouncement was a sucker punch. "American," Leif repeated in disbelief. "You're sure? Did they give names?"

"The leader call himself—augh!" He jolted against Saito's ministrations, then fell limp.

Saito growled. "I need more light—the torch in my ruck."

After retrieving the small lamp, Leif twisted and pulled it. Light bloomed through the room and elicited a curse from Saito. The smell of antiseptic hit the air.

"He needs an evac."

Leif keyed his comms.

"Chief, I'll be honest . . ." Saito went quiet, shaking his head. "This is bad. Not sure I can—"

"Just do it. Make him better."

"Best thing we can do is pack the wound and get him to a hospital."

"Then do it. I'm not letting him—"

"Runt," Ausar muttered, his face sagging under the oppressive pain and infection. "Save them . . . children. Make . . . leave . . ." He went still, and Leif tensed.

"He's out," Saito said, packing the wound.

"Mercy," Leif called, moving to join Habiba outside the thin curtain that served as a door.

She sidled up.

"Call Iliescu. We need to get Ausar to a hospital and relocate this village."

"See what you have done?" Chibale yelled. "What you—"

Leif leapt off the stairs and charged toward Chibale. "Why did you not get him help?" he asked in Arabic. "Why are you letting him die? Is that how you care for your people? Is that how you take care of those who depend on you?"

Chibale skidded a nervous glance around. "He would not leave. He refused."

"If you want to be a leader, then you *make* those depending on you understand why it's to their benefit that they leave. If you don't get them out of here, Chibale, they will die of starvation."

"Other villages will not take us. To them, we are cursed because we let Colonel Nesto do this." Chibale looked very much like the little brother to the real leader of this village.

"Nesto." Leif let his brain catch up. "Is that who came?"

"Not him," Chibale said, "but the soldiers, the colonel send them."

"Runt." Lawe touched his mic. "Water and supplies from El Gorah are en route."

Glad Lawe had taken care of that without being ordered to, Leif nodded. "Good. Thanks." Overwhelmed, he turned to Chibale.

"They promised to make our water more clean." Chibale's attitude was different from their initial confrontation. "We give them our trust. The rains stopped a week after the machine. In a month, the lake is dry. They come to take the machine, but Ausar argued with them. Told them to leave. Go away. We fight and they leave. But Ausar was shot." The whites of the man's eyes went red. "He would not leave. Said they would come back and he must be here to protect us."

Leif clamped a hand on Chibale's shoulder, speaking volumes without a word. Then he stilled. "Wait. The machine—it's still here?"

"In the field. By the well."

"Show me."

TWENTY-EIGHT

TWO HOURS SOUTH OF EL GORAH, EGYPT

Heading down the path that led away from the homes to the long fields, Leif thrummed. If they could find—

"Chief!"

He turned, searching for Lawe among those who had followed him down the dusty path that circled the parched fields.

The big guy stood to the side, pointing to Chibale, who had a cell phone to his ear. Not just a cell phone, but a *satellite* phone.

"What is that?" Leif growled, storming toward him, facts rolling in on top of one another.

Chibale's face fell. He shook his head. Lowered the phone. "They say they come."

Leif frowned. They? Who?

"Now."

As if on cue, a repetitive *thwump* sailed through the air, rattling eardrums and the ground. Leif checked the sky and found the black dot.

"Medical?" Culver asked.

"Not enough time to scramble, get airborne, and be this close."

"Then—"

"Go!" Leif threw himself down the path, sprinting for all he was worth to get that machine before the chopper did. Chibale was with him, hoofing it to the well. They broke off the path and shoved through the dried-up husks in the fields.

"There! There!" Chibale shouted, stabbing a dark finger at Leif's two-o'clock position. Leif diverted in that direction, leaping and sailing over as many of the waist-high stalks as he could. It was tougher than one might think, trying to barrel through a dried-up wheat or corn field. He couldn't remember which had been planted here, and he wasn't a farmer who could tell from the brown shafts.

He leapt over a depression and landed near the stone encasement of the well, once fed by a natural spring. At the same moment, he registered the sign jutting up from the cracked earth. LAND MINE. In the very middle of the field lay a metal orb the size of a football, its sides a network of octagon panels. Dust caked it.

A curse fought Leif's restraint even as he heard the frantic approach of Chibale. The leader skidded to a halt, and their gazes met, revealing guilt in Chibale's eyes. Or was it disappointment that Leif hadn't been blown apart?

"You knew about this," he said.

Chibale faltered.

"Do you know a safe path in?"

"I-I do not."

Leif swiped a hand over his face. When the others appeared, he threw out a hand. "Land mines!"

Devine didn't flinch, shrugging out of her pack. She swung her weapon around and detached the scope. "Thermal." She motioned like she was going to toss it. "Mines warm the sand around them."

She'd better know how to throw well. He nodded, and the scope went airborne. He caught it and put it to his eye. The field altered before him into a multicolored schematic, revealing not two inches from his right boot a bloom of red. He muttered a curse, realizing how close he'd come to losing a leg, if not his life.

He swept around to be sure there weren't more near his feet, then stepped into the field, keeping to the darker colors, until he reached the orb. Squatting, he eyed the orb to determine if it was rigged with a pressure plate underneath.

"What're you waiting for?" Lawe growled.

"I can't tell if it's on a plate."

"One way to find out."

Right. He checked one more time with the scope before pocketing it. He reached for the orb, surprised at the way it vibrated and hummed. What was that thrumming? Electricity?

"Uh, Runt?" Mercy was watching the sky.

No. Not the sky. The chopper marring the blue expanse. From its belly birthed a plume of smoke.

"Missile!" Lawe shouted, waving everyone to the village. "Go!"

Resisting the urge to run, Leif placed the scope against his eye again. Picked his way through the field with careful but hurried steps. Death by mine and death by missile weren't in his plans for the day.

Searing heat rushed over him as the missile screamed toward its target. He sprinted, using his toes to sprint faster and faster.

The missile impacted with a heavy thump. A shockwave punched his back. It violently smacked his ears, making them ring. Heat seared his spine. His legs lifted, carried him up and over. He thudded into the ground, knocking the air from his lungs. Leif arched his back, groaning. Turned onto all fours.

Warbling sounds reached him through the ringing in his ears. Adrenaline shoved him up. Safety—get to cover. A split-second recon told him he was alone. He couldn't see the others. Couldn't see . . . anyone. Being in the open field made him a sitting duck. He spun back toward the village, only to see the huge black hull of the gunship bearing down on him.

The orb! Where was the orb?

He glanced around, his hearing hollow. Disoriented, he tried to shake it off. Blinked against the cloud of dirt. Searched the ground. Light flashed on the orb to his three. He dove for it.

Ground spit and chewed at him as he hooked it into an arm hold. Bullets!

He low-crawled, hugging the orb and hoping against reality that the chopper couldn't see him. They had the advantage in the air. He had the *dis*advantage of his ears still being plugged. He shimmied through the stalks, trying to avoid as many as possible so he didn't create a swaying pattern that would give him away. The ground didn't seem to be vibrating as hard. Peering up revealed nothing but tan stalks and blue sky. Staying eyes out, he dragged his ruck around. Retrieved his gun and set the orb inside.

Weapon ready, he eased up, scanning. Where was the helo? It'd either swung around for another run or left. Maybe they were convinced they'd destroyed the orb. Job done. Head home.

A guy could hope.

He pushed up to a knee. The chopper careened over a hill, heading straight for him.

Leif shoved himself down, feeling the weight of the orb against his back. Weapon across his forearms, he scrambled in a low-crawl away from that position. Dirt and stalks spit at him. Bullets chewed up the land.

A trail seared his arm, narrowly missing his weapon, not to mention his elbow and main artery. As soon as the vibrating thunder dissipated, Leif punched to his feet and sprinted toward his only chance for cover and survival—the village.

Each step felt like kneading dough. He dug in. Shoved off. But the adrenaline made his legs rubbery. His heart rate amped. The Black Hawk arced around, and the gunner in the jump seat was ready.

Leif dove into the field. The stalks jerked violently beneath the spray of cannon fire.

Knowing his ruck would be a dead giveaway, he shifted onto his side. Used his feet to push him through the rows, keeping his gaze and muzzle skyward. As the belly of the beast buzzed the ground, he took aim, waiting . . . waiting . . . until he saw the gunner. And fired a short burst.

The shooting stopped. Had he actually hit the gunner?

The chopper veered up, then dove straight back down.

Great. Tick 'em off. Make 'em really *want to kill you.* Nothing like a little added pressure.

He threw himself backward. Smacked his head against something hard—and his eardrums popped. Blinding pain exploded in his skull. He buried his face, hunching his shoulders against the searing. When he could think through it, his vision snagged on a dark blur. He squinted through the dust and stalks. Something moved. Was it the orb? No, he still felt it against his spine. What was out there, then? It was small. Moving away or closer?

He watched. Felt the violent wash of the rotors, but something told him to focus on the blur. Blinking to clear his vision, he realized the blur was moving away. Then the shape came into focus. A face.

A small, round face with terrified, marble-black eyes.

Farid. *Out here alone?*

Where was Habiba? Leif scrabbled toward the little girl, doing his best to keep his movements controlled yet fast. In his panic, he couldn't betray his postion. Or hers.

The thunder returned, leaves snapping violently beneath the rotor wash and bullets. Though he couldn't hear Farid, he saw her face screwed tight in terror. Tears gouging rivulets down her dusty cheeks. Mouth wide in silent screams. She wriggled away from him.

The chopper! Her movements—

God, please—no! The chopper would hit her, thinking it was him.

Leif shot forward. Erased the last fifteen yards between them. Hauled Farid into his arms, undone when he felt her trembling sobs against his chest. He scuttled away from that spot, knowing their only chance was to beat the enemy. Outrun the chopper.

He really had lost his mind.

Weapon in one hand, Farid in the other arm, he loped sideways through the stalks. He had no idea if his comms were working because he couldn't hear over her wails. Skeletal legs clung to him but weren't enough, so he had to hold her as he shuffled through the field.

It'd be great if the chopper gave up. "Nothing to see here. I'm not the rogue operator you're gunning for."

But the big black bird swung right at him. He didn't want to shoot it down and have it crash in the village—not that he had artillery big enough to take it down. But he could try to hit the pilot. Or the gunners. He couldn't lie down and let them rip his—or Farid's—life away. Bullets made tiny explosions in the dusty earth, beelining straight toward his boots.

Crap crap crap. He sprinted, clutching Farid.

Something thumped his boot. The unmistakable chill of the chopper blotting out the sun felt too ominous. It streaked overhead.

Munitions sprayed from its underside. Dirt vomited around him. Peppered his cheeks. He ducked, covering Farid. Praying nothing hit her. She'd gone rigid. Leif blinked. Aimed and fired. Sparks flew off the helo's hull in several directions.

The gunship veered away.

As the thunder receded, he dropped to his knees. Surveyed Farid. Verified she was alive. Unharmed—as much as could be. Then he clambered to his feet, legs rubbery. He slung his weapon crossbody, because he had more precious cargo to protect. Curling himself around Farid, he made for the village. Sprinted for all he was worth. Lawe and Culver were taking a bead on the gunship. Vultures circling for the kill.

Someone lay on a roof. He smiled at the Devine intervention.

Peyton fired. The chopper's windshield cracked. Splintered. They veered off again, this time in a wide arc. Tail tucked. Running.

Leif slowed to a trot then a walk. Resisted the urge to collapse to his knees. Out of exhaustion, not relief. But Farid's renewed shrieks matched those coming from the village and forced him on. Several huts were missing chunks of wall and thatch. Bodies littered the road. Including Habiba's.

Chibale came toward him, pale despite his dark skin. Expression wrought, he reached for little Farid, who lunged into her uncle's arms. "Ausar is dead."

Leif shuddered to a stop. "No," he breathed, looking at the hut where Saito sat on the step, head in his hands. "I'm sorry, Chibale."

"You are a better man than me. He was a better man."

That was true. But saying it wouldn't help. He could steer the new village chief in the right direction, though. "Honor your brother," Leif said. "Be the leader he knew you could be."

Chibale started. Then agreed as he handed Farid off to one of the women. "You found the machine?"

Leif nodded.

"Think the crops will grow now?"

"Not this year. And if they return, it will not be pretty." Could he ever convince them to leave their homeland? "I can talk to my people, see if we can get a team out here to assess the water and soil. See if any of this can be reversed."

"It would be very good of you, Runt."

He wasn't sure what to say. Chibale had always been set against him and Western influence. "I'll make it happen."

Never in her life had she watched something so heartrending. The team had rushed her back to the relative safety of the village, nobody sure where Leif had gone after collecting the orb—and that had been terrifying to watch, Leif with the scope tucked to his eye and picking his way across the minefield. She'd anticipated a loud explosion with each step he took. But he'd trusted the woman who'd tossed him the scope. Followed her instructions. And retrieved the orb.

Then things went crazy.

Her heart still hadn't settled. He'd delivered the child to her family, talked with the man who would lead this village, then turned. And looked right at her. Right into her soul.

She wanted to hug him. Kiss him. All out of relief that he'd survived. But it was stupid. She had survived worse. He probably had, too. Yet she still wanted to do it. It was just emotion. A reaction to a situation that had nearly gutted her, expecting each pass of the helicopter to kill him. But he was alive. Scratched up, but alive. Those blue eyes reaching for her, it seemed, the way the child had reached for her uncle.

She ached to go to him. Wrap her arms around him.

But that wasn't her place. He wasn't hers. And what would happen if she opened not only her arms but also her heart?

He'll die.

Iskra hugged herself, hand over her mouth. Choking back the buzzing in her veins. She hadn't made that perilous journey with the little girl, but it felt like she had. Because that little girl, in her mind, was Bisera.

Would Leif do that for Bisera? Would he crawl through a minefield, fight an attack chopper, and get her to safety?

Don't be foolish, Iskra. Men cannot be trusted.

But Leif could. The team trusted him to make it to safety with the child. Told her to wait. That he'd be angry if she went out. That she'd just be another worry or body to retrieve. She resented their lack of confidence in her abilities, but in all honesty, she wasn't sure she would have been as strong or as successful as he'd been.

The men clustered around Leif, patting his shoulder. Saito checked Leif's arm—he must've been scratched up bad. The sniper came down from the roof, and Leif congratulated her. Hugged her.

It became too much. Iskra turned away. Wandered the road that led out of the village. She wanted out. Wanted to get away. She was toeing a dangerous line. One that could rip out her soul.

But she tasted something in the air here. Something that bred off the fight from the last hour for the survival of this village and its people. Of Leif and that little girl.

Hope.

It teased her. Taunted her. Dared her to step from her cocoon and lay everything at his feet. She scoffed. The boots of a man—

Who had just stepped in front of her. Her thoughts embarrassed her, forbidding her to look up at him. She stared at his dirt-caked boots, surprised to see a hole in them. "I . . ."

"You okay?" he asked, his voice thick.

"Yeah, sure." She nodded.

"Then why are you crying?"

She wiped at her cheeks before she realized what she was doing. Before she realized he was right. "I'm fine."

"Iskra." He inched closer. Touched her shoulder.

"Chief, our ride's inbound," the brawny guy called. "Chibale wants to talk."

Leif muttered something, then squeezed her arm. "I have to deal with this." And he left.

Minutes later, as the chopper approached, the children and women screamed, running to shelter, fearing another attack.

But the helicopter, which had been called to take the now-dead chief to the hospital, landed without incident. Medical personnel rushed to assist the injured villagers into the bird. There was so much grief here. It weighted Iskra's limbs, her thoughts. She watched, mute, as people were loaded up and another chopper approached, this one to ferry the team back to the base.

Robotically, she obeyed the big-chested guy who directed her onto the nylon strap seat along with the others. Leif sat across from her. Touched her knee. But she ignored him.

She couldn't do it. Couldn't trust him—not with Bisera's life.

He swatted her knee again. This time, she saw the blood on his shirt. The torn sleeve. His flesh grazed. The scar. He rotated his forearm, as if trying to shrug off the attention it had drawn.

She shoved her gaze out the door to the desert. In the far distance glowed a pyramid. On the other side, the Nile. Soon, that gave way to city lights. Then the base, where a team brought them to another building. There, the orb was taken into custody, and they were debriefed. Four mind-numbing hours that allowed her to recover from a near-lapse in judgment.

Afterward, Iskra headed to the showers and savored the hot spray that only lasted a few minutes. They definitely didn't want soldiers lingering. But she couldn't keep her mind from returning to the sight of Leif and that little girl.

Anguish rose in her, aching for him to carry Bisera to safety. But that was left to her. Nobody else would care. Nobody would fight for Bisera like Iskra. Nobody would understand. Wanting to be alone with her misery, she dressed and went to her bunk. The lonely white halls were—gratefully—empty and seemed to escort Iskra to her room's solitude.

Except there was no solitude. Mercy and Leif stood by the small metal desk, whispering back and forth. The glow of a tablet washed over their faces, defiant against the sunlight restrained by plastic blinds. Their unrepentant expressions struck her. Had Iskra not seen her empty water bottle from earlier, she would have figured she had the wrong room.

Mercy came toward her, touched Iskra's shoulder, then left without a word, which seemed ominous.

Fist to his mouth, Leif touched the electronic screen.

"I thought you were supposed to be resting," she said softly, playfully—nervously. Clearly something on that tablet had brought them both here.

He shifted toward her, and a storm hung in his eyes. A dark, terrible storm. He planted his hands on his belt. "What is it—the trade?"

Iskra frowned, confused. "The what?"

"The *trade*," he repeated, his voice firmer, sharper. "You give them the book, and what do you get?"

Cold dread rushed across her shoulders and threw her gaze back to the device. What had he found? Why was he asking? Why did he even care? She eyed him, mind reaching, scrambling. The trade.

With purpose and intention, he picked up the tablet and held it out to her, almost defying her to look at it.

"You're angry," she realized, surprised. Scared.

He clenched his jaw, the muscle popping.

She reached for the device and forced herself to look at the screen. An inbox waited—and with it came roiling nausea. "She hacked my email." But even as she said it, heard there was no animosity in her words, she noted the newest email. From Lesya. And it had been opened.

Objection poised on her tongue. She swallowed it. Maybe this was for the best. Maybe . . .

Don't be a fool!

She skated a glance at Leif, who hadn't moved. His presence smothered her defiance, but she refused to cower. Not in front of him. She opened the email.

A video sprang to life. Her heart skipped a beat as the setting came into sharp focus—the estate. Someone holding a camera walked through the halls of the residence apartments. That was her wing to the right. Straight ahead, Hristoff's. As soon as the person aimed left toward the two large suites, she couldn't breathe. The first was an apartment for Lesya and her secretary, Duscha. The second for—

When they bypassed the first, Iskra let out a tremulous breath.

Duscha stood there, frantic and terrified. *"These rooms are private—"*

"Do not tell me about my own home!" The voice came from behind the camera—was Hristoff filming? *"Now, where is she?"*

"I don't know what you are talking about."

"Tell me or I will beat it out of you!"

"I don't—"

"Sir, there!"

The camera spun toward the door, and a blur rushed through the hall.

Since Iskra was on mission, there was only one "she" Hristoff would be looking for—Bisera.

"No no no." Iskra watched helplessly as the blur—Lesya—darted down the marble hall.

"Give her to me!" Hristoff roared. He stalked ahead of the camera, his strides long and powerful. His frame seemed preternaturally large. Terrifying.

The camera was high—same height as Hristoff, which meant it must be Ruslan following. The pace slowed and stopped jarring, blurring, revealing the horrible truth—the small child Lesya carried to safety. But there was no safety from Hristoff's rage. Only pain.

Lesya collided with a bulky man—Maksim had appeared from a side door. She screamed. *"No, you've hurt her enough already."* Twisting away but not breaking free, she aimed her begging at Hristoff. *"Please!"*

No. He wouldn't hurt Bisera. The thought rattled through Iskra, shaking loose her courage and confidence. He protected his property. "He wouldn't," she breathed. It had been her one morsel of sanity, knowing he didn't injure what was his.

Hristoff lunged toward Lesya. Snatched a shrieking Bisera from her.

Iskra sucked in a breath. Covered her mouth. *No no no.* Tears ran down her cheeks. She blinked them away, furious with how they blurred her vision. This was a mistake. "A mistake. No, he . . ." He wouldn't.

But he is! It's right there!

Hristoff backhanded Lesya, sending her sprawling into a marble column. The sound of her head hitting was hollow and violent. She collapsed, unmoving.

Iskra choked on a gasp. Froze, unable to take her eyes from Bisera now cowering on the floor. "No," she gulped.

Innocent wails filled her ears as Hristoff motioned for the camera to face him and display his fury. *"See what happens, Iskra? See what you have done? Look at her!"* He pinched Bisera's round face between his thumb and fingers. *"Look what you've done, running off with that American."* Bisera's brilliant little face was blotched with cuts and bruises.

A strangled cry clawed through Iskra. Fury churned through her, rising and growing. "I will kill him," she growled through her sobs. Though she tried to look away, she couldn't. She could not let go of the tablet, of her terrible failure. That precious baby girl!

She pitched the tablet on the bed and spun away. Buried her face in her hands. She'd waited too long. She should've gone with him in Turkey. Should've—

"I think it's time you came home. Don't you? We wouldn't want any accidents to happen, would we?"

His words reached through the device and gripped her throat. Because they weren't just words. They were a promise. She collapsed against the wall. All these years . . . all her hard work . . . all her plans . . .

Leif approached.

"No!" she barked, holding out a palm. She shook her head, a sob choking her. "Stay there."

It was too late. He wouldn't be the one to carry Bisera to safety. He couldn't. Why had she even entertained the insidious belief that there was hope? That Bisera would be safe?

I have to go back. Placate Hristoff. Do whatever he wanted. For Bisera. She had to.

"Hey . . ." Leif came closer.

She threw herself at him. "You!" she growled through gritted teeth. "Stay away from me! Get back! This is your fault!"

"How do you figure?" he demanded.

"Because of you—" She couldn't finish it. Couldn't think. Couldn't see past the tears.

"Iskra—"

"No! Do not . . ." The grief was too much. She'd hoped. Fool that she was, she'd hoped. And been crushed. Again. She held her palm out to him again as an agonizing sob seized her. "Just . . . don't . . . talk." Eyes burning and thick with tears, she glared. "Ever again." She should never have let herself believe . . . "I believed—"

"What? What did—"

"*You.* That you were different. That you could—" She pressed the back of her hand to her mouth. Something ripped through his expression and shattered the thin veneer holding her together. Grief turned to fear. To anger. "I hate you."

"Iskra, that's not fair."

"*Life* isn't fair. I hate you. I hate everything you represent. Everything you—"

He came forward.

"Stay—"

But he came.

She shoved him back.

He rebounded.

"Get back! Get away! Never aga—" A wail cut off her raging, but she still had fists. She punched him. Slapped. "I hate you! Hate you!"

He deflected.

Her fists pounded his chest. "If you hadn't been at the facility, if you hadn't come to the club and the hotel, tempted me to run—"

Leif caught her wrists. Held them. Drove them behind her—but gently.

Which only fueled her rage. She writhed, bucked. Thought of Bisera being hit by that monster. Because Iskra had left her there.

"No," she moaned. The things he'd do . . . "No. No no . . ."

Everything she'd worked for was collapsing.

Iskra's full weight sagged against him. Surprised, Leif hooked an arm around her shoulders for support, both physical and moral. Uncertain what to say, he held her. Sobs shook her lithe frame, her tears drenching his tactical shirt.

Her words had blown him away. Cut him to the core. He struggled to understand, to fathom what she had been through. What terrors had carved her into the woman in his arms. Out of his depth, Leif cupped her head against his chest. Searched for a perfect phrase or words that would reassure her, but after that video, everything *he* believed had upended.

And then, as quickly as Iskra had collapsed into tears, she was straightening. Shaking from the violence of her reaction. Gaze down, she pulled her shoulders square. Shuddered through breaths. Her fingers uncoiled from his shirt, leaving a hand on his chest and one on his arm. A long, tremored breath closed her eyes.

He wasn't willing to let go. Not yet. And it seemed she wasn't either.

Though he had an instinct to pull her close again, he knew she'd resist.

"She's what you wanted to trade," he managed. "The girl—your daughter for the book."

TWENTY-NINE

NORTH BASE CAMP, EL GORAH, EGYPT

"You want freedom." Leif's ominously quiet voice was tinged with an edge, "for you and your daughter."

"No," she said with more vehemence than she'd intended. Then she laughed. "Not for me." Nobody could understand. Not even the noble Leif Metcalfe with his perfect manners and heroic character. Though he'd try.

When only silence hung in the air, when he didn't ask her to clarify, she glanced at him. Something in his pale eyes tore at her, tugged on loose threads attached to her control, her entire life. One more tug and . . .

She shoved off the wall, moving away from him and the vulnerability he seemed to siphon from deep within her soul.

"Why not for you?" he asked. "Your daughter needs you."

"She doesn't need me." She wiped her nose.

"How can you say that? Look what he did—"

"He wasn't supposed to—" She bit off the words. "Hristoff protects what's his." *You sound idiotic.* Iskra shrugged, trying to avoid the images that played havoc in her mind. But all she could see was Bisera's terrified, tear-stained face. The cuts. Bruises. All she could hear were those pitiful cries and heartrending shrieks. What nightmare had she been experiencing because Iskra was gone?

That question pushed Iskra onto the vinyl mattress, and she covered her mouth. As if she could stifle the grief. As if she could keep it in. She'd been keeping it in for so long.

Leif knelt before her. "Iskra, help me understand."

"Help *you* understand? How—when *I* don't understand?" She shook her head, looking down again. "He wasn't supposed to—it's worked. It's worked all this time."

"What's worked?"

"Hristoff protects what he sees as his." She hugged herself tightly. "I shouldn't have run with you in Turkey." She'd made a fatal decision there. She'd been weak. Desperate. "If I had gone back with him, she would be okay."

"But for how long? Iskra, this isn't going away. You have to do something. For you and your daughter."

"Bisera has a chance," she conceded. "If I can get back there with the USB—"

Leif screwed up his face. "You seriously think handing him that corrupted USB will buy freedom for you two? He's not the type of man to let things go, especially not—"

"*Don't* think you know anything about him or me."

"I know his kind, Iskra. I've fought them."

She gave a morbid laugh. "Not Hristoff—you haven't faced him. Trust me, you'll lose. Every time." She'd blamed Leif, but she needed to blame herself. How could she have thought *anyone* would make a difference? Mean a different outcome? "I need to go back."

"I thought you intended to work with Veratti."

"There is no time—going to Veratti uses up whatever time Bisera has left. The corrupted scans will appease Hristoff, buy me a chance to get her out." Yes, this could work. She touched her forehead, planning. Hristoff would see it. He'd understand she hadn't betrayed him. See that she'd brought him something priceless. "Then, once I get the book back, I'll find Veratti. Somehow. Get Bisera to safety." She nodded, convincing herself. "It's the only way."

"You're not that stupid."

His words seared like a hot dagger, running through her armor and straight into her thundering heart. "Obviously I am," she growled, "because I'm here with you instead of back there where I can do something. Keep Hristoff distracted. Happy."

Revulsion washed through Leif's face, and he drew back, shaking his head. "How long? How long have you been living like that?"

"When haven't I?" She laughed, but it was empty. "And it never changes." She could feel venom heating her words. "Every man wants the same thing, and when he's done, when he's gotten what he wants, he's gone. Finds a new adventure."

"Is that what I am now?"

She lifted her chin. Shrugged.

"So I've gone from the one man who tempted you to hope, to being relegated to 'every man'?"

"You are every man, because Hristoff will kill you like the others."

"Others." His eyebrows rose. "Wow. How many have you—"

She slapped him.

He surged closer. "*That*—that wasn't the slap of someone who just sees me as 'every man.'"

She swallowed. Rose and stepped away, too startled that he'd again homed in on her true feelings. That line of conversation wasn't doing anyone—especially her—any good. "I . . . I must go back. It's the only way Bisera will be safe."

"*Safe?*" His eyes flared. "Listen to yourself. How does this even make sense to you?"

"It is the only sense that exists," she hissed. "What would you tell me to do? Escape? Run with her?"

"Yes!"

"I *tried*." She tugged aside her shirt, revealing the scar along her shoulder. "He taught me a lesson. Is this"—she stabbed a finger at the discolored flesh—"what you want for a child? Is that what I'm supposed to give Bisera? Tell me, Leif. You've already called me stupid. You've already said I'm not making sense. Tell me what I'm supposed to do!" Her screams bounced off the walls, smacking back to her and loosing tears. "Because I'll do it. I've tried! Tried everything!" In the silence after her railing, she sagged. Saw the disgust on his face. "You think me a demon to leave a child with him."

"I don't," Leif said, frowning.

She didn't want his sympathy. Or his chastisement. "Just . . ." She drew in a shaky breath, her throat raw. "I . . . I have a plan. So I have to go back."

"Peychinovich just beat the crap out of your daughter, and you think he's going to listen to anything you say?" Leif shoved a hand through his hair.

"I know how to placate him." She disembodied herself from the words. From the repulsive truth.

"No," he said definitively. "No more of that."

"I appreciate your testosterone-laden heroism, but I will do what I have to so Bisera has a chance for a good life. I have a plan. It'll . . . work." She hated her own uncertainty.

"For how long?" he challenged.

"I don't need long." She tried to convince herself that she could do anything for a while. "I have a friend," she finally explained. "She'll take the child. Hide her."

"I'll help."

Iskra started. Toed the edges of that dangerous line again.

"Just one thing." His tone was soft. His gaze was soft. His touch was soft as he traced her face and jaw, vibrating jitters through every nerve in her body. "Tell me why you don't call her your daughter."

She sniffed.

"You call her 'Bisera,' 'child,' and 'little girl,' but I've never heard you say 'my daughter.'"

"I've spoken of her, what, two, three times?" she scoffed. "And you're making a judgment—"

"Maybe she's not really your daughter."

Fury erupted through her. "Of—"

"But you've perfected the art of *not feeling*, so I think she *is* your daughter." He thumbed his jaw. "Owning her like that, using the words 'my daughter,' makes it personal. Affirms that connection. But you keep everyone at bay. You refuse help from people because they'll fail you one way or another. Deny attachments because they only mean one of two things: a threat against your person, or that you present danger to them."

She should not be surprised—he had read her soul since they first met. But this was insanely accurate. "So not only heroic but a psychologist, too?"

"I know what it looks like because I've lived it, too."

And another surprise. He was racking them up today. What did he mean, he'd lived it? "I really doubt that."

He stepped closer. "Why do you think I know you so well?"

"You have my dossier."

"Ancillary details not connected to your character." Inching forward, he smirked. "Let me help, Iskra. Let me do that for you."

It was hard to think with his nearness. He'd erased all proper distance, making her acutely aware of his presence. His eyes and their earnestness. His lips and the promises they spoke. His hands and the way he'd saved her in the ocean, held her in Burma. Brought that child to safety in Egypt. The memory staggered through her resistance. His gaze bounced around her face, probing the depths of her soul.

"Why?" she asked, swallowing. Wishing—despite the gravity of their conversation—to kiss him again.

He angled in, and she realized they were having the same thoughts, the same difficulty with those thoughts. "Because." His breath whispered at the edge of her mouth. "We make a good team. We're on the same wavelength."

Could he hear the unsteady cadence of her breathing? Of her heart? Her defiant heart that said she couldn't trust him. *Was* he like every other man who'd wanted *this* from her, then vanished?

Therein lies your out. Distraction was easy. Effective. He wanted to help. Wanted to believe he could do what no man had done before.

"How?" she asked.

The tension in his brow surrendered, like storm clouds giving way to sunshine. "I promise you," he said, words taut with conviction and—oh mercy!—attraction as his hand landed on her waist, "we'll figure it out. Together. Get you out. *Both* of you, Iskra." He leaned forward, their noses touching. "Both."

Curse her body and its reaction—mouth opening as he spoke. Tasting his words. She berated herself. He would only repeat the words if he didn't believe them. Or if he thought *she* didn't believe him. "Not fair," she whispered, "using my weakness against me."

His hand slid around her waist. "Am I your weakness?"

He was. Had been from the start. It was a side of her—the weaker, *less* side—that felt a stirring of giddiness at the way he looked at her now, his longing obvious. But also at the words he'd spoken. The injection of that accursed hope. At the ridiculous notion she could actually be free. That Leif was different.

He's not. Distract and desert, Delilah.

The tingle of his whiskers against the edge of her lip made her pull in a breath. And she hated herself for it. He was distracting *her*, his touch hot against her waist. His lips searching for a landing.

But she already had her own plan. Deviating meant risking all she'd worked for. That couldn't happen. Bisera *had* to be free.

Trust him, Iskra. He's better than the others.

Maybe. But if she was wrong? If it was merely attraction to the man who had her nearly pinned to the wall, was it worth Bisera's freedom?

"I saw you rescue that little girl," she said.

He searched her eyes.

"I wanted so badly for that to be Bisera you were rescuing."

A hesitant frown flicked through his handsome features.

"So . . . yeah." She cupped his face. Rose on her tiptoes. And kissed him.

He tensed. But Iskra lingered, surprised at the magnetism that shocked her system, syncing them. His mouth captured hers, and she arched into him, circling her arms around his shoulders. He caved. His hands spread to the small of her back, tugging her closer as he deepened the kiss. He was electric. Different, beautiful. Strong. Intense—but also kind. Honest. Funny.

He moaned, but then it turned to a growl. He jerked back. Fingers locked behind his head, he turned away.

Bereft of his touch, Iskra swallowed. *What are you doing? You were just supposed to distract him. Not offer him what Valery took.* Her cheeks heated, stunned by herself.

"I won't—" His voice cracked, and he faced her. "Sorry."

"Sorry?"

"I think we both had an ulterior motive that just backfired on us."

The truth startled her. She lowered her head. "Guess it wasn't good enough. You jerked away pretty hard."

He rumbled a laugh. "That was because—first, kissing you is like falling into the ocean—almost no chance of getting out alive."

Wow. That was some compliment.

"Second, I want you to believe that when we kiss, it's not because I want to sleep with you. I mean—yes, that's where that act starts, but . . ." He shoved a hand over his shorn hair. "I'm screwing this up."

"If that's not what you want, what *do* you want, Leif?"

Sincerity tugged at his features. "To reach you, Iskra. The real you. Not Viorica." He shrugged. "When you look at me, I see the wounds that keep *her* at the forefront. I see the frightened girl who thinks she only has one way to get what she wants." He pointed to the mattress. "The woman crying after seeing her daughter beaten? *That*'s Iskra Todorova. I want *her*."

They'd only known each other for a short time. And he expected a person she barely recognized anymore to show up in his arms?

"I know the entire basis of what we have has been embroiled in opposition and confrontation, but"—he let out a sigh and shook his head—"I want you to trust me."

"Trust is overrated." She hated the acid in her words, but it kept her alive.

"Trust is vital," he countered, "especially if we're going to get you and your daughter to safety. Or are you too selfish to try?"

"For her—*everything* I do is for Bisera."

After another smirk, she realized his point: she still hadn't called Bisera her daughter.

"Runt." Mercy appeared at the door. "They've got something. We need you in the briefing room. I think they're going to send us out."

"The orb," Braun said from the live feed as the team gathered, "is sophisticated. We've never seen anything like it. What we can decipher is that it has a receiver and a transponder."

Leif groaned, his thoughts echoed by Lawe. Admittedly, it was hard to yank his mind out of the conversation—and that kiss!—with Iskra. But if they were going to defeat ArC and its psychos, he had to get his head in the game.

"That means, as you're already guessing, that it can receive and send information, but it's not the *origination* device. That's what we need to find. Where is the device communicating with it, the one delivering the silver iodide? And who's controlling it? Who came up with it?" Braun looked to Iskra, eyebrows raised.

"That I do not know. I only heard the conversation once," Iskra said. "Hristoff had a piece—an orb, I guess, though I never saw it myself."

"Is it possible there are other orbs?"

"I suppose it's possible and would also make sense. If they gave him the orb but refused him the mechanism—that would anger him."

She'd seen a lot of anger from him, hadn't she? That was probably how she'd become so skilled at working people.

"You have no idea what I've had to do to survive."

That pig was sick. He'd bought her. Raped her. Fathered a child on her.

Anger corkscrewed through Leif, thinking of Iskra's daughter, whom the perv had held to the camera. Displayed her bruises. Proud of the injuries. Proud he had a way to tighten the shackle around Iskra's neck.

Because of men like him, God had made warriors like Leif. To do violence on behalf of the innocent.

"I've had Cell monitoring activity and unusual patterns," Iliescu said. "Unsurprisingly, more locations around Africa are getting hit."

"Any word from ArC or any hint as to their end game?" Leif asked. "Why are they altering the weather in these areas? I mean, so far we've seen Burma, Egypt, and now you're saying more in Africa?" He didn't like being on this continent. It was too close to his missing answers.

"No word, and trust me, we're digging deep and hard," Iliescu growled. "Assets on the ground are pushing and probing. We've put out word that we're willing to pay big for intel about these artificial storms. Hopefully, applying that heat will force them to rush their timeline and make mistakes we can seize upon. I want to get in front of this thing before they destroy the world."

"Bit dramatic, ain't it?" Culver asked.

"That's the point, I think," Iliescu said. "If ArC can show people they control the weather, they'll put the fear of God in them. People, governments, and countries will do whatever ArC wants to stop the destruction. And I think that's what they're after. Bringing down these locations, seizing the land. I doubt they even care about the people."

"I still cannot believe we're battling someone who wants to make Armageddon happen, rather than stop it." Lawe scratched his beard as he tipped back his chair.

"The places you're sending us—what're you seeing out there?" Saito asked.

"Purcell?"

"We all know about the unusual weather patterns, so I refined the search parameters to add the strange smell," Cell explained. "A few hot spots came up, but the biggest concerns right now are the Angolan coast and Botswana. There are increased storms there, a rapid escalation of tornadic activity, and general chaos because it's Carnival in Angola."

"Carnival?" Saito asked.

"Shrove Tuesday," Leif said.

"Right," Cell continued with a nod. "Shrove Tuesday is the last day before the long fast for Lent. It has many names, including Fat Tuesday, Mardi Gras, the Tuesday of Carnival, and Pancake Day. Huge celebration. The bigger the better. The shinier the better. Parades and parties galore."

Saito shifted. "A big storm with tornados could produce hail. Injure or kill all those partying people."

"Exactly the problem, not to mention whatever nefarious purpose ArC has for hitting the coast." Again, Cell nodded. "The other possibilities were either too late or didn't have enough intel to confirm. So for now we focus on Angola and Botswana. See what we can find."

Braun shifted in her creaking seat back in Maryland. "Chopper will take you from El Gorah to the USS *Mount Whitney*. You'll have their sophisticated instruments at your disposal, and Mr. Purcell will run a small command center from that location. The team will then launch from the ship at 0300, infil to the coordinates he provides." She nodded. "Good luck. And good hunting."

THIRTY

USS *MOUNT WHITNEY*, SOUTH ATLANTIC OCEAN

The ocean was a fickle mistress. She could lull his senses to sleep with her beauty, expanse, and openness. And she could thrash a ship to slivers in a rage. But there was nowhere Leif liked better than riding her waves. Canyon loved to surf, and their brother Range had gone Coast Guard, so love of the water ran in the Metcalfe veins.

Delivered to the Blue Ridge–class command ship of the United States Navy by a Chinook, the team had first met with the captain of the boat before being sent belowdecks to wait for their briefing. "The Voice of the Sea," as she was called by her crew, was also the flagship of the Sixth Fleet. With a complement of one hundred fifty enlisted personnel, twelve officers, and one hundred fifty Civilian Mariners from Military Sealift Command, the *Mount Whitney* had been one of the first ships to accommodate women on board.

Mercy cornered Leif as they waited in a conference room. "So, it seems Ororo is more a storm than ever now."

Leif gritted his teeth, deducing she had some other point to make. "What?"

"Well," she said, tucking her dark hair behind her ear, "I'm just wondering—Peychinovich is some kind of seriously messed-up villain, but . . . this whole thing with him hurting the child? It seems . . . not right for him. All those years he provided for Iskra—"

"And raped."

"Okay, that . . ." Mercy blanched. "Besides that"—she shook her head—"Peychinovich is all about appearances. Pride and arrogance are his hallmarks—millions poured into renovating that estate. His guards drive very nice rides, and so on."

"Iskra said as much. So . . . *why*? Why hurt the kid?" His mind raced.

"I think he had reason to believe Viorica *wasn't* coming back."

"She wouldn't leave her daughter there."

Mercy nodded, lips pursed. "I think I agree, but does Peychinovich know that? Or is he just seeing Viorica race around the globe with a handsome American operative?"

His thoughts hammered. "He thinks I've turned her. No wonder he sent that video. But . . . why just hurt her? I'd think he'd make it retaliatory—kill the girl."

"Because she's his child."

"Think that matters to an animal like him?"

Mercy shrugged. "I have no answers there. Just lots of ques—"

"Ms. Maddox?"

Mercy pivoted toward the hatch, where a seaman waited.

"You're requested abovedeck, ma'am."

Leif stood.

"*Just* Ms. Maddox," the seaman clarified, then added, "Vice Admiral Manche insists, sir. Said you could take it up with Director Iliescu later."

"I will." Leif didn't like his team being called up by officers on a ship. "As long as Vice Admiral Manche recognizes he has no authority over my team."

"He does." The seaman skipped his gaze to Mercy, motioning her into the passage. "Ma'am."

"Being fought over," Mercy said with a smirk. "How medieval. You're adorable." She wrinkled her nose. But he saw her nerves and uncertainty at being called out.

Mercy followed the seaman out of the belly of the beast to a smaller, cozier series of conference rooms huddled in dim lighting.

Activity thrummed beyond the glass wall in a communications hub.

Eat your heart out, Barc.

"Miss Maddox," a deep voice boomed behind her.

She spun and took in the uniformed officer addressing her. Eyed his name tape. "Admiral Manche."

He nodded to a seat as he closed the door. "Sorry for the surreptitious methods, but I wanted to talk with you alone."

"About?"

He smiled as he settled at the table—not in a chair, but by parking his hip on the edge. "The Bahamas."

What about it? She didn't detect malicious intent. "Is this—"

"Good game of beach volleyball with your team," he said, arms folded. "You're a strong spiker."

"Yeah, this isn't creepy at all."

"Amaretto sour for you. Martini for your . . . guest."

"I didn't have a—" Mercy snapped her mouth shut, recalling the man she'd had drinks with. Andrew. Her pulse skipped a beat.

"I see we understand each other."

"Quite the contrary," she said calmly, ready to rip the anonymous off Andrew's cover. "Is this where you warn me to keep my nose out of your business?"

"*American* business," he corrected. "You've seized on an asset we've been able to move around very easily for years . . . until you, like a rabid dog, bit the bone."

"Bit?" she repeated, then pursed her lips. "You haven't seen my bite yet." Nothing made her angrier than threats, veiled or direct.

"Mercy Maddox, Lara Milton, Mina Lauren . . ."

Her breathing shallowed. Nobody knew those names save Dru. Was he in on this? It didn't matter. She had a sudden and vicious hatred for Manche. She also hated the next name about to leap out of his mouth and into the open. But what if she was wrong? She couldn't show her hand if—

"Ar—"

"*What* do you want?"

He let her question linger for several long seconds that had her heart pounding the warning drums of the past. "You're tenacious," he said, "but my asset is more so. That name you didn't want me to speak?" His eyebrow arched. "Remember that."

Indignation scampered up her spine. How had she slipped up? What mistake had given her away? "I remember a lot of things." She tossed her own threat onto the sparring mat.

Manche flashed his palms. "To be clear, we intend you no harm, Miss Maddox. But you are poised to help us in a profound way."

"Hel—" The word caught at the back of her throat as she recoiled. "I will not work against my team."

"I wouldn't dream of asking you to," he said. "No, what we want is for you to pursue a name. You're intelligent and determined. We're confident in what you'll find. It'll help you. It will even help Miss Todorova, though she may argue that viciously."

Viorica? Was he kidding? "And you'd like that—for me to help *her*?" she asked, nearly laughing. "You might know a lot about me, but you don't know *me*."

"Miss Todorova needs help, whether or not she would agree," Manche said frankly. "Right now, it's important that she get the help."

"Then help her."

"That"—he seemed remorseful—"we cannot do."

This made no sense. Why would they help a Bulgarian operative? "Your asset." She snorted a laugh. "You're giving me this information so I'll leave him alone."

The vice admiral held her gaze, his gold eyes sharp.

"One condition."

"You believe you're in the position to negotiate?"

"No," Mercy said, "not negotiate. Understand."

His eyebrow quirked, and she took it as a good sign.

"Tell me this—this *asset*, is he on our side?" If she wasn't betraying her team, would she betray Iliescu by pursuing this tip? She couldn't live with herself if that happened.

Another annoying smile. Which meant yes. Didn't it? "What side is that?"

Ah. "Clever." Another stab at the fact that he knew her true identity. This was going to drive her mad. But only because she knew he wouldn't divulge anything. Fine. "Sorry, were you going to give me a name?"

Now a smirk. She really didn't like this admiral. "Valery Kuznetsov."

Mercy frowned. "One of the twins."

He moved to the door. "Good day, Miss Maddox. We have work to do now." He left without another word.

Why on earth would he tell her to look into Kuznetsov? What had she missed? Mercy looked through the smoky glass to the bustling communications room—and she saw a face staring back. *His* face! Andrew! She hauled in a breath. He drifted out of the room.

No, not the room. A reflection. From behind!

Mercy whirled to see him slip down the gangway. She darted out of the room and pivoted around the corner. And slammed into the seaman who'd escorted her.

"Sorry, ma'am," he said, squaring his stance. "Restricted area."

She thumped his chest in frustration, then realized what she'd done. "Sorry." She patted his chest in apology. Down the gangway, two sailors stood guard in front of a thick door, weapons held capably. Security. Okay, but what were they guarding?

Better yet—why were they protecting *him*? Who was he that he'd have an admiral's ear and protection? And what did he know about Viorica or Kuznetsov? Her gaze hit a camera mounted in the corner of the passage, just above the door.

Perf. Cyberocity really did love her.

"Ma'am," the seaman said, his voice edgier.

Mercy lifted her hands. "Just leaving."

"There a problem?"

She turned to find Leif and the team entering the passage, then gave the seaman a smile. "None at all." Amazing how a hackable camera feed made her so lighthearted.

"Briefing," Leif said, indicating the very room the asset had escaped into. Hope leapt anew as they were granted access. She hurried in, scanning the dimmed interior, quickly realizing it was the hub beyond the glass wall where the admiral had confronted her. Techs speaking into comms and hovering over light boards, illuminated Plexiglas wall maps visible from both sides, and row upon row of computer terminals.

But where had the asset gone?

THIRTY-ONE

USS *MOUNT WHITNEY*, SOUTH ATLANTIC OCEAN

Leif rounded the light table, studying the topographical map of the African coast and the South Atlantic Ocean. An animated overlay came to life, rolling a radar image over the area.

"In the time since you departed El Gorah, we've made some determinations," a uniform said as he waded around the team and stood at the head of the table. A captain. Name plate: Aznar.

Leif went rigid.

Aznar. Aznar reported to Reimer. Didn't he?

Why couldn't he remember? He never forgot. Only then did he realize Iliescu had never clarified the connection. But this man had been feeding them information from the beginning.

"The entity known as ArC is working in the region to destabilize Angola and Botswana," Aznar said.

"We already knew this. You have anything new or actionable?" Leif asked.

Aznar's face twitched. "We added the information you've gleaned and the efforts you've made to what we've already seen and projected. Landlocked Botswana is significant. With a population of just over two million, it's one of the most sparsely populated countries. Only ten percent of the population lives in Gaborone, the capital and largest city. In the last fifty years, it's gone from one of the poorest countries in the world to one of the richest in Africa, perhaps the fourth-largest economy on the continent. Mining, cattle, and tourism dominate. It has a relatively high standard of living and the highest Human Development Index of continental sub-Saharan Africa. That makes it a problem, especially for ArC, who is trying to buy South Africa's loyalty by offering funds to provide food and potable water to the region, granted only when they comply."

"What's the end game?" Lawe asked.

Aznar glanced at his device, made a few clicks, then nodded to the wall, where the face of a lanky, dark-skinned man appeared. "This is Bandile Botha, who—"

"Hold up," Leif said. "As in the Botha Revolution?"

Aznar nodded. "Botha rose swiftly to power across the eastern half of South Africa. Though officially he holds no recognized office, assets on the ground confirm that Mozambique, Zimbabwe, and Zambia are heavily under his influence. They refer to him as the 'governor.' He has had tremendous luck, too, swaying key UN members to vote in his favor."

"These countries going under?" Culver asked.

"Negative. In fact, Botha is active in advocating for his governorates. It looks good on the surface, but with the addition of Angola and Botswana"—he pointed to the bottom tip of the continent—"ArC will be one large step closer to controlling one of the most pivotal ports in the region."

"Cape Town." Leif crossed his arms and tucked his hands in his armpits.

"Exactly." Aznar motioned to the weather radar overlay. "We've isolated what appears to be two separate focal points to the unexpected storms."

"Okay," Leif said, confused. "What's the connection between Botha and the storms? How do we even know he's part of that? I mean—he's not in power in Burma or Egypt."

"Correct. But what we have repeatedly seen is heavy influence by individuals who are key to locations or countries. Botha has made or received visits from this man, Alessio Greco."

Leif touched his fingertips together. "Italian." His gaze hit Iskra, thinking of another Italian.

"A powerful man. He served their executive branch as the president of the Council of the Ministers and is now the ambassador to the UN and good friend of Ciro Veratti, the prime minister."

Leif and Iskra shared a long glance, but neither said anything.

"Any other questions?" Aznar sniped. "Or can I proceed?"

Leif indicated for him to go on.

"Since Botswana is flat, they're battling high winds and tornadic activity. Angola is a coastal country, so its storm is developing into a land-based hurricane. Our problem is that I can't send you in."

Leif blinked. "Come again?"

"The storms." Aznar nodded to the illuminated map at their fingertips. "The waters off Angola are too treacherous to take the ship in."

"Which means choppers are out, as well," Culver noted.

"Roger. Winds are too high. We already have reported sightings of tornadic activity on the ground," Aznar explained, flipping around to another screen that held footage. "This storm is unprecedented. High winds alone make it too dangerous. At this rate, we'll be dealing with a land-based hurricane by 0600. I won't put my sailors at unnecessary risk." He gave an apologetic shrug. "You'll have to wait it out. When this dies down, I'll send you in with an escort."

"Wait it out?" Saito asked.

"Our mission is to stop it," Leif said. "We wait it out, and there'll be nothing left."

"Which is exactly what ArC wants," Lawe agreed. "We have to go—*now*."

"Fighting against the storm will cost time," Culver said. "Even if we made land, we couldn't interdict in both countries. We're going to lose one."

"Not if we split up." Devine shouldered closer, face intent. "Split us up. Two teams. Half to Angola, the rest to Botswana."

"I don't think you're hearing me," Aznar growled.

"Agreed." Leif focused on the captain. "Give me a boat—"

"Excuse me?"

"Give us a boat," Leif repeated. "Half will hit Angola, try to stop this storm before it rips apart the coastal villages. The rest will go inland to Botswana to interdict there. We'll do it on our own. No cost to your sailors."

Aznar glowered.

"Unless you have a reason you don't want this resolved, Captain Aznar." Something in Leif begged the captain to argue.

"Are you accusing me—"

Leif tapped the table. "When I was attached to the SEALs, we conducted noncompliant maritime interdiction ops." When the captain didn't argue, he went on. "Do you have a Zodiac CZ7 or other RIB?" A rigid-hull inflatable boat would be perfect, especially a CZ7 wave buster. Costly, but effective. "I'm offering a solution at no cost to you or yours."

"Unless you lose the SWCC trying to get in there."

"Take it out of our pay." Leif had a crush on special warfare combatant-crafts. Maybe he'd lose it intentionally . . . have it turn up back home. Magically.

"You've had a burr in your saddle since you walked in here, son. Want to explain why?"

"Reimer."

Aznar didn't flinch. "Sorry?"

So maybe Leif had it wrong. But why did he remember Aznar, and why was there a tenuous connection with Reimer in his mind? "Look." Leif bypassed that conundrum. "The deputy director and DIA sent us out here with orders to get this done. To interdict where you can't as an official arm of the United States military. You can't go in and dirty your hands." He shrugged. "We get that. But that's what we're here to do."

"Hooah," Lawe grunted.

"I'll even call it in for you."

Challenge set.

"Your butts, not mine," Aznar finally grumbled.

"Done." Leif weighed which of his team were the best swimmers in case the water rejected their approach to the coastline. "Culver and Saito with me to Angola."

Lawe twitched, used to being with Leif as first.

"I need strong swimmers, Lawe," Leif said.

"I can swim."

"Dog paddling doesn't count," Culver said, eliciting a scowl from the big guy.

"Culver and I were SEALs," Leif explained. "I need that experience."

"And Saito?"

"Smaller, lighter to carry when he passes out in the water," Culver snarked.

Interbranch rivalry never ended. Even when you were combat brothers.

"So that leaves me babysitting two chicks and an Arab."

Lawe really hadn't learned much.

"Devine, you have my permission to leave him behind when he gets tired," Leif said.

"With or without an extra hole or two?" Devine asked.

"Imagine how I feel," Baddar put in, his accent thick but English clean, "having to help the Army Ranger come out alive." He clicked his tongue. "Please. Be sure to stay alive. It will look bad on my record if you die. It is hard for an Arab to gain trust in America, and that will not help."

"Shut up, man," Lawe groused.

"We're short on time and long on trouble." Leif pushed away from the table. "Gear up."

Heading belowdecks, he drew Mercy aside. "What happened up there with Manche?"

She skated a look around. "Nothing I can't handle." She watched Iskra thread her arms through a life vest for the choppy trip out. "But I'd keep a close eye on her."

What did that mean? He couldn't spend time on it. Right now, he had to get moving. Leif drew out his phone and hit a speed-dial number as he pulled his ruck to the side and started checking weapons and supplies.

"Iliescu."

"Tell me Aznar's good meat."

Silence.

"Tell me trusting this captain isn't going to leave me high and dry or dead."

"It won't, but don't count on much more."

"Understood. We're heading into the storm."

The flagship of the Sixth Fleet had made good time bringing them in as close as possible to the approaching storm without endangering itself. They were lowered down the gray hull by the starboard umbilical arm, the ship's side painted with *CZ7* in large black-and-white stenciling. Before they'd even cleared the wake of the *Mount Whitney*, water lurched upward, reaching for them.

Leif eyed the Chinook lifting from the helipad, carrying the other half of the team to Botswana. As he visually tracked their departure, Leif noted Iskra behind him in the RIB. She gripped the handles of her seat, hunched against the pelting rain.

Culver took the saddle next to him, sitting on a ten-grand piece of the shock-mitigating craft. The helm was sexy with its Raymarine electronics suite, and twin Evinrude 150s packed power that made Leif feel at home. He pushed the throttle wide open to reach the craft's max 52 miles per hour, giving them a gut-churning ride and the best hope of reaching shore before it was too late. Head down, Saito seemed ready for the confrontation. Probably praying, too.

With each nautical mile they ate up, the wind whipped and rain spat at them. As if the weather was telling them to go back, that this was a bad idea. Leif lowered his goggles and used the compass to guide them in. Dawn fought the storm in a valiant effort that ended in defeat, rays blotted out by thick rolling clouds.

Lightning splintered the sky. Leif counted. One-one-thousand. Two-one-thousand. Three-one-thousand. Four-one—

Thunder cracked, thumping against his chest.

Four seconds. Which meant they had just minutes to hit the beach before the storm unleashed its fury. Unscientific, but with the way things had gone, he expected Mother Nature wouldn't mind a bit of unscientific measuring.

Iskra's head came up at the thunder. She glanced at him. Why wasn't she fighting him harder?

She wants to be here.

No, she wanted to be with her daughter.

"Chief!"

His attention snapped to Saito, who indicated the wall forming to their nine. Leif's breath backed into his throat—water rose over them. Towering.

Oh crap.

No power steering on the CZ7 made the hard turn a brutal effort as he fought to get away from the swell, aiming for a small valley that sneaked between the big wave and another. They bounced over the water. He sighted the land. At least two more nautical miles, if what he saw through the thick clouds, rain, and surging waves was actually land.

Leif braced himself. They came out the other side, and he breathed a little easier at the smaller waves. The winds were a little—

Iskra's shout mingled with the din of a roar. He checked over his shoulder to see her pointing to their six. Leif started to look but sensed the empty silence of the wave that hovered over them, waiting . . .

The boat was twanging. Jouncing. A futile effort, like a fish fighting upstream. As if someone had grabbed their tail, forbidding escape.

Then it came. Roaring. Howling.

The wave slammed into them.

Leif was lifted and pitched forward. Dunked. Held under. Shoved deeper. Breathing was impossible.

The RIB danced on the surface, conquering the violent waves. Leif righted himself, scrambled for the boat. Caught the rear deck like a lifeline. Where were the others? He looked around, but the merciless storm continued its assault.

A squall leapt at him. Punched him backward. Another ferocious hit came from a different wave. It shoved him deep into the ocean's vicious hold. Panic gripped him—in the lashing surge, he was losing his orientation.

You trained for this.

He steadied his thoughts. Defied every inborn instinct to thrash. To breathe. Leif relaxed. In doing so, he felt it, the seeming surrender of the ocean that allowed him to drift. He paddled his feet. Then . . . he was rising.

He broke the surface and sucked in a gulp of air, knowing it would be short-lived. The ocean was a tempest, eager to devour those who dared enter its domain. His eyes stung, but he blinked away the water and searched for the others.

Instead, something large tumbled right at him. He threw up his arm to protect his face. Pain detonated through his arm. Cracked his skull. Punched him into darkness.

THIRTY-TWO

ANGOLAN COAST

A wood plank shot up out of the water and struck Leif in the head, shoving him full force at Iskra. Treading water in the suddenly calm storm, she readied herself but registered that he'd gone limp. He'd drown! Scrambling as he impacted her, she grabbed the strap of his vest. It burned her fingers, the water furiously trying to drag him down. He was heavy. Bigger than she was. And the ocean more powerful. Hooking an arm around his neck, she fought to keep them both above water.

"Leif?" she called, hoping to rouse him. "Leif, please! Wake up!" But it was no good. He was unconscious, and the storm was eating her words.

Was he even breathing? He had to be. Because she couldn't do anything about it until they got to shore.

"Leif!" Her limbs were quickly tiring as she swam for two people. She grunted, a whimper crawling through her chest, but she refused it voice. No whining. She had to keep him alive.

Arms aching, she kicked and aimed toward shore. Due to the strain and the cold, her limbs felt like anchors. How had he done this in Cuba? How had Leif gotten her to safety, held her in the water so long and not given up? How had his body not quit?

She glanced toward shore, a blur of grays and browns. A plume of foam caught her attention—someone swimming toward them.

A wave dunked her. Fingers tightening on Leif, she clamped her mouth shut too late. The water hit the back of her throat and forced a cough. But she broke upward. Sputtered. Gagged.

Something thumped into her.

"Got him?" a voice barked against her ear. Culver. A weight tugged her vest.

Nearly in tears at the assistance, at not being left to drown, she nodded but kept her mouth closed to avoid the salty spray.

"Hold tight. I'll bring us in," Culver ordered.

Her system flooded with relief. And exhaustion. She looped her other arm over Leif's shoulder, his bloodied face pressed to hers, and dug her fingers under his front vest strap.

The water fought them. Of course it did. Everything in life fought her.

"Get your feet under you," Culver boomed.

Iskra startled that they were already at shore. Her boots sank into the sludgy beach. She pushed up, shifting so she could stand but keep Leif's head up. Culver moved in, lifted Leif over his shoulder in a fireman's carry, and trudged up out of the water. The deluge was heavy and they had no shelter, no reprieve from the rain, but she didn't care. They were out of the Atlantic.

Culver went to a knee, setting Leif on the ground near a patch of grass. Saito rushed toward them and dropped at Leif's side, assessing. Taking his vitals.

Iskra collapsed, watching. The ridge above Leif's eye was split, compliments of the plank that had knocked him out. She scooted closer, unnerved when Saito started compressions. Breaths.

Leif wasn't breathing? No. Her heart skipped several beats. He could not die. He'd promised her. Promised he'd be there. When she was ready.

She just hadn't realized she'd been ready for a while. Back of her hand to her mouth, she wrestled the terrible fear that Leif would die. That the glimmer of hope that had awakened at his incursion into her life would die with him.

It was crazy. She barely knew him. But somehow she knew him better than she'd known anyone. He would always be there for her, if he lived.

Compressions continued, Culver taking over so Saito could do the breaths. Leif's chest was forced to rise beneath the air Saito puffed into his lungs. Then more compressions.

Tears burned as Iskra sat helpless, begging those blue eyes to once more spark at her. For that stupid smirk to reappear. He could not die now. He could not.

A bark startled them.

Convulsing, Leif coughed. Sputtered. They turned him over, and he vomited. His hands dug into the ground, limbs trembling.

Culver grunted. "Had us worried, Runt."

Rolling onto his side, Leif suddenly howled, holding his arm to his chest. An injury? Veins bulged at his temple as he battled the pain. "Son . . . of . . ."

Saito reached in. Gently lifted the arm.

Leif went crimson.

"Broken," Saito said. "Probably both bones." He dug an inflatable splint out of his pack.

"No," Leif growled, pulling himself upright. "I'll be okay."

"Bull," Saito argued. "That's likely a double break. You—"

"We're screwed," Culver said.

"We're . . . not." Leif pressed the heel of his other hand to his head. Shook it. His gaze hit hers, and his unfocused eyes suddenly sharpened. Darkened. "You okay? What happened?"

Iskra startled. "Yes, I—"

"It's *your* blood on her, from that gash in your temple," Culver said. "When debris tried to take that thick head of yours off, she hauled your sorry carcass to shore. We'll need to glue that."

Leif scowled. "But you're okay?" he asked her again.

Now that you're alive. "Yes."

Reticence marked his expression, but he finally seemed to relax.

Culver snickered. "Never thought I'd see the day where a leaf beat a plank of wood."

"You need new jokes," Leif muttered. "That didn't even make sense."

Saito stuffed the splint at him. "Put it on. Now." He pointed to his temple. "I'm going to glue that now."

Irritated, Leif huffed. "It's raining."

"It'll just take longer to dry," Saito said.

Leif let the medic work. He grimaced and tensed as the splint immobilized his arm. Then he looked at her again. Reached toward her. Rough fingers swept her cheek. Did it again. Wiping away the blood. Apparently, it bothered him to see blood on her face.

When the medic shifted and assessed his temple, Leif waved him off. "We need to get moving."

GABORONE, BOTSWANA

"This isn't looking good." Lawe braced himself in the cockpit of the Boeing CH-47 Chinook, a twin-engine, tandem-rotor, heavy-lift helicopter that was ferrying them to the edge of Gabs, as locals called Gaborone. Situated between Kgale and Oodi Hills, it was fighting a massive storm with tornadoes and hail, but there was a bigger problem near the center of the storm.

"The rivers are swollen." The pilot flew them around the capital to the confluence of two rivers. "Much more rain, and it'll flood the city. Displace two hundred thousand people."

What were they supposed to do with two hundred thousand people if they didn't stop this nightmare? Adam swiped a hand over his beard, watching the rivers collide, shoving water into a raging chaos intent on swallowing the capital.

"Look." Baddar huddled behind him and pointed to their nine.

To a place the storm didn't exist. A halo-shaped rivulet of sunshine and calm in the middle of an ebony void. The epicenter. That was where the experts believed the device would be located.

Adam keyed his mic. "Drop us to your eleven, captain. Just over that ridge." As the helo swung around, he returned to the belly of the chopper where Peyton and Mercy waited on the red-strap seats.

He nodded to the rear of the fuselage where the loading bay door yawned wide.

The skilled pilots circled back, descended, then aimed the tail down. A spray of rain and mud spewed from the engine wash, but in a few seconds they were only a soft jump away from the ground.

Adam glanced at the others, at Peyton, affirming they were ready, then adjusted his weight as he approached the downward-sloping ramp.

Without warning, he was thrown to the side. He grabbed for support, but the cant of the chopper made it impossible. Peyton rammed into him as they swung away from the drop zone. He held her fast as they both gaped at the churning, tumbling water that slapped the lowered bay door.

"Sorry about that," the pilot's voice carried through the comms. "River broke over the ridge, slammed into us. Nearly took us down."

Adam cupped Peyton's head to his chest as the cauldron of water exploded through the city. Chewed through walls, like carpenter ants eating table legs, and forcing the steel giants to their knees. It swept cars and poles into its frenzy. Snatched people from safety.

Holding him, Peyton whimpered over her shoulder. "All those people . . ."

"We're too late."

"Maybe not," Baddar said as the bay door closed. "What if we shut it down?"

Adam glowered. "Maybe you missed the memo, but the floods—"

"The *storm*. What if we shut it down? Slow the damage." He nodded to something behind Adam.

Lawe looked back, confused . . . then saw them. Gunners. Perched in the side doors. Who knew if it would work? They had nothing to lose.

Adam shoved to his feet. "Hey." He clambered toward the gunners. "Can you target that calm area?"

The 7.62-mm M60 machine gun on a pintle mount wouldn't fire

rockets, but since it fired 500 to 650 rounds per minute, it was an area-effect weapon.

The gunner shrugged. "Why not?"

After conveying the plan to the pilot, who lined them up, Adam nodded to the gunner. "Light 'er up."

Bullets pelted the ground, plumes dancing and jittering through the unnatural calm. It was impressive. But ineffective. As he'd expected. Yet Adam wasn't ready to give up. He had the other gunner do the same. This time, a spark ignited in the center of the calm spot. Gave him hope.

"You got anything else?"

The first gunner grinned. "Incendiaries." He lifted a shoulder in a shrug. "A bit farfetched, but . . ."

"Try it."

With Baddar's help, they assisted the gunners in feeding the incendiary rounds. Then crouched and watched as the fiery rounds hit and . . . did nothing.

Hope fading, river rushing faster, Adam huffed.

Boom! Crack-boom! An explosion erupted in the eye of the storm.

The Chinook came around, and through the front windshield, he saw the black sky receding.

"Yeah!" Adam high-fived Baddar. "We did it!"

"Command will not be happy we destroyed it," Baddar noted.

Claxons sounded. The Chinook veered sharply left. Then right.

"Command," the pilot shouted, "we're under attack and taking fire."

Adam's mirth vanished at the sound of the alarms for the targeting system. Someone on the ground with the device was firing countermeasures.

ANGOLAN COAST

Hiking up the slick, grassy hillside and across the muddy road, Leif knew the glue wouldn't last. Not because of the rain—that excuse had been a feeble attempt to dissuade Saito from worrying about his injuries. They'd heal on their own. Faster than normal, of course. But Saito wasn't one to take a hint. And he'd had that look that told Leif to avoid suspicion. It was why he'd allowed the splint. He didn't need questions about a quick-healing fracture. It wasn't like it'd be healed tomorrow. At least not completely.

He couldn't explain. Didn't want to try. Things had been different since he and the team had fought their way out of the desert over five years ago. *He* had been different.

Touching his comms piece, he tested it. Confirmed it still worked after he'd nearly drowned. "Storm center is there. We'll hike north about five klicks." He motioned in the general direction. "Take out the device."

"How do we get out of here?" Culver asked. His red hair was dark, plastered to his face and skull. "We lost the Zodiac."

"One thing at a time," Leif said. "First: stop the device."

"Let's do it," Saito agreed.

They broke into a jog and headed toward the calm. Leif's skull throbbed from being hit by the plank. His ego was bruised, too. *She hauled you to shore.* What he wouldn't give to talk to Canyon. Find out how he'd won his wife over. How he'd broken down the walls she'd put up after being held captive for months in Venezuela. Because when push came to shove, it was kind of the same thing. Captivity was captivity, and that was the life Iskra lived. Wasn't it?

Wind tugged at them. Rain pelted needling reminders that they were entering the dark corridor. But they warriored on, heading straight to the epicenter. It was ominous, strange, and otherworldly, seeing the great black clouds swirling over the villages and city to the south, but straight ahead lay an unaffected clearing. Still another two-point-five klicks to go.

Leif hoofed it over uneven terrain, careful not to twist his ankle or crack another bone. The run turned into a jog, the natural progression of a long march on bodies. He told himself to slow down—for the team's sake if nothing else—but they had to get to the drive.

His near-death had cost them time. And the cloud tumbling overhead didn't look like a patient master.

"Augh!"

Leif glanced back and dropped out of his jog.

Hobbling, Iskra babied her right ankle, her face screwed tight.

"What happened?"

"Wrenched it. The rain and ruts—" She shook her head.

Saito crouched beside her while she steadied herself using a thin tree. He cupped her heel and then rotated it. She strangled a cry.

Cracks and booms from the sky rattled the ground.

"Go," Iskra said. "I'll catch up."

Leif eyed the device strapped to his wrist. "Just another one-point—"

"Go," she growled. "Stop that storm!" She waved them on.

Leif hesitated, knowing he *should* get moving. They had to. But leaving Iskra . . .

"I'll stay with her, Chief," Saito said. "Get her some painkillers and tape, then we'll catch up."

Wariness crowded his mission focus.

A sound carried on the stinging wind, stilling Leif. He scanned the area, confused. Had he—

"I heard it, too," Culver said, ear trained to the air. "Gunfire."

Leif pivoted. "But . . . where?"

"And who?"

Only one possibility. "ArC operatives." He nailed his gaze on that clear patch of sky. As if someone had forgotten to paint a spot on the canvas. "Defending the device."

"From who? Because they sure ain't shooting at us." Culver looked worried.

"Good question."

Daggers of lightning shot out of the storm.

"Go." Iskra straightened, shuffled toward him. "Go! Stop it. You have to."

Leif twisted around and nodded to Culver. Then burst into action. Even as he let his feet carry him away, his mind stayed with her. Worried she'd get hurt without his protection. But thousands were depending on them stopping the device. Eager to confront Peychinovich, he hoped that was who he was headed toward.

Wind battered them as they ran. Made them feel like they were running uphill during a tornado. Which . . . they were.

A gust caught Culver. Yanked him backward. The sight reminded Leif of football dummies in high school. One man against an entire mechanical line pushing him away from the goal. Fighting his progress. Preventing a touchdown.

He hadn't been named homecoming king just for his good looks.

He turned into the threat, entrenching his toes in the sodden earth.

Crack. Crack-crack.

Silvery strands of light skewered the sky. His hair stood on end, the electricity in the air unlike anything he'd ever encountered.

Pop pop! Pop! Pop-pop-pop!

Gunfire to his right. He veered that way. The sound was closer, yet sounded farther away because of the wind's howl.

"There." Culver pointed to a knoll. Then—he flipped up into the air. Slid a dozen feet.

Leif scurried back, digging in. Ducked against the torrential rain. He snagged Culver's drag strap and helped him find his feet.

They trudged together up the hill. Went flat, the automatic result when Mother Nature provided a reprieve. Leif peered through the binoculars, not because of distance but because of the elements.

Three trucks. Men braced on this side of them and shooting at someone the vehicles blocked from view. Who were they fighting? He tried to assess the position of the area and the trucks. Realized fighting the storm had pushed them off the direct track they'd plotted.

"Are the trucks good guys or bad guys?" Culver asked.

"Unknown. Can't tell if they're defending themselves or the device."

"Or both." Culver nodded. "Check your eleven."

Four dark shapes—stealthy, experienced fighters—were closing in. Elite, judging by their movements. Leif scanned back. The shooters by the truck hadn't seen the foursome. They were too focused on their twelve.

Leif attempted to zoom in more. No-go. The truck had a dozen or so guys ducked behind it. He tried to see their weapons, but there were too many shadows from the thick clouds. He turned back to the foursome. Black tactical, if the blurred-by-the-rain image was right. Which he couldn't guarantee.

The leader lifted his left arm. Gave signals. Straight. Two klicks. Stay low.

And how did Leif know that? The arm . . .

Shouts. Screams. A voice—a familiar timbre. He could hear it, but he couldn't make out words. His hearing was plugged. A shape loomed over him. A hand on his chest, holding him down. Shouts. Being defended. Protected. "Remember," the voice growled around a laugh, "I will—"

"—always rise."

"Come again?" Culver frowned.

Leif shrugged away the memories. "You take the four."

"Leaving you to handle a dozen fighters." Culver pursed his lips. "Either stupid or brave."

"Both. Did you forget?" Using his splinted arm for a stabilizer, Leif targeted the shooters behind the truck. "We're heroes."

THIRTY-THREE

USS *MOUNT WHITNEY*, SOUTH ATLANTIC OCEAN

Unable to forget the raging river devouring Gaborone and its people and feeling the full brunt of their mission failure in the fatality of three hundred and counting, Mercy had pushed herself into the thing she knew best: cyberocity. The team had destroyed the orb, the storm clouds had dissipated, but they'd been too late to stave off the raging rivers. Though they had stunted the storm's full force, the team had barely escaped a ground-to-air assault, returning to the *Mount Whitney* with a bullet-riddled fuselage.

The efforts to evacuate the city in Botswana were colossal, occupying the *Mount Whitney*'s sailors and crew. Mercy had spent the last hour in the briefing room with Peyton and Lawe, who'd suddenly gotten real cozy with each other. Facing a catastrophe sort of put things in perspective, she guessed.

But Mercy just needed air. And strong Wi-Fi. She'd find out about Valery Kuznetsov if it killed her. So far, she'd unearthed the obvious—twin to Vasily, worked for Peychinovich as CEO of—*ha, imagine that*—Viorica Steel out of Nizhny Novgorod in Russia's Volga District.

Okay, nothing mind-blowing there. So . . . parents?

The twins were born to Edik and Ilia Kuznetsov forty-one years ago. Valery had served in the Russian army, rising through the ranks. Shortly after the death of his parents, he left the army. Found his way into the good graces of one Hristoff Peychinovich. No pictures, since he was Russian army. Too much to track.

So maybe Vasily's history would be more forthcoming. A scholar of the sciences. Went to university, then found his way to Greece. "Ah yes," Mercy murmured as her eyes hit a familiar location. "Aperióristos Labs. Fancy that."

Viorica had been on Vasily's boat. So, yeah, she definitely got the intel on the Book of the Wars from him. Probably. Could that be proven? He had an impeccable record so far, but how had he known about the book? Or had he? Had Viorica just shown up with it?

She'd check Vasily's employee record. Another firewall to breach. She always had loved Greece. It was easy work, diving into their system and doing a search for all things Kuznetsov. A string of emails. Preserved, no doubt, because of his position at the company and the sensitive things he worked on. Which really meant nothing to Mercy. Languages. Artifacts.

She scanned his emails, searching subject lines. Thousands. "*Boring*," she said, holding the down arrow for . . . ever.

Baddar appeared with a tray of chips, hummus, and fruit.

"You really are cruel, eating in front of me," she taunted.

"I have already had my meal. This is for you. In case . . ." He nudged the plate toward her. And there he was, his gorgeous Afghan self, worrying over her again. Charming.

Lawe hovered behind Baddar and clapped his shoulder. "Aww, look at that. The big fierce commando hand-delivers food to the feisty intel analyst." He playfully smacked Baddar's face. "Next time, bring me some grub, Baddy. Remember, I saved your butt."

Baddar gave a nervous laugh, his face reddening. "I think it was Runt who saved me."

Mercy had no idea what to do with that. It was easy to forget the gentle, softhearted Baddar Amir Nawabi had once been an Afghan commando. A very good and effective one, from what she'd heard. Having his attention directed at her . . .

His rich eyes came back to hers, and he gave her a shy, almost sheepish grin. Then he nudged her laptop. "Anything yet?"

Thankful for the out, she swung her attention to the intel. "If only this were as simple as TV shows and movies, with one good twin and one evil."

"The one who work for the Russian—he is good?"

"Well, I wouldn't call Valery *bad*, even though he worked for that piece of dirt," she said. "His record seems clean—as in redacted or erased—so I shifted to his brother. That's where I am now. Vasily used to work at the lab in Greece where the Book of the Wars was held."

To avoid meeting those inviting, caring eyes again, she clicked on files. Found a picture. "Oh." The twins on a yacht. One held a bottle of champagne. They were celebrating something. "'Double, double toil and trouble,'" she murmured.

Baddar leaned in, and Mercy . . . well, it was hard to pay attention to intel with smooth olive skin sliding into her view. She was a sucker for the darker tones. Like Ram. But Baddar was a little more rough-edged, despite his tender personality. And had a stronger jaw. A perpetual smile that, if she were truthful, penetrated her heart.

"When was this—" His gaze rammed into hers.

Mercy started but couldn't move. Refused to flinch. Yes, she'd been staring. Yes, he now knew. No, she wouldn't act guilty or pull away. By all the powers of the universe, she wasn't sure she cared anymore. His eyes went crazy-soft. His smile caressed her, somehow told her it was okay.

What was okay?

Lawe cleared his throat—loud. Long. Then did it again.

Peyton slapped his chest. "Leave them alone."

"Just trying to help them past this awkward silence. Looks painful."

Mercy dropped her head, smiling.

Baddar touched her shoulder in solidarity, then nodded to the picture. "When was this taken?"

"Right. Uh." She eased forward, her face near his. And man, he smelled good, too. *The date, Mercy. The date.* "Five years ago. Why?"

"Look what he is holding," Baddar said quietly.

Mercy squinted at Valery, hand upheld. She drew up straight. "A baby rattle."

It hit her brain like Thor's hammer. She sucked in a breath. Clicked back over to the email.

"What is it?" Baddar asked.

"I think . . ." She scrolled, killing the down arrow again in her attempt to hurry. Then it flashed past. "Vasily was a scientist, working with artifacts. Pottery, scrolls, manuscripts. Yet . . ." More scrolling. *C'mon, c'mon.* Where had it gone? "There!" She slid the trackball back up a few lines. And smiled. "Right under my nose."

Her mind ricocheted off the subject line as she clicked open the file labeled WILD ROSE.

ANGOLAN COAST

Dark clouds birthed twisters like nobody's business, dropping them right between Leif and Culver and that confrontation. So much for getting involved in the fight.

Culver grabbed his shoulder. Tugged him.

The device.

Staying low to the ground in a crouch-run made it easier to avoid most of the higher wind. More than once, it tossed them back a dozen feet. Futility coursed through Leif, staring through his goggles at the clearing that was less than a half klick away. Yet despite their every effort, they couldn't make it.

Lightning corkscrewed and daggered out of the clearing. Streaked across the sky. Stabbed the land. As Leif ran, he could've sworn a freight train was coming at him. Then he remembered. He threw himself into the muck. Covered his head and prayed like he'd never prayed before. Tornados were said to mimic the sound of freight trains. *Incoming!*

Debris whipped and pitched, stinging his head and hands. This was hopeless. Once the tumult dropped a degree, he glanced at the clearing. Two more twisters danced around the edge. Entire huts swirled in the air. A truck pitched into an intact wall, spitting shards in every direction.

There was no hope. How was he supposed to get through that?

"Shots are closer," Iskra noted as she struggled toward the opening in the sky. The painkillers had worked, but minimally—the brace helped more.

"Yeah," Saito said slowly, his weapon coming around in front of him.

Then the familiar *rat-a-tat* of automatic rounds peppered the air. Very near. Instinct pushed Iskra down, the rain-soaked dirt suctioning her knee.

Saito went for cover, too, listening. He keyed his comms. "Beta Actual, come in."

But the only sound to reach them was the progressive closing-in of gunfire. What they were shooting at, she couldn't tell. The storm's surge had increased, so Leif probably hadn't yet reached the device.

Like a determined predator, wind ripped across the open plain toward them. Dark clouds covered the entire area, dropping dozens of funnels to the earth. Like a demon unleashing her spawn.

Iskra watched, stricken. Terrified.

A crackling screech buzzed in her ear. She ducked and touched her comms piece. Looked to Saito, who was doing the same. Whispering something.

Her heart skipped a beat. No, he wasn't whispering. He was shouting. Less than a foot away from her. And she couldn't hear his words.

Then his eyes widened, looking over her shoulder. He swung around, then slammed backward. The ground rushed up at Iskra.

Culver's face was muddied and streaked with rain rivulets. Determination gouged his expression. He motioned behind them. Across the open field, back where they'd left Iskra and Saito, a lanky man strode from a vehicle. Bent and jerked someone from the ground.

Leif's heart kick-started. Iskra!

He jolted forward, but Culver caught him. Held him. Forced him to watch helplessly as the man carried her limp body to the vehicle.

Roaring, Leif bucked. Though he knew it was right for his buddy to hold him back, Leif couldn't just stay here. "No!" The storm ate his words. "Nooo!"

Culver hauled him back. Slammed him to the ground. Put a knee in his chest. He was shouting, but the winds deprived his words of their power. There was enough in his expression, though, that Leif knew they had no time to go back. The storm was their priority.

Fury shoved him free of Culver's hold. He staggered, throwing one more glance at the now-empty plain. Whoever had come for her—it meant they were blown. The team was being monitored or had been recognized. It meant they may have already lost.

Bolts of lightning shot out of the opening.

They had to try. They had to. No choice. Even if they had to low-crawl. Then he'd find Peychinovich. Make him hurt. A lot.

Teeth gritted, he prostrated himself like an offering to a tempestuous god. Weapon guard resting over his firing arm—which throbbed like nobody's business—he low-crawled, pushing his arms ahead and then sliding his firing leg forward. Pull with his good arm. Push with his legs. Sliding over the snot-like terrain. Eyes on the lightning storm. On the only place that provided both light and darkness. Life and death.

Halfway there, he grew more intent, numb to the pain. Determined to do this. He'd survive. Then he'd take out his fury on Peychinovich. He'd save Iskra and her daughter. He wouldn't fail her.

Something sailed toward them.

Leif balked, realizing what flew through the air. A body. Swirling above them. A sickening epiphany hit him—the tornado had snatched this man into its chaos and spit him out. The storm had a will of its own.

Static hissed and crackled in a dome-like arch forty-five meters ahead, creating a literal line in the sand where the storm raged outside and peace reigned inside.

"Chief, this is base, come in," came Cell's voice through the comms.

"Go ahead," Leif shouted, covering his open ear.

"We have an intermittent signal fifty yards from your position. It's growing in intensity. They've started evacuations of the city, but Aznar's screaming about you being too slow. We're pretty sure the device is in there."

He'd kinda figured that out. "Heading in." Leif scurried forward. Got his feet under him and surged at the calm spot with Culver.

They broke through the barrier. The enormous struggle to even move instantly evaporated. They stumbled in, nearly falling. Tripped, no longer needing the power of a Goliath to move a muscle.

As he righted himself, Leif noted a strange tickling along his arm. His face. Neck. He held out his arm, fascinated by the electricity zapping along the hairs. He looked at Culver, who was just as amazed.

A bolt streaked between them. Hot. Searing. He smelled something burning and yelped. The hair on his body was singeing.

"Look!" Culver shouted.

Freaked, Leif glanced at the center of the clearing, where the orb lay on a stone foundation. But it wasn't the orb Culver was indicating—it was the duo on the opposite side. A third guy in the center, holding a weapon Leif didn't recognize, wore a heavy jacket. A *rubber* jacket. As if—

"The middle—take him down!" Leif ordered. The only reason he would wear a rubber jacket was if he knew what he'd face at the center. He had to be ArC's man.

Culver fired a short burst.

Which somehow drew the currents from the orb. They converged and snapped at him. Shot him backward out of the bubble.

On the far side, the two men were down. One rose to a knee, but his buddy was laid out.

The man in the rubber jacket raised a hand. "Stop shooting," he shouted, "or you'll kill us all."

"He's lying," the kneeling man countered. "We came here to stop him—*he*'s controlling it."

Leif's gaze bounced to Rubber Jacket, who was extending something toward the device. "No. Hands!" He took aim.

"That is stupid," Rubber Jacket growled, nodding at the body. "Thought you would've figured that out."

Leif had no idea if they'd killed a good guy or a bad one.

What's the call?

Hanged if he knew. Rubber Jacket had come prepared. Stood closest to the device. Survivor guy had a dead buddy. Leif tightened his lips, frustrated. Only a mind reader could call this.

Leif advanced, but when he did, the orb reacted. He leapt away as it spat a bolt of lightning at him. The spot where he had stood was now a sizzling scorch.

"Can't shoot it," Rubber Jacket called. "I can't get any closer either. It reacts to electrical charges."

Which human bodies had. So obviously he couldn't touch it. The charge could kill him.

". . . ctual. Come in." At the crackle in his comms, Leif stilled. Glanced back at Culver's unmoving form and subvocalized, hoping the other guys wouldn't see him talk. "Go ahead."

"Blow it," Aznar's voice sailed through, surprisingly clear. "Destroy the device. The evacuation in the cities was a ruse to get as many people in one location as possible. ArC is using the device to kill millions."

Stunned, Leif trained back on the orb. Shrugged out of his ruck, eye on Rubber Jacket, who watched warily.

Leif drew out a brick of C-4. "You might want to back up."

Rubber Jacket took several steps away. When he halted, Leif set the timer—but a spark shot from the orb. The electrical current neutralized the timer—and amazingly didn't ignite the C-4. What on earth . . . ?

Hissing at the sizzle in his hand, Leif saw the surviving loner had lifted a weapon. The survivor shot toward Rubber Jacket, who pivoted to Leif.

"The brick. Throw it—now!"

Hadn't this guy seen what happened to Culver? The orb reac—

Yes. He had seen. Brilliant.

In a split second, Leif realized several things. Survivor was trying to stop Rubber Jacket, who wanted the C-4 thrown. Throwing the brick—they hoped—would draw instincts from Survivor, who'd fire at it. They could all die, but so would the Meteoroi.

He fastballed the brick at the device.

Spider-like branches of electricity converged over the orb. They grabbed the brick, wrapped around it. Suspended it.

Even as he rotated and threw himself away, Leif heard the report of a weapon.

His legs felt like they weighed a thousand pounds as he shoved himself away. His right foot dug in. Pushed. Left foot. He aimed toward Culver's prone form. His pulse whooshed in his ears with each step.

One . . .

It was like running in water.

Two . . .

His movements were sluggish. The ground unforgiving.

Crack! Boom!

A shriek pierced his ears.

The air punched him. Lifted him. Vaulted him out of the bubble.

THIRTY-FOUR

ANGOLAN COAST

Warbling thrummed, beckoned him to answer its call.

Leif groaned—and even that hurt his eardrums. He shifted, his back sticky.

"You . . . me?"

Pushing onto all fours, Leif registered the wet earth. The acrid smell of burnt flesh. The colossal pounding in his head, as if he had the hangover of a lifetime.

"You good?" warbled Culver's voice.

Leif moved onto his haunches and squinted at the man before him. Not Culver. It was Rubber Jacket. He had a marred mess across his cheek now. Sandy brown hair.

"Nice throw. He shot the C-4. Blew him and the device to smithereens."

Leif looked past him to the partially melted body of Survivor and winced.

"You did good," Rubber Jacket said, patting his shoulder.

Leif put a palm over his aching ear. "Who are you? The device—the jacket. How'd you know? Who—" Man, it hurt to hear himself talking.

The man extended his hand. "Call me Andrew."

Jolting at the name, Leif gawked. The same guy Mercy had seen at the facility? In Burma? "Where's the book?"

With a smirk, Andrew offered his hand again, angling away even as he did.

Leif glanced down. Andrew's sleeve had tugged back, revealing his wrist and a small tattoo inked there. The sight of it shot barbs through Leif's mind.

The hand stretched past Leif and pointed. "Your buddy is there. Alive, but needs medical. Might look to that."

Culver. Leif struggled to his feet, feeling top-heavy because of his plugged ears and pounding headache. His back stung. He staggered a step, his mind catching up with his circumstances. The rain had stopped. The clouds were receding. But he had no evac. No Zodiac to clear out. Did he even have a team anymore?

"Culver!" He trudged to his buddy and dropped to his knees.

His red beard was coated with ash and mud, but Culver's chest rose and fell steadily. His shoulder bore a scorch mark. He moaned.

"Yeah, me too." Leif watched Andrew walk across the field in his rubber jacket. A little less confident. A little slower. Like Leif. He did not know what to make of the guy. The tat—it hurt to think about it.

His mind careened back to Iskra. He sagged. Turned to where she'd been taken. Spotted Saito moving on the ground.

"Augh!" Culver jolted forward, blinking. Gasping.

"Easy," Leif said, letting out a weighted sigh. "It's over. It's over."

"Holy batch of cookies, my shoulder hurts." Culver groaned as he cupped the injured joint. "What . . . ?"

"Second, maybe third-degree burns from the lightning." Leif touched his comms. It crackled, sounding in his ear worse than someone firing a weapon. "Augh!"

"Beta Actual, we are en route," Lawe's voice boomed. "Good work."

No. Good work would mean they were all going home. Leif paused. Looked back at where he'd last seen Iskra. "I keep my promises."

USS *MOUNT WHITNEY*, SOUTH ATLANTIC OCEAN

Fifty lives lost in Burma.

Three hundred thirty-two in Botswana.

Fifteen in Angola.

One device retrieved. Two destroyed.

Culver was down in the med bay, getting treatment for the second-degree burns on his back and shoulder. Lawe, Devine, and Baddar had listened with rapt attention as Saito recounted their harrowing ordeal.

"Stacking up the losses," Leif said as he sat in the briefing room. "Mercy, the guy at the middle of it was your guy, Andrew."

"Wait. What?" Her expression brightened. "Seriously?"

"He helped me blow the device."

She frowned. Everyone frowned. "I don't—" She shook her head. "Why would he do that?"

"I have no idea."

Braun cut in, giving them status updates on Burma, Botswana, and Angola—all tentatively destabilized. Efforts were underway to undo the work, but the admiral said it'd be a long road. She dismissed them, and Leif headed out, ready for some downtime. He wanted to figure out the quickest strategy for going after Iskra.

Mercy came around the table. "I think you'll want to see what I found."

He had to admit she had a way of baiting a guy. "Andrew?"

She deflated. "No." She shrugged. "Remember you asked why Viorica kept going back to Peychinovich?"

Just had to bring that up, didn't she? Now that Iskra was gone, back in the hands of that man, Leif wanted to strangle someone. He might as well start with Mercy. "Her daughter," he said, annoyed. "You took pleasure in bringing that to my attention."

Mercy faltered. "You're right. I did."

"Go away, Mercy. It's a bad day—"

"I was wrong."

Leif eyed her, gauging her words.

"Well, I wasn't wrong that the child is her daughter."

"I really don't have the time or energy for this." He wanted to take a long soak . . . in the Atlantic. Never come back. But first, he needed an aggressive strategy for finding Iskra and getting her daughter to safety. If they were still alive.

"Did she tell you who fathered Bisera?"

"Peychinovich."

"She said that?" Mercy asked, her tone urgent. Surprised. "That the girl was his?"

"Yeah," Leif grunted. Then realized . . . scanned back through their conversations.

"Hristoff protects what he sees as his."

"Not directly," he conceded. "It was understood. All those years of him raping her eventually got her pregnant."

Nodding, Mercy opened a file on her laptop. "Look. It's a paternity test." She scrolled to the bottom and tapped the screen.

Leif read the results. Two pieces of info melted his brain:

MATCH PROBABILITY: 98%
FATHER: KUZNETSOV, VALERY

"I . . . no." That couldn't be right. The brother of the guy on the boat Iskra went to after Greece. The guy she sought help from. "Peych isn't the father."

"Valery Kuznetsov was murdered," Mercy said, "and everyone thought it was a rival of Viorica Steel. But what if it was Peychinovich himself? What if he killed Valery because he found out about him and Viorica?"

Leif smoothed back his hair, feeling the brittle ends of the singed strands. "He killed Vasily because he helped Iskra in Greece. Probably fell in love with her, too." He roughed a hand over his mouth. "I'm going to guess Peych was so angry in Turkey because he'd found out about the child."

"It would explain a lot," Mercy murmured.

"Too much."

"Why he beat the girl."

"Hristoff protects what he sees as his."

If Peych had figured out Bisera wasn't his, that was why he wasn't afraid to hurt her. But would he do more than that? What if that was why he demanded V come back? He wasn't even worried about the book.

No. No no no.

Leif came up out of his chair. "I have to go to Russia." He bolted for the door. "He'll kill them. He'll kill them both."

THIRTY-FIVE

VOLGA DISTRICT, RUSSIA

There had been a time Iskra savored the view from the room he'd given her. Relished the way the sun glistened like diamonds on the water. It spoke to her. Told her there was an entire world beyond.

I am winter.

For a brief moment, she had dared to believe that the winter of her life had ended. That its claim on her, the one that sealed her dreams, hopes, and heart, had finally surrendered to the warmth of spring.

In the salt mines, she'd made a vow to bury any who opposed her or the goals she set within—what she then believed to be—winter's last embrace. But now? Now she merely wished to lay herself within its folds.

It was over. She was done fighting. If only Leif had let her drown. Let her find peace.

Footsteps in the hall.

Lesya, Iskra's assistant and closest friend, rose from the sofa where she'd silently sat. She'd been Iskra's only company since Hristoff had dragged her back to his estate. Locked her in her suite. Threatened not her but Bisera if she attempted another escape.

Lesya's worried face, marred with an ugly green bruise from being thrown into the marble column, considered her.

"Do not be afraid," Iskra said. "I will do whatever he wants."

Tears pooled in her friend's eyes. "I know. You always do." She squeezed back a sob. "I hoped it would be different. I'm so sorry. I don't know how—"

The door cracked open.

Instead of the forbidding form of Hristoff, a flutter of fabric and dark hair whirled into the room. Beautiful innocence. Bruised face. A scabbed cut. But alive and fiery as ever.

Bisera flew at her. "Mama!"

"You don't call her your daughter." Leif's words chastised her. Again.

Iskra knelt, heart melting at the exuberance of the child she'd made with Valery. "Darling." She gathered the small frame close. Tears pricked her heart.

Leif had been right. She *had* held Bisera at arm's length, afraid to be attached. Afraid to let her seize a piece of the organ Iskra had long thought dead—her heart.

Because she'd known Hristoff would harm Bisera if he discovered the truth. He'd killed Valery to smother her so-called infidelity.

"My sweet," Iskra muttered into the thick hair so like her own.

Arms hooked around her neck, Bisera held tight. "I'm glad you're back. It's always better when you're here."

She closed her eyes, hating the truth. Hating that her daughter knew the difference.

"Ah, isn't this grand?" Hristoff's gravelly taunt cut through the tender moment. "A reunion of mother and daughter."

Iskra swallowed. Mustered what remained of her strength and faced him, glad Bisera could not see the lasers of his eyes cutting them apart. He knew. She did not know how, but he knew.

"I visited Vasily Kuznetsov." Hristoff slid his hands into the pockets of his expensive slacks. "Did I tell you?"

Iskra tried to calm the unsteady cadence of her heart. She passed Bisera to Lesya. "Go with her, my sweet. I'll be along soon." She tensed when Hristoff did not argue.

Carrying Bisera, Lesya hurried in a wide arc around Hristoff and slipped out.

Iskra freed a captive breath and clasped her hands. "I cannot pretend to understand why you would kill Vasily. He was a good man. He did nothing to harm you."

Hristoff squinted as he lifted a small crystal elephant from a stand and considered it. "Didn't he?"

Iskra was never comfortable when he held sharp or fragile objects. She braced herself. And anticipated when he pitched the figurine at her. She caught it—mistakenly focused on the elephant and not the monster in the room, who flew at her.

Hristoff cuffed her throat. Slammed her backward. Her head cracked against the window.

She cried out.

"Didn't he?" he growled against her face. "I went to him, confused as to why you would be there. Alone on his yacht, the *Taissia*," he hissed.

He wasn't choking her. Hurting, yes. Which meant she still had a chance—

"We took his files to be sure nobody could trace it back." His nose pressed to her cheek. "Do you know what I learned, Iskra? The *Taissia* was named after your daughter! I wondered how that could be, when your daughter—our daughter—is named Bisera."

She flinched—he was toying with her. He knew. Taissia was the name she and Valery had chosen for their daughter, but "Bisera" was Hristoff's preference.

She gripped the hands clamped around her throat, her toes barely touching the marble floor. Thought to fight him. To hurt him as she had dreamed. Over and over. But Bisera . . .

"Then do you know what I found on his computer?" His grip tightened, strangling.

The test. Vasily had sworn he'd deleted it. Destroyed it.

"Yes." He smirked. "I see you do."

Struggling, she tried to wrest free, but he was strong. "Please—"

Bisera screamed in the hall, drawing his attention to the door.

Iskra flailed. "Hristoff, no. Please. You can't—"

"Can't I?"

Crack!

Something hit the glass. Hristoff started, gaze focusing behind her. She could see his expression from the corner of her eye. And it frightened her.

He jerked away, staring in disbelief at the white crater and spiderweb crack in the bulletproof glass. In his shock, he lessened his grip.

Iskra responded. Lifted her left arm up and over his. Drove her elbow down against his forearm. Snaked her arm around his and gripped the back of his neck. Drove her other elbow into his face. It happened in a split second.

He howled.

Still holding his neck, she rammed her knee into his nose.

Hristoff staggered, hands covering his bloodied face.

The door bucked open. Shoving free of Hristoff, Iskra assumed a fighting stance.

Ruslan stopped short. Gaped at Hristoff, bloody and stumbling. Enraged.

"A sniper just took a shot at me!" Hristoff growled nasally, pointing at the window.

"And we have trouble at the front gate," Ruslan said.

They rushed out of the room. Locked the door from the outside.

Seriously? Did he think that would stop her?

She waited until she was sure he had cleared the hall, then drove her heel at the door. It bucked, but she repeated the kick. Wood splintered. One more time.

It popped open. Banged against the wall. She sprinted toward the cries of her daughter down the hall. Toward the shouts of Lesya.

Shots peppered the air. Plaster splintered, someone pursuing her. She ducked and used the wall to push off to her left.

Ahead, a door slammed. Bisera's room.

A masked figure rounded the corner. Iskra slid to a stop, hands up—not for defense. For offense. No longer would she wait for the attack.

Until—the eyes. Familiar. Weapon tucked against his shoulder, pale blue eyes blazing with rage, Leif hurried toward her. "We have to go."

"My daughter!" She ran at the door to Bisera's room. Sailed sideways into the air, drew her knee to her stomach, and shoved it out. Her heel connected with the jamb. The door cracked open.

Iskra landed and scanned the room.

Maksim stood in the corner with a wailing Bisera crushed to his chest. Lesya lay in a pool of blood at his feet.

Fury drew Iskra up straight. "Release her," she growled.

"Not a chance," he growled back.

A side door flung open. Hristoff, eyes swollen nearly shut from her strikes, stalked in. "Kill the child."

"No!" Iskra rushed between the men and held out her arms, pleased when Leif and his team filtered into the room. "Nobody hurts her." She dared them to try. "These men are prepared to"—she didn't want her daughter to see or hear any more than necessary—"do whatever it takes to make sure Bisera and I leave alive."

Rage boiled through Hristoff's gaze. "You dare—"

"I do," she said around a tremulous breath. "That's all I want. To leave. Alive with Bisera."

His lip curled. "You belong to me."

Iskra lifted her chin, then turned to Maksim. Gave him a look that warned he knew her abilities. "Give me my daughter before you have a very unfortunate accident."

"I'd think twice about causing that little girl any harm," Leif warned.

Maksim faltered.

Iskra seized his hesitation. Took Bisera, who shuddered as she wrapped her legs and arms around Iskra. Buried her little nose against Iskra's neck. "It's okay, baby." She walked toward the door but sensed movement. She broke into a run.

A burst of gunfire chased her into the hall—who had been shot?

"Don't move, Peych."

Hearing Hristoff was still alive quickened Iskra's pace. She ran as fast as she could, forbidding Bisera from lifting her head. She did not want these images burned into her daughter's mind.

The presence of Leif's team cocooned her as she reached the kitchens, but a quick glance revealed Leif wasn't there. She stopped.

"It's okay," Mercy said.

"Do it," came Leif's growl from the bedroom. "Give me a reason."

At the corner of the corridor, Mercy and Baddar nodded and escorted Iskra out through the halls. She was stunned at the way the guards allowed her to exit without resistance. The team led her to the servants' entrance.

Iskra shook, each step an effort. Each breath treacherous—would she really make it? Was this really happening? She hadn't dared hope. Hadn't believed it possible.

A shout from behind made her look back. Leif was there, a shadow against the glare of the hall lights. Weapon pointed up, he shouldered open a door, his back to them, eyes on a threat she couldn't see. He arched forward, taking aim. Fired.

"C'mon," Mercy whispered, luring Iskra out into the side courtyard. She hustled to a white, nondescript van.

Leif jogged to them, yanking open the vehicle door. "You okay?"

With a nod, Iskra climbed in, still forcing Bisera to keep her head down. The others filled in around her. Leif last. He tugged the door closed.

"Iskra!" Hristoff roared from the front stoop, aiming a gun at the van as they careened around the house.

She sucked in a breath, tucking her chin against Bisera's hair.

But then Hristoff tripped and tumbled to the ground. And didn't get up.

"What . . . ?"

"A little Devine intervention," Lawe murmured as the van tore down the long drive and barreled to safety.

Epilogue

UNDISCLOSED LOCATION, ITALY

The team had holed up at a safehouse. Eaten. Rested. Showered. Caught up on badly needed sleep. Iskra was in the back room with her sleeping daughter. Leif and the others were talking with Cell, who'd brought supplies and bad news.

"What we know is that, despite the blow we delivered to ArC, they aren't slowing down. We might've destroyed the devices, but the fear they unleashed and the damage they did were enough to force local governments to lend at least one ear to Botha. They're determined to bring about Armageddon and establish their caliphate."

"Bring about Armageddon," Culver snorted. "That is some messed-up thinking, there."

"They don't believe the Christian Bible, but they do believe in the End Times. So, to them, if they can set up this caliphate, they prove the Bible wrong." Cell shrugged. "But I've been going over the scroll, working overtime to piece together the corrupted pieces."

"Any luck?" Leif asked.

"Not really." Cell sighed. "And while we'd like to say we have some downtime before the next war, I'd be lying."

Leif pinched the bridge of his nose. "All right." He folded his arms over his chest. "Give it to us."

"Has anyone heard of the Neiothen?"

"They're just legend, myth," Lawe countered.

"What legend?" Saito asked.

"A story conjured on the backs of vets who returned from Afghanistan and Iraq changed." Lawe scoffed. "Congress tried to accuse the DoD of experimental procedures. It all turned out to be a hoax."

"It's not a hoax." Wrapped in the shadows of the darkened hallway that led to the bedrooms, Iskra hugged herself. "I've been looking for my brother for over ten years. He was part of a black ops super-army."

"Super-army." Leif lifted his chin, recalling when she'd brought that up at the facility. He sat forward. "You said the Pearl of the Antilles is in the book."

She nodded.

"And that it was the location of a super-army."

Another nod. "That is what I was told. I have been unable to find proof of that, which is why I so wanted to find that book. Vasily was a language expert, and he deciphered it. He said the super-army was mentioned there."

"What're you thinking, Usurper?" Cell asked.

Leif frowned, then shook it off. Sat back, tapping a pen against the table. "I don't know what I'm thinking. But a super-army . . ." Why did that word feel like the electrical charges of the dome? "How do you know your brother was with them if he was MIA?"

"A friend told me to find the book, that it would help me find Mitre." She hunched her shoulders. "When I found it, Vasily verified they are mentioned in the scroll."

"But they're not," Cell said, confused. "Not as far as we've been able to translate or decipher—which is why I'm here. In that other section Harden and I were able to piece back together—and granted, it's a bit messy because the level of corruption was high"—Cell pointed to the screen—"there's a mention in the fourth war John wrote about. Let me find it. Here." He nodded to his screen. "Actually, we weren't sure if it was a fourth war or part of another. A chunk is too corrupted to tell."

"Yeah. Corrupted." Leif waved his hand in circles. "Tell us."

"Okay, here goes. '*. . . garbed in authority lost their lives, breath snuffed like lamps doused. Rage in the right hand, vengeance in the left, there was naught but blood upon the lands. Kingdoms shifted. Countries collapsed. Chaos seized and reigned in answer to the summons of the enemies of kings. Upon those from below is marked the quest that tethers their soul in darkness . . .*'"

"If that's not ominous, I don't know what is," Mercy said.

"This sounds like some twisted Humpty Dumpty," Culver said. "I mean, are we seriously going to try to stop another war that hasn't happened—one involving kingdoms? Not sure I'm ready to get burned again."

"So, the next war," Leif said, pinching the bridge of his nose, "is kings falling."

Ronie Kendig is the bestselling, award-winning author of over twenty novels. She grew up an Army brat, and now she and her hunky hero are adventuring on the East Coast with their grown children, a retired military working dog, VVolt N629, and Benning the Stealth Golden. Ronie's degree in psychology has helped her pen novels with intense, raw characters. Visit Ronie online at www.roniekendig.com.